PRAISE FOR *CHARLOTTE*

'*Charlotte* is elegant and sophisticated but also completely gripping. Martina Devlin brilliantly creates the world around this iconic writer, with characters who have the power to surprise and compel. I loved it.' – Emily Hourican

'In her fiction, Martina Devlin has a rare gift for reconstructing the past and bringing real historical figures to life on the page. In *Charlotte* she uses the substantial research her readers have come to expect from her in inventive and compelling ways' – Lia Mills

'I was utterly enthralled by this fictional rendering of *Charlotte* Bronte's life—and its aftermath—as viewed through the eyes of her husband's second wife. This powerful and compelling novel expertly imagines the lives and times of those closest to Bronte, and captivates the reader with its cleverness and eloquence.' – Mary Costello

'In *Charlotte*, the raw gold of Charlotte Bronte's marriage to Arthur Nicholls has been wrought in a wonderful artefact – a beautiful novel full of mystery, intrigue and story.' – Carlo Gébler

'Gorgeous and innovative, *Charlotte* does what biographical fiction does best – it vivifies the past and brings the reader close. Here, Martina Devlin weaves a beautiful spell where objects are as important as people, and two wives – one gone, one living – vie for the reader's loyalty and affections. A lively story of memory, love, and loss.' – Nuala O'Connor

CHARLOTTE

Martina Devlin

THE LILLIPUT PRESS
DUBLIN

First published by
THE LILLIPUT PRESS
62–63 Sitric Road,
Arbour Hill,
Dublin 7,
Ireland
www.lilliputpress.ie

Copyright © Martina Devlin, 2024

10 9 8 7 6 5 4 3 2 1

All rights reserved. No part of this publication may be reproduced in
any form or by any means without the prior permission of the
publisher.

A CIP record for this title is available from The British Library.

Paperback ISBN 978 1 84351 904 1
eBook ISBN 978 1 84351 905 8

Lilliput gratefully acknowledges the financial support of the Arts
Council / An Chomhairle Ealaíon.

Set in 11pt on 14pt Garamond Pro by Compuscript
Printed and bound in Sweden by ScandBook

In memory of Niall Devlin of Omagh (1958–2024).
Beloved.

Also by Martina Devlin
Edith

'Life must be understood backwards; but ... it must be lived forwards.'

Søren Kierkegaard, *Journals and Papers* (1843)

This story does not claim to be the truth but is inspired by real events.

PARTIAL FAMILY TREE OF THE BELLS AND NICHOLLS

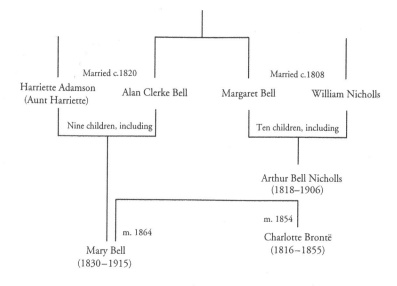

Married c.1820

Harriette Adamson
(Aunt Harriette)   Alan Clerke Bell

Nine children, including

Married c.1808

Margaret Bell   William Nicholls

Ten children, including

Arthur Bell Nicholls
(1818–1906)

m. 1854

m. 1864

Mary Bell
(1830–1915)

Charlotte Brontë
(1816–1855)

1854

CHAPTER 1
BANAGHER, IRELAND

'Jane Eyre is getting married to Arthur. And they're coming to Ireland on their honeymoon.' Mama, known the length and breadth of King's County for her composure, was wide-eyed with astonishment at the news in her letter.

'Our Arthur?' I asked.

'Yes.'

'Marrying Charlotte Brontë?'

'That's what I said. The *Jane Eyre* authoress.'

'The most famous writer in the world?'

'Don't exaggerate, Mary.'

'She's caused a sensation!'

'If you say so, my pet.'

We were drinking tea at the breakfast table – me considering whether to choose pale blue or pale pink for my new summer gown, Mama reading her letters. I had noticed one from Arthur among her stack, but he was twelve years my senior and his communications rarely interested me. They droned on about Sunday school prizes and godless parishioners, or walks on the moors with the parsonage hounds. Mr Brontë this and Mr Brontë that. I'd have paid attention to any mention of Charlotte Brontë, but it was always the old parson he talked about. If not for that memorable surname, we'd never have joined the dots when the novels were published. Arthur had said nothing about the parson's daughters being writers.

Mama threw down the letter and tested her fingertips against her coronet of plaits. 'How could he!'

'You're always saying it's high time he took a wife, Mama.'

'But not just any wife. You, Mary! He's meant to marry you!'

'He's never shown the least interest in me.'

'That's because you don't encourage him.'

'Arthur's like a brother to me. Kinder than a brother – he never dropped earwigs down the back of my neck like Richard did. Besides, I don't believe I'd care to be a minister's wife.'

'What you get and what you want are two different things.'

'You got what you wanted with Papa.'

'Your poor papa. He was the kindest of men. Goodness knows what he thinks of Arthur's marriage plans, looking down on us all.'

'I expect he'd say it's a suitable match.'

'I hope she doesn't find us too provincial here. I don't know how we're supposed to keep her entertained.'

'At least we've read her novels.'

'I cast an eye over them, I admit. But I prefer poetry.'

'You devoured them, Mama. Especially *Jane Eyre*. You can't have forgotten Denis Coughlan driving us into Parson-stown to buy each instalment?' I quoted my favourite passage from memory. '*Do you think, because I am poor, obscure, plain, and little, I am soulless and heartless? You think wrong! – I have as much soul as you, – and full as much heart!* It's – I don't know – it puts me in raptures! I long to press herself between the book's pages like a dried flower!'

'Don't gush, Mary.'

'When I read it, I fancied Jane was confiding in me. We were sitting together, and she was trusting me with her story.'

'But who are you meant to marry now? Arthur's perfect for you. How *can* he be so inconsiderate?'

'Mama, I've never wanted to marry Arthur. I can't imagine being his wife. It's too silly for words.'

'You don't know what's best for you.' A gusty sigh. 'Too late now.'

'What else does the letter say?'

She picked it up from the table and read aloud. '*In the course of our trip, I hope to show Banagher to my new wife. May we spend a week with all of you in Cuba Court, Aunt Harriette? I can't wait to introduce Charlotte to my family.*'

'It's nice he's bringing her here to pay her respects to you.'

A sniff. 'It means we aren't invited. He won't have any of his kin standing beside him on his wedding day.'

'Hasn't he asked Alan?'

'Apparently not.'

'You'd think he'd want his brother as best man.'

'One of those parson friends of his is doing the honours. He says it's because everything's happening quite soon, on the twenty-ninth of June. He's in a tearing hurry.'

'That's not like Arthur. Usually, he takes a mortal age to make up his mind to anything.'

'It must be that Jane Eyre person, afraid he'll slip through her fingers.'

'Charlotte Brontë, Mama. You mustn't keep calling her Jane Eyre. She might take offence if you do it to her face. You'll write back and tell Arthur to bring her, won't you? Think of the excitement in the parish!'

'Arthur's wife will always be welcome here. This is his home.'

'May I read the letter?' She handed it over.

I wish you could be with us, Aunt Harriette, but time is in short supply, and Haworth is remote – it takes a determined explorer to reach the Yorkshire moors. If we marry quickly, Mr Brontë can spare me from my duties for a month's holiday. I intend us to do some touring. My bride-to-be, while otherwise perfect, is woefully ignorant about Ireland's charms, and we can't have that.

'Arthur will be in his element poring over train timetables and drawing up their itinerary, Mama. I wonder where else he'll bring her? Dublin, I suppose, to stay with Alan.'

'I remember him telling me her father's an Irishman, from County Down. I expect they'll go north.'

'Of course. Arthur likes to do the right thing.'

'The right thing would be marrying you. Oh, no use crying over spilled milk. Is there time to sew a new counterpane for the Blue Room, do you think?'

Counterpanes! At a time like this! 'I wonder how it can have happened, Mama?'

'What, dear?'

'Arthur bagging Charlotte Brontë.'

'He's good-looking and good-natured. Why shouldn't he win her?'

'But poor, like most curates.'

'After donkey's years as her father's curate, I suppose proximity led to affection.'

I handed back the letter. 'But he resigned his position last year. The last time we saw Arthur, he was talking about becoming a missionary. Maybe he intends to make Charlotte a missionary's wife. That would certainly inspire another novel!'

'A missionary's wife has no time to write novels. In any case, I suspect he's given up that notion. Can't say I'm sorry. The missions tend to break a man's health.'

I was envious of the idea of a wedding tour – I'd never gone further than Dublin. Mama had an aversion to travel because Papa, who was asthmatic, had died waiting to take ship to the south of France. A daring idea caught hold of me, and I became dense with longing. 'May I meet them off the boat?'

'His brother in Dublin will do that, Mary. You'll have an opportunity to become acquainted with your new cousin in Banagher.'

'Please, Mama. If we're not going to the wedding. It's so humdrum here!'

Mama gave me an indulgent smile. 'Very well, my pet. I'll write to Alan's wife and ask if you can stay a few nights. She's in a delicate condition, but one more guest won't make much difference. In fact, Julia might be glad of your help.' She stood up, all bustle and business as usual. 'Who will you travel up with? Richard's the obvious candidate, but I don't want him getting up to mischief in the city. One of your Adamson cousins might chaperone you. But it means them coming to Banagher to fetch you. Perhaps if I have a stern talk with Richard …'

Having won the battle, I knew better than to protest about escorts, and left Mama to her machinations. Meanwhile, I hugged tight my elation.

*

I wanted to meet Charlotte Brontë off the steam packet at Kingstown. It seemed fitting to witness her stepping onto Irish soil there, the restless sea at her back. Ropes thrown by sailors to men waiting on the dock. A gangplank laid from ship to quay. Sails rolled and lashed. The crew with tattoos on their arms and necks, calling to one another in a variety of languages. But the men in my family pointed out that boat trains were always crammed and the quays slippery, so instead we waited for the newlyweds six or so miles away, in Westland Row railway station.

And there we made three spokes in a welcoming wheel: Arthur's older brother, Alan Nicholls, my brother Richard and me, keen to greet Charlotte – not because she was a fêted writer, but as Arthur's wife. We Bells and our Nicholls cousins are family-minded. The two Nicholls boys were planted within our household, and my parents had raised all of us together in Cuba Court with no difference in treatment.

Arthur's robust shape was easy to spot, but she was harder to spy. First, I saw an arm reaching out from the train: he took her hand and guided her onto the platform. Still, I couldn't quite distinguish her, half-hidden by his frame. Usually, Mama was indignant about Arthur's worn appearance when he came home on holiday. 'A dogsbody, they make of him, in that English parish,' she'd say. This year, he looked rejuvenated.

Alan rushed at them, but Richard held back and nudged me. 'Look at the smile on Arthur's face. Cupid's arrow's found its mark.'

'What would you know about Cupid?'

'More than you.'

'There's a difference between love and your, your, buccaneering.'

'Miss Prim.' He tweaked my hat ribbons, deliberately lopsiding my bonnet, and strolled over to join the others.

Fuming, I hovered on the sidelines, while Richard clapped Arthur on the back, raised his hat to Charlotte and kissed her hand. Arthur couldn't help but look drab beside my dashing brother, who peacocked about Cuba Court even when we had no company.

'Mary,' said Arthur, 'what a pleasant surprise. Come and say hello. There's someone I want you to meet.' He reached his arm around Charlotte's waist and gave her a gentle push forward. 'Mary's like a sister to me,' he said.

At that word sister, a shadow ghosted across her face. But when I smiled, an answering smile tiptoed between us, and the darkness cleared. Charlotte bowed to me, and held out a hand for a feathery handshake, her lace mittens rubbing against my white gloves. I felt angular and lanky beside her – she reached no higher than my ear lobe. But my diffidence evaporated when our eyes met. Then, everything was forgotten in the scorch of her singularity.

I saw a ladylike person, everything just so. She wore dove-grey, yet appearances were deceptive, because her silk dress was woven with thin white stripes and had a mauve sheen, suggesting sunlight as it hits ice. Her spectacles indicated eyes weakened from novelizing, but a person not burdened by vanity. Most brides would have left them off, at least temporarily, to meet their husband's relatives. Overall, she gave an impression of youth but not bloom.

'Welcome to Ireland, Mrs Nicholls.' I presented her with a spray of white heather, picked from the gardens at Cuba Court. 'For luck.'

Charlotte accepted the posy with a smile, peeping at me from under her bonnet. 'I've set aside the idea of luck, whether good or bad. But I would like life to be ...'

'Yes?'

'Smoother. I'm tired of thunderbolts and crises. I want less drama and more peace.'

I glanced around to see if Arthur had heard this aspiration, which owed more to candour than romance. However, the Nicholls brothers were competing to give a porter instructions about the luggage, and my brother had inveigled into a conversation with a mother and two pretty daughters who appeared to have missed the person due to meet them. I bit my lip and turned my back on Richard.

Charlotte missed nothing: 'Your brother seems to have taken those ladies under his wing.'

'Indeed.'

'How charming he is.'

'So people say.'

'What does Mr Bell do? Other than help damsels in distress? I think Arthur said he lives with you and your mother.'

'He's headmaster of the Royal Free School in Banagher, where we live. Papa was headmaster there before him.' I risked a glance at Richard, offering his services to those attractive strangers, and felt the need to defend him. 'I don't know that he cares for schoolmastering, but he took it on for us. So Mama and I could stay on at Cuba Court. The school's on its grounds, you see. We'd have lost our home otherwise.'

'Women are tossed about like corks on water. I'd have to leave the parsonage if anything happened to my father. But Arthur will succeed him. So all's well that ends well.'

How detached from romance it sounded. She could be describing a business arrangement. 'Transferring your trunks from the luggage car to a hansom cab will take a little while, Mrs Nicholls,' I added. 'Nothing happens quickly in Ireland.' Their trunks could have followed them – Alan's house on Sir John Rogerson's Quay was close enough to walk to, but he was determined to do things in style. His sister-in-law was a feather in his cap – if he could, he'd have fashioned wings to fly her there.

We stood in companionable silence. I noticed how she turned her head left and right, observing the tangle of humanity in the station: joyful family reunions, passengers dodging obstacles as they sprinted for trains, insults traded between rival porters, cabbies touting for trade. Her reactions suggested surprise, a reminder that we Hibernians are said to be an exuberant race compared with the English. Even our boisterous seagulls drew a glance from our visitor. Yet she was married to an Irishman. Arthur was the reserved version, obviously. Still, every stewpot requires a variety of ingredients. Could we really be so different to England, a short strip of sea away? Ireland wasn't Arabia or the New World.

Just then, a hollow-chested girl carrying a baby almost as large as herself approached us through the scramble and swarm. Both skulls were outlined, as though skin was barely able to contain bone. The sour smell of unwashed bodies oozed from them, along with the smack of exhaustion.

The girl held out her free hand and spoke rapidly. '*Níor ith muid le trí lá. Is muid an t-aon bheirt atá fágtha as ochtar.*'

'I don't understand,' said Charlotte. 'Is it Irish?'

'She's saying they're hungry. They're the only two left from a family of eight.'

Charlotte's eyes clouded, and she placed some coins in the girl's palm. 'For my sisters, in Wanderland. And because you're taking care of yours. God bless you.'

Following her example, I wedged a shilling in the baby's fist, although I wanted that money for dress trimmings. But I knew I must guard against allowing my heart to harden – it needed Charlotte's gaze to fix on what was common here. Evidence of destitution was everywhere since the Famine. The people had become walking skeletons – those who'd survived. Between death and emigration, the country had emptied out.

Hoping to distract Charlotte from Ireland's sorry state, I pointed to a monkey in an embroidered waistcoat and tas-selled hat, clinging to a man's shoulder. 'Look who's dressed in his holiday best to meet someone off the train.'

'My sister Emily would say that little captive belongs in the wild, where God placed him.'

'But see how he's petted. He wants for nothing with that owner.'

'Except his freedom. Most precious of all.'

Now I noticed the chain around the monkey's waist, and he no longer looked cosseted. 'I never thought of it that way.'

Her eyes grew brilliant. 'I expect I wouldn't either, but for Emily. Beasts lack dishonesty and vanity – unlike people,' she said.

'That's the luggage taken care of.' Arthur bustled back. 'My brother's gone out to find a cab for us. Come along, Charlotte. You too, Mary. You must be famished, dearest, I know I am. Alan says his wife has breakfast ready for us.'

'Where's Richard?' I asked.

'Sir Galahading again.'

I caught sight of Richard surrounded by the women, bluer-than-blue eyes sparkling. Charlotte noticed my wrinkled nose. 'Don't worry. It's kind of your brother.'

'Yes.'

'He'll join us later, Mary,' said Arthur, and the three of us descended the station steps.

'Yours is a name I take pleasure in, Miss Bell,' said Charlotte.

'Because of Currer Bell?' I asked.

'Just so. I seem to have helped myself to your name. I hope you don't mind.'

'I'm happy to share it with you. What made you chose it?'

'My father's a parson. Church bells often ring while I plot my books. I suppose Bell suggested itself.'

'And it's Arthur's middle name, of course.'

'Arthur! Over here!' Alan was standing beside a dappled grey horse harnessed to a hansom. Arthur shepherded us towards him and guided Charlotte into the cab. Left to fend for myself, I skirted around to the door on the far side and clambered in.

For a few moments, it was just the two of us inside. 'It had nothing to do with Arthur,' said Charlotte. 'A coincidence. He was just another of the holies.' A mischievous smile spread across her face. 'That's what my sisters and me called Papa's curates.'

The cab tilted with Arthur's weight as he climbed in and settled opposite Charlotte, the better to gaze at her. I knew him for every day of my life, and never saw Arthur Nicholls look at man, woman, child or animal with as much devotion as he showered over his new wife.

I found Charlotte harder to read. Her heart was a locked room to me – yet like a glimpse through a keyhole, I understood his cherishing manner pleased her. Fatigued though she was, her head lifted on its stem, and I realized that she loved his love for her.

'Here you are in Ireland,' he said.

'I've often wondered about it,' she answered. 'And now life has carried me away like a child's balloon – swept me here to Ireland.'

1913

CHAPTER 2

Until now, I have shared the specifics of that first meeting between us with no one. If I let them, people would pore over every detail, handle each scrap. Shop-soiling with their touch. Strangers can be inclined to pry – scholars, collectors, journalists, biographers, admirers (the curious go by all manner of names). Sooner or later, once the link is made, they swamp me with questions. Usually, I say she was Arthur's wife a decade before he married me, that they lived in Yorkshire, and I was never there. It suggests I didn't know her without telling an outright falsehood.

People who never laid eyes on Charlotte tell third-hand stories about her. A welter of false reports has taken root, tenacious as lies can be. For decades, I saw no reason to make free with my memories, like a human echo. Why should I satisfy the snoops? People who respect no boundaries?

Remembrance has been a burden, on occasion. In my middle years, there were times when my memories gusted over me – buffeting blasts that flayed all before them. In old age, my memories aren't the sort I can burrow into for comfort. There are days when I seethe because all I seem to do is convert life into memory. But there are days, too, when I am twenty-two again and the world is garden-fresh.

I see her now as clear, as clear – that bride on her wedding tour. Charlotte was particular about her appearance, toned bonnet ribbons to her gown, buttons to gloves. Others have called her a Quakeress, but my Charlotte dressed neither plainly nor gaudily – she combined simplicity with elegance. The portraits bear little resemblance to the Charlotte I met. They capture her hair, a silky brown kept enamel smooth, but any likeness to her face is a distant one. The tendency is to fit it out in a melancholic sweetness – a Sunday-morning hymn made flesh. The truth is, her face was plain: an overhanging forehead and a nose like a shoehorn. Yet it was unforgettable because of her fine hazel eyes, which kindled with hidden fire when something interested her. Then she magnetised the room.

What else? Not shoulder-high to Arthur, and inclined to cling to his arm – perhaps it was the novelty of having a husband's arm to hold. Brittle, from her glass-thin voice to her delicate wrists, yet burning with a steady white light. A well-stocked mind. Kept herself busy. Sat over her sewing – fairy stitches – for hours while we conversed. Short-sighted, peering at things like some timid but curious woodland creature. Reserve and inquisitiveness battled one another in her. Nothing escaped her attention – I suppose it's the way with novelists. They store up names, faces, happenings to fatten their books. She tended towards silence with strangers, but a waterfall of words flowed when she forgot herself.

Yes, Charlotte Brontë was cut from original cloth.

Once, I overheard my brother Richard say, 'Mary's a sly puss. A watcher.' It's true, I am an observer of small things – it's in my nature. A mosaic of patches can be stitched together into one large shape; the contours of someone. Nobody is entirely knowable – elements are always withheld – but it is possible to make informed guesses.

Some people might suspect my motives for telling our story now, considering we shared a husband. Even a saint would find it impossible to avoid the occasional dart of jealousy. Arthur was married to her for less than a year, and me for forty-two years, but Charlotte was his only sweetheart. She kept us constant company during our marriage: Charlotte and Arthur and me. Some might regard that as punishment, but I never resented her presence. I understood the terms when he proposed to me. I could have said no to him.

But I was unable to refuse Charlotte.

I'm an ordinary person – not false modesty, but clarity. As Ecclesiastes tells us: *And some there may be, which have no memorial; who are perished, as though they have never been.* I have something extraordinary in my life, though – a cord joining me to her. Meeting her transformed me, not just because I felt more significant in her presence, but because she gave me a purpose.

I'm not clever like her – facts seep through the cracks in my mind and evaporate. But at least I was sharp enough to fathom this. From the day I encountered Charlotte Brontë, I knew I had a job to do – to see, listen and remember.

*

Brontë/Ireland recording: number one of two
Interviewee: Mrs Mary Nicholls, widow of the Revd Arthur Bell Nicholls, formerly curate of Haworth, Yorkshire
Date: Made on the 19th day of August 1913
Location: Hill House, Banagher, King's County, Ireland
Interviewer: Mr Harry Graham of the *Illustrated London News*
Present: Mrs Nicholls and Mr Graham

[some crackling, a series of squawks and whistles]
Mr Graham: Could you state your name, please?

Mrs Nicholls: Mrs Arthur Nicholls. So this is the famous talking machine.

Mr Graham: Edison's Perfected Phonograph, no less. And your maiden name?

Mrs Nicholls: I was born Mary Anna Bell. What an enormous apparatus. I can't begin to fathom what it's all needed for.

Mr Graham: It's a device to capture your voice, Mrs Nicholls.

Mrs Nicholls: So many ingenious inventions nowadays. But that huge horn-shaped object is rather off-putting.

Mr Graham: I'm afraid it's an essential part of the equipment. As I explained before we began, a wax recording will be made of your words. To enable them to endure indefinitely.

Mrs Nicholls: Yes, I've been thinking about that. I must say, it sounds like you're embalming me while I'm still alive!

Mr Graham: Nothing so macabre, I assure you. If cameras can fix images, why shouldn't a mechanical ear fix sounds?

Mrs Nicholls: A voice without a face. Won't that be rather ghostly?

Mr Graham: I suppose that's one way of putting it. But the phonograph is useful. We'll have your voice, rather than simply a transcript of what you say. Your account will be preserved precisely, for future generations.

Mrs Nicholls: I can't imagine why future generations should care thruppence ha'penny for me.

Mr Graham: Let's press on, Mrs Nicholls. Now, the subject of our interview is your memories of Charlotte Brontë. Let me start by –

Mrs Nicholls: I thought it was to disentangle truth from fiction.

Mr Graham: Absolutely, that, too. She's someone who continues to draw a lot of attention because of her family circumstances. It's fair to say tragedy dogged the Brontës' footsteps. How would you –

Mrs Nicholls: I see sensationalism is your goal. Very well. I've changed my mind – I no longer wish to do an interview.

Mr Graham: Don't say that! I'm sorry if I offended you – we got off to a bad start. That was stupid of me. Mrs Nicholls? Can we try again? I've travelled a long way, Mrs Nicholls.

Mrs Nicholls: I'm under no obligation to you.

Mr Graham: I know that. But I'd be very grateful if you'd continue. Truth is, I'll catch it from my editor if you call a halt. He'll think I did something to upset you. And I wouldn't do that for the world. I'm throwing myself on your mercy, Mrs Nicholls. Please, have a heart!

Mrs Nicholls: Oh, very well. Proceed. But nothing lurid, young man, or I shall ask you to leave. I give you fair warning, you can expect nothing titillating to chew on. Kindly note that on your phonomajig.

Mr Graham: Duly noted. Believe me, Mrs Nicholls, titillation is the last thing on my mind. [recording makes a warbling noise] Now, your husband was Arthur Bell Nicholls, is that right?

Miss Bell: The Reverend Arthur Bell Nicholls.

Mr Graham: Your first cousin?

Miss Bell: Correct.

Mr Graham: And he had been married before, I believe?

Mrs Nicholls: I can't understand why you're asking me questions if you know the answers already, young man.

Mr Graham: To get your response on the record.

Mrs Nicholls: He was married for nine months to Charlotte Brontë.

Mr Graham: Did you ever meet her?

Mrs Nicholls: Of course. He brought her here on their honeymoon. I spent, I suppose, ten days in their company.

Mr Graham: And what were your impressions of her, Mrs Nicholls? [a pause, crackling on the recording] Mrs Nicholls?

Mrs Nicholls: I'm at a loss why you're picking over this. It's the shadow stuff of an old woman's memories.

Mr Graham: You had a ringside seat on literary history.

Mrs Nicholls: I'm quite unimportant. A bystander.

Mr Graham: Bystanders have eyes and ears. They observe. With luck, they remember. As time passes, the number of people who had any meaningful contact with Charlotte Brontë is dwindling. Your eyewitness account is invaluable.

Mrs Nicholls: She was always cordial to me, although far superior in experience and achievement. I liked her on sight – and even better as we became acquainted. Indeed, I flatter myself we struck up a friendship during her visit. Circumstances parted us, unfortunately.

Mr Graham: Some people say the portraits in existence of her are flattering. May I ask, what did she look like?

Mrs Nicholls: There was a general sense of chin and nose. Yet she was woven from quality fibres. Her way of looking at the world was the most distinctive thing about her – it wasn't like other people's.

Mr Graham: What else can you tell us? Anything at all that shines some light on who she was.

Mrs Nicholls: Oh my goodness, I can't remember. I didn't know I'd be expected to repeat it all into a machine one day. Let me see. She had a brave and faithful heart – she was no plaster saint, but trickery was beyond her.

Mr Graham: Did you recognize her genius as soon as you met her? If you hadn't already read her novels, would you have known she was out of the ordinary?

Mrs Nicholls: She was her own woman – that's no ordinary thing. She knew her mind's worth. Smart as a brass button. Not exactly a bluestocking, but her brain worked quicker than Arthur and Richard's, for all their university degrees. 'I try to practise intellectual self-improvement,' she told me once. There now, I've made her sound an awful prig. All I mean is, she'd have liked more learning.

Mr Graham: Was she as shy as people say?

Mrs Nicholls: She was reserved with those she didn't know well, but small eruptions could break through the surface.

My brother had that effect on her. He was headmaster of the Royal Free School at Banagher when they met.

Mr Graham: Can you recall the circumstances?

Mrs Nicholls: She had views on education. Disapproved of rote learning, but Richard disagreed. He liked to drill the boys in declensions and dates and whatnot. Also, she believed women should have more to occupy them than running a household. She said women shouldn't have to confine themselves to making puddings and embroidering samplers. It startled my poor mother, who said some ladies enjoyed those pursuits. And some don't, said Charlotte. Some waste their God-given talents, which could be put to better use. Richard asked her how marrying our cousin Arthur was putting her God-given talents to use – 'Any woman can snare a husband,' he said – all the while smiling as though he was funning.

Mr Graham: What did she answer?

Mrs Nicholls: Nothing. Women learn to harness their tongue – life forces it on them. A rowdy sigh is as much as most of us allow ourselves. But it was clear she felt she knew as much about education as Richard did. He was relieved when Arthur carried her off on the rest of their tour. Said she had an iron will beneath a conventional surface, and it was bound to emerge during the marriage. I don't know if that proved to be the case. Or, indeed, why it should be regarded as a character flaw. My brother preferred his women … Never mind.

Mr Graham: Did you have any sense of how tattered Charlotte's health was becoming during her marriage?

Mrs Nicholls: She looked well on her honeymoon. A little tired after the journey, to begin with, and she had some cuts on the back of her hands. But my mother healed them with a honey remedy – Mama kept bees – and Charlotte soon perked up. It was the following January, or maybe February, when Arthur wrote and told us she was shrivelling away before his eyes. He had hopes of her rallying if she could only hold on till spring. But I understand springtime is a latecomer in

Yorkshire. Afterwards, he said Charlotte's body turned against her, but consoled himself that she looked down on him with heavenly serenity. Personally, I never thought serenity was part of her nature.

Mr Graham: What did she do here in Ireland? Which sights did she and her husband visit?

Mrs Nicholls: Oh, the usual. The Ring of Kerry and so on. It was a very successful holiday. Apart from …

Mr Graham: Yes?

Mrs Nicholls: A tragedy happened. There was a very sad death while she was staying with us in Banagher. A drowning. Inevitably, it cast a shadow. She and Arthur left Cuba Court a little sooner than intended because of it.

Mr Graham: Did Charlotte know the victim?

Mrs Nicholls: Well enough to give evidence at the inquest.

Mr Graham: What sort of evidence?

Mrs Nicholls: About the deceased's state of mind. I don't care to talk about this any further, Mr Graham. I was on quite close terms with the person in question. I shouldn't have dredged it up.

Mr Graham: Was Charlotte – forgive me if this is indelicate – was she happy with her husband?

Mrs Nicholls: I believe so.

Mr Graham: Did Mr Nicholls often speak of her? In later life?

Mrs Nicholls: To me, yes. With others, he was circumspect. Learned the hard way how every little morsel is chewed over. Charlotte's biographer, Mrs Gaskell, was responsible for spreading some unkind stories. Her account vilifies both Mr Brontë and my husband. It caused my husband pain, but he never uttered a word against Mrs Gaskell. Nor will I, since it's a sin to speak ill of the dead, and she's long gone to face her Maker. Arthur opposed the biography, but his father-in-law was determined, and so my husband gave way. Mr Brontë feared the world would forget his daughter.

Mr Graham: Elizabeth Gaskell's book was certainly indiscreet.

Mrs Nicholls: I dare say a discreet one wouldn't sell.

Mr Graham: Hearsay puts down roots, and we're reliant on those who knew her to confirm or deny accounts. You're telling us theirs was a happy marriage?

Mrs Nicholls: I know there are letters in circulation where Charlotte wrote unkind things about Arthur. But that was before their marriage. When she changed her name to his, she changed her mind about him. People are allowed to. With my own eyes, I saw how con – contented [sound of a sniff] they were in each other's society.

Mr Graham: Take my handkerchief, Mrs Nicholls. Please. I certainly didn't mean to distress you. [indistinct noises] Do you need a glass of water?

Mrs Nicholls: I have my own handkerchief, thank you. [sound of a nose being blown] Yes, some water, please. [sound of liquid pouring into a glass] You may continue.

Mr Graham: After she passed away, Mr Nicholls stayed on with Mr Brontë in the parsonage. That must have had its moments.

Mrs Nicholls: They were the best of friends. Both loved her, you see.

Mr Graham: No friction? [silence] Mrs Nicholls, I need you to say yes or no when I ask a question. The machine picks up only sounds. When you shake your head it's not recorded. I'd take it as a great favour if you'd keep this in mind.

Mrs Nicholls: The only friction came from the outside world. The two were widowers who ought to have been left in peace. Instead, they were pestered by biographers and souvenir-hunters.

Mr Graham: Was Mr Nicholls sorry to leave Haworth? Following Mr Brontë's death?

Mrs Nicholls: He always missed the moors. Said they were glorious, although relentless. But he never shed any tears over the villagers. As for the oglers – that's what he called the tourists – he was well rid of them. They leave us in peace in Banagher. Too far off the beaten track.

Mr Graham: Yet your life and Charlotte Brontë's continued to intersect through your husband. Even after his death. How conscious of that connection were you?

Mrs Nicholls: I suppose I was always aware that Charlotte and I had Arthur in common. It struck me first when I met her, as a girl, and then later, when I found myself sharing a roof with her possessions. Arthur was like a brother to me before he was a husband: he was raised with us, you see. His mother and my father were brother and sister. Arthur's parents struggled – a brood of children, an unprofitable farm. Not that profitable farms are commonplace these days. Anyhow, to help out, Mama and Papa took Arthur and Alan in.

Mr Graham: Forgive me for being direct, but, well, the fact of the two of you sharing a husband … not simultaneously, of course … [sound of nervous laughter] that's quite a link between two ladies. Especially if they knew one another. How do you imagine Charlotte would have reacted? If she had a crystal ball and saw you'd both marry Mr Nicholls?

Mrs Nicholls: I refuse to speculate. Are we nearly finished?

Mr Graham: A little longer, please. Did people recognize her in Ireland? Ask for her autograph? Or souvenirs – hair clippings, and so on? There are reports of strangers approaching her in the street. What can you remember?

Mrs Nicholls: I remember everything.

[silence]

Mr Graham: In your own time, Mrs Nicholls. Speak about whatever you're comfortable with.

Mrs Nicholls: I'm not particularly comfortable with any of this. The world is overrun with Brontëmania and this interview will only fan the flames. They pretend to an interest born of reverence but really it's nothing more than voyeurism.

Mr Graham: People are spellbound. Which keeps Charlotte Brontë's work alive. Did she cast a spell over you?

Mrs Nicholls: I was only a girl. Meeting her was the most remarkable thing that ever happened to me. I never expected to earn my own living – indeed, I'd no skills to do so. Yet here was a lady who'd made her way in the world. I confess, Mr Graham, I admired her independence. But she allowed Arthur to believe she relied on him far more than she did.

Mr Graham: The Haworth years were a crucial period in Mr Nicholls' life. He met a remarkable family there, and an exceptional woman who became his wife. I mean, ah, what I'm trying to say, the first of two exceptional …

Mrs Nicholls: Don't go tying yourself up in knots, young man. I know I'm nobody.

[sound of a throat being cleared]

Mr Graham: Haworth is where Charlotte Brontë drew her inspiration. It's difficult to imagine her here in Ireland, or anywhere else.

Mrs Nicholls: To my mind, she missed Haworth when she was away, and felt lonely when she was there.

Mr Graham: I understood she had a strong attachment to the parsonage.

Mrs Nicholls: She talked up that house as though it were heaven on earth. But I suspect at times it stifled her. She quizzed me about Cuba Court – that's where we lived when she stayed with us. Would it be our 'always home'? I told her that depended on my brother Richard retaining the mastership. As it turned out, he lost it, and we had to move here to Hill House. That happened some years after Charlotte's death. But I digress. She said she'd no memory of any home except the parsonage, but once her father died she stood to lose it. Arthur changes all that, she said. He was expected to take over as perpetual vicar of the parish after Mr Brontë. Haworth decided otherwise. Still, their loss was our gain. Naturally, he came to live with us.

Mr Graham: Let me turn to something else now. Something of particular interest to my editor, Mr Shorter. I wonder, Mrs Nicholls, whether you still have any of Charlotte Brontë's possessions?

Mrs Nicholls: Some trifles. Nothing of substance.

Mr Graham: A range of Brontë artefacts, historically and culturally significant, have turned up in this house. Is there anything you haven't been able to part with?

Mrs Nicholls: They didn't just turn up here. Everyone knows Mr Nicholls brought them with him when he moved home to Ireland. It's no secret.

Mr Graham: May I ask what you have?

Mrs Nicholls: I really don't know. I'm past eighty years of age. I can't clamber about attics rummaging in boxes. I understood you were interested in my memories of Charlotte Brontë. But now I see you want to ferret about with her relics.

Mr Graham: Your memories are gold dust, Mrs Nicholls. Anything you can share adds to the sum of our knowledge about this gifted woman. But Mr Shorter is anxious to establish –

Mrs Nicholls: What's important about her is visible in the work. Read her novels and you'll see who she was.

Mr Graham: Her belongings also reveal something about Charlotte Brontë. The things she owned –

Mrs Nicholls: For heaven's sake! I'm out of patience with this business of her possessions! With the veneration the world attaches to them!

Mr Graham: With respect, Mrs Nicholls, you wouldn't be able to sell them without that sense of veneration.

[sound of a clock bonging]

Forgive me, Mrs Nicholls. That was rude of me. [silence] I always find clocks a friendly sound. [silence] May we proceed, please? I've lost my train of thought. Ah yes, Charlotte Brontë's possessions, which wound up in Ireland. They –

Mrs Nicholls: We must distinguish between two types of items attached to her name. There are the parsonage contents which Mr Nicholls transported to Ireland after Mr Brontë's death. And there are her own things. So, for example, the birch-wood rocking chair in that corner came from the parsonage. All the family would have used it. But her sewing box, or little writing desk, or a cloak of hers I came across one day – those have a more personal ... a kind of presence, I suppose.

Mr Graham: How soon did you realize there might be monetary value in Brontë materials?

Mrs Nicholls: Not as fast as those grasping villagers in Haworth. Sold stuff to all and sundry as soon as the visitors began arriving. I've never understood why people collect. It feels gloating. Mine, mine, mine!

Mr Graham: Her belongings allow people to step into Charlotte Brontë's world and become intimate with her.

Mrs Nicholls: But it's not real closeness. They can't know her because of it.

Mr Graham: They can know something of her.

[sound of a heavy sigh]

About the memorabilia. Mr Nicholls sold some items. And you have, too. Yes?

Mrs Nicholls: We parted company with a number of her possessions. Reluctantly, I must stress. Land prices collapsed. Bills mounted. Times changed. But some things we kept. And some decayed or deteriorated and were lost.

Mr Graham: It's wonderful to see these Brontë treasures valued in a family with links to the authoress.

Mrs Nicholls: If you say so.

Mr Graham: You don't regard the memorabilia as treasures?

Mrs Nicholls: They take up a great deal of space. But possessions can be prized in families because of dear associations, young man, and not because the owner was celebrated in the wider world.

Mr Graham: Still, one can imagine Charlotte and her sisters –

Mrs Nicholls: One can imagine a great deal. People do, in my experience. Often on baseless conjectures.

Mr Graham: You're quite right, let's stick to facts. The George Richmond drawing of Charlotte Brontë – Mr Nicholls brought it with him to this house, I believe?

Mrs Nicholls: That's correct. He told me she wore a green dress for the sitting. Although it's a charcoal, so no colour is apparent.

Mr Graham: And it hung in your home for decades. A constant companion to all of you.

Mrs Nicholls: Yes.

Mr Graham: A consolation to Mr Nicholls in his untimely loss.

Mrs Nicholls: Yes.

Mr Graham: Did you find it –

Mrs Nicholls: I don't know there's anything more to say about it. It's no longer in my keeping.

Mr Graham: But you shared your home with the portrait. You didn't have to do that. You could have asked your husband to pack it away.

Mrs Nicholls: Gracious me, why would I do that? It would have deprived Arthur of a long-standing pleasure. Every morning, he greeted the portrait, and told it – her – how he slept, and whether he dreamed of her. Every evening, he wished her sweet dreams. If he had overnight business away from us, he always made a beeline for the portrait on his return. There were times he greeted her before me.

Mr Graham: That must have needled you sometimes.

Mrs Nicholls: I had – have – nothing but admiration for Charlotte Brontë.

Mr Graham: But you wouldn't be human if you didn't feel second-best on occasion.

Mrs Nicholls: My feelings are none of your business.

Mr Graham: Mr Nicholls' actions, in saving so much from the parsonage, give us a clearer picture of the Brontës' lives. But at some personal cost to you, obliged to live with it all. [silence] Mrs Nicholls?

Mrs Nicholls: The detritus of other people's lives is peculiar. I doubt if anyone will bother about my knick-knacks once I'm gone. My treasures will be jumble.

Mr Graham: Do you miss any of the Brontë relics you parted with?

Mrs Nicholls: I'm rather sorry we sent the grandfather clock to Sotheby's. It gave faithful service to both households. Space looks bare when something goes.

[sound of a door opening, footsteps approaching]

Mr Graham: That clock face must have been as familiar to Charlotte Brontë as her own.

Mrs Nicholls: You could put it that way.

Mr Graham: For years, you heard the same sounds as Charlotte did. Saw the same sights.

Mrs Nicholls: Up to a point. Our boglands are not the Yorkshire moors.

[two women's voices, indistinct words]

My memory must be starting to fail me. My housekeeper, Miss Porter, reminds me I used to stop, sometimes, and stare at the clock

Mr Graham: What were you thinking?

Mrs Nicholls: Strange to think how it endured – and she didn't. How all of them who heard it telling the hours are dead – Charlotte, her sisters, her brother, their father. The talented Brontës, all turned to dust. My Arthur, too. I claim too much in calling him mine. *Our* Arthur, let's say.

[sound of knuckles rapped on a table]

Best day's work I ever did, clearing out that tatty pile of junk!

Unknown woman's voice: Miss Mary! You don't mean that! Turn off your machine please. Turn it off! Now!

[recording suspended for half an hour]

Mr Graham: Earlier, you expressed some resentment at Brontë belongings teeming through your home for four or five decades. It must have been difficult, at times.

Mrs Nicholls: I was being silly. Of course I was glad Mr Nicholls had his souvenirs. It consoled him to see her spectacles sitting on a shelf in the room where he read his newspaper, and so on.

Mr Graham: This is a ticklish subject, so I must beg your pardon in advance. Some people question the propriety of Mr Nicholls' actions, although not his entitlement, in removing everything from the parsonage and transporting it to Ireland.

Mrs Nicholls: That's rich coming from people who cast him off like an old shoe! Arthur inherited everything from Patrick Brontë, aside from some minor bequests. Had he seen out his days in the parsonage, I dare say things would have been different. But he had to empty out all personal effects before his replacement arrived. He'd no choice but to take everything away. Four days' notice, he was given. I ask you!

Mr Graham: It does sound heartless when you put it like that. You mentioned a grandfather clock. Is there any other Brontë memorabilia to which you have a particular attachment?

Mrs Nicholls: A vanity set Charlotte left behind in our house by mistake. She loved it because her sisters bought it for her. I offered to post it, but she said she'd be back to collect it in person. I've never been able to part with that.

Mr Graham: About her wedding dress. There are persistent rumours Mr Nicholls took it with him to Ireland. Do you have it? [silence] Mrs Nicholls? Do you?

Mrs Nicholls: I do.

Mr Graham: May I see it?

Mrs Nicholls: You may not.

Mr Graham: Mr Shorter is especially keen on this. He suggests you might be gracious enough to allow us to arrange for someone to sketch it?

Mrs Nicholls: Impossible.

Mr Graham: Oh, but surely –

Mrs Nicholls: I said no.

Mr Graham: What kind of condition is it in?

Mrs Nicholls: I take excellent care of all the Brontë artefacts, Mr Graham.

Mr Graham: No one can doubt it. But Mr Shorter, who is a great admirer of the Brontës, is worried because cloth is delicate. Really, he's enormously concerned about the wedding gown.

Mrs Nicholls: Because he's such a romantic.

Mr Graham: He's thinking of posterity, Mrs Nicholls.

Mrs Nicholls: Posterity can jump off a cliff, as far as I'm concerned. Arthur and I had quite enough of it dogging our tracks.

Mr Graham: Charlotte describes the dress in letters. But imagine if it went on display in a cultural institution. The Victoria and Albert Museum, for example. Think of the queues to admire it!

Mrs Nicholls: To gawk, you mean.

Mr Graham: It all helps to preserve her legacy.

Mrs Nicholls: The gawpers don't care about her books. It's the melodrama they want. Misfortune and heartbreak and wuthering winds. A wedding dress fit for a sprite wafted in from the moors. I'm tired now, I need to rest. When you reach my age, young man, you'll understand how exhausting it is blowing the cobwebs off the past.

Mr Graham: May we pick this up again later, Mrs Nicholls?

Mrs Nicholls: Very well. Tomorrow morning, same time.

[sound of a bell]

Recording ends

CHAPTER 3

'Come and eat a bite of luncheon now, Miss Mary. That young man's questions have worn you out. I reheated yesterday's meat pie.'

'A few parings of cheese and a lettuce leaf would have been enough, Hope. The pie could have done for dinner.'

'It's a false saving to skimp on meals. Doctor's bills are dearer than the butcher's, Miss. You need to keep your strength up.'

'Very well. But no dessert or coffee.'

I went into the dining room, to a place setting for one, and picked at my food. Eating alone was dreary. A daughter would have been company for me, and a son could have contributed to the household income. But childlessness was something else I shared with Charlotte. Along with a need – belated in my case, admittedly – to practise economies. After Mama's death in 1902, our income had dwindled. The yearly allowance settled on her by my grandfather at the time of her marriage ceased when she did.

Worry shredded my peace of mind. Since Arthur's death almost seven years ago, I had been holding on by my fingernails. But my financial situation deteriorated year on year, and now

I could no longer make ends meet. The house was tumbling down about our ears – holes the size of cabbages in the roof, and the window frames were rotted through. They need replacing, every last one of them. I was faced with selling Hill House and moving into rented rooms, or begging for a bed in my brother's home. Worse was the prospect of parting company with Hope Porter after her lifetime in our family's employ. Towards her, I owed a particular duty.

From my pocket, I extracted Arthur's list. I scanned it so often I was almost word-perfect. Most of the prized items had been disposed of already, but something valuable to a collector might still remain. If so, I needed to translate it into money – nostalgia was an extravagance. Keeping her possessions was an act of loyalty. But loyalty was an unaffordable luxury with Hope's wages unpaid and the insurance policy on the house left to lapse.

HAWORTH PARSONAGE CONTENTS TRANSPORTED TO HILL HOUSE, BANAGHER

One wedding dress Charlotte Brontë
One mantle to wear over wedding dress
Black shoes, white gloves - part of wedding costume
One framed engraving Charlotte Brontë by George Richmond
One framed profile Branwell Brontë
One framed photograph Haworth Parsonage - glass cracked en route
One engraving Duke of Wellington
One engraving William Makepeace Thackeray
Two rocking chairs
Three laptop writing desks
One long case clock
One long gun Revd P. Brontë
One plaited hair bracelet with amethyst clasp Charlotte Brontë

One carved wooden swan signed HB Charlotte Brontë
One Bible Charlotte Brontë previously Aunt Branwell's
Various first editions by Currer Bell, Ellis Bell, Acton Bell and Revd P. Brontë
Selection of pamphlets by Revd P. Brontë
Five boxes books belonging to Brontë family library
Six boxes Brontë papers and letters
One box miniature books by four Brontë children
Three sewing boxes
Items of clothing, bonnets and shoes Brontë family
One album of ferns collected by Charlotte Brontë
Drawing of Keeper her dog by Emily Brontë
Drawing of Flossy her dog by Anne Brontë
Various watercolours by Charlotte, Emily and Anne Brontë
Various samplers Charlotte, Emily and Anne Brontë and Maria Branwell Brontë
One vanity set comprising mirror, brush and comb made of bone in case with pink silk lining Charlotte Brontë

Signed: Arthur Bell Nicholls,
Monday 18th November 1861
This is an incomplete list, compiled by Martha Brown and Hope Porter. To be added to.
NB Martha Brown and Plato, the Parsonage dog, also came with me to Banagher.
Martha Brown returned to Haworth.

Mama's face when the wagon pulled up and begun unloading the parsonage contents. *He'll clog up the entire house!* Mama had told Arthur to bring what he wanted, not anticipating how much he'd carry away. He kept the whole caboodle for decades, until life became grainier for people like us – landlords. The government had ordered us to part with our land to the tenants who farmed it. Even when we retained a few fields, rents dried up and earnings from our property plummeted. Britain was turning its back on us while Ireland was turning militant – we were there on sufferance. Our fortunes were in decline.

For Arthur, it was like losing a limb to part with anything of the Brontës' but especially Charlotte's belongings. However, he knew we'd taken him in after Haworth – without a word being spoken, he understood where his duty lay. And so he began the process of selling Charlotte's possessions piecemeal, with Clement Shorter as one of his intermediaries. After parting with something, he used to shut himself up in his study.

As for me, I was sorrier to let some things go than others, but needs must. Faced with death duties after Arthur's passing, I put Charlotte's and Emily's desks into a Sotheby's auction, and peddled the child's tea set the three small girls and their brother had played with to the Brontë museum in Haworth – *Ladies all I pray make free/And tell me how you like your tea* said the legend along the side.

I squinted at the list. Hardly anything left on it to sell now. I rang the bell for the table to be cleared. Hope Porter entered unobtrusively, as always. She had an economy of movement, which was just as well because she did most of the household's work – apart from the laundry, which we sent out, and occasional repairs and gardening handled by Ben Coughlan.

Hope's build was along fine lines, with a delicate face. As a child, we used to think she'd never grow bigger than the doll she lugged everywhere, but a spurt at sixteen left her almost matching me for height. *Strange little creature. Woeful as a raincloud.* Richard was dismissive of her. He could charm most females, but Hope was immune to him, even as a tiny girl. She'd been owlish, accustomed only to the grown-up world. Arthur alone had been able raise a smile in her, with his sugar treats and juggling tricks. I counted back to work out her age. Why, she'd be sixty-six at the end of the month.

'Hope, I'm presuming the first Mrs Nicholls' wedding outfit is still safe where it's stored in the house?'

'Naturally, Miss Mary.'

'And the moths haven't nibbled on it? Have you checked it recently?'

She primmed her face at me. 'It was right as rain last time I looked. I take proper care of it.'

'Where is it?'

'In the box room. In an old brown chest with leather straps.'

'I haven't laid eyes on it since …'

Hand lapped in hand, she raised her eyes to mine. 'I remember.'

'I'd like to see it again.'

'I wouldn't, Miss Mary.'

'Why not?'

'It'll only set you thinking about what's gone. And that makes a body sad.'

'Show me where it is, Hope.'

'Stairs'll make your hips ache, Miss.'

'That's my business. Besides, I can rub liniment on them.'

'And what'll you rub on your heartache?'

'That's enough, Hope.'

She wiped her hands down the front of her skirts, as though washing them of me, and led the way up to the box room, to a chest with *Haworth Parsonage* painted on the lid. The H and P were decipherable, the other lettering barely visible. A scent of beeswax polish rose up from the wood. I made the polish myself, the way my mother taught me, a household job I liked – and not only because there were fewer servants than in her day. Hope Porter was the only full-time one now, whereas once we had a household.

Gingerly, I lowered myself into a kneeling position and lifted the lid. Stale air escaped, the smell mixed with lavender from the dried petals we used to deter moths. Hope hovered at my back. 'Thank you, Hope, I can manage from here.'

'Please don't, Miss Mary.'

'Don't what?'

'Sell it. Master Arthur, he prized it.'

'Indeed he did. It's an heirloom.'

'I've kept it safe all these years. For the master's sake.'

'You've kept it safe? This is my house. Surely it's me who's preserved it!'

'Maybe you've mixed feelings about it, Miss. Maybe that's why you'd think about selling it to that London fellow.'

'I haven't a notion what you're talking about.'

'I'm thinking … Miss, I'm sorry to say it … the dress stands for everything she had and you didn't.'

'Really, you forget yourself, Hope Porter!'

'I know I'm speaking out of turn. But it's no secret we're hard up. And them hoarders with money would love to get their hands on her wedding dress.'

'I think you've said quite enough. Kindly attend to your duties elsewhere. Close the door behind you.'

'Poor gentleman, he moped over it. 'Twasn't healthy, the way he made something holy out of that wedding finery. Many's the time I thought of begging him to let it go, but I never had the heart – I knew it would pain him to lose it.'

'He felt that way about every blessed thing she owned. This house was jammed with her belongings.'

'Ah, Miss Mary, but the dress was … I hardly like to put the word on it.'

'Go on. You may as well finish what you started.'

'It was sacred to him. When he looked at it, he saw her wearing it. She wasn't a corpse, but a bride, standing in the church at Haworth.'

Winded, I had to shove some boxes off an old chair and sit down. Hope stood watching, arms folded. 'How do you know?'

'Master told me himself. Regular as clockwork, he used to get me to unpack it all for him, and spread it out on a clean bedsheet. You didn't know?'

I shook my head. 'On their wedding anniversary? June the twenty-ninth?'

'Never then. He didn't want you upset. It wasn't always the same date, but a day or two either side of it. When you'd be gone from home for a few hours.'

'What did he do with the wedding clothes? Stroke them? Smell them?'

'I wouldn't know. I'd leave him alone with his thoughts. But I'd watch the clock. After an hour, I'd go back upstairs and stand outside the door. There were times I could hear his sobs, other times there wasn't a sound. I'd knock and call – Master Arthur, I've left a cup of tea for you outside. Drink it up, and take yourself off for a good long walk with the dogs! I'd wait nearby, out of sight. When I heard him stamp down the stairs, I'd go in and put it all away again.'

'How did I never know this, in four decades of marriage?'

'He'd get up in the morning and know in his own mind it was time to look at the dress again. Then he'd ask you what your plans were for the day. If you had none, he'd beg a favour, one to take you out of the house. Sometimes, he'd pick my brains for an errand he could send you on.'

The pair had conspired against me. I breathed hard through my nose. But maybe it was as well I'd never noticed that annual ceremony.

'Don't be hurt, Miss. He was the best husband he could be to you. Only ...'

'Only he buried his heart in Haworth Church, with Charlotte.'

A sliver of time elapsed between eye blinks, while we took the measure of one another. 'You knew the bargain you were making, Miss Mary. He never hid how he felt.'

I had no answer to that. My gaze fastened on the trunk. 'I suppose if you helped take care of this' – my mouth drooped of its own accord – 'bridal array, you've seen it dozens of times?'

'I have. It never loses its power to …'

'No. I don't imagine it would. Seeing it once was enough for me.'

'I remember, Miss. Just before your own wedding day. You'd a fancy to try it on.'

'I was already walking in a dead woman's shoes. What a fool to add her wedding dress to the load. Is it all there, Hope? Everything she wore that morning in Haworth?'

'Apart from her wedding bonnet and a short veil that went over it. Prettiest bonnet ever to circle a face, according to Master Arthur.'

'Charlotte told me about it. A symphony of white lace and silk rosebuds, apparently. I'm surprised the bonnet isn't with the rest of her things.'

'The master give it to that Martha Brown for one or other of her sisters' weddings. Pearls before swine.'

'He was fond of her.'

'I never had any time for that Martha Brown. She'd no refinement. Will we go downstairs now, Miss Mary? Leave the dress and whatnot in peace?'

'I'd like to sit here a while. That'll be all, Hope.'

As soon as I was alone, I rolled back the patched sheet covering the chest's contents. Each item was wrapped in tissue paper. On top lay a pair of child-sized gloves with a pearl button fastening at the wrist. Underneath, a web of lace was folded into squares – a shawl as insubstantial as Charlotte. Arthur said she wore a mantle so I supposed that's what she called it. Tentatively, I rested one hand on the garment, and heard a rustle that was almost a sigh. I moved it aside to reveal a soap bubble of a gown.

Certain objects have the capacity to bridge time and distance. 'Oh Charlotte,' I whispered, and fluttered it out. The dress was as beautiful as I remembered, although its colour had changed – darkened from snowdrop white to bone. I held it at arm's length and gazed.

For a minute, maybe two, I yielded to sentiment. Strange, to think it was only my second time examining Charlotte's bridal regalia in more than half a century of sharing a home with it. Now, my skin was as frail as the coating on boiled milk but the gown remained youthful. I draped it over one arm and knuckled my eyes, waiting for my breathing to steady.

I knew better than to jam on Charlotte's dress this time – even if I could lift my arms high enough to attempt it. No borrowed plumes for me. If I couldn't fit into it back then, it was pointless to try now. The Mary Bell I'd been, last time I looked at this dress, was young still – possibilities glinting. A tender charge for my youthful self coursed through my blood.

Even if I couldn't wear the gown, I could admire it. I could hold it against me, as I'd done before, and look in the mirror. And so I did. The looking glass reflected a silver-haired woman in borrowed finery. By some trick of fancy or the light, Charlotte filled out the dress in my arms: hands emerging from the sleeves, head pushing up through the collar, tiny feet pointing from the hem.

I could never quite grasp the nature of her love for him. His was easy to comprehend. Hers was more complicated. She had arrayed herself in ceremonial fashion when there was no need – he'd have been happy with any version of Charlotte Brontë walking towards him at the altar. Why put such effort into her wedding dress? It must have been because she found his love for her irresistible.

I bundled away the mantle and other items, but instead of packing the gown, I carried it to my bedroom. Tenderly, I stroked the cloth, fitted a padded coat-hanger between the shoulders, and hung it from the window rail. I left the curtains open, and the dress moved gently in a drift of air through some gaps between wood and glass in the frame. Sleep overtook me as I lay watching it swish from side to side.

*

That night I dreamed I saw her standing with Arthur on the moors, bound together as tight as a lover's knot. I saw him bending towards her, his palm against the small of her back, listening closely. She was telling him something, her face flushed with vitality. I strained to hear their conversation but the dream was soundless.

A fox's bark in the garden, with an answering howl from the gravedigger's dog, startled me awake. I opened my eyes to moonbeams silvering Charlotte's gown. The dress dipped, coquettish. We were low on oil – a bill too long unpaid had dented our credit with that shopkeeper – so I struck a match and lit the candle on my bedside locker. The moonlight was so bright I almost didn't need the flame. But at my stage of life, a misstep could lead to a fall, and a fall to broken bones which might not heal.

Pool of light in hand, I approached the dress. Captivating. Candle held high, my eyes caressed the narrow bodice and minuscule waist. What wren bones she'd had. But the heart of an eagle. Just short of sixty years since she wore it. A panelled underskirt was visible through the gauzy muslin, and I carried the candle closer to admire the seamstress's handiwork. Closer. How delicate a confection. How vulnerable to a crooked nail. My hand shook. 'Careful, Mary,' I whispered. My hands had a palsy, I was starting to drop things. I set down the candle and reached up, lifting the gown off the rail. Then I laid it across my arm, retrieved my candle, and processed to the bathroom like a high priestess.

I placed the candlestick on the rim of the bath, creaked into a kneeling position, and spread out the dress inside the tub. Lovingly, I smoothed its folds against the enamel, straightened collar and sleeves. It occurred to me to wonder where she'd hung it in the parsonage in the days preceding her wedding. Perhaps on the back of a door, covered by a cloth wrapper. Or laid across one of the other girls' empty beds, since she was the only Brontë sister left. Had she felt a metamorphosis when she slipped it on and her friend Ellen Nussey hooked her up? Perhaps she had told me once. Memories were like butterflies. Bright when they chanced by, but fleeting.

This was a dress with power. 'Do it quick before it tricks you into changing your mind,' I said, my voice grating through the empty room. I lifted the candlestick again and bent over the bath. One of my own beeswax candles. The flame ruffled, and steadied itself, but a teardrop of wax slid from the column. It alighted just above the hem of the gown and, quick as thought, cooled and hardened. How pretty it was – like a honey-gold pearl. I leaned lower, candlestick tilted. Another wax droplet touched a sleeve. Now one on the bodice. My hand dipped down and I rippled the flame, oh so delicately, against the collar. It kindled at once. A quiver of fire sprang up against the surrounding material – kissing the cloth, I fancied. It flickered to the shoulders, caught on the bodice, arched towards the sleeves and danced onto the skirt. Soon, its touch embraced the entire dress.

Fire has always had the power to mesmerize. The way the flames flex, their sinuous movement, their sense of purpose. Their hunger. The spectacle hypnotised me: I had to force myself back. The blaze was intense – exhilarating. But it was also brief, and soon began to dwindle, snapping and sputtering. Smoke crimped upwards and chafed my throat, but I waited while the fire burnt itself out. Only a few blackened rags curled at the bottom of the bath, their edges glowing.

It was done.

'Miss Mary! Are you in there? I smell burning.'

'Just taking care of a little housekeeping, Hope. No need to be alarmed.'

A rattle on the doorknob. 'At two o'clock in the morning? In the bathroom?'

'It's a good time to burn something private.'

'Miss, it's not safe for you to lock doors. What if you fall?'

'I'm finished now. I'll be out presently.'

The door knob twisted back and forwards. 'Let me help you back to bed. Open up, Miss Mary.'

'Hope, there's no need to be alarmed. Off you go. I'm perfectly fine.'

I heard footsteps receding. Only then did I stretch out my hand and stir the remnants of Charlotte's wedding dress with my fingers. A few vestiges clung to my skin. Pain gouged my leg and hip as I levered myself to my feet. At the sink, I washed my blackened hands, collected the candle and returned to bed. I managed a few hours' rest. A sound conscience has a knack of encouraging sleep.

When dawn announced itself, I awoke with an instant memory of what I had done. Stiff from neck to knee, I eased from the bed, nudged my feet into slippers and arms into a robe, and returned to the bathroom. A mound of ashes lay in the bottom of the tub. Contented, I viewed my handiwork.

Like her, it was gone – it belonged to the realm of the imagination now. The house felt purified, as if an offering had been made to some deity.

The door handle squeaked, and Hope Porter stood beside me. 'I looked in the trunk. It's not there.'

'Don't sneak up on me, Hope. Mama taught you better manners than that.'

'What did you burn last night?'

'None of your business.'

She glared at me, hands clenched into fists. 'Her wedding dress. You set it on fire, didn't you?'

'It's my property. I can do what I like with it.'

'It's not yours.'

'In law, it is.'

A sniff. 'That's as may be. But you did a wrong thing. I'm surprised at you, Miss Mary.'

'Because the dress was worth money?'

'No, Miss. Because you've always done your best with her things. Setting fire to it wasn't like you.' A beat. 'And her as nice as can be to you when she was the master's wife. How would she feel about it?'

'You don't know everything, Hope. Don't jump to conclusions. Now, I'm ravenous this morning. I believe I'll have two eggs for breakfast. Soft-boiled, please.'

The skin tightened around Hope's eyes. Words simmered on the tip of her tongue, but she fought them back.

CHAPTER 4

Brontë/Ireland recording: number two of two
Interviewee: Mrs Mary Nicholls, widow of Revd Arthur
Bell Nicholls, formerly curate of Haworth, Yorkshire
Date: Made on the 20th day of August 1913
Location: Hill House, Banagher, King's County, Ireland
Interviewer: Mr Harry Graham of the *Illustrated London News*
Present: Mrs Nicholls and Mr Graham

Mr Graham: Mrs Nicholls, yesterday you were kind enough to share some personal impressions of Charlotte Brontë. Despite the passage of time, interest in the Brontës keeps growing. Newspaper articles, books, scholarly dissertations.

Mrs Nicholls: A lot of what's printed is servants' tittle-tattle dressed up as fact.

Mr Graham: Paper never refuses ink.

Mrs Nicholls: But some of what's published is utter tripe. That Branwell wrote *Wuthering Heights*. That the sisters were love rivals for a curate who died. That their father banned any mention of Ireland in the parsonage. Charlotte told me they prayed for Ireland during the Famine.

Mr Graham: How aware of her Irish roots was Charlotte Brontë?

Mrs Nicholls: She seemed surprised we weren't a bunch of backward savages. But Irish colour certainly intrigued her. She heard the *caoine* during her stay in Banagher – the lament for the dead – and said it made the hairs on the back of her neck stand on end.

Mr Graham: Scholars say they can detect the Celtic heritage in some of her themes – a tendency towards spectral undercurrents. As when Jane Eyre hears Mr Rochester call to her across hundreds of miles.

Mrs Nicholls: She'd a passion for ghost stories. Told me one she heard in Ireland, from – well, never mind who. Something about a phantom house, occupied by a rather unnerving brother and sister.

Mr Graham: Imagine finding that tale among her papers!

Mrs Nicholls: You never know.

Mr Graham: Can you call to mind the story?

Mrs Nicholls: There's a housekeeper in a new position, who gets lost out walking when a mist rolls in. She's given shelter in a mysterious property and spends an eventful night there. I really can't recall anymore. It was gripping, I know that much. Charlotte had me write it out for her, because she'd cut her hands and couldn't hold the pen, you see.

Mr Graham: It may turn up yet. Some lost work of hers could be lining a forgotten croquet box or trunk in an attic. Perhaps unfinished work. That has its own weight. It's full of possibilities. If she'd lived longer, there might have been a story with an Irish setting.

Mrs Nicholls: I believe you're right, Mr Graham. Charlotte said something I've never forgotten when we were out walking by the bog one day, admiring the spark of colour from the flowers. Snipe were nearby. Have you heard the noise they make? No? They go *hu-hu-hu*. An otherworldly sound. She squeezed my fingers – she'd often do that when she was moved – and, oh, it sounds foolish when I say it now.

Mr Graham: No detail is foolish, I assure you.

Mrs Nicholls: She said, 'In Ireland, I feel something stirring deep down inside me. Sometimes we remember things we never knew.' That may have been her Irish blood calling to her.

Mr Graham: 'Sometimes we remember things we never knew.' How … strange.

Mrs Nicholls: Or perceptive. 'Don't look back,' Charlotte said to me once. 'It makes us too sad. And sadness is something we have to try and avoid.' But I seem to do little else *except* look back.

Mr Graham: You're doing it to good effect here, Mrs Nicholls. Let me turn to photographs. No verified photographs of Charlotte Brontë exist. But there are two which people claim to be of her. I have copies here. Could you look them over and confirm whether they're genuine? I'll start with the Henderson one –

Mrs Nicholls: It's not her.

Mr Graham: Are you certain? Take another look. For the record, it shows a lady in a checked dress with a book open on her lap.

Mrs Nicholls: It's not Charlotte.

Mr Graham: My editor will be deflated. He paid a considerable sum of money for that photograph.

Mrs Nicholls: He was rooked. She looks nothing like Charlotte. Apart from anything else, Charlotte was extremely near-sighted and habitually wore spectacles. If she had a book to hand, she'd either be wearing or holding them.

Mr Graham: It's not unheard of for a lady to whip them off for a photograph, perhaps push them out of sight.

Mrs Nicholls: True. But anyhow this individual is much larger. Charlotte had a narrow frame. Thin as string.

Mr Graham: I also have a Yorkshire Moors picture. Two versions of it, in fact, you'll see why in a moment. Let me – I'm all fingers and thumbs today – get it out of the folder. Experts agree it bears a strong likeness to a painting of Charlotte and her sisters in the National Gallery in London. Branwell Brontë's *Pillar Portrait*. Which I gather you discovered here in Banagher after your husband's death?

Mrs Nicholls: Arthur had relics squirrelled away all over the house. Yes, I stumbled across the painting in a box room where he kept some of his Haworth things. Folded up inside brown paper, on top of a wardrobe. Looked half-finished, to tell you the truth. Striking, I'll grant you. But not to everyone's taste. I suppose Arthur didn't care for it. It went to the London gallery. They have the Richmond drawing, too. I'm told the world beats a path to Trafalgar Square to view Charlotte's face.

Mr Graham: Here we are, I have the moors photograph for you now, Mrs Nicholls. Two walkers in bonnets and cloaks. As you can see, one has her back to the camera, and hasn't been identified, but her companion is visible in profile. We've studied it under a magnifying glass and believe it may be Charlotte Brontë. What do you think?

Mrs Nicholls: Let me hold it, please. There's a slight resemblance. But it isn't her.

Mr Graham: I have a magnifying glass here if you'd like to take a closer look?

Mrs Nicholls: Very well. [sound of rustling] No, it's not Charlotte. The fact is, she was never photographed. If there was any chance of that happening, it would have been when Lady Rosse of Birr Castle asked her to sit during Charlotte's honeymoon. Lady Rosse was quite the pioneer with a camera. She sent word she'd call on us at Cuba Court to meet the bride. Mama was in a tizzy – no one from Birr Castle had visited us before. Or since. Her ladyship tried very hard to persuade her to pose, but Charlotte was adamant. Mama would have liked her to oblige the countess, and appealed to Arthur, but he said he knew better than to interfere on such a delicate matter.

Mr Graham: Delicate, how?

Mrs Nicholls: Are you single, Mr Graham? I suspected as much. Until then, Mama had been the principal female in Arthur's life. When he declined to intervene, it told her she'd been toppled from the seat of honour.

Mr Graham: So no photograph was taken?

Mrs Nicholls: None.

Mr Graham: Are you quite certain? Things can get misplaced and misfiled.

Mrs Nicholls: Please understand, young man, there's no photograph. Charlotte was horrified at the suggestion.

Mr Graham: It seems an awful pity.

Mrs Nicholls: Lady Rosse exerted every iota of her personality, but Charlotte dug in her heels. I should know – I was present.

Mr Graham: Another of life's if-onlys. I suppose it was down to modesty, or shyness, or something like that.

Mrs Nicholls: The idea of a photograph was repugnant to Charlotte Brontë. She made the best of things, but was, how shall I put it? Self-conscious about her appearance. She couldn't abide people looking at her. I remember asking about her wedding day, when she must have been the focus of attention, and she said she tolerated the fuss because she knew it would only last a few hours. I spouted some twaddle about how every bride is beautiful, and she let fly a peal of laughter. 'I put my best foot forward, but one is as one's made,' she said. 'I try to keep myself neat. Anne, now, she was the pretty one.'

Mr Graham: But those are wonderful details, straight from life. They show how unassuming she was.

Mrs Nicholls: I wouldn't call her unassuming. You misunderstand what I'm telling you.

Mr Graham: Help me to understand, then. I'm puzzled because she posed for artists – Branwell Brontë, and the society artist George Richmond.

Mrs Nicholls: Her publisher coaxed her to the one, to sell books, and her brother to the other because he'd hopes of becoming a portrait painter. Sometimes, we do things we'd rather not for people we care about. But I'm guessing, which I'd prefer not to do. Our interview is meant to put facts on the record.

Mr Graham: Indeed. Compared with other people of your acquaintance, was she more advanced on issues to do with love and marriage – or love without marriage?

Mrs Nicholls: Really, young man!

Mr Graham: Hear me out. When you consider the novels were published more than sixty years ago, some of her heroines are astonishing. Inside six years, between *Jane Eyre* in 1847 and *Villette* in 1853, she produced a memorable group of independent-minded women. Did she draw on memory as well as imagination? Could there be a clue in the title, *Jane Eyre: An Autobiography*?

Mrs Nicholls: I think you're reading too much into a book title, Mr Graham.

Mr Graham: But here's what I'm driving at: do the novels reflect Charlotte Brontë the woman as well as the authoress?

Mrs Nicholls: I'm afraid I couldn't say.

Mr Graham: Some of her letters suggest she was no Victorian miss.

Mrs Nicholls: No one expects their private correspondence to be pawed over, and published, the way Charlotte's has been.

Mr Graham: But the letters do tell us lot about her.

Mrs Nicholls: People put her on a pedestal after she died. Arthur complained to my mother about it. 'I don't want my wife up there because it pushes her beyond my reach, Aunt Harriette,' he said. And no sooner is she up there than some scoundrels come along and try to knock her off with innuendo and allegations. Are we nearly finished? I'm starting to tire. I'd no idea you meant to quiz me at such length.

Mr Graham: Just a little longer, please. When you talk about people trying to topple her from her pedestal, do you mean the Heger letters and the rumpus they caused?

Mrs Nicholls: Under no circumstances will I discuss them. Rumours about Charlotte Brontë are ten a penny.

Mr Graham: This is more than a rumour. Four letters in her own hand support it.

Mrs Nicholls: Mr Graham, please don't play me for a fool. There were two conditions to our meeting. The interview material to go to a reputable public institution, after your Mr Shorter gets his pound of flesh, and no mention of the Brussels letters or Charlotte's professor.

Mr Graham: It's a chance to scotch misleading reports, Mrs Nicholls. If Charlotte Brontë didn't write the letters – if the Hegers have pulled a trick – we're happy to print anything you can say to support that.

Mrs Nicholls: I grew up in an era where it was considered vulgar for one lady to discuss another in public. And nothing I say will change people's minds if they're determined to believe the worst. Charlotte's private letters – published in the *Times*! It's monstrous! Utterly indefensible! And that's my final word on the matter.

Mr Graham: Naturally, the *Illustrated London News* respects your reticence. But discoveries like this keep her name alive. As you said yourself, Mr Brontë feared the world would forget his daughter.

Mrs Nicholls: I hardly think he'd want her remembered for those letters.

Mr Graham: Maybe so, but if the letters tell the truth – and the experts believe they do – then it's right to publish them. The truth should always take priority.

[sound of a cane rapped twice on the ground and chair legs scraping]

Mrs Nicholls: I've had quite enough. Good day.

Recording ends

Recordings and written transcripts held in the private collection of Mr Napoleon Witt of Austin, Texas, United States of America. Access restricted.

Other Brontëana known to be in the Witt Collection includes:

First editions of *Jane Eyre*, *Shirley* and *Villette* by Currer Bell and *The Professor* by Charlotte Brontë

First edition of *Poems* by Currer, Ellis and Acton Bell

Juvenilia by Emily and Anne Brontë in form of two miniature books and sketchpad

Watercolour of the Reverend Patrick Brontë by Branwell Brontë

Charcoal sketch of Emily Brontë with dog by Branwell Brontë

Ivory vanity set in black leather case belonging to Charlotte Brontë plus letter of authentication in author's hand

Notebook containing notes made by Mr Harry Graham of the *Illustrated London News* following a series of meetings with Mrs Mary Anna Bell Nicholls of Banagher, Ireland, in 1913.

Typed note pinned to list:
Harry Graham died in an explosion in France in 1917, aged twenty-eight, leaving a widow and four-month-old son. His newspaper set up an annual prize in his memory. It was discontinued after 1927 following the death of the editor, Clement King Shorter, the previous year.

CHAPTER 5

Harry Graham left me fuming with his sanctimonious utterances about the truth. I had read and re-read the letters reproduced in the *Times* sent to me by Clement Shorter the previous month. His accompanying note had pressed me to agree to a phonograph recording. Normally, I'd have refused, but those old letters of Charlotte's had overridden my reservations. Her passion-soaked pleas for love, flaunted across news-sheets, needed to be counteracted. 'She's Jane Eyre, not Bertha Rochester,' I'd cried. Jane was prudent – she resisted temptation. It was Bertha whose urges tipped her into insanity. Wasn't it? After poring over those letters I'd no longer known what to believe. But I was in no doubt about the message I hoped to convey to Harry Graham. Except journalists were slippery customers.

In the parlour, I spread out the odious newspaper on the desktop of my walnut bureau. It was dated 29 July 1913. Charlotte's letters were printed in French, apart from one postscript in English, just as she'd written them. Translations had been added and notes prefaced the letters, the word 'copyright' prominent to deter duplication. This must have been my fifth or sixth reading, but their emotional charge winded me once again. Charlotte's desolation coiled its tendrils across the years.

I am in a fever – I lose my appetite and my sleep – I pine away
Day and night I find neither rest nor peace
Disappointment flings me down again into overwhelming misery
I find it difficult to be cheerful so long as I think I shall never see you more
If my master withdraws his friendship from me entirely, I shall be absolutely without hope – if he gives me a little friendship – a very little – I shall be content
To forbid me to write to you – to refuse to reply to me – that will be to tear from me the only joy I have on earth.

This Belgian professor had pushed ajar the door of her heart, whether intentionally or accidentally, and once it was opened she had hungered for love beyond any capacity for self-restraint. The letters suggested she was immoral. But wasn't it equally immoral to print her innermost thoughts for voyeurs to feast on? There could be no justification for this violation. My fingers itched to tear the newspaper into shreds. But it was only one among thousands of copies.

A knock. Hope Porter stood in the doorway with a tea tray, although I hadn't ordered any. 'This'll perk you up, Miss Mary.'

'Thank you, Hope. You take good care of me.'

'I'll pour it out for you, Miss. The day you've had, would annoy a saint.' Before I could stop her, she added two spoons of sugar.

'You know I'm trying to give it up. It's an unnecessary expense.'

'You need it this day. You look worn out.'

When I accepted the cup and saucer, the spoon fell to the ground.

'A dropped spoon – Lizzie Nolan always said that's a sign of a visitor,' said Hope.

'I hope not. I've had enough of visitors.'

*

'It's that Mr Graham. Sends in these. Asking to see you.'

I cast an eye over the nosegay of violets. 'I thought he'd gone back to London.'

'Seems not, Miss Mary.'

'Put them in water and tell him I'm indisposed.'

Hope Porter left but returned a few moments later with the flowers in a crystal vase. 'He's given me this letter. Had it ready in his pocket.'

Banagher, Friday August 22nd

My dear Mrs Nicholls,

Allow me to apologize unreservedly for any offence I caused you during our last encounter. In my eagerness, I trespassed on your good nature. It was unforgiveable of me – yet I hope you will be gracious enough to do so. I am loathe

to part company on such a sour note. Would
you kindly afford me one further meeting for no
purpose other than to apologize in person?

Yours sincerely,
Harry Graham
International Affairs Correspondent
Illustrated London News

The man was a mosquito for persistence, but the violets' woodland scent suggested renewal and possibilities, and life in an Irish midlands town could be dull. 'Send him in, Hope.'

Civilities were exchanged. For a few moments, we looked each other over – which tends not to be flattering at my stage of life. As for my visitor, beneath the deferential veneer I detected a rakish air. Perhaps it sprang from the boater under his arm, the houndstooth waistcoat beneath his jacket. I tried to see the room through his eyes: a few muddy oil paintings on the walls, an elderly woman feeling unvalued and eroded.

'We haven't had much of a chance to chat. You're a Londoner, am I correct, Mr Graham?'

'Guilty as charged. Born in Southwark, south of the Thames. Ever been, Mrs Nicholls?'

'The only time I left Ireland was to go to Wales, following my wedding. Long before you were born, young man.'

'Ain't that a shame. London's a pearl – the empire's chief city.'

'London will have to manage without me. I'm plaited into Banagher like a twisted straw rope. How's your phono-thing? Packed it all away?' I was testing him, to see if he was here to apologize, or return us to a business footing.

'I could bring it in again and pick up where we left off?'

'Certainly not! It will mean one impertinent question after another.'

'Impertinence is the last thing on my mind, Mrs Nicholls. But I crossed the Irish Sea with expensive equipment, it makes sense to put it to use. I'm sorry if I was too forward yesterday. What's good copy to me is a different kettle of fish to you.'

'It's the stuff of my life.'

A whorl of hair sprang free from the wax pomade he had used on his curls. They were almost black, a similar colour to Emily Brontë's. I knew, because Charlotte had worn a plaited hair bracelet on her wrist, the narrow braids held in place by a purple amethyst the size and shape of a raindrop. One plait was dark and the other light brown.

A wobble disturbed the air, a sense of the past butting in. Charlotte, Arthur and me, in a hansom cab on the Dublin quays. Charlotte stroking the hair bracelet. *It means I can have my sisters with me always. When I touch it, I touch them. This bracelet cheats the grave.* I'd found the mourning jewellery among Arthur's things, recognized it, and started to pull it onto my own wrist. But a spasm of aversion had overtaken me. Dead women's hair – my skin had crawled.

'Mrs Nicholls? You were miles away! I was just saying, why don't we chat here for a while without the phonograph? I can understand how it's off-putting.'

I shook myself back to the present. 'I've told you everything I'm able to recollect. Everything of importance.'

'Sometimes it's the trivial particulars that shed most light on a story. We can talk off the record, if you like. Just background information.'

'You're a born salesman, young man.'

'Let's try it and see. Did you ever think to yourself, *How did I end up married to Charlotte Brontë's husband?*

'You mean her widower. He wasn't a bigamist.'

'Be a twist straight out of *Jane Eyre* if he was!'

I couldn't help a gush of laughter, and the ice between us began to thaw. I noticed the symmetry of his features, and the white of his collar against the tan of his skin. I liked people to be well turned out. 'It wasn't always a case of *reader, I married him*, but we had a happily ever after. Of sorts. When he forgot to wallow about her.'

'Did he go in much for wallowing?'

'Regular as clockwork, every March the thirty-first. The date of her passing. *Love is stronger than death*, he'd say. Next day, he always picked me daffodils, or whatever he could find in the fields. Truth be told, I felt he should mark her anniversary.'

'You're a right sort, Mrs Nicholls. Not many second wives would be as generous.'

'I've been fortunate. I feel sorry for second wives who never meet their predecessor. No need for me to imagine mine.'

'Did you never think it odd she used your maiden name as a pseudonym? That she was Currer Bell before the secret of her identity seeped out?'

'I wasn't the Bell impersonated by Charlotte and her sisters. It was Arthur's middle name she borrowed. She denied it, of course. Called it a coincidence. But if you ask me, Charlotte noticed Arthur long before she loved him – despite her brains, there were times she was blind. She had her own small fictions, as we all do. I imagine you have some yourself, Mr Graham.'

'Ouch! What was she really like? Go on – now the phonograph isn't recording. No one alive today knows her as well as you did, Mrs Nicholls.'

'Flatterer.'

But it had been decades since a smooth-skinned man with sculpted features was riveted by anything I said, and it made me feel as if the world's dust had blown away. 'She was witty, acidic, inquiring, and sometimes submissive. But when she was compliant, I always had the sense she was play-acting. She had a forthright streak – that's one of the reasons I liked her. She didn't rein back the way my mother schooled me to do.'

'Give me an example.'

'My brother Richard could be roguish. Once, he referred to Charlotte and Arthur as being tethered together in marriage. She told him they weren't a pair of goats.'

'I expect he thought twice before he opened his mouth after that. Anything else?' Graham slid a notebook from a pocket and flicked it open.

'She was fond of claiming she awaited God's will, which was right and proper for a minister's daughter – I was taught the same. But I always had the sense God's will came second to her own. Don't even think of writing that down, young man.'

He pushed the notebook back where it came from, and held his hands up in surrender. 'It's all off the record, no word of a lie. I just wanted to make a note of what you said. Can't rely on my memory.' Knuckles were rapped against his forehead. 'You've a perfect knack for bringing her to life, Mrs Nicholls. What did you like best about her?'

'Her imagination. It ran riot – as reckless as any rebel.'

'Glad you mentioned a rebellious side to her. I heard a story about her visiting her father's home place when she was in Ireland. Much to the displeasure of the old reverend. Apparently, someone called Hugh Brunty made contact with her. A brother of Mr Brontë's.'

'I can't imagine how these rumours spring up. It never happened.'

'No?'

'I'm sorry to disappoint you, but there was no visit north. From Dublin, she went south-west, to Limerick and on to Kilkee in County Clare.'

'Mr Shorter was offered some material for publication, from a neighbour of the Bruntys in a place called Ballynaskeagh. The individual in question insists she gave him a two-shilling bit because he sang a song for her, an old Irish lullaby. He was woken out of bed, and carried in his father's arms to the Brunty farmhouse, especially to perform for their important visitor. There was a party under way – music and dancing. He remembers her face, although he only saw her by rushlight. That's some kind of lighting they used, not very bright, with rushes dipped in melted tallow.'

'I know what rushlights are, Mr Graham.'

'Apologies, Mrs Nicholls. It's a new one on me. The men were drinking whiskey, but the lady was sipping a sort of peppermint tea they made locally, laced with milk and sugar. Our informant was just a boy at the time, but says he never forgot her funny way of talking. Says she wore spectacles, and tiny boots with laces up the side.'

'That could be anyone. Why presume Charlotte Brontë?'

'He was told she was a famous lady novelist from England. His sister was with him, and the visitor gave her a coin, too, and asked her name. When she said Anne, the lady looked sad. "Look after your Anne and always be kind to her," she told the boy. "Annes are the best of sisters." Our informant says she was a near relation of the Bruntys, farmers in a small way in County Down. Apparently, no one called them Brontë there. Name was an invention on the old reverend's part after he left Ireland.'

'I've heard something to that effect. Vanity, or a new leaf, or warding off anti-Irish sentiment – take your pick.'

'Ever visited Haworth, Mrs Nicholls?'

'Never. We looked into it once. But it wasn't convenient.'

'That's a shame.'

'I'm told an army of Brontë admirers go there every year.'

'I'm sure my newspaper would be happy to arrange a visit to Haworth, if you'd like to see the parsonage and Charlotte Brontë's resting place in the graveyard beside it.'

'As a matter of fact, she's buried in the church where she was married. In a vault, surrounded by family members.'

'And Mr Nicholls?'

'Arthur's grave is on the far side of the road outside this house. You can almost see his headstone from our front windows.'

'Not reunited with Charlotte Brontë in death, then.'

'No.'

'Even so, we'd cover your expenses to Haworth, in return for an article and photographs. A tasteful write-up, naturally.'

'You're incorrigible, young man! Once, I longed to go, but those days are past. Parsonstown is as far as I care to travel.'

'I'd be glad to accompany you to Yorkshire myself. Surely you're tempted to pay your respects to Charlotte? You strike me as devoted to her.'

'I've a fondness for her, certainly. Our lives overlapped.'

'Forgive me for being blunt, Mrs Nicholls, but you won't always be here. Your –'

'The same applies to you, Mr Graham, fresh-faced though you are at present.'

'Your loss would be greater than mine. You have precious memories of Charlotte Brontë. Some you've been good enough to share, but others, I suspect, you're keeping to yourself. Are there any of those private ones I could coax you to divulge? In the service of literary history?'

'My memories are mine, not literary history's.'

'Still, it would be an awful shame if they were forgotten.'

'Memory isn't obliged to voice its lines. It can choose to be silent.'

'Don't be cross, Mrs Nicholls.'

'I'm not cross – it's something else I feel. This Brontë obsession. It's incessant. And no one can give them what they're after.'

'Information?'

'Intimacy with genius. They want to come within touching distance of the divine flame.'

A hush fell. Overhead, the roof timbers creaked – there was no wind, it must have been a large bird hopping across the ridge.

'Mrs Nicholls, you're a bridge to her. When people meet you, they're talking to someone who talked with Charlotte Brontë. For them, it's a thrill.' He hesitated, scratched under his collar. 'But for you, it must feel like a responsibility.'

How intuitive this young man was. Yes, I owed it to Charlotte Brontë to speak up on her behalf. Who was left to do it, if not me? I levered myself to my feet and tap-tapped over to the window. A blur of wings, a black-and-grey shape whirring past. The click of a beak against the path, and a hooded crow scooped up an unwary insect.

Let that be a lesson to you, Mary Bell, I told myself. Despite his charm, or because of it, I needed to keep my wits about me with Harry Graham. 'What does your Clement Shorter want from me, young man? Why has he really sent you to Ireland?'

'Shall I be direct, Mrs Nicholls?'

'Please.'

'Anything of Charlotte Brontë's. Memorabilia, preferably, although he says most of the good stuff's picked over. But he's after memories, too. He likes writing books. They appeal to his vanity – he sees himself as a man of letters.'

Just as I suspected. 'And what do you want, Mr Graham?'

'To be a war correspondent. No offence, Mrs Nicholls, but I'm not particularly interested in your Charlotte Brontë.'

'Ah, war. We've heard the drumbeat here in Ireland.'

'Tensions are brewing across Europe, especially in the Balkans.'

'When Mr Shorter wrote to me proposing our interview, he said all the young men of his acquaintance were fired up at the prospect of combat. But his wish was for wiser heads to prevail.'

'If war's declared, I hope to cover it.'

'Don't be in any rush to volunteer your services, Mr Graham. But if you won't listen to your editor, I don't suppose you'll take advice from me.'

'Our neighbours on the continent are quarrelsome. England may have no choice but to wade in.'

'What will you do if there's no war to cover? Mind you, when you've lived as long as me, you'll realize there's always a war brewing somewhere or other.'

'These phonograph recordings are quite a nifty line for me – Mr Shorter fancies commissioning others. You see, Mrs Nicholls, if I don't make my way in the world, I can't marry the sweetest girl who's waiting for me. Her name's Elsie, we grew up on the same street. Would you like to see her photograph?' He brandished a picture of an insipid young woman with a flat hat tilted on her head, its enormous brim weighed down with feathers and artificial flowers.

'Delightful. Who else does the *Illustrated London News* have in its sights for recordings?'

'Literary types.'

'And do you know much about literature, Mr Graham? Are you a reader?'

'I prefer the music hall. But I know how to do my job. Ask the right questions.' He nodded towards a glass-fronted case with first editions of the Brontë novels. 'Read all them?'

'Naturally.'

'All three sisters?'

'All three. Plus four books of poetry and prose by the Reverend Patrick Brontë.'

'Never knew he did anything in the literary line. Any good?'

'Heavy on virtue being its own reward – it never is, in my experience.'

'I flicked through Charlotte's novels when I heard I was being sent here.'

'And?'

'Full of spinsters and schoolrooms.'

'There's more to them than that.'

'She relied too much on coincidence, the uncanny, and violent happenings – storms at sea, madwomen setting houses on fire. Mr Shorter says Charlotte Brontë's life experiences hadn't the breadth of Dickens or Thackeray. And it shows in her novels.'

'Does he, indeed.'

'But he also says she's one of the greats. That Charlotte Brontë belongs to the nation – to the world.'

'She belongs to herself. Nobody else.'

'Mrs Nicholls, you're a game old lady. I'm going to tell you something I think you should know. Out there in the world, a battle's under way for Charlotte Brontë's story. For the version of events surrounding it. You know those letters of hers in last month's *Times*—'

'I thought I made it clear I wouldn't discuss them.'

'Let me finish. Those letters – they've changed how people think about her. Have you seen them? I mean, no offence, but do you realize how incendiary they are?'

'Your Mr Shorter was kind enough to send me a copy of the newspaper in question. Charlotte's niche in the temple of literature is secure, apparently – he does prattle on, rather – but he indicated the cache of letters are, let me think of the term he used, heady stuff. Written to a married man, and so on. Four of them, I believe.'

'And every one a sizzler. Pardon my French, Mrs Nicholls.'

'The letters predate her marriage to Arthur by a considerable stretch of time.'

'True. But the daughter of the parsonage reputation – that's taken a knock.'

'It's possible the letters are forgeries, Mr Graham.'

'The British Library believes they're authentic.'

'Perhaps further study of the letters will prove the library mistaken.'

'Who knows? For now, the general view is they're genuine. A lonely lady, pouring out her heart to the professor who befriended her.'

'Intolerable!' I protested.

'Unrequited love, Mrs Nicholls. It can drive people crazy.'

'How did the letters end up in the British Library's hands?'

'Through a Belgian brother and sister named Heger. They donated them. Very generous, if you ask me. Those letters are worth a bob or two.'

The world is full of places I long to visit, Charlotte.

Travel leaves its trace, wherever we go. We're changed by it.
Which place changed you most?

She leans into me, forming a conspirator's bubble. Brussels. I was a pupil-teacher at a boarding school there. I met a brilliant, unforgettable man. He showed me what was possible.

Who was he?

My master. Professor Heger. We were kindred spirits.

I become aware of Harry Graham's scrutiny. 'The name means something to you, Mrs Nicholls.'

'Not particularly. I read the newspaper article. I know the so-called Charlotte letters are addressed to a Professor Heger.'

'Father of the donors. Seems she had a mash on him.'

'Tangled stories. People don't know truth from fiction.'

'Nothing tangled here. They show Charlotte deeply smitten with the professor who took pains with her education.'

'She was determined to improve her French because she hoped to open a school with her sisters. I can't believe she had designs on her teacher. It's out of character. The Charlotte I knew would never have thrown herself at a man. Let alone a husband and father.'

'All work and no play makes Jill a dull girl. She seems to have mistaken his interest in a promising pupil for something else entirely. It was an infatuation. One-sided, apparently.'

'She was far from home. All alone. It can be …' I abandoned my efforts to offer an alternative explanation. I'd been riveted by the same newspaper article as Harry Graham. I knew they were love letters.

'People say she left Brussels abruptly. Under a cloud, Mrs Nicholls.'

'People say a lot of things.'

He spread his hands. 'The letters are out in the world now. Stirring things up. We can read them and judge for ourselves.'

'It's tasteless to publish private letters. She's dead nearly six decades.'

'But honoured the world over, Mrs Nicholls. Not dead in the usual sense. Interest in Charlotte Brontë is stronger than ever. It's a miracle the letters survived.'

'That's one way to put it.' I made a final attempt to speak up for Charlotte. 'Even if the letters are bona fide, whose business is it but hers? I suppose that professor led her on.'

'Not according to the Hegers. They say he stopped writing to her because her tone embarrassed him. Tore up her letters and threw them away. But his wife found them in his wastepaper basket and stitched or glued them together.'

'Rather odd behaviour.'

'The family say she felt they might be necessary as evidence, to counter any suggestion of wrongdoing on his part. Presumably, it wasn't the first time pupils or teachers fell under his spell. Madame Heger told her daughter about the letters, and she came across them in her mother's jewellery box after her death.'

'At which point, Mademoiselle Heger should have done what her mother neglected to do.'

'I have a friend on the *Times*. He says the Heger brother and sister debated the best course of action. They used an intermediary, and made a gift of them to the British nation. If the letters were hoaxes, they'd have been looking for payment. But there were no strings attached. Handsome, if you ask me. At least Mr Nicholls didn't live to see the day.'

My mind thrust up Arthur's faithful face. Faithful to her, of course, not me. Still. 'I believe it's time for my nap, Mr Graham. I didn't sleep well last night.'

'The thing is, Mrs Nicholls, Mr Shorter was hoping you might have some similar letters in your possession. Rough copies, even, made before dispatching the fair copy.'

'More sizzlers?'

'Or Professor Heger's replies?'

'No, nothing like that.'

'He said to tell you not to see it as disloyalty. Any letters of that nature would give a more rounded picture of a complex,

brilliant woman.' The attempt to manipulate me was ludicrous –
I almost laughed aloud, but muffled it with a yawn. 'Do you,
Mrs Nicholls? Have other letters like those?'

'No.'

'Something else to bear in mind. Interest in Charlotte Brontë
is running at fever-pitch since the *Times* article. So now's a good
time to place any Brontë curios you may be holding onto. The
wedding dress – you could name your price for that.' He rubbed
forefinger and thumb together.

'Let me reflect on what you've said. Come back tomorrow.'

'To talk about letters? Relics? The wedding dress?'

'We'll see.'

'So you still have some items?'

'What do you think?'

An arc of teeth gleamed. 'I think you're a Sphinx. You do
know Mr Shorter could help you dispose of your Brontë what-
nots?'

'He's taken some things off our hands in the past. Doesn't
pay very well.'

'He likes a bargain. You're probably too ladylike in your
dealings with him. Between you and me, you should hold his
feet to the fire, Mrs Nicholls. Anything to do with the Brontës
is worth money.'

'The last time he was here, your Mr Shorter persuaded us
to part with some miniature books created by the Brontës as
children. Pronounced them Lilliputian and paid us an equally
small pittance.'

'Crafty devil. He made a packet on them, you know, old
Shorter.'

'I didn't know.'

'Probably shouldn't tell you this, but they caused a stir in the
literary world.'

'Really? Arthur and I were mystified by them. The Brontës
were only children when they devised their tiny books. Wrote
and illustrated them, sewed the pages together, cut out cloth

covers. I suppose they'd something of the elfin world about them.'

'That's why people with deep pockets were sniffing after them. As soon as he read the lie of the land, Shorter started sending them to the salerooms, staggering their release. Let his friend Wise get his hands on some. Wise talked them up, and the price rose too.'

'I haven't come across a Mr Wise.'

'Thomas J. Wise, collector and rare books expert. Bit of a schemer, if you ask me. But old Shorter and him, they're thick as thieves.'

I wished I had more of those diminutive books in faded brown handwriting, loaded with the adventures of dukes and generals, battles and elopements in make-believe lands. But Shorter had seized the lot. Since it couldn't be helped, and I might need him again, I decided to be magnanimous. If only in front of his employee. 'I see. Well, the books were just mouldering here. At least Mr Shorter recognized their potential.'

'What else you got mouldering here, Mrs Nicholls? Want me to take a look at anything? You might have dynamite, for all you know. And I don't mean the kind that comes with a fuse!'

His words unsettled me, and I injected a sliver of ice into our farewell. 'Let's talk further tomorrow, Mr Graham. *Sufficient unto the day is the evil thereof.*'

The undertow of my mind disturbed, I watched for his departure from the window. Ben Coughlan was outside with a scythe, cutting the grass. It was a sign – I could send him into the attic. There was still one parsonage box I'd never rummaged through. Arthur had said it was jumble from Charlotte's time in Belgium, exercise books littered with essays and so on. But what if it held more of those dreadful *Times* letters? Or compromising letters back from that professor? Details of assignations? Further proof of the allegations people were making? I wasn't getting any younger, and couldn't risk the contents of that trunk falling into the wrong hands.

All at once, I realized Harry Graham hadn't appeared on the front path. He must be in the house still. Heartbeat racing, I crept out to the hall. He was huddled in conversation with Hope Porter; scattered phrases were all I could detect.

'House this size … nooks and … bound to be old boxes … worth your while … Royal Shannon.'

He pressed something into her hand, at which I must have made a sound, because both of them looked around. Graham lifted his hat and left.

'What did he want, Hope?'

Rosy-cheeked, she hurried across the tiled floor to my side. 'To meet me, Miss Mary. I said no.'

'You took your time saying no.'

'He's … you know yourself, Miss.'

'He gave you something. Money? Is he trying to buy you?'

Her fingers opened to reveal Graham's business card. She tore it into quarters, and jammed the pieces into her pocket. 'He's after her wedding dress. And anything else he can get his hands on. But the dress is gone now, isn't it?'

Perhaps I'd been too brusque with Hope – it wouldn't hurt to explain my actions to her, in the interests of harmony. Of course, there was no need, being her mistress. But ours was hardly a typical mistress–maid relationship. 'I did what had to be done, Hope. Better burn it than make an exhibition of it.'

She searched my face, and gave a slow nod.

CHAPTER 6

'How was your nap, Miss Mary?'

'I nodded off while Ben was clomping about upstairs. Did he fetch the box?'

'It's in the parlour, where you said. I gave it a wipe – thick with dust, it was.'

'The right one?'

'Wooden, handles on the side, CB on the lid.'

'Did you open it?'

Her mouth disappeared. 'No, Miss.'

Something drove me on. 'I heard the front gate swing open. I saw you in your hat. Going out.'

'I'd shoes to drop off at the cobbler's. I knew there was time while you were napping.'

'So you went into town?'

'Yes, Miss.'

'Did you stop by the Royal Shannon Hotel?'

'Why would I do that?'

'To see that young newspaperman.'

Hope's eyes snapped. 'I've no business with him and he's no business with me.'

The trust between us had been punctured by Graham. I tried to repair the damage. 'Being interviewed seems to have shaken loose something inside me, Hope. I lay in bed remembering, or dreaming, or a compound of both.'

She looked wistful. 'About a happy time?'

'I was young again, in Cuba Court. Happiness always seems more potent when we're young.'

'Who was in your dream, Miss?'

'Charlotte. And you.' Hope brightened. 'It was one of her last days in Banagher. I dreamed about a time we sat by the riverbank watching Arthur tickle trout. It was after a visit to the Rosses. In my dream you ran down with a message from Mama.'

'What was it?'

'I woke up just as you were about to tell us.'

'Isn't that always the way. Disappointing things, dreams.'

I stretched, and heard my bones crack. 'Hope, I know you've been in town already, but I'd like you to go back on another errand. If it's not too much trouble. Could you call to Ned Dermody's? I have a commission for him. Tell him I'd be obliged if he'd take care of it without delay.'

'As you wish, Miss Mary.'

'I've written out what needs to be engraved. It's best if you wait till it's ready.'

'It'll mean mealtime running late.'

'Don't mind about that. Put your hat on while I fetch the item.'

It occurred to me that Hope would have time to meet Harry Graham while waiting for the silversmith to finish. 'Take some flowers from the garden for Lizzie's grave, if you like. The lilies are looking well.' There, that would give her another errand. I knew Hope was incapable of a quick visit to St Rynagh's – she'd wander the rows, reading familiar names from the past. Mrs Foley, our Cuba Court cook, and Ben

Coughlan's father, Denis, the coachman, were buried in the same graveyard.

After Hope left, I went into the parlour to inspect the chest, which had leather straps across the circumference. Charlotte Brontë's life was stacked inside boxes and folded into drawers all around the house. The trunk was sea-stained and reeked of decay. Did it contain secrets? Kneeling, I gritted my teeth against the pain, and opened the lid. I rummaged past a New Testament with foxed edges, an ivory-handled fan, French essays in Charlotte's hand and someone else's and lists of German verbs. A bunch of samplers emerged, including one worked by Charlotte's mother, Maria Branwell, dated 1791. *Flee from sin as from a serpent, for if thou comest too near to it, it will bite thee. The teeth thereof are as the teeth of a lion to slay the souls of men.* I felt for that small girl in Penzance. Mama had chosen gentler texts for me to practise my stitching.

Halfway down, wrapped in cloth, I came across a cheap pocket notebook, spine buckled and dark stains spotting the pages. On the inside cover was written *1843*, followed by *Charlotte Brontë, Pensionnat Heger, Rue d'Isabelle, Bruxelles.* Beneath it, Arthur had inked NOT FOR MRS GASKELL'S EYES. My antennae twitched.

Six lines in Charlotte's handwriting were on the flyleaf. Might they be a quote from Keats or Coleridge, or possibly her sister Emily's work?

> *To love unloved is a cruel fate*
> *Yet even so I live in hope*
> *It is not a strong hope*
> *But it beats its wings*
> *Against my breast*
> *And I know it to be there.*

The words had a revelatory ring.

I leafed through the notebook, and saw the entries were mostly pencilled. The contents ranged from notes on classroom exercises to personal accounts. Expenditure was modest: a bar of orange-blossom soap, some liquorice sweets, a skein of blue thread. Useful tips were itemised.

> *To take Ink Spots out of Linen.*
> *To cure a Nosebleed.*

A hand-drawn map outlined streets, with a steep flight of steps leading down to the Pensionat Heger. *Slippery when it rains* was logged beneath the drawing. Here was the address of a shoe-mender, there were church service times. A recipe for baking a gingerbread house included an illustration.

On I browsed, through lists.

> *Write to Ellen*
> *Take a walk every day*
> *Work out cost of trip to Paris*

A page was devoted to a sketch of a dark-haired man, floppy bow at his throat, lost in thought. It has an arresting quality. Some stand-alone sentences followed, a series of desperate thoughts heaped one on top of the other.

> *My mind is a messy kitchen table of half-cooked meals. I must become more methodical. Have squandered the entire morning – why why why must I be profligate with precious time?*
>
> *Madame must not be allowed to provoke me. I will <u>not</u> give her that power over me.*
>
> *Aesop's fable about the tree and the reed – by bending like a reed we can survive storms in which mighty trees are torn up by their roots.*
>
> *Only 32 more days until I am back in Haworth where I shall be safe and I fear sorry.*
>
> *He says my English reserve is bogus. Inwardly I simmer with passion. He sees into my SOUL.*

Near the back, I encountered a longer passage of writing. At first, I thought it was the draft outline of a letter. Closer inspection revealed it to be a diary entry. *Ostend* was written at the top, and the date, *Monday 1ˢᵗ January 1844*. Before the end of the first page, realization rushed over me: I was on the brink of a discovery. The air changed – solidified. My body recoiled, my fingers lost their grip, the book fell from my hands. I could hear the desolation in Charlotte Brontë's voice, sense the derangement in her being. Her life was unravelling. These words lodged at a midpoint between supplication and confession, and I was spying on her by reading them.

My gaze circumnavigated the room, where objects were chiselled into unfamiliar shapes. Outside on the road, a cart trundled past, and a voice floated in through the open window, '… best way to cure a stutter is …' I tried to summon the strength to do right. The dead were due respect. But almost of its own volition, my hand fumbled on the ground for the dropped notebook. I resumed my trespass, and read quickly – consumed the sentences, you might say. Shock tasted metallic in my mouth.

> *Today I leave Brussels. I sit on my bunk bed in the ship's cabin listening to the cries of the sailors preparing to cast-off, and a crushing loneliness weighs on me. I should have gone in October when I knew there was no hope – by now, the pain of parting would be lifting. A crust would have grown over the wound. Instead, I listened to my master. It was hard to refuse him when he entreated me to stay. Consider how much you are learning here, he said.*
>
> *By Christmas, I knew it was impossible. Madame accepted my resignation in silence, no pretence at changing my mind.*
>
> *I must make a record of our parting while it remains fresh in my mind. My master insisted*

on accompanying me to the railway station.
Madame was displeased when he told her. He said
it casually while I stood in the hallway in cloak
and bonnet, trunk beside me, as though it had
only occurred to him. But I think it was always his
intention. He did not want to say farewell with his
wife watching.

    —Zoë, j'irai avec Mademoiselle Brontë jusqu'à
la gare.[1]

    —Mais pourquoi, Constantin?

    —Elle a un long voyage, et elle est seule. C'est
une gentillesse. Allons, Mademoiselle.

She turned away to hide the arrowpoint of
anger. But I knew it ripped through her – I saw
how her eyes flamed, her knuckles whitened. She
was jealous of the way he showed his preference
for me. In the hackney, I took my courage in my
hands.

    —Puis-je vous écrire, Professeur?[2]

    —Bien sûr.

    —Et allez-vous répondre?

    —Quand je peux.

At the station, I tried again. I was bold, I did
not use the formal vous. The French tongue gave
me the freedom to say what was impossible in
English.

---

1 –Zoë, I will go with Miss Brontë to the railway station.
  –But why, Constantin?
  –She has a long journey, and she is alone. It is a kindness. Let's go, Miss.
2 –May I write to you, Master?
  –Of course.
  –And will you reply?
  –When I can.

—Vais-je te manquer, Professeur?[3]

—Cela va sans dire.

—Mais non, if faut le dire!

He stared. I was too direct. By now, we were on the platform. A puff of steam hid him, but I knew he was close by – I felt his presence.

We found my carriage, but I could not bring myself to climb on board. I felt his hand on mine, an object was pressed into my fingers – a parting gift. No time to open it. The train let loose its long whistle, guards responded with short blasts, my master bundled me through the carriage door and shut it behind me.

—Vite ! Il n'y a pas de temps à perdre.[4]

I could not restrain myself. Just as fast as he'd pushed me in, I tugged down the window and leaned out. We were face to face.

—Priez Dieu que je te reverrai, Professeur.[5]

Engine brakes squealed, releasing the wheels. I caught his hand to my lips and kissed it.

—Monsieur! Reculez! protested the guard.[6]

My master and I looked one another in the eye, and our spirits voiced what our tongues could not. The train began to move.

—Soyez heureuse, Charlotte.[7]

---

3 –Will you miss me, Master?

  –That goes without saying.

  –Oh no, it must be said!

4 –Quick. There is no time to lose.

5 –Pray God I'll see you again, Master.

6 –Sir! Step back!

7 –Be happy, Charlotte.

  –Every evening at nine o'clock I'll think of you, my master. If you think of me then, too, my heart will speak to yours.

*—Chaque soir à neuf heures je penserai à toi,
mon professeur. Si tu penses aussi à moi, mon cœur
parlera au tien.*

*I held on to the rim of the window, keeping
him in my sights. He lifted his hat and walked
away.*

*We were some miles down the track to Ostend
before I remembered the farewell present. Half-
blind with tears, I opened my fingers. A packet
of bonbons lay there – as though I was a child to
console with treats, instead of a grown woman
whose heart was splintering.*

*This cannot be the end for my master and me.
Fate would never be so niggardly. I will not believe
it. Be happy, Charlotte, he said at our farewell.
Never before has he spoken my name. Always, I
am Mademoiselle Brontë. But now I am Charlotte. His Charlotte. His and no other's. Oh my
master, my master! I will cling to hope! You say
I have a turbulent heart, which I must learn to
quell. But at least there is a heart inside me and
not a block of ice. It beats for you!*

Back, I skipped, to the date at the top. New Year's Day 1844,
more than a decade before her marriage to Arthur. Perhaps only
three sets of eyes had read this: Charlotte, Arthur and now me.
A mean thought ambushed me – he knew his goddess had feet
of clay!

It was followed by another realization. The commonplace
book was worth a small fortune, especially in the Heger letters'
wake – this diary entry corroborated her love for the Belgian
professor. Hopeless, yes, but insistent. Mechanically, my fingers
squeezed the notebook. I possessed something men (I knew it
would be men) were bound to covet.

Undoubtedly, I owed something to Charlotte. If I parted with it, her reputation would be desecrated. The Heger letters were already a violation, and this diary entry would salt the wound. *But her obsession with the schoolmaster is already public,* I argued with my conscience. *The notebook adds more texture, that's all.*

I'd been tested already over the wedding gown and done the right thing. But I had to find something to sell if I wanted to stay on in Hill House; give Hope Porter a roof over her head, a modest income. Where would she go if we had to part company? A home with us was all she'd ever known.

This discovery could rescue me. But I had to decide whether my primary responsibility rested with the dead – or did the living have a stronger claim?

CHAPTER 7

That night, preparing for bed, I blacked out. The next I knew, Hope was dabbing at my temples with a damp cloth and a button was biting into the back of my head. It seemed to be a rolled-up cardigan, pressed into service as a pillow. My gaze travelled around the bedroom, which looked somehow strange. Oh, I was lying on the floor, covered by the blue counterpane from my bed.

'Miss Mary! Thank goodness you're alive. Don't try to move. Just stay where you are.' Gingerly, I touched my forehead. 'You must have tripped, or taken a turn. I heard the thud when you fell. I think you caught your head on the corner of the bed. You're going to have a bump the size of a goose egg.'

My tongue felt too big for my mouth. 'Don't remem –'

'It'll come back to you. Here, drink this.'

Hope's cool fingers stroked my hair back from my face, and coaxed me into sips from a glass of water. Gentle as a mother with her child, she helped me into my nightdress, unpinned my lace cap, let down my plait and led me to bed. A pounding had started up inside my skull, and I gestured weakly.

'I'll get you some headache powder.'

'Don't leave me –'

But she was already sprinting to the medicine cabinet. She had to prop me up to take the medication, but before long it gave me something approaching clarity.

'I think I had a dizzy spell when I stooped to unbuckle my shoes.'

'I don't like the sound of that. I'm going to run out for Dr Mills.'

'No, it's late for a house call that isn't about birth or death.'

'He won't mind.'

'Time enough tomorrow.'

'Very well, Miss Mary, but I'm going to spend the night on a chair in your room. If you need me, I'll be right here.'

I stretched out a hand, she took it and gave it a squeeze.

*

Dr Mills prescribed bed rest for a day, a tonic, and no more bending over or sudden changes of position. 'You've poor circulation and low blood pressure – they can cause dizziness,' he said. 'Try to avoid stress or insecurity. Worry could have brought this attack on. But overall, you're in reasonable shape for your time of life. Miss Porter takes good care of you.'

Hope had begged not to be sent out of the room during my consultation, and looked gratified now. 'I do my best, doctor.'

'I don't doubt it.' He was freshly shaven, scented with bay rum cologne, but his eyes were pouched with tiredness. 'Last time I was here it was to see about Mr Nicholls.'

'You were attentive during my husband's last illness. I haven't forgotten it.'

'He was a stoical patient. I suppose his training as a minister helped.'

'That wasn't why he –'

'Miss Mary.' Hope's voice crackled with warning.

'Right, I'll be off. Do you want me to drop that into the Royal Shannon? I've to drive past.' The doctor nodded towards the envelope with Harry Graham and the hotel's name on it. I'd scribbled a few lines advising him I was in no state to receive visitors that day, but expected to be back on my feet tomorrow.

'Please.'

Hope showed him out, and returned with some mending to keep me company in the bedroom. Yesterday's stockings were among her pile – I'd ripped a tear in one of them. 'The doctor doesn't need to know why the master was ready to die, Miss Mary.'

'I wouldn't be surprised if Arthur told him.'

'His mind wandered towards the end. Any mention the master made of the other Mrs Nicholls – it didn't have to mean much.' She shuttled a cautious glance at me.

'You know as well as I do he was pining for Charlotte in his final weeks. His sleep was fitful. Night and day, he never shut up about being reunited with her.'

'Don't upset yourself, Miss. Remember what Dr Mills said about avoiding stress.'

'Open my bedroom window, Hope. I'll listen to the birds for a while. Birdsong always relaxes me.'

She did as I asked, then lifted the blanket she'd dozed under the previous night and tucked it around me. For a while, I lay engrossed by the bird calls – it always surprised me how much noise such tiny creatures could make.

'By the way, I never asked how your visit to Lizzie Nolan's grave went yesterday?'

'It was grand. I sat and thought about her. Her face stays with me, but I can't summon up her voice anymore.' With a sudden snap, she bit off a length of thread with her teeth. 'I never understood why she did it.'

'Some people lose the power to bloom, Hope.'

'Every All Soul's Night, I leave a candle inside a jam jar on her grave, so she isn't lonesome.'

A robin landed on the windowsill and peeked in at us.

'Aren't you the brave fellow. I wish I'd some breadcrumbs for him.'

'I could go down to the kitchen, Miss?'

'Ah no, stay. Do you recall that day everyone was out looking for her?'

'I'll never forget it.'

'You never saw ... after she was found?'

'No, the old mistress kept me by her. She wanted to spare me that.'

'I'm glad.'

'The mistress took me on her lap and held me there when the men carried Lizzie in. In case I'd run out. To distract me, she showed me how to plait hair. My fingers remember what hers taught.'

'Then something of Mama's lives on in you.'

'Ah now, Miss Mary. That's not fitting.'

I hesitated, on the brink of confiding something to her, but too many years had passed. Let sleeping dogs lie. 'Mama was fond of you, Hope.'

'She took pains with me. Taught me how to be a lady's maid so I'd never want for a position.'

'You're my housekeeper now. Not a lady's maid. It's a step up.'

'You know as well as I do, Miss, I'm housekeeper, cook and parlourmaid.'

'I wish I didn't have to work you so hard.'

'Never you worry about that.' She pursed her lips. 'You remember Lizzie had the second sight? It ran in her family.'

'Much good it did poor Lizzie.'

'They say you can't use the gift to look into your own future. Lizzie told me something, Miss Mary. Swore me to secrecy afterwards. But maybe, after all this time, it doesn't matter anymore.'

'What was it?'

'That me and you, we'd make old bones, but Miss Charlotte wouldn't. And she said you'd never get the one thing you wanted most in life.'

'Love? But I was happy with your master, Hope. Wasn't I?'

'That's not for me to say, Miss.'

'Everyone wanted us to marry. Mama, especially.'

'I don't think it was a husband's love Lizzie meant.'

'You're speaking in riddles, Hope. Did Lizzie tell you I shouldn't wed?'

'No, Miss. I've repeated her words exactly as she said them. Anyhow, she was long gone by the time Master Arthur made you his wife.'

Reflexively, my fingers began pleating a swatch of my night-dress. 'What else was I reared for but the marriage market? I only did what was expected of me. I wasn't like Charlotte, I couldn't governess.'

Hope's fingers kept patching my stockings. 'Lizzie Nolan told me, "You put your faith in your own two hands and don't be looking to anybody else, *a leanbh*."'

Poor Lizzie, I thought. If only she'd been less trusting herself. 'I worry about what'll happen to you when I'm gone, Hope.'

'I've saved what I can against that day.'

'How long will it last? There used to be money galore in my family. And now look at me. But I'll do my best for you, Hope – make what provision I can. I won't leave you high and dry.'

'You've always done right by me, Miss Mary. Ever since I was no bigger than your thumb. I'd never have known what a home was, but for you and your mother. I get down on my knees and pray for the two of you every night, so I do. Master Arthur, too.'

Her natural simplicity and trustfulness shamed me. Had she never suspected the truth of her situation? 'Did it ever occur to you to get married and have a family of your own, Hope?'

'Never, Miss. I was born into service. It's the only life I know.'

How contented she looked, sitting over her mending. There was scarcely a worry line on her face. If she'd wanted to find out about her background, she could have gone to Dublin and made inquiries. But she'd never asked for anything beyond the story we'd told her. Besides, what good would it do her to know?

'Hope, I know Arthur gave you a few things of Charlotte's. If you run short of money after I'm gone, you might think about selling them.' Her forehead rumpled, but I refused to be deterred. 'Do you still have her wooden swan?'

'Sure, it's not worth anything. Not like letters and frocks. How's anyone to know what it meant to her?'

'I'd love to see it sometime. Don't be alarmed – it's yours, Hope. No one would dream of taking it from you. I'd just like to look at it. I was there when it was given to Charlotte.'

'She was fierce taken with that swan, wasn't she?'

'Fierce taken.'

There's something magical about swans, Mary.

I suppose it's because they're so graceful. The country people believe it's unlucky to kill one.

He made it himself for me. A doubly precious gift.

Your uncle hasn't just given you a little wooden swan, Charlotte. He's given you a story.

Nothing has more power than a story. Her eyes glow.

'Miss Mary? Did you say something?'

'Just talking to myself, Hope.' I gathered the memory and tidied it away. 'Here's a thought. If I wrote out a testimonial describing how I saw Hugh Brunty give it to Charlotte, the swan might be considered valuable.'

'But then you'd have to admit she met her father's people. And I heard you tell that reporter from London she never did.'

'I was obliged to say that. To stop people raking over Charlotte's family history. What business is it of theirs what she did or who she saw in Ireland? They'd only twist it for the scandal sheets. Alice Brunty would be turned into some kind of madwoman in the attic.'

'Alice Brunty? Who's she, Miss?'

'Nobody.' I dropped my eyelids. 'I believe I could manage something to eat now. Find me a slice of stale bread, too, in case that robin comes back. And why not bring a plate for yourself, Hope? We could eat together.'

'No, Miss Mary, that wouldn't be right. I'll have a pick at something later.' Hand on the doorknob, she paused. 'I'll never part with that swan, you know.'

'Quite right. We've let too much belonging to her go to strangers.'

After she shut the door behind her, the suggestion hissed in my mind that I'd missed out on what I most wanted in life. Lizzie Nolan had looked into the future and read that fate for me.

Hadn't I wanted to be Arthur's wife? Maybe, but given the choice, what I'd longed for above all was Charlotte Brontë's friendship. I was pulled to her like metal to a magnet. And she'd treated me as a friend. *My lass*, she called me, and *cousin*. But how had I repaid her? By hawking her belongings to pay bills I couldn't meet otherwise. By reading a diary entry depicting her in a state of despair. By tallying how much it might fetch at auction. Unworthy Mary Bell. Barefaced Mary Bell. Faithless Mary Bell. Shame settled inside me like a dropped anchor.

*

Hope drew the curtains and lit the lamp. 'Will we take a turn about the room to stretch your legs, Miss Mary? Your knee's bound to be stiff from all day in bed. Some exercise might help you sleep.'

'Good idea, Hope.'

'Take my arm, Miss. Just in case.'

Pins and needles attacked my left leg as soon as I put weight on it, but I shook them out while Hope held me upright. Slowly, we circled the bedroom, then out into the corridor, and back to pace the room again.

'Why don't I tidy your hair?'

She sat me on a stool in front of the dressing table, her deft fingers unpicking my plait and straightening its kinks. I watched her in the looking glass. Hope's red-gold hair was faded to a sandy shade, but in a certain light its colour reminded me of Charlotte's. Oblivious to my regard, she took the comb from its box padded with pink lining and began to tease out a knot.

'Is this a new set, Miss? I haven't seen it before. Some of the teeth on the comb are broken.'

'Not new. But new to me. I don't mind the teeth, it's only a couple, and the little hand mirror is easier to hold. I came across it in one of the parsonage boxes, looking lost and forlorn, and thought I might as well put it to use.'

'The old kit was handsome. It did you solid service.'

'Mama's. Papa presented it to her when Richard was born.'

'All the more reason to keep using it.'

'I felt like a change.'

'As you wish, Miss.' She put the comb back in its case, gathered a skein of my hair and began weaving it. 'You still have lovely thick hair.'

'All the fair's parched out of it.'

'You were such a beauty in your day.' She tied a ribbon around the plait's tail. 'There now, all done.'

'I take after Mama's side of the family.' Her voice rang in my head. *The Adamsons have Viking blood, it's where our blonde hair comes from. Your name may be Bell, Mary, but you're a Dane like me.*

'Must be nice to know your seed and breed.'

'I suppose.'

'It matters, Miss Mary.' Hope's voice was wistful. 'You'd know all about it if you were a foundling.'

I swivelled around on the stool to face her. 'We're your family, Hope.'

She turned over her hands and looked at the calluses on their palms. 'Not exactly, Miss.'

I offered an olive branch. 'Shall I tell you about Arthur finding you?'

Her expression cleared, and she nodded. Hope never wearied of the account.

'It was one of the worst of the Famine years. Black Forty-Seven. Arthur was passing through Dublin, on his way to Banagher, and had a package to collect from Richard, who was a student at Trinity College. Richard had arranged to leave it at the porter's lodge. Arthur went in under the arch – and there you lay outside the porter's door, wrapped in a shawl. The scrawniest wee scrap of humanity he ever laid eyes on. Too weak even to mewl or kick your heels. Holding on to life by a thread. Not but a day old. H-O-P-E was written on a sheet of paper pinned to your shawl. Poor mite, said Arthur. He picked you up and carried you into the porter, who insisted he'd seen nothing, heard nothing. So Arthur took you home to Banagher with him. It was either that or the foundlings' hospital, and it was stuffed to the rafters. Arthur always had a soft spot for babies. That's why he saved you.'

'Finding a baby makes you responsible for it,' prompted Hope.

'Indeed it does. Forever responsible. He called you Porter for the porter's house where he found you. No one knew your real name. And he landed at Cuba Court with you. Asked Mama to take you in. Arthur, she said, we'll be swamped if we give a home to every abandoned waif and stray. But she moved the shawl away from your face, and you melted her heart.'

'Mrs Foley did most of the mothering.'

Another name from the Cuba Court days. Our cook. 'Mrs Foley was very good to you. But we all made a pet of you, really. That first day, Mama rang for Lizzie Nolan to carry you down to the kitchen for milk. Lizzie hadn't long joined us. She was only twelve, but she lifted you up in her arms and said she'd mind you. And so she did, as long as she worked for us. Seven years, I think it was.'

'Poor Lizzie,' whispered Hope.

My conscience scratched. Our family hadn't done right by Lizzie Nolan in the end. Almost a lifetime later, it still mortified me how we'd forsaken her when she was in need. Not that I'd grasped the extent of our failure – too preoccupied with entertaining our famous visitor. Still, I knew Mama could have watched out for Lizzie with more diligence, and I ought to have spoken up for her when it happened. As for the one who'd wronged her ... well, he had his own conscience to deal with.

I doubted if it caused him much disquiet.

CHAPTER 8

Instead of Harry Graham, his editor presented himself at Hill House. Clearly, he'd been alerted to the possibility of a deal. 'I was anxious to pay my respects in person, gracious lady. It's been some years since we met.'

Clement King Shorter was a wheeler-dealer in a frock coat – but needs must. Characteristically dapper, with a rosebud in his lapel, he bowed over my hand. His eyes were every bit as shrewd as I remembered, although they assessed me behind gold-edged spectacles now. His moustache was still luxuriant, if flecked with grey.

'You've come a long way to make a social call, Mr Shorter.'

'Banagher isn't exactly on the Piccadilly line. But I'd travel to the ends of the earth to show my esteem to any connection of Charlotte Brontë.'

'Oh, my link with her is glancing.'

'Hardly that. But this isn't entirely a social call.'

'I didn't imagine so.'

'I've been conducting business in Dublin. As you know, Dora, my wife, is Irish. A poetess of some renown.'

'We're a backwater here. I wasn't aware of it.'

'Dora Sigerson Shorter. *The Faery Changeling and Other Poems*? *The Story and Song of Black Earl Roderick*? *The Sphere* hailed her latest work with "Fe, fi, fo, fum! She grinds Shakespeare's bones to make her bread."'

'Don't you edit that publication, Mr Shorter?'

He blinked, and shifted into a different register. 'Young Graham mentioned you discussed those *Times* letters. I'm afraid they may have disturbed your peace of mind. I want to reassure you, Mrs Nicholls. Charlotte Brontë's place in the pantheon of greats is secure. Regardless of anything written about her in the newspapers that lesser minds might think sullies her.'

He blathered on about the Brontë genius. It always sounded as if he were dictating a newspaper article when he spoke about them: daughters of a poor parson but rich in talent, declining into death with melancholy swiftness yet leaving imperishable work behind. I absented myself mentally while he continued in that refrain, the churn of my thoughts grappling with the transaction I needed to make.

'I'm a little confused, Mr Shorter. Am I to expect Mr Graham as well? Or has he passed the baton to you?'

'My protégé is packing to return to London, we require him for other assignments. But he's acquainted me with the tenor of your conversation.' A finger pad touched the ruby fastening his cravat. 'About her wedding dress. Mr Graham mentioned you still have it in your possession.'

'My husband dreaded it falling into the hands of souvenir-hunters. He instructed me to destroy the garment after he died. It would have unmanned him to torch it himself.'

His eyes popped. 'Have you?'

'Not yet.'

'So the dress is intact?'

'For now.'

'Capital.' Another fidget with his cravat. 'Is it here in this house?'

'Safely wrapped in tissue paper. I looked at it only the other night. Good as new.'

'May I have first refusal, if you decide to sell?'

'Of course. Arthur valued his business relationship with you, and you've always been very kind about sending magazines and newspapers. But I'm not quite ready to part with the gown, Mr Shorter. Soon. But not yet. However, I have something else which may interest you.'

'I'm all ears, gracious lady.'

I put my hand behind the cushion on my seat, and extracted a black Morocco case. 'Our Brontë belongings are muddled up and scattered through the house; put to use in the kitchen or sewing room. But last night, preparing for bed, my eye caught this. It's been sitting on my dressing table for years. Not used, I should say – it's too precious for that. But looked at, certainly, and loved.'

He stood up to take the vanity case and returned to his seat, fingers sure as he unhasped it. 'What have we here? A mirror, hairbrush and comb. Dear me, some of the teeth are broken.'

'It's Charlotte Brontë's vanity set. As you can see, her possessions have presence and eloquence – they call to mind their owner.' His shoulders moved in a slight shrug. 'She left it behind in Cuba Court by mistake. Those strands of hair caught between the bristles are hers.' His attention ratcheted up. 'The story behind the set is rather touching.'

'A gift from Mr Nicholls to his bride?'

I shook my head.

'From father to daughter?'

I could almost hear the click and whirr of coils and springs in his brain. 'No, Mr Shorter. Look closer. Start with the brush.'

From the red velvet interior he lifted out an ivory hairbrush, strands of brown hair with a hint of gold coiled at its base.

To CB from EJB was etched on a silver disc on the handle. Next, he fingered the comb, its teeth also made from ivory. It had a detachable top, ornate silver, which Hope Porter had polished to a gleaming finish. The glass on the mirror was foggy, but that didn't deter him from admiring his reflection.

'Look at the back, Mr Shorter.'

He turned it around. *To CB from AB* was inscribed on it. The tip of his tongue poked out and moistened his lips. 'All three sisters have a connection with it!'

'Their brother, too. Those broken teeth. One day, while she was staying with us, I attended to Charlotte's hair with that set. Naturally, I noticed the damage to the comb, and asked how it happened. Emily hurled it at Branwell when he wasn't himself, is the way she put it.'

'I say!'

'I thought I should give you an opportunity to acquire it.'

'And you'd sign a paper to authenticate it?'

'Naturally.'

'These objects are curiosities, certainly. But a little outside our usual sphere of activity. I was really hoping for letters.'

There was no help for it. My fish was nibbling rather than biting. 'I have a letter from Charlotte which mentions it. She confirms Emily and Anne bought the kit as a gift for her. To cheer her up, at a sad time in her life.' I paused for emphasis. 'After she left Brussels.'

His eyebrows raised at the mention of the city, but he fondled the wings of his moustache and held off from answering for half a minute or so. 'If I were to purchase these pieces, I'd require the letter, too. I must have both.'

'I don't know. I value it above money.'

'Letters offer unique insights; telling details revealed. More than one author's been immortalized by an aptitude for letter-writing. Especially if there's a hint of malice?'

'Certainly not!'

'Do, please, show it to me. Just a peep.'

'It's personal. I'm sorry I mentioned it now.'

'Gracious lady, you do an injury to the world of literature by withholding it.'

'And an injury to myself by sharing what's private.'

'You've trodden in the footsteps of greatness, Mrs Nicholls. That carries a certain responsibility.'

'Fiddlesticks!'

'I'm afraid I can't make an offer for the vanity set without the letter. Now, you were telling me about a conversation you had with Charlotte while attending to her hair with this brush.' He produced a pencil and small notepad from an inner pocket.

Nettled at finding myself in the squalid position of having to bargain with this huckster humbug, I sailed into battle to extract as much as I could from him. 'One afternoon, during their stay at Cuba Court, I happened to be passing Arthur and Charlotte's bedroom. Its door lay ajar, and by the angle of the dressing table mirror, I saw Charlotte. Her hair was loose, covering her face – she appeared to be in a state of dejection. Naturally, I knocked, and she was good enough to invite me to enter. In her hand, she held a hairbrush, as though misery had paralysed her mid-stroke.

–Let me do that, I said. I took the brush and smoothed it over her long fine hair.

–I don't know how Papa will take to sharing a roof with Arthur.

–I'm sure they'll manage.

–I just have to hope for the best. I'll never get any writing done if they don't. I have scribblemania, you know – writing is my life.

–Don't worry, Charlotte. Arthur will weather a great deal for your sake.

–But I want him to feel at home in the parsonage. I had our old peat room behind the parlour emptied, and fitted out as a study for him. So he and Papa have one apiece.

–Do you have a study, too?

–Good heavens, no. There isn't space. I always do my composing at the dining room table.

Mr Shorter's pencil hovered over his pad. I spread my hands to indicate there was nothing further. 'I must work this into an article. Or even another book.'

'*Another* book on Charlotte Brontë?'

'Her story fills an emptiness inside people.'

'But it isn't particularly happy.'

'No, but it's eventful. People whose existence feels flat or dull are drawn to the lives of notable people. Admirals, lords and ladies, artists – even murderers! Please, dear lady, let me see the letter. If nothing else, I can advise you on its significance. There's no requirement to sell.'

'Very well. But I warn you, Mr Shorter, I can't part with it easily.'

'Understood.'

'It's in my bureau next door. I'll only be a moment.' My leg was more troublesome than usual, the pain stretching its shoots towards my left hip. Despite my best efforts – *try not to limp, Mary, it's inelegant* was a constant refrain from Mama in the early years after my accident – my left leg dragged on the short journey to and from the parlour. 'It's the only letter I ever had from Charlotte. You'll see it's dated Monday the first of October 1854, and she signed it. She mentions that it pleases her to picture the hairbrush, and so on, awaiting her return to Banagher. This is the relevant passage: *Emily and Anne pooled their resources to buy it for me at a time of trouble and unhappiness. I felt a failure because I came home early from Brussels, where I was a pupil-teacher. I know you will keep the set safe for me, dearest Mary.*'

Shorter read the letter twice, and returned it to its original folds. 'Now, to business.' He tore a sheet of paper from his notebook, scribbled some figures, doubled over the page and handed it to me. 'I'm prepared to offer this sum for the mirror, brush and comb along with your letter.'

I opened the paper. 'I couldn't possibly let them go for that.'

He repeated the exercise. I shook my head. 'I've developed second thoughts, Mr Shorter. It feels as if I'm feeding the curio industry, like Chaucer's Pardoner.'

'But your vanity set is genuine, unlike the Pardoner's Romanist shams: "And in a glas he hadde pigges bones," and so on.'

'That's not the point. I'm worried about fuelling Brontë idolatry.'

'You mustn't think that. Your touching memento embellishes the legend of a singular family.'

'In that case, I may try to place it elsewhere.'

'Buyers, like omnibuses, can keep you waiting, Mrs Nicholls. With me, you have a bird in the hand. Very well, I detect steel beneath the velvet. I need to send a telegram to my associate, Wise. The history of the items is affecting, I confess. Three humble objects with connections to all four of the Brontë children, confirmed by her own hand. Apart from the Branwell incident, which she doesn't reference, but I've no reason to doubt you. I hope to make another offer after I consult with Wise. But it will be our final one, gracious lady.'

He sprang up, and insisted on kissing my hand. I pulled the bell cord for Hope, and walked him to the drawing-room door. His gaze inspected walls and tabletops. 'Such a shame no one thought to make a death mask of the great Charlotte.' With a supreme effort, I contained the spike of sarcasm which roiled on my tongue, and handed him over to Hope to guide him out.

I left the door ajar and listened while Shorter bombarded her with questions while they walked down the hall. 'How long have you been in service with the family? Since Cuba Court? Does that mean you met Charlotte Brontë? Do you have any souvenirs of …?'

Hope shut the front door in mid-interrogation and hurried back to me. Her eyes flew to the vanity set. 'He didn't take it?'

'No, but he'll be back. He's greedy. Greedy people always return for more.'

'Why do people want these things so badly, Miss Mary?'

'Because to possess any of Charlotte Brontë's belongings is to possess something of her.'

Hope straightened the cushion on the chair where Shorter had sat, and went back to her household duties. As for me, I had other Charlotte business to attend to, wearied though I was from duelling with Clement Shorter. I lurched my body next door to the bureau. Her commonplace book lay on its desktop, and I picked it up and hugged it against my breast. If Shorter took the bait, that vanity kit would buy me time. But how long could I keep Charlotte's *cri de cœur* away from other eyes?

CHAPTER 9

I went looking for Hope, and found her kneeling on an old sheet, shining door knobs with a rag. 'Mr Shorter gave me a cheque. I'll be able to pay your back wages as soon as it clears.'

'There's no rush, Miss. What do I need money for?'

'It's owed to you. You can't work for bed and board.'

'I will if it comes to it. Didn't the old mistress see me right in her will?'

'Mama's bequest has lost value, Hope. She thought it would provide more security in your later years than may prove to be the case, I'm afraid.'

'It was generous of her, whatever the outcome. The other servants weren't a bit pleased at me being singled out.'

'She wanted to show she cared about you, Hope.'

'Did she, Miss?' Her hands stilled, and her face blossomed, the way a flower opens to the sun. 'I thought the world of her. Though I never forgot my place.'

Hope's words gave me a pang. 'You'll be crippled from kneeling. The door handles are glossy enough.'

She hauled herself up. 'It was Lizzie showed me the right way to polish things, Miss Mary. She taught me well.'

'She was a good worker, a quick learner. Best parlour maid we ever had.'

'You know she never learned to read or write? I used to show her the A, B, Cs on a slate you gave me. But time ran out for Lizzie.'

My heartbeat's rhythm stammered, and righted itself. 'Not for you, though, Hope. One small girl was saved.'

She puffed out a breath of air. 'I wish someone had kept the shawl the master found me in. It must have come from my mother.'

'It had to be burnt, in case of famine fever.'

'They could have kept the scrap of paper with H-O-P-E on it. Maybe 'twas her own hand wrote it.'

'Everything had to be burnt. The fever was terrible, Hope. People fell down dead in ditches. The whole country was an open grave. Those who could, cleared out. The emigrant ships were packed. Burning your things – it couldn't be helped.'

'If you say so, Miss.' Resigned, she picked up the sheet she'd been kneeling on, folded it, and turned away. At the end of the passage, she looked back and saw me watching her. An expression I couldn't decipher crossed her face, and she retraced her steps. 'I always wondered something, Miss.'

'Yes?'

'Why you walked into the church so plain, Miss Mary. Why there were no bridal fancies? Nothing but a bouquet of white heather.'

'I had my reasons.'

'You looked stern going up to wed Master Arthur.'

'I was concentrating – I didn't want to limp on my way to the altar. I saw you there in one of the pews, Hope. When I was going down the aisle after the service. But not outside, when the bells were carolling.'

'I'd to hurry back to the house, to help with the reception.'

'You should have had the day off. A wedding guest.'

'The other servants would've been slighted. You have to treat everyone the same. Though I always had the notion you threw your bouquet straight at me, Miss. That 'twas no accident I caught it.'

'I knew what you'd do with it. Put it on Lizzie Nolan's grave.'

'So I did. There's not much you don't know, Miss Mary.'

'There's one thing I don't.'

'Miss?'

'Whether I made your master happy.'

'You were good to him, Miss Mary. He was in a desperate state when he came back to us from over there.'

'It's too bad we'd left Cuba Court by then. He loved the place.'

'Master Richard couldn't fill his father's boots.'

'They were big shoes to fill. Just because Papa could manage headmastering didn't mean Richard could. He took on too heavy a load at too young an age. It was all for the best, him giving up the school and the house.' Even as I offered a defence of Richard, I called myself a fool. My breezy big brother had a knack for finding people to smooth his path through life, and was indifferent to those left stranded in his wake. Better to save my breath than make excuses for him.

'The old mistress missed Cuba Court.'

'I never did. It's a whale of a place. Hill House is more convenient. And at least we were able to stay in Banagher.' But perhaps I missed Cuba Court's rose garden, where I'd roamed in the twilight, sharing confidences with Charlotte.

'It's a mortal pity Master Arthur didn't come back to us sooner. He could have helped Master Richard run the school.'

'You know he couldn't leave Haworth while Mr Brontë was alive, Hope.' Just as well he hadn't gone into business with my brother, I reflected. It would have ended badly – Arthur was meticulous, if somewhat plodding, while Richard was slapdash and irresponsible.

'And by the time he came back to us, Master Arthur couldn't even help himself. The old mistress saved him.'

'Not me?'

Pity was visible on her face. 'Hush now, Miss Mary.'

*

That night, Hope checked up on me at bedtime, as she had taken to doing since my fall. I was sitting at the dressing table and she lifted the bone-handled brush, placed her palm on my scalp, and began to stroke the bristles along my hair.

'This set isn't as good as the mistress's. Ned Dermody admired the ivory.'

'I have other things of Mama's. She took care of her belongings.' A beat. 'It was a shame I had to break a few teeth on her comb.'

Hope nodded. She had expressed no opinion when she returned from the silversmith with Mama's vanity kit, silver discs with initialled inscriptions added to it. Nor had she asked any questions when I begged a few strands from her hairbrush. Perhaps I imagined the gleam of approval as she held out her hand, a coil of hair more brown than red twined in its palm. But neither of us had acknowledged what I was doing.

Not that I was ashamed – the counterfeit set was good enough for that scavenger Shorter, not to mention the millionaire collector he and Wise would fleece. But I didn't have it all my own way. To show provenance, I had to part with my letter from Charlotte, which was genuine. Most of the letter: I kept the postscript, written on a separate page. It contained confidential information about Hope Porter, which neither Shorter nor his infernal posterity had any right to know.

The deception was wicked, obviously, but it gave me a punch of glee. At my stage of life, you took your pleasures where you could. Besides, it was gratifying to see my reflection in Charlotte's mirror, and have her brush and comb to smooth through my hair – their use allowed some atom from her to enter me.

*

Two months passed, during which I grew more housebound, more dependent on Hope. But if my body was deteriorating, I was thankful my mind, at least, remained clear. One morning, I woke knowing exactly what had to be done. Charlotte's words in the commonplace book had tunnelled to my mind's surface. *I have known the scorch of passion … If I don't tell someone, I'll be obliged to do like King Midas's barber and whisper it into a hole in the ground.* They gave me an idea. The fact I had parted with Charlotte's only letter to me, despite vowing to keep it always, was a warning I could no longer trust myself to protect her green notebook.

Still in my nightgown, I creaked out of bed, lifted my keys and retrieved it from the bureau. One last time I opened it, touching dents left on the paper by the intensity of her confessional. *Today I left Brussels – perhaps never to return … a crushing loneliness weighs on me.*

A burst of compassion flared for Arthur. A stand-in's lot was threadbare, as I knew myself. My eye snagged again on Charlotte's pencil sketch of a vivid, dark man, his expression alert. Her master, I was convinced of it.

It wasn't true that she was gone to a place where nothing could hurt her when her reputation could be vandalized. I caught sight of my reflection in a mirror: I was wan, jittery. And no wonder. I held a tinderbox in my hands. Some secrets, if discovered, should be wrapped up again and put back where they were found. For as long as he could, Arthur had kept safe the skeleton in Charlotte's closet – her love for a married man. But those letters in the *Times* meant it was loose in the world, and this commonplace book would fill its sails.

'Why didn't you tear out the pages and rip them to shreds years ago, Arthur?' I cried. But I knew the answer. He could bear to destroy nothing Charlotte treasured. Not even her delirium for another man. Despite her anguish, these sheets contained an outpouring of love.

I enveloped the book in oilcloth and leaned out of the window to call to Hope, who was taking a chance on the autumn weather by pegging out washing. She was singing a song about winding roads and sweethearts, although Hope had never kept company with any man in all the time I knew her. She blew in, windswept from the garden, and stood there with one hand folded in front of the other, looking ageless and infinitely capable. It was innate in her. Even as a child, Hope had a collected air.

'I have a favour to ask, Hope. I want you to dispose of this in the bog. It's something Arthur wouldn't have wanted found. Ever.'

Her eyes glittered. 'I'll take care of it, Miss Mary.'

'You'll be careful? I'd hate you to disappear into a bog hole.'

'The bog's meat and drink to me, Miss. I'll come to no harm there.' Barely glancing at it, she slid the oilskin into the big front pocket of her apron.

'Aren't you curious to know what you'll be burying?'

'No, Miss. Not if it's something the master didn't want people knowing about. Will I do it now? Or later?'

'No time like the present. Oh, and Hope?'

'Miss?'

'If I ask you in future, never tell me where you hid it.'

A nod, and she was gone. The bog revealed its secrets occasionally, but that was out of my control now – it could keep this book or part with it. The responsibility was no longer mine.

*

A month or so later I awoke with a start, as though slapped. My heartbeat was fluttering, and I felt woozy when I attempted to get up. I pressed the heel of a hand against my chest, monitoring my heart's skip and falter. Hope was alarmed when she carried in my morning tray, and urged me to spend the day in bed. I couldn't afford such procrastination, but allowed her to prop me against a bank of pillows, drank my tea and watched a patch of sky through which starlings plunged and looped.

My mind, too, was circling. I had two final decisions to make about items from the Charlotte years, and my heart's fumbles were a reminder not to postpone them. I needed to rouse myself and take care of obligations. One concerned a photograph, the other a set of letters, both housed in drawers beneath my bed. That was convenient, at least. I inched across the mattress, slid off, and landed on my hands and knees on the rug. Head spinning, I managed to do an about-turn and rest my forehead against the bedframe, where the metal's cold sting helped the dizzies to recede. Still holding onto the bed, I pulled out one of the drawers and removed a framed photograph plus a tin box.

Back under the covers, I held the photograph close to me and stared at it. My emotions were mixed, yet I couldn't prise my eyes off the girl in the picture. The composition was charming: a young woman leaning against a tree, flowers underfoot. She was wearing a striped summer dress and bonneted in a straw hat with dangling ribbons. How fresh and pretty she looked. How innocent of the stale ways of the world. One of Mrs Foley's sayings strayed into my mind. *The afternoon knows what the morning never suspects.*

A knock on the door. It was Hope with some beef tea and thin slices of bread and butter. 'I want you to eat every morsel, Miss. You'll never get your strength back otherwise.'

I held out the silver frame. 'I never gave you a birthday present this year, Hope. I want you to have this. Lady Rosse took it.'

She received it from my hand and looked at that long-ago girl. 'I've not seen this before. Is it – is it you, Miss Mary? But where are you? I don't recognize the place.'

'Birr Castle. Charlotte and Mama and me were asked to tea there one afternoon. We knew Lady Rosse had an ulterior motive, but it was a compliment to be invited. I never liked to have the photograph sitting out. Because of Lizzie Nolan. It was taken the day she went missing.'

'God be good to Lizzie. Thank you, Miss. It's a lovely souvenir.'

'Pull off the back of the frame, Hope.'

Surprise pinched her eyebrows, but she did as I instructed and found a second photograph pushed in behind the first. Although blurred, it showed the same girl, this time with a companion. The second woman was petite, wore spectacles, and pointed upwards into the tree branches. The two seemed to be laughing at something outside the picture.

'Oh, Miss Mary!'

I put my finger to my lips. 'Say nothing. It's an insurance policy for you, Hope. After I'm gone. To do with as you think fit.' By some trick of the light, as she stood there smiling, Hope called to mind her father. He was dead now, but I saw him in her and winced.

'Are you in pain, Miss?'

'Just a little stiff. Put the photograph somewhere safe. Now, off you go, I'll ring if you're needed.'

I forced down every drop and crumb of the meal she carried in to me, and prepared to do the needful. There were too many times in my life when I went along with what other people wanted, rather than follow my own inclinations. But on this matter, I was determined. I wouldn't be seaweed flung about on the current, I'd choose my direction.

The tin box was behind my pillows. It measured some eight inches by six inches and had been painted once, but only a few blue flakes remained. The lid resisted my first attempts to tug it open, but I persevered and had my way. Inside, tied in mildewed ribbon of an indeterminate colour, were Charlotte and Arthur's courtship letters. Three from him and three from her.

I put on my spectacles and browsed the letters. I'd discovered the hoard decades earlier, but had only managed to read them once while Arthur was alive. Increasingly bedbound now, I found myself reading and re-reading them – imagining it was me he addressed. Arthur's outpourings were dog-eared phrases of the two-hearts-beating-in-rhythm variety, yet I envied Charlotte those pages. He sent me no notes melting with tenderness during our courtship, such as it was. I hadn't known whether to laugh or cry at his gift to me on our first Christmas morning as man and wife. The past lurched in with its usual insistence.

I had Martha Brown bring these from Yorkshire for you.

Clogs! Like a mill girl!

They'll keep your feet dry. I bought myself a pair, too. Wet feet are dangerous. He puts his arms around me, and I rest my head on his chest. I couldn't bear to lose a second wife. You won't desert me, will you, my Mary?

I threw a woollen shawl over my shoulders and went downstairs gingerly, gripping the banister. Somewhere at the back of the house I could hear Hope singing. Charlotte's workbox was in my parlour, and I took her stork scissors from it. One after another, I snipped Charlotte and Arthur's letters into confetti, and transferred the scraps back into the tin. Now I considered my next step. I could open the window, or chance going outside to the apple orchard. The orchard, I decided – it was where Arthur had proposed to me.

In the hallway, watery sunshine illuminated the fanlight above the door, painting diluted rainbows on the wall. I hobbled past them, and was outside. Tap-tap, careful not to trip. Opposite was St Paul's Church and graveyard, where Arthur lay. A tethered donkey belonging to the vicar cropped our grass. It threw me an indifferent glance, and returned to tearing and chewing with its strong yellow teeth.

A breeze was blowing, its breath chilly on my face. *My sister Emily said the wind swept her mind clean.* 'Not wuthering, Charlotte, but sufficient,' I said aloud. Making a scoop of my hands, I held them out, and a light gust lifted the fragments and carried them away. Let birds and field mice use them to line their nests – they'd line no one's collection, biography or dissertation. These love letters would never become public property like the Heger correspondence. I'd prevent it.

Slivers of paper wafted here and there, including a mouthful scooped up and gulped by the donkey. I laughed aloud at that outcome for their *billets-doux* – I've never claimed to be a saint. But I've done what I can to be the guardian of Charlotte and Arthur's love. The same impulse had caused me to burn her wedding dress rather than allow it to become a museum exhibit for every Tom, Dick and Harry to ogle. I'd put it out of reach for private collectors, curio hunters, museums, cultists and gawkers. If I'd sold it, the new owner might have used it to turn her into Snow White entombed in glass.

I'd parted with too much belonging to Charlotte already, financial need overcoming scruples. The truth was, I couldn't trust myself. What I didn't have, I couldn't sell. No matter how tempting the offer or straitened my circumstances, I'd never have to put a price on Charlotte's wedding gown. And now her love letters were safe, too.

'Miss Mary! What are you doing outside in your night clothes? You'll get your death.'

'I wanted to stand in the orchard again, Hope. It's where Arthur proposed to me.'

I looked at a tree weighed down by bronze-red discs, windfall apples dotted about the grass near its trunk. It had been early summertime when Arthur asked me to be his wife, fruit not yet bulging on the branches but the blossom melted away. As the seasons did, one year folding into the next. It was nearly half a century since Arthur had walked me around the orchard and spoken of marriage. That tree, a witness to his proposal, had outlived Charlotte, Mama, Arthur, Richard, and would outlast Hope and me. 'Did I make him happy, Hope?'

'Ah now, you know perfectly well –' The donkey's raw call rang out, and Hope didn't finish the sentence. 'You're trembling, Miss Mary! And look at your legs – they're blue with the cold.

No wonder, and you with no stockings on!' She fussed at the shawl, which had come loose, tightening it around me. 'Let's get you indoors.' Her strong arms guided me. 'You mustn't risk your health this way, Miss Mary.' A catch in her voice. 'What would I do without you?'

I wanted to tell Hope she was my rock. That all these years, she'd been faithful and true, and I loved her. But my teeth had begun to chatter and I couldn't pin down the words, which shifted this way and that. A puff of air tossed a paper ribbon at me, which snagged on the knot in my shawl. I pulled it off and read *y heart's treasure, we*. My fingers felt for Hope's, and I pressed the fragment into her hand.

1906

CHAPTER 10

Frost etchings were blooming on the bedroom windowpanes when I lit the lamp and hustled into my clothes. Arthur rolled over and watched me beneath his eyelids.

'Aren't you getting up, Arthur?'

'I don't feel myself.' His breathing was laborious.

Immediately, I stopped what I was doing and hauled him into a semi-upright position, a couple of pillows propped behind his back. 'Bed's the best place for you. Nice and cosy on a winter's morning.' I held a glass of water from the bedside table to his mouth. He coughed, spilling fat drops. 'Slowly, dear.'

'I'm afraid you hadn't much rest, Mary.'

'I don't need a lot of sleep, Arthur.'

He had been wheezy in the night, and I had risen to boil water. It was the most effective remedy when his lungs troubled him. Fill a basin, drape a towel over the head and breathe in the steam.

'My bronchitis is getting worse.'

'Too many comings and goings this week. Shall I send Pauline up with a cup of tea? Or can you get back to sleep?'

'I'd like some tea. Nothing with it.'

I pinned on my white lace cap. In the mirror, Arthur's reflection pressed his thumb to his inner wrist, checking the pulse. I pretended not to notice – he'd been fretting over his heart rate since the day we wed. The secret to contentment in marriage was to choose not to see certain things – such as the signet ring he always wore, with a compartment containing her hair. He thought I didn't know about its contents. 'I wish you'd stayed home from church yesterday, dear. No one would've thought any the worse of you. Least of all the Lord above.'

'All I did was go to a neighbour's funeral.'

'And stand about chatting to people afterwards. The tail end of November's too cold for that.'

'I'll stay put today. I don't feel able for the Dodds.'

'I'll send our excuses. They'll understand.'

'You go. They'll be disappointed if we both pull out.'

'You don't look well. I'm sending for Dr Mills.'

'Don't. A day in bed will cure me.'

'We'll see. Close your eyes and rest. I'll dim the lamp.'

'Wait, Mary. I've a favour to ask.'

I tidied his rucked nightshirt collar. White hair curled at the gap below his throat, but his eyebrows remained black. 'Name it.'

'Say no if it's –' A fit of wheezing cut him off.

I leaned him forward and pounded his back. 'I'm definitely sending for the doctor. No arguments.'

Arthur's breath whistled. 'Don't. Be. Hurt.' His nostrils flared and collapsed. 'Portrait. Wife. Here.'

'In the bedroom?'

A nod. 'Miss. Her. Face.'

An itch of jealousy prickled across my skin. He always called her his wife. I ought to be accustomed to it by now, but some things you never reconcile yourself to. Because what did that make me? His almost-wife? I stepped away and fussed with the curtains. Sharing the drawing room with her portrait was one thing, but our bedroom was another matter entirely.

Arthur's eyes pleaded – even when I turned my back to him, I could feel their clamour. I relented. After all, Charlotte had been grafted onto our married life for more than forty years. 'I'll have it carried up after breakfast. Can you wait that long?' A tiny yank at his beard to show I was teasing.

*

When it came time to leave for the Dodds, I checked on Arthur again. How whittled away his body looked beneath the bed-covers. He'd always been a vigorous man, even in old age, but this bout of illness was shrivelling him up. I tried not to disturb him, but he heard my walking stick against the floorboards, and opened his eyes.

'Will you send Pauline up to light a fire?'

'In here?'

'Please.'

How strange – Arthur disapproved of fires in the bedroom, insisting they were unhealthy because they sucked in air people needed to breathe. 'Do you want extra blankets as well?'

'Just a fire.'

'I'll tell her to bring a screen in case it sparks. Good, I see the portrait's here.' I nodded towards the sketch of Charlotte, propped on a chest of drawers directly opposite the bed. 'Is this where you want it?'

'Thank you, Mary.'

Arthur's eyes rested on it, his devotion transparent, and it caused me to ask him a question I should have shied away from. 'Have you been happy with me, Arthur?'

'Happy enough.' My face must have betrayed me because he tried to make amends. 'Happier than I expected, Mary. I miss Aunt Harriette. The three of us muddled along well together.'

'I know I can't tell a sauceboat from a saucepan, but I always did my best to make you comfortable and see you wanted for …' I was going to say wanted for nothing, but stopped myself in time.

'You did, my dear. You always did. You've been …' I waited. 'Constant.'

Some words shouldn't be spoken aloud, yet I said them anyway – it's human nature to make comparisons. 'Except I wasn't Charlotte.' He didn't respond. 'I hear carriage wheels. Goodbye, Arthur. Keep resting. It's the best medicine.' I left without kissing him, an act of rebellion I don't suppose he noticed.

We could no longer afford to keep a carriage, but the Dodds had kindly sent theirs. While it rattled downhill, I dwelt on Arthur's reconstruction of Haworth life. Charlotte was an angel. Patrick a benevolent country vicar. Emily and Anne were children of the moors. Branwell fell in with evil company but felt remorse for his behaviour before he died. Such a narrative involved elaborations, distortions and omissions. But it allowed him to save her memory within a scented net of perfection, the same way he preserved her wedding clothes.

*

I returned home before Arthur expected me, to find him riddling the flames with a poker in one hand, the other braced against the mantelpiece to hold himself upright. Grime was smeared on his face and hands from burning papers, whose charred remains whirled up the chimney. Time enough for reproaches – first, I concentrated on helping him into bed, where he flopped against the pillows. He looked more spent than I'd ever seen him. Yet there was a trace of satisfaction, too.

I kept my voice gentle. 'You need to rest, Arthur. And now your skin's all clammy. Let's get you changed.' I contrived to pull the sooty garment off his sweat-soured body, sponge him down, and tug on a fresh nightshirt. He was as docile as a newborn.

'I hope you're not running a fever. Standing over the fire hasn't helped.'

'Set my mind … at rest.' Arthur was descending into himself.

When his eyelids drifted shut, I returned to the fireplace. The blaze was collapsing. I crouched down and used tongs to retrieve a notebook with a green card cover, followed by a few charred scraps of pages. They looked like letters. On the loose paper, only the odd phrase or broken sentence remained visible. *personne ne le saura jamais;*[8] *I promi; the two of us c.* It was Charlotte's handwriting – having lived for so long with her belongings, I was familiar with it. On another page, the script was larger, bolder. *Chère Mademoiselle Br.* Even as I pieced them together, the words curled up and blackened. Arthur began mumbling, and I glanced back over my shoulder. 'Pansies,' followed by another word I couldn't quite catch, but it sounded like courtship. His breathing slowed. A long sigh, and another word tumbled from him, clear as sunlight. 'Brussels.'

A series of crackles returned my eyes to the salvaged pages. They were crumbling to ash, words erased before my eyes. If they were letters of Charlotte's, they were gone now. But the notebook was more or less intact and I picked it up, alert to Arthur's breathing. Its texture had altered – he was asleep. For a few moments, I watched the rise and fall of his chest. Instinctively, my glance flicked to Charlotte's portrait. She was wearing her Mona Lisa expression.

'Well, Charlotte?' I mouthed, waving the green book. 'Remember this?' The eyes in the picture seemed to grow luminous. 'Forgive me, Charlotte dear. You'd do the same in my shoes.' I wrenched my stiff limbs upright and took away the notebook to read privately. Inspecting it beneath her gaze was an intrusion too far.

---

8 nobody will ever know

In the passageway, I met Hope Porter, the picture of a model housekeeper in her black dress with white collar and cuffs. 'I was just coming to see if Master Arthur needed anything, Miss Mary.'

'He's sleeping. Perhaps in an hour or so you could bring him one of your tinctures. Something for his chest. His breathing catches.'

'I'll see to it now.'

'No, let him rest. He's been overdoing it. I found him going through his Haworth papers. It's best if he doesn't do that, Hope – it agitates him.'

She reddened, and I knew she must have gone to the attic on his behalf, because he was no longer able to climb up there. 'He knows his own mind, Miss.'

'No matter how he begs you, don't bring him any more of those boxes. Please, Hope. For his own sake.'

She moved her head in a gesture that was neither yes nor no, and I had to make do with that. Hope Porter could refuse Arthur nothing. I left her loitering in the corridor, knowing – whether I liked it or not – she'd check for herself on his condition.

In my dressing room, I poured water into a bowl and soaped away the soot traces from my hands, then rubbed ointment on my leg – kneeling caused the kneecap to ache. The soap was made by Hope, scented with lavender from our garden. She had numerous talents, but following my instructions was not among them. Subtleties of feeling were beyond her: Arthur had always been her primary concern. I lit a lamp and began to examine what I'd salvaged. There were pages of lists, some sketches, and a long passage of writing at the back.

Oh my master, my master! I will cling to hope! You say I have a turbulent heart which I must learn to quell. But at least there is a heart inside me and not a block of ice. It beats for you!

It must be a scene from a novel – the voice had a Jane Eyre ring. I slipped the notebook into my jewellery casket and returned to Arthur's bedside, where I stroked his hair, still thick at eighty-six years of age. He stirred, edged into wakefulness.

'Will you know Charlotte in heaven?'

'Anywhere.'

'How?'

A twitch of the lips. 'Her tiny, cold feet. Heels rough. From walking.' He opened his eyes. The smile tapered away.

'We never had a child, Arthur. It always grieved me.'

He sat up, knuckling his eyes, and drank some water. 'If anything went wrong, I couldn't have borne your loss.'

'I'd have chanced it.'

'Women do.'

'I feel I failed you.'

'Never think that, Mary.'

'I can't help it. You've always loved children, Arthur, I know you have. I saw how you were with Ben Coughlan's granddaughter the other week. When he came to see about the roof.'

'A fine wee lass.' He chuckled. 'She liked my trick with the penny.'

'You paid more attention to her than the state of our tiles.'

'Roofs are depressing, Mary. But children lift the spirits.'

Arthur had caught the little creature staring at him. Solemnly, he'd produced a penny, held it in the air, transferred it to the left hand, closed his fingers over it, opened them – and the coin was gone. He'd flashed his right hand, and there was the coin.

'Again!' she'd cried, shyness forgotten.

Arthur had repeated the trick, before giving her the penny to keep.

'Where did you learn to do that, Master Arthur?' Ben had asked.

'My Trinity years weren't all study.'

In all the time I'd known him, Arthur could never resist giving children sweets or coins. No wonder I'd followed him about, Pied Piper fashion, as a small girl myself.

'I have something to show you, my dear. I never meant you to see it. But perhaps you ought to.' He nodded towards the drawer in his nightstand. 'Take out my Bible.'

Arthur read from the New Testament every night. The copy he used was old Mr Brontë's, which was enough to deter me from ever leafing through it. No matter how Arthur praised him, I had never warmed to Charlotte's father.

I handed it to Arthur, and he removed a yellowed page from a flap inside.

'Read this, Mary.'

The paper was heavily creased, folded into quarters beginning to tear from age, or handling, or both. It was a letter, ink withered to brown, signed by Charlotte's father. I checked who it was written to – Arthur – and glanced at him. Expressionless, he waited. I began to read.

Haworth Parsonage
Tuesday 27th June 1854

Dear Mr Nicholls,

I write to you on the cusp of your wedding day, relying on your discretion. Let me stress my intention is not to prevent your union with my beloved daughter. I accept I was an obstacle in your path. She is an exceptional individual, which the world now recognizes, and I would have been negligent had I not forced you to prove yourself disinterested in your pursuit of her – which I now believe to be the case. In short, Mr Nicholls, I do not doubt the sincerity of your feelings for her.

That acknowledgement is not the purpose of this letter, however. As your wedding day nears,

I must issue a warning which I hope you will take in the spirit, not of an interfering father, but a loving one. My daughter is too frail to be your wife in the fullest sense. If you attempt to live as man and wife with Charlotte you will construct a coffin for her. Each time you exert your connubial rights will drive a nail into that coffin. She is not built for motherhood. The strain of carrying a child would apply intolerable pressure to her fragile body. Childbirth is a hazard for any woman, but for my Charlotte I am convinced it cannot end well.

As a clergyman, I know that intimacy between man and wife is sanctioned by God and licensed by the Church, and you would be within your rights, and indeed your natural desires. Nevertheless, I beseech you to leave her untouched. If you choose to disregard this plea, I regret to warn you, Sir, you will not long be in possession of a wife. Regard this, not as an instruction from the Vicar of Haworth, but an appeal from the heart and hand of a devoted father. The Lord has tempered me in adversity – my only hope is for one of my six children to be spared to me.

These words cannot find favour with a bridegroom. Yet I know you will afford them the

consideration they deserve, and pray for guidance
on the matter.
Believe me to be,
Ever truly yours,
Patrick Brontë A.B.,
Incumbent of Haworth

Two men haggling over Charlotte. Her expressive face swam up at me, eyes brilliant with hope for the future. It was almost more than I could bear. A couple of crows set up a tetchy din outside and returned me to my senses. Arthur was waiting for my response, a just-scolded expression on his face.

'Written two days before your marriage, Arthur. It reads like a last-ditch attempt to thwart it.'

He cleared his throat. 'I took it in that light, I admit.'

'But you triumphed in the end – you made her your wife.'

'Only because Charlotte willed it.'

'That gives you relief, surely? The knowledge she smoothed away obstacles to your union.' I held out the letter.

Mechanically, his fingers accepted it. 'Imagine the use Mrs Gaskell would have made of this for my wife's biography. Merry mayhem, she'd have caused. She never could abide Mr Brontë or me. Yet he insisted she should be the one to write the book.'

'It's a mystery to me how you managed to live with that obstinate old man after your marriage, Arthur.'

'I made allowances. I knew I'd reached high in aiming for Charlotte. And she wanted us to be friends, so both of us tried, for her sake. I didn't find it much of an effort. Patrick Brontë was a remarkable man. He gave his children newspapers to inform them, books to fire their imagination, paper to write with. His daughters had an education, as well as his son. They were ambitious because he nurtured it.'

I was pulled up short. *There's no one like Papa, Mary. He made something of himself. It's why I want my life to mean something, too.* 'Still, that line about Charlotte's frailty ... it's unseemly. He's using any weapon he can.'

'Ah, but he was right. My love killed her, Mary. That's a burden I've had to live with.' He threw down a look that was all challenge. 'I don't suppose you know what I mean.'

'I think I do.'

'Impossible. I've never talked about it. I couldn't. Charlotte was expecting a baby when she died – that's what killed her. She couldn't keep food down. Everything she ate came back up again, until she was throwing up her own stomach lining. My poor darling grew weaker and weaker. Dwindling into thin air before my eyes. Until finally ...' He gulped, and rested one hand across his eyes, fingers splayed.

Arthur was not an imaginative man – that bridegroom of half a century ago wouldn't have seen the darkness hurtling towards him. Not even when Mr Brontë recognized the danger and pointed to it.

I took his hand away from his face, forcing him to look at me. 'Martha Brown told me. I've known for years.'

'Martha! I'd never have believed it. I thought she was loyal.'

'She *was* loyal, Arthur.'

'Yet she betrayed ...'

'It wasn't a betrayal. She knew I'd never speak about it to anyone.'

'Not even Aunt Harriette?'

'Not a soul. But others knew, Arthur. Martha wasn't the only one.'

'My life reduced to fireside gossip! Who else knew?'

'Martha's mother. Mrs Brown attended Charlotte when pregnancy was suspected. And Charlotte wrote to Ellen Nussey. I expect Ellen told Mrs Gaskell – she didn't hold much back from her.'

'The biography alludes to her pregnancy. But it's not made explicit. I've never had the impression people knew, in general. Mr Brontë never mentioned it. Not once, in all our years together.' A tremor caught him, and he burst out, 'Why did Martha tell you?'

'She meant no harm. She loved Charlotte – she loved all the Brontës. But she felt I should be told.'

He relapsed into silence, looking inward. When he spoke again, his voice was strained. 'I was warned. I didn't listen. You've read the letter.'

'Dearest, don't blame yourself. You only did what ...'

'She was expecting our child and the pregnancy put an intolerable strain on her body. If I'd exercised restraint, I'd never have lost her. She had her whole life ahead. But I robbed her of it because of my, oh good God, I can't endure it, my urges.'

I took both of his hands in mine and held them firmly. 'Arthur, don't punish yourself. It happened a lifetime ago.'

'I can't bear thinking about it. If only I could turn the clock back.'

'It's a woman's lot when she becomes a wife. It's a risk Charlotte was ready to take.'

'The risk was entirely on her side. All I thought about was my pleasure. I shouldn't have –'

'Stop it, Arthur! You're punishing yourself to no purpose. Physical love is part of marriage. And Charlotte was willing to have a baby, she talked about it to me. "Other women manage so I dare say I can," she said. "It would be a relief not to be the last of the Brontës." And she hoped a child might seal the friendship between its papa and grandpapa. But her death secured that, in any case.'

A quiver passed through his body. Hoarse, broken sobs erupted, and his hands flailed the air. I held him against me, his tears wetting my blouse, and rubbed between his shoulder blades. When the sobs had turned to hiccups, and his tremors quietened, I blotted his face with my handkerchief. Exhausted, he lay back against the pillows.

I kissed his forehead. 'Arthur, I do have one question about Mr Brontë's letter. Why show it to me now, after all these years?'

'So you'd understand why I never wanted you to have a baby, Mary.'

Something chill entered the room, and now I was the one trembling. 'But we … there was. Intimacy occurred.'

'Full consummation was rare. I tried to regulate myself. The way I should have, with Charlotte.'

My body reacted before my brain. Winded, I stumbled to my feet and backed away, arms wrapped tight across my chest. When my thoughts began to move, they went forward slowly, waders through mud. Over the years, the times we were together as husband and wife had dwindled. Sometimes, we'd begin the act, only for him to leave the room hurriedly. Once or twice, I'd suggested his caresses would be welcome, but was rebuffed. All I'd seen was a man who no longer desired me as once he had.

'Mary, don't look at me like that!'

'I need to un … You didn't want …?'

'I did it to protect you. Not hurt you.'

'But I longed for … You took …' It felt as if a chicken bone was wedged in my throat. I coughed and tried again – a croak but the words struggled out. 'I could have been a mother!'

'The danger was too great.'

'You never discussed it with me! This was my life too, Arthur. My hopes.'

'It was for the best, Mary.'

'Best for who? Not me!'

'Charlotte and I never talked about it, either. We let nature take its course. And look what happened.' His eyes swam. 'You must see, Mary. It was because I couldn't bear to lose you, too.'

It was the closest he'd ever come to talking about his feelings for me. Dependence was a kind of love – it had to be. Still smarting with shock and resentment, I released a sigh. Unfolded my arms. Yielded. Both of us had paid a price for Arthur's reluctance to expose me to childbirth. The peril to Charlotte was past, but a different kind of threat loomed over our husband.

'Give me the letter, Arthur.' I took it from his hand – snatched it is closer to the truth – and dropped it into a half-full water jug on the chest of drawers. It took two heartbeats, maybe three, for Patrick Brontë's words to dissolve, tinging the water a brackish shade. Arthur's shoulders relaxed.

'Nothing good can come of a letter like that,' I said.

*

The Midland Mercury – Friday 7th December 1906

ONE OF BANAGHER'S LEADING CITIZENS LAID TO REST

FASCINATING BRONTÉ CONNECTIONS HIGHLIGHTED IN EULOGY

BANAGHER came to a standstill earlier this week for the funeral procession of one of its most venerable citizens. The streets were thronged for the interment of the Reverend Arthur Bell Nicholls of Hill House, and many business premises closed for the morning as a mark of respect.

At the eleven o'clock service on Wednesday, parishioners joined mourners comprising family, friends and household servants to fill St Paul's Church, where Mr Nicholls worshipped for most of his life.

He reached the enviable age of eighty-seven before being taken to his eternal rest, and was in excellent health until six months ago, when his much-regretted decline began. Throughout, he was cared for with unstinting devotion by his wife of forty-two years, Mrs Mary Anna Nicholls *née* Bell, a member of one of Banagher's leading families. Mrs Nicholls was by his bedside when Mr Nicholls expired last Sunday, December 2nd, shortly before seven o'clock in the morning.

The Church of Ireland funeral service was conducted by the present incumbent, the Revd J.J. Bowes, who returned early from a trip to perform this final service for the worthy old gentleman.

In his eulogy he told how Mr Nicholls was licensed as curate at Haworth in Yorkshire, synonymous with the exceptional Brontë family. That appointment led to his first marriage, to renowned authoress Charlotte Brontë. The proud bridegroom made a point of bringing the writer of *Jane Eyre*, *Shirley*, *Villette* and other works of genius

to Banagher soon after their nuptials in 1854. She pronounced herself delighted with local scenes.

The couple spent a week in Cuba Court with Mr Nicholls's widowed aunt Mrs Harriette Bell, whose husband Dr Alan Bell was formerly headmaster of the Royal Free School in Banagher. Subsequently, the newlyweds continued their wedding tour in Limerick, Clare and Kerry, returning home to Yorkshire via Dublin.

Unfortunately, they were to know only a fleeting taste of marital joy before the untimely demise of the illustrious authoress. Thereafter, Mr Nicholls became the custodian of her legacy, regularly consulted by Brontë scholars.

Mr Nicholls no longer held an active ministry following his return to Ireland from Yorkshire in 1861, instead turning to farming and managing his aunt's affairs. However he frequently read the lesson at St Paul's Church on Sundays.

He was predeceased by his brother-in-law, the Revd Richard Bell, formerly master of the Royal Free School at Banagher, and by Mrs Harriette Bell.

Despite inclement weather, a large cortege was formed to convey the deceased to his final resting place, where Mr Nicholls's remains were consigned to the earth with all due reverence.

Turn to page 12 for more on the close Brontë connections of Mr Nicholls and full text of the eulogy.

1864

CHAPTER 11

'You've waited long enough, Mary,' said Mama.

'For what?'

'Arthur to propose marriage to you.'

'Mama, marriage doesn't interest me.'

'Nonsense! What else will you do with your life? I see I shall have to take the situation in hand.'

'Please don't, Mama. Arthur's happy as he is, and so am I.'

'But you could both be happier. The fact of the matter is you'll suit one another. A husband and wife are like an egg: one is yolk and the other is white. Different, but bound together. And marriage is the shell that keeps them in place. A shell offers protection.'

'I don't want his protection.'

'You goose, Mary – when I'm gone, where will you live? With Richard, whose wife will make a servant out of you, although you're a gentlewoman? It's what happens to the spinster sister. No, my pet, marrying Arthur is the solution. You're serene and capable – exactly like me. He prizes those attributes in you.'

How little Mama knew me. I kept my tone reasonable, although one pays for outward calm with an almost unbearable inner struggle. 'Mama, my expectations about the future are modest. Even so, I must protest. Arthur loves Charlotte still. He can never forget her subtraction from his life. There's no space in his heart for anyone else.'

'It's better to marry *to* love than *for* love. And you can make him comfortable.'

'He'll never love me like her. Even if I give my every waking thought to his needs. That will become my function, and he'll be incapable of looking past it. He won't see me in my wholeness.'

'You're parroting romantic novels. It won't do, Mary.' I turned away from her, but she caught me by the elbow. 'I want what's best for you, child. Arthur's sober, dependable and honourable, he'll take care of you when I'm gone. He's ideal husband material. Not quite there yet – he's not a man to be rushed. But I'm confident his eye will light on you soon.'

'Oh Mama, I don't want to be a second-best Mrs Nicholls.'

'There's no shame in sharing a husband. Lots of wives have predecessors.'

'Not like Charlotte. She's unforgettable.'

'Are you jealous of Charlotte Brontë, my pet?'

'No! Arthur's devotion is admirable. He's a man who loves only once. I respect that. But as for me loving him – that would be a doomed project.'

Mama crackled with impatience. 'Stuff and nonsense! You listen to me, my girl. I've watched over Arthur since I took him in at six years of age. Trust me, you'll match well together. Arthur has no subtext, he takes everything literally. That makes a husband easy to manage. He's not one of those weathervane men – he'll be affectionate.'

'Affectionate? With no place for love? I want more, Mama.'

'You're thirty-two. Those days are gone, and if you've any sense you won't miss them. He'll be reliable. The kind of man who'll order his doors painted and chimneys cleaned before they need it. When you've lived as long as me, you'll realize a steady husband is worth more than a starry-eyed one.'

'Other men have offered for my hand. I said no to them. There are alternatives to marriage.'

'Not many. Patience is better than pride, Mary. You're waiting for Arthur, whether you admit it or not.' She touched two fingertips to her coronet of plaits. 'Besides, you can give him something his first wife couldn't.'

Blank, I looked at her.

'A baby, you ninny. Arthur's besotted with children. Give him sons and daughters, and he'll be yours for life. Even one would do.'

Mama was no fool. Grudgingly, I had to admit she was right. And so the smudged thumbprint of fate was set upon our marriage. One afternoon in late June, Mama had me change into my best gown on a pretext. I saw she was exhilarated, but didn't have to wonder for long.

'It's time. Try not to limp. Concentrate, my pet.'

'I don't do it to amuse myself, Mama.'

'Arthur's waiting for you in the orchard. Off you go. No, don't bother with your hat.'

'But what about the sun?'

'Just for today. A hat will only get in the way. Take your parasol instead.'

Off I went, to be marched between the trees, to the annoyance of the hens pecking about there. At first, I could barely keep up. But when Arthur noticed, he slowed down, and put a question I never liked to be asked.

'Is your leg troubling you, Mary?'

'Just a little. Mama says I've been slack about my exercises.'

'It's the left leg, isn't it?'

'Yes. My knee.'

'You never complain. We could do exercises together, if you like. I do mine every morning.'

'I've seen you at them, Arthur. They look rather demanding. I just do some knee and hip stretches.'

'I might take your regime in hand. I could devise something suitable for a lady.'

Side by side, we meandered now, the spire of St Paul's visible above the Hill House perimeter wall. A proposal hovered in the air – yet still it didn't come. But Mama had schemed for it, and when she put her mind to something, generally she prevailed.

'You used to have a horse, didn't you, Mary?'

'Starlight.'

'It had to be shot afterwards.' The parasol dropped from my hands. He picked it up and gave it back to me. 'You didn't know?'

'I – no – Mama said she sold her. I had a fever for days afterwards.' Regret for that skittish mare's fate spurted up in me. She'd shied at a hare, caught one of her front hooves in a hole, fallen and rolled on my leg. I'd wept for Starlight's loss, and even now felt a pang.

We did another circuit of the orchard, while I waited for Arthur's proposal with a degree of curiosity. Would he mention Charlotte? Instead, he spoke about her moors, his hand stitching pictures through the air. 'They never look the same from one day to the next. The sky moves, clouds balloon or shrink, the light shifts and something alters in the landscape – sorceries of colour and shape.'

'I thought it was meant to be a bleak, windy place.'

'Winds as stirring as a trumpet blast. But the moors have gentle times, too.'

His description had the ring of Charlotte. He didn't mention her name, which in itself was noteworthy – clearly, he was being tactful. Yet in conjuring up her moorland, he was resurrecting her. Even on this day, ours was no lover's tryst. Something revolted inside me.

'I understood Yorkshire's big towns and cities hiccup smoke, Arthur.'

'But there's an austere beauty to the countryside. On the moors, you inhale air no one's ever breathed before. So clean it polishes your lungs. Look up and you see hawks and falcons – look down and it's rabbits and foxes.'

While he gabbled on, I watched a bee land on a climbing rose pinned to a trellis against the wall, and listened for a step change into courtship. We can't all find second selves in marriage – it would be too claustrophobic – but surely I was entitled to some words of molten silver to tide me through the years ahead. Some tribute to my cornflower eyes, my flawless complexion. When I realized I could expect none, a small hollow dented my heart. Finally, I was obliged to use the missing word myself. 'You sound as if you love the moors.'

His eyebrows hiked up. 'I do?'

'You do.'

'I suppose I must.'

'Why?'

'Because the moors are a living presence.'

'Or perhaps you love them because the one you love did?'

'You know me so well, my sweet cousin. You're right, I do love the moors. But landscape is one thing, the people we live among, another. You're part of the tapestry of my life, Mary. You represent harmony and balance. I've never liked change, I confess – not that I've been able to escape it. I prefer quiet, and the countryside folded around me. You understand that, don't you?' I nodded. 'Is such a life to your taste, Mary? Would you be content to live here always?'

'I've nothing to compare Banagher to, Arthur – it's the only life I know. I've lived nowhere else. Unlike you.'

'Haworth.' The name whispered from his lips, and his eyes grew distant, probing the past. 'It was full of drama. There wasn't much tranquillity there. Much ease. Except for a few months. I've found peace again, here, in Banagher. You have a woman's touch, Mary. I see how you look to my comforts. You're thoughtful as well as beautiful. I know you can pick and choose – Aunt Harriette tells me you've turned down proposals of marriage from other suitors.'

He stopped and removed his hat. We were face to face now. A declaration was imminent. I could bat it away with a playful sentence, no harm done. Instead, I matched his gesture by folding my parasol, and chose to hear him out.

'I'm a bumbling member of the male species, with no silken phrases to woo you. I can only speak from the heart. You're everything a man could want in a wife, and I don't deserve you. But I ask the question anyway. Will you be mine, Mary?'

Heightened awareness of my surroundings caught hold of me. Bands of soft green light filtering through the trees, sweet grass layered with a woody tang, the measured pace of Arthur's breathing. A clump of ferns flapped, catching my eye.

What are you drawing, Charlotte?

Aunt Harriette's ferns.

May I see?

She turns the sketchpad around – she's caught the leaves' intricacies, the coil of the stems. Charlotte! You keep surprising me! An artist as well as a writer.

Hardly. But I dash off a sketch when I can. There's a vulnerability to ferns that appeals to me. I try to capture it, before they melt away. She laughs. I sound woeful. But I'm happy here in Ireland. I'd forgotten what happiness was like.

'Will I make you happy, Arthur?'

'I believe so, Mary. With luck, we can make each other happy.'

I gave my assent. Arthur kissed my cheek, replaced his hat on his head, and we resumed walking. Except now his arm was slotted around my waist.

And so I found myself engaged. Destined to be a make-do-and-mend wife. I knew it, and went along with it. Mama had the sherry decanter and glasses sitting out, confident of the outcome. Arthur drank soda water for our toast.

*

That summer, Mama was in seventh heaven. The Prince of Wales had married Princess Alexander of Denmark the previous year in Windsor, and she pored over their wedding arrangements, debating bridesmaids and flowers. Having agreed to be the bride, I had no choice but to become involved in her machinations, but Arthur was more interested in a new cricketing manoeuvre, recently legalized. Richard paid a visit to congratulate us, and the pair of them spent the entire time debating the pros and cons of overarm bowling.

Richard and I didn't have much to say to one another these days, although he gave the impression of having turned over a new leaf. He'd taken holy orders to borrow gravitas, and had the living of a parish in Kilkenny. The idea of him as a clergyman wearied me now, although I had been incensed when it was first proposed. Mama continued to indulge him. When he told her he felt guilty about losing the headmastership, she insisted we were snug in Hill House, and running Cuba Court was beyond her powers. At that, I had to leave the room. If my brother wanted to convey remorse, there were more pressing examples.

Once, Richard tried to engage me in one of our former, friendly conversations, but I snubbed him. Perhaps it was by accident, or maybe it was pique at my coldness, but he let slip something about the financial arrangements surrounding my marriage. 'Sale agreed' was the phrase he used. I wouldn't lower myself to quiz him, but tackled Mama.

She refused to admit her part in engineering our union. 'How you do take on, Mary. Count yourself lucky. Fortune's wheel has turned and Arthur's landed in your square.'

'Don't you mean our square? He's marrying both of us, Mama. Tidying things up in Hill House.'

'Crosspatch. You won't spoil my pleasure in this marriage.'

'Shouldn't I be drawing some pleasure from it, Mama?'

'Indeed, you should, my pet.'

'And what if I'm not?'

'Then you don't know when you're well off.'

'Mama, did you offer Arthur any inducement to marry me?'

'Don't be so modest, Mary. You'd make any man an exemplary wife. I should know, I trained you myself.'

'I have a right to know, Mama.'

'Very well. I promised him the deeds to Hill House and farm on your wedding day.'

'Mama! You sold me to him!'

'A dowry. Why not?'

'I feel humiliated!'

'My papa paid yours a dowry for me.'

'Only after he asked to marry you. Grandpa didn't pin Papa down and say take my daughter, I'll make it worth your while.' Rage and humiliation welled up.

'Mary, calm yourself. I didn't do that with Arthur, either. I simply told him the facts of the situation. That I could delay no longer in finding you a husband, that he was my first choice but your cousin Joseph Adamson would take you gladly if he was unwilling, and that your future spouse would find me inclined to make generous provision. Then I outlined what I could offer. Now, enough of these tantrums, my pet. I've been thinking about your wedding dress. The Princess of Wales made a radiant bride – we could replicate some elements of her gown. Stiffened cream silk and Honiton lace is a little sumptuous for a country wedding, but those sweet puffed sleeves would work. And that drawstring neckline exposing the shoulders would suit you – you have a lovely neck and arms, Mary. No harm reminding Arthur of it. Perhaps a white gown rather than cream, with your complexion.'

I brooded, and hatched a plan.

*

I suppose I should blush to admit it, but I was shameless. I told myself I was stepping into a dead woman's shoes, and needed to know if I'd be wearing them forever. This was a lie. Really, I was giving myself permission to spy on Arthur's love for Charlotte. It was fair day, and I knew Arthur would be gone until nightfall, while Mama was paying a sick call and had mentioned several other errands.

I rang for Hope Porter. 'Hope, fetch me Charlotte Brontë's wedding clothes.'

'I don't know what you mean, Miss.'

'Don't play-act, Hope. I know my fiancé' – I used the word deliberately, to establish my rights in the matter – 'brought them here when he emptied out the parsonage.'

'If he hasn't shown you them, he must have his reasons.'

'Hope, stop arguing. Just do as I say.'

'I wouldn't advise it, Miss Mary.'

'Why not?'

'It'll only set you to thinking.'

'Are you refusing to get them?'

'I can't refuse you. You know I can't. But I beg you, Miss, for your own sake. Don't do it.'

'Where are they? The attic?'

'The box room.'

I stalked off, Hope trailing behind.

In the crowded little room on the top floor, she tapped her foot against a trunk with *Haworth Parsonage* painted on the lid. 'It's that one. But please don't open it, Miss. A bride-to-be gets odd notions.'

'How would you know?'

'I know there's no use comparing yourself to a dead woman.'

'You presume too much.'

Colour crept upwards on her neck but she stood her ground. 'Miss Mary, hear me out. I don't like to see you made miserable. Why are you marrying Master Arthur when he'll never stop loving Miss Charlotte? It's not too late to change your mind. Tell him you can't go through with it.'

'It's for the best. Everyone else seems to want it.'

'What do you want?'

I blinked. No one ever asked me that, and I didn't have a ready answer. 'That'll be all, Hope.'

Alone, I took out the gossamer dress, fabric airy as a cobweb. It must have been white once, but was ivory now. Soft collar nestling at the throat. Cinched-in waist. Puffed sleeves drawn tight at the wrist. Invisible hook-and-eyelet fastenings, hidden by a box pleat. Mother-of-pearl buttons at the back. Bell-shaped skirts, loosely pleated for volume, designed to sweep the ground – its wearer would have appeared to float along. Charlotte must have looked enchanting in her once-worn wedding gown.

I held it against my body, stroking it. A mottled old pier glass lurched in a corner, and I went over to look at my likeness. 'Charlotte's. And now mine.' But they were empty words and I knew it. Charlotte's wedding dress was hers, and hers alone.

Even so, I was curious to see what I'd look like in the gown. The evidence of my own eyes told me it wouldn't fit. My body bulged around its slender waist and narrow shoulders. The hem barely reached mid-calf. But desire mastered me, and I tried to slip inside its flimsy folds. It caught at my neck and shoulders, where seams strained and the material protested. A giantess was tearing into a fairy garment.

I capitulated, threw the gown back into the trunk in a heap, and called to Hope. She arrived so fast she must have been hovering outside. Sheepish, I exited the box room.

'Could you put it away, please?' My back was to her. 'It didn't fit.'

'No, Miss.'

'I shouldn't have tried. It was vanity. Or something.'

'Are you all right, Miss Mary?'

I half-turned, slid a glance in her direction. Pity would be intolerable. But her expression was neutral. 'Fine. I've been a little careless with the dress, you might restore it to its original folds.'

'Very good, Miss.'

I should have left Hope to her work, but lingered to watch. 'Her taste is deceptively simple.'

'She'd have taken the master's breath away when he saw her in it.'

I chewed my lip. That stung, but I deserved it. 'Charlotte wasn't the sort to flaunt herself. But when you look at her things closely, you can tell how fastidious she was.'

'She was particular, Miss Mary.'

'She told me she had her wedding clothes made up quickly, but I suspect she'd thought long and hard about the gown.'

'Never you mind about the dress. Try this.'

Hope had shaken out the mantle and was holding it towards me. Something complicit flowed between us. I approached, bent my head, and she draped it over me like a veil. 'You'll be a beautiful bride, Miss Mary. You'll make your mama proud.'

I noticed she didn't mention Arthur, but let it pass, engrossed in my reflection, which sent a jolt of pleasure to compensate for the dress. A woman wearing a veil is transformed: her features concealed, imperfections blurred. Artifice is created. I allowed myself to sink into the illusion. Our marriage would be a success – I wouldn't be a poor substitute for Charlotte. I pirouetted, smiled, and let my misgivings be packed away, along with my predecessor's wedding finery.

*

'Mama, I've made up my mind. I'd prefer a simple ceremony. Just you, me and Arthur.'

'And Richard, of course. He's to be Arthur's best man.'

'I won't have him there.'

'But he's your brother! Besides, if we invite neighbours and cousins, we might find him a suitable wife.'

'My wedding is not being used as an opportunity to match Richard off!'

'But a clergyman needs a wife.'

'No!'

'How peevish you are, my pet. I suppose it must be pre-wedding nerves.'

'Also, I'm not wearing white, Mama. Tell the dressmaker.'

'But she's already working on your gown.'

'It'll have to be dyed.'

'Cream, then.'

I shook my head.

'Pale gold? Light fawn?'

'None of this is what I want, Mama!'

'Really, Mary, I don't know what's got into you.'

'You're making a bride of me, but I won't let you trick me out like one. I'll walk down the aisle in a colour of my choosing. Without flounces, or lace trimmings, or orange blossom, or music. I'll have a plain-Jane wedding. Or none at all.'

'Ingratitude!' Mama blinked hard, and rummaged for a handkerchief.

'It's tempting fate, Mama.'

'All I've ever tried to do is my best for you. It hasn't been easy since your papa died. You were only nine, Mary. The dear man was waiting in England for a ship to the south of France – he was chesty, the sun would have helped. I was meant to join him. But out of the blue, I was a widow. The shock was like a …' She gulped, cupped a hand around her throat.

'Tree falling on you!' I was word-perfect on the story. Widowhood didn't suit Mama, the way it agreed with some women, yet she'd never remarried. She was manipulating me, but I couldn't stay testy with her. Other young widows might have gone to pieces, but she'd stayed strong for her children. I rested my cheek on her circlet of plaits.

'All right, Mama, I'll wear fawn. But no lace and no veil.'

'And Richard … ?'

'He can host the wedding breakfast here in Hill House. But I'm not having him in the church.'

'I can't imagine why you've taken against your brother, Mary.'

'Can't you, Mama? Think hard. I'm sure the answer will come to you.'

*

Martha Brown, the Haworth Parsonage servant in Charlotte's time, paid us one of her occasional visits to coincide with the wedding day. 'Minister writ and invited me to see thee and e wed, Miss Mary,' she said. 'I've no likin for weddins, considerin lives ma married sisters lead. Never mind poor Mother. But I wunt disappoint im for world.'

'You're very good to answer his call. Mrs Bell will be glad of an extra pair of hands.'

'Baked you a wedding cake. I'm famous for ma cakes.'

'Wonderful. That means we'll have two.'

'Mine'll be tastiest, tha'll see. I baked Miss Charlotte's.'

'In fact, we had some – she brought us a few slices to taste. Delicious.'

'Aye, I done er proud. Now, I were going to wear one of Miss Charlotte's frocks to tha wedding. But then I thought best not fo fear minister recognized it. Might give im a land.'

'I imagine it would.'

'Though mebbe e wunt recognize it?'

'I'm afraid he's bound to. I didn't know you had any of her dresses, Martha.'

'Oh aye, minister gev me a few bits and bobs. Dresses and bonnets.'

'And do you wear them?'

'Not i front of minister. Good stuff in them dresses but I ad to let em out. I'm skinny but she were a sparrow. I got er going-away frock, a funny kind of grey that changes colour, and another wi flowers and leaves on it.'

A memory butted through: Charlotte stepping off the train at Westland Row station in Dublin, in a grey dress with mauve sheen. How had it ended up with Martha Brown? Down to chance, I supposed, the same way her wooden swan was in Hope's possession. 'I can let you have a dress if you need something to wear, Martha. Though I'm afraid you'll have to take it up.'

'Thank yus, Miss Mary. Aye, you be on tall side. But I can tek a needle and thread to it.' She folded one hand in front of the other and her eyes, so brown they were almost black, travelled over me. 'Minister said twa fittin to ave me at both is weddins.'

'Did he, indeed?' I hesitated, but curiosity prevailed. 'How was he, at the Charlotte wedding? Elated, I suppose.'

'E were a man walkin on eggshells goin int chapel and walkin on air leavin it.'

'He'd won his heart's desire.'

'Aye. But wur short-lived. Minister wanted more. He got er and then e wanted a bairn. Wunt meant to be.'

'We don't always get everything we want. Charlotte wasn't able to –'

'Oh, she wur able, Miss. Up to a point. She wur carryin a bairn. That's what done for er.'

Shock smarted through me. 'She was pregnant when she died?'

'Mebbe two or three months gone.'

'Arthur never mentioned a baby.' I swallowed. 'He always says she just wasted away. We supposed a form of consumption.'

'Nay, nay. Miss Charlotte's monthlies ad stopped. She'd a sick stomach, wunt able to keep food down. Mother called up to look about er in parsonage, said she wur in family way. Minister never wanted to admit she died from it, but tiny mite inside er drained away what morsel of strength she ad.'

'What a tragedy, Martha! Arthur must have been devastated.'

'Minister never forgive imself, if you ask me.'

My brain was close to bursting point with the information being spilled out. All I could manage was a pious, 'Marriage is a perilous business.'

'Aye, for women. Me, I've next to no learning. But I were born wi more sense than to mess wi marriage.'

'I suppose there may be compensations.'

'Appen so. I know Miss Charlotte wur well matched wi Mr Nicholls. Hadn't much time with im. But she were reet content wi time she ad.' A sniff. 'Minister took er loss ard, but not as ard as old parson. Day she died, e come into ma kitchen, a thing e never done. Leaned on chair like is legs wunt fit to old im. Said Miss Charlotte wunt able for marriage. Said is daughter wud still be alive if she'd stayed unwed.'

'He blamed Arthur ...'

'Easy for parson to say. E never give is wife much peace when e wur a young man – six bairns in as many years. And er a tiny wisp of a lady, too. Birthed Miss Anne and downhill from there. That wur the end o Mrs Brontë. Poor lady wur coffined and gone when little ones wunt much more'n babes in arms.'

'History repeating itself. Except at least she had babies.'

'Much good it done er lyin in vault under church floor.'

'Mary!' For a few moments, my name didn't register. It sounded again, closer. 'Mary! I need you.' The summons came from Mama.

'Miss, tha's as white as a sheet. Mrs Bell wunt tek kindly to me tellin tales.'

'Don't worry, Martha, I won't breathe a word about this.'

'Aye, she wants tha wed. And never tha fret, Miss Mary. Tha's a strong sort. Marriage wunt best thee.' A pause. 'I aven't given tha second thoughts?'

Suspicion snaked through me. 'Do you want to?'

'Nay, Miss. That's not ma intention. But thee as a reet to knaw the truth before thy weddin day.'

CHAPTER 12
CONWAY, NORTH WALES

'Silly thing, you weigh nothing at all.'

My new husband's mumbling jangled me awake in the middle of the night. 'Your writing box weighs more.' He was tossing about, captured by a dream. I was on the brink of rousing him when he spoke again. 'I like you on my lap ... wee sprite ... know where to find you.'

I propped myself on an elbow. A strip of moonlight captured his indulgent smile while he talked to her in his sleep.

'Pop you in my pocket ... parish work ... improvement ...' On and on, he went. Not captured by his dream, but captivated by it. 'Playful kitten, tugging my whiskers.'

Aghast, I could neither stop my ears nor his tongue. 'You smell of apple blossom, Sharlie.'

He had a pet name for her – and none for me! Never once was I invited to climb on his knee. Here we were on our honeymoon, where we had become one flesh, as the Bible said should happen when a man took a wife. Yet his thoughts teemed with her. I wanted to throw back the covers and run, run, run from this marriage bed of ours. But I couldn't wander the hotel corridors by night. 'Stop! Stop it at once!' I squawked.

Arthur jolted awake. 'What's the matter, Mary?'

I made my voice furry with drowsiness. 'Mmm, what?'

'You're shouting, Mary.'

'Sorry … asleep.'

He curved his arm around my waist. 'It's been a long day. And more travelling tomorrow. You must rest. Otherwise, you'll doze off when I'm pointing out mountain peaks and passes!'

I gave a mock yawn and sat up in bed. He fumbled for matches and lit an oil lamp, whose yellow beam turned the room into a place of dark patches and strange oblongs of light.

Arthur looked closely at my face, his expression rueful. 'Did I hurt you, Mary? When we were together?'

'I, no.'

'My dear, I'll be gentler in future, I give you my word.'

Arthur kissed me on the mouth, a lover's embrace. The moment to speak had passed. Perhaps such a dream wouldn't happen again – the repetition of a wedding day may have rekindled memories. He pressed himself the length of me, body heat rushing through my clothing, his hand reaching beneath my nightgown. But afterwards, when he lay back down to sleep, his hand heavy against my hip, the huddle we made was shaped like a question mark. In the throat of the night, I lay awake with my thoughts chugging. Did other newlyweds fall asleep wearing their nightclothes? Had he slept naked with her?

When morning landed in on us, Arthur sprang up, rang for water to shave by, and relieved himself in the chamber pot with his back to me, his urine pungent. Marriage was nothing if not intimate. He dressed quickly – still wearing clerical black, despite no longer holding a ministry – and was lacing up his boots when a jug of hot water was handed in at the door.

He soaped his face in front of a mirror. 'All set to tour North Wales? The reservations are made. Snowdonia, Bangor, glorious sights.'

'Yes. But. Must we?'

Surprised, his hand stopped scraping. 'Is there somewhere you'd prefer to go?'

'Haworth.' The name skidded off my tongue of its own accord.

He lowered the razor. 'Yorkshire is nowhere near Wales. But if you want to go there, I'll check the train timetable. I don't know if it's viable but let me look into it.'

'You'd bring me there?'

He lifted the blade to his cheek again. 'Of course. If you'd mentioned it earlier, I'd have arranged it.'

'I didn't think of it before. But last night, I realized I'd like to visit her grave.'

'Why?'

'To ask for her blessing. And ...' I bit the inside of my mouth, and threw back the bed covers.

He anchored me with a look. 'And?'

'To see what she saw, hear what she heard.'

'She saw the moors. And heard the wind whistle straight off them. As for her blessing, we have it. I feel it in here.' He tapped his chest. 'But Charlotte doesn't lie in a grave. She's in a vault below the church.'

'It seems wrong. She should sleep in the earth, where the heathers grow.'

'I'd no say in it.'

'Still, she's with her family. That's something.'

He frowned, shook himself, and bent to stroke my hair. 'Up you get, lazybones. We'll have breakfast, then walk over to the railway station and inspect the timetable. I'll wait downstairs for you. I expect you'd like privacy to dress.'

'I don't mind, Arthur. We have to get used to each other.'

'Gradually is best, my dear. Unless you can't ... hooks and buttons, and so forth?'

'I can manage.'

'Of course you can, Charlotte. You're a born manager.'

A buffeting at my heart. 'I'm Mary.'

'That's what I said.'

'You called me Charlotte.'

'Don't be silly. Why would I call you that?'

'But you did.'

'It's not a competition, Mary. I loved her, and now I, ah, love you.'

That morning, three days after our wedding, a narrow vein of hatred for Arthur pulsed alongside the affection I felt for him. 'No, Arthur!' I flared up. 'You love her. There's no past tense where she's concerned.'

'You're tired, my dear. Would you like breakfast in bed?'

Mama's words on the morning we were married rattled in my ears. *Broken hearts mend, Mary. Arthur's will, too.* I breathed in, set aside the kink of jealousy, twined my arms around his neck and pressed my cheek against his. 'Let's not argue, Arthur. I'll join you downstairs directly. And don't worry if Haworth isn't possible. It's just a fancy.'

The sleeves of my nightgown, embroidered with myrtle by Mama, fell back above my elbows and he ran his hands along my arms. 'A bride deserves to have her fancies indulged.' He dropped a kiss on top of my head, took a book from the trunk and went downstairs.

Left alone, I washed myself with a flannel and leftover, lukewarm water from Arthur's jug. On one of my inner thighs, I found a bruise caused by the thrust of his body. It was a sign of something. Desire. There was that, at least. I felt it for him, too. Arthur was handsome, passionate – there was a loosening deep inside me when he touched my flesh. Perhaps hunger for one another's bodies would give our marriage texture. And if it led to a baby, as I hoped, our union would ripen still further. Buttoning up my dress, I daydreamed about a honeymoon baby, conceived here in Conway. Good fortune would make me generous – if it was a girl, we'd call her Charlotte for a middle name. A boy would be Arthur.

Ready now, I smoothed my hair and checked my appearance in the mirror. The same face as usual, which people seemed to admire. An adjustment to my cuffs, and I crossed to the window to inspect the view. We were staying in a hotel in this ancient walled town, in the shadow of its medieval castle made spectacular by eight towers, where Arthur and Charlotte had honeymooned. It wasn't his idea. He'd offered me anywhere in Europe. 'Wales,' I said, 'to tour Snowdonia.' Because she'd praised it.

But I didn't bargain for the impact this palimpsest honeymoon would have on both of us. Signing the register at the Castle Hotel, he'd mentioned it was the same inn where they'd stayed ten years previously. Somehow, that nugget of information had shocked me. 'I knew the inn was a decent one,' he'd explained.

A thought barbed in my head. Possibly, I was standing in the same room where they'd embraced. Seen one another's nakedness. Made love. Hard on the heels of that thought followed another. However long or short a time we had together, Arthur would never love me as he loved her. But there was justice in that. Because he would never spellbind me as she did.

In my mind's eye, I saw a tiny version of the two of them, hand in hand – like something viewed the wrong way through a telescope. These nips of jealousy are natural, I told myself. Don't be resentful. But you'll have something Charlotte never did. You can never be loved as she was, fêted as she was, but you can carry a baby without dying from it.

*

We were lovers during those days in Wales – it was time out of time. But all things must pass, and the final day came. Arthur left me in our hotel room, to buy a present for Hope Porter – a length of lace suitable for a shawl I'd drawn his attention to earlier in the trip. It was extravagant, for a member of the household who was neither family nor servant, but I was feeling well-disposed towards the world. My hopes were high that this marriage could work, that happiness wouldn't prove elusive. Arthur was thoughtful and generous, even if it was Mama's money he was indulging us with.

On the bedside locker lay a bulky tome he'd been reading. Bored, I lifted it.

British Manly Exercises
Containing
Rowing and Sailing
Riding & Driving, &c. &c.

Its author, Donald Walker, urged physical training for everyone for the prevention and cure of disease, prolonging life and promoting happiness. It seemed an extravagant set of claims. The pages were peppered with engravings of manly men engaged in vigorous pursuits, vaulting and boxing, climbing ladders and poles, all without risking their hats. I wondered what was their secret? I could barely manage some bending and stretching for my stiff leg without losing my hairpins.

Arthur lugged the exercises manual everywhere with him – he'd be distraught if he forgot it. His trunk lay in the corner, battered and seawater-stained. It was unlocked, and I raised the lid to put the book inside. How orderly everything was. He had refused my offer to pack for him, saying he was accustomed to shifting for himself – which may have been true when he lived in Haworth but certainly wasn't the case in Banagher. I placed the book on top, but as I closed the trunk, my eye caught a flash of colour. It was a tin box painted blue. Intrigued, I lifted it out. Had it been locked, I'd like to think I'd have left well alone, but the lid opened at my touch. Inside was a page of notepaper: *To be retained semper* in a hand I recognized instantly as Arthur's.

Sheltered beneath that lay a cache of letters tied with a pale green ribbon. I untied the bow and fanned out the contents.

Six letters in total, some with stamps, postmarks and broken wafer seals, others presumably delivered by hand. All were carefully preserved. Two sets of penmanship. Three letters were to Miss Charlotte Brontë from Arthur. A further three letters were addressed to Revd Arthur Nicholls in what I thought might be Charlotte's script, although I wasn't certain until I checked the signature.

A skim of their substance revealed them to be correspondence between the pair during their courtship. All of Charlotte's were sent from the parsonage. One of Arthur's was hand-delivered from Oxenhope a few miles from Haworth, where he stayed with a parson friend in the days preceding their wedding. His others were marked Kirk Smeaton, which I knew was forty miles away, where Arthur had held a curate's post after resigning when his first marriage proposal was declined. Without a single scruple, I settled down to read. Arthur's first letter was dated Friday 30 September 1853, addressed to *Dear Miss Brontë*.

Being six-times-six cleverer than me, you will have fathomed already that what moved me first about you was your insight. That day in the laneway, when I spoke to you about my boyhood in Banagher and you said, why, both of us were raised by aunts, I was overcome. My aunt Harriette is goodness personified, but to lose a mother's loving presence is a wrench. I push on too fast, I know, but I am only flesh and blood despite this priest's collar. Foolishly, I spoke of marriage before I had even wooed you. Might you consent to rectify that by agreeing to a meeting? It would afford you an opportunity to study me, in my role as suitor rather than curate, and afford me much joy because I would be in your presence.

By the second letter in the pile, dated Tuesday 14 February 1854, an understanding seemed to have developed between them. Clearly, his soft words were not falling on stony ground. He had the confidence to reference St Valentine's Day and by now she was

My dear (dare I say dearest? I dare!) Charlotte, You listen to my babblings with infinite patience – sometimes I think I spy a smile. I cannot blame you, because I stumble about, a great oaf, in the courtship maze. Now I have a favour to beg. Won't you call me Arthur? I long to hear my name on your lips. You would not refuse me if you knew how much rigid self-control I exercise in your presence. You would think it little to ask. The body obeys its own logic, and when we meet it takes every ounce of my willpower not to seize you and

Disappointingly, any subsequent sheets were missing. I turned to the third letter, dated Wednesday 28 June 1854, the day before they exchanged their vows.

Thrice dearest Charlotte, I scrawl these hurried lines while a boy waits to deliver them before nightfall. In a matter of hours, my heart's treasure, we will be man and wife – that is the important thing. Do not fret over the disappointment you wrote to me about. It changes nothing.

I pray God will bless our union. I read your final words with pleasure, as a man rather than a minister, but I should warn you I am no romantic hero in a novel. I am merely a human being who loves you and is truly convinced we are meant to spend our lives together. My dearest, in order to protect you, I will burn the final page of your letter before I leave for church in the morning.

Soon, the world will know you as Mrs Arthur Nicholls. Until then, my darlingest Miss Brontë, I take a reluctant leave of you. But this is our last farewell. From tomorrow, we two will never be parted. I kiss this letter before I seal it.

Believe me to be, Charlotte
Your most constant Arthur
Faithful for all eternity

I folded up his letters, keeping them in order, and scuttled to the window to check for Arthur's return. People were darting in and out of white shop fronts, or scudding along the High Street's footpaths, bristling with intent. I looked left towards the castle, and right in the harbour's direction. No sign of Arthur's sturdy shape. I told myself the passion I had uncovered was my punishment for snooping on their wooing. Yet despite Arthur's fever, love was voiced in stock language – she was a sorceress, he was enslaved. Not everyone could Shakespeare their beloved. Still, at least he'd tried. Unlike his proposal of marriage to me in the Hill House orchard.

'Well, Mary, have you had enough of spying?' I asked my silhouette in the window glass. The answer was a foregone conclusion. I turned to Charlotte's letters. The first was dated Thursday 6 October 1853. He was *Dear Mr Nicholls* and she did not regard him as a lover.

I can no longer allow your letters to go unanswered. I know, from experience, the deadening sense of hopes thwarted which comes from watching for post destined never to arrive. I would not inflict such misery on another soul. However, I urge you not to continue wishing for the impossible. It will destroy your peace of mind. I have no thoughts of marriage.

In the second letter, dated Monday 2 January 1854, he was still *Dear Mr Nicholls* but a gift had been accepted.

Thank you for the New Year's present of pansies, an underrated flower. You must have gone to enormous trouble to source them out of season. I fear I was a little tongue-tied on receiving your posy, because they catapulted me back to a time in my life when I spoke and perhaps thought in the French language. Pansies are pensées – symbols of thoughts and dreams. You chose well, Mr Nicholls.

Sir, I can make no promises except one: I will give you a fair hearing and reflect on your words. In return, you must give me time.

Yours very respectfully,

C. Brontë

It was clear she welcomed his attentions. Ear cocked for Arthur's return, I handled the third and final letter from Charlotte. By far the longest, it was a revelation. Like his, it was written on the evening before their marriage. By now, she had graduated to *My dear Arthur.*

I write to you this evening so that you won't be alarmed by Papa's absence from church tomorrow. Just an hour ago, before going to bed, he sent word by Martha for me to visit him in his study. I arrived laughing, from some bridal nonsense or other of Ellen's, expecting a few words of fatherly advice on matrimony, or something sentimental about his and Mama's wedding day. Instead, he told me abruptly he could not bring himself to attend the ceremony, let alone give me in marriage. To say it came as a bolt from the blue is an understatement. He had been in loquacious form when my dear friends arrived, and I believed him to be quite reconciled to our match. When he told me of his decision, I could scarcely credit such a volte-face. I reproduce our exchange here, as best I can recall it.

But Papa, we agreed you wouldn't have to conduct the marriage service. Surely it's not too much to walk with me up the aisle? As fathers have done for their daughters since time immemorial?

I'm an old man, not long for this world. I've consulted my conscience, and prayed over it. The duty is too onerous. I cannot undertake it.

Don't consult your conscience – consult me! Papa! Think what I need!

I'll be there in spirit. On my knees praying for you as you make your vows to Mr Nicholls.

This is cruel, Papa!

Cruel is losing the final wee chick where once there were six nestlings. I'm frightened, Charlotte. Scared I'll be unmanned when the Wedding March strikes up. That I'll break down and howl my grief. Think how that would overshadow your day. Spare me that indignity in the church where I've preached for more than thirty years.

There was no more to be said. Once Papa's mind is made up, nothing can shift him. I returned to my wedding guests.

Tyrant! said Ellen.

He's suffered so much, Ellen. Don't attack him.

It's a father's sacred duty. I've never heard of anyone shirking it.

Does he think this will prevent the marriage? asked Miss Wooler.

I suppose it must. A woman has to be given in marriage by someone. What are we but property? If not a father's then a husband's! If Emily was alive she'd catch Papa by the lapels and shake him till he relented.

It's a shame Branwell isn't here to step into the breach, said Ellen.

Branwell wouldn't be able to stand upright long enough.

He wasn't always like that, Charlotte, said Ellen.

I know. I'm unkind. It's the shock.

I'd never have believed it of Mr Brontë, said Miss Wooler.

Me, me, me, said Ellen. That's what he's saying.

Ellen continued to fulminate against Papa. I couldn't contradict her because, in my heart, I agreed. But Miss Wooler turned her brain to possible solutions, left the room and returned with an idea. I do hope you approve, Arthur. It is this. Miss Wooler checked the wording in The Prayer Book. It said a woman's hand should be received by the officiating minister from 'her father's or friend's hands' — nothing specified the friend's sex. Resourceful Miss Wooler, ever useful in an emergency, volunteered to give her old pupil away, and I have accepted with deepest gratitude.

I realize it is unconventional, but why let custom and practice limit us? Please don't be alarmed or dismayed when you see her step forward to undertake the role. We must not allow such impediments to deter us if we are sincere in our determination to couple our lives together. I know you will be provoked on my behalf, as my friends are, but for my sake accept it.

This time tomorrow night, my hair — which you have stroked, and longed to unpin — will be lying across your chest. Skin will be pressed against skin. There will be no barriers between us. Tonight, I intend to fall asleep (if sleep I can) anticipating those bonds of intimacy soon to exist between us. I cannot bring my pen to order — perhaps the scene with Papa has unsettled me. Arthur, my pen, my hand, my heart insist on sharing this intelligence with you. I want you to know that I am eager to *cross the Rubicon into the conjugal state and experience the fullness of earthly union with you.*

Your impatient wife-to-be,

Charlotte

How direct she was! How taken aback Arthur must have been! Women were meant to desire their husbands after the marriage ceremony, not before. Now I understood the unease in his last letter: he didn't know what to make of a woman who expressed ardour. Yet he remained loving; his reference to burning the page in which passion had burst through was the only hint of disapproval. Why hadn't he done so? The lover in Arthur – who kept faith with her even when she was indifferent to him – must have needed that written confirmation.

A door banged in the corridor. Fingers flying, I returned the letters to the box in Arthur's trunk, and drank some cold, stewed tea from the pot sitting on the table. My skin was overheated, my pulse speeding. Poor Charlotte, grappling with such a setback on the night before her wedding. Yet she was receptive to any solution, however unusual. Arthur was a fortunate man having Charlotte in his camp.

But what did I have? She had the flame and I had the embers. I'd known that before my marriage.

CHAPTER 13

The day we returned to Banagher from our wedding trip, a wedge of geese flew overhead, against a rumpled sky – the flocks beginning their winter migration. Mama looked into my eyes with a question in hers, and when I nodded, she hugged me. 'The first flush of marriage is a special time,' she whispered. No point in telling her I had accepted my lot. Ours would be no Romeo and Juliet pairing, all rapture and rupture. I knew Arthur liked me well enough, and would always be kind to me – apart from the particular unkindness of loving his first wife more.

He went out to walk the land, while I climbed upstairs to my bedroom to check minor alterations had been made for my new husband to join me there. Another bedside locker, a chair at his side of the room, and so on. It was strange being back in my home as a wife.

And perhaps, in time, a mother, too. On the Irish Sea between Holyhead and Kingstown, Arthur had stood beside me at the packet's rail watching white furrows foam up and collapse into the great mass of grey. I'd been happy to have him there, because it meant he wasn't retching with seasickness, from which he suffered horribly. Over the sea's roar, he said, 'Motherhood is a sacred duty.'

I burrowed into his shoulder. 'And a joy.'

'But not without risk.'

'I'm strong, Arthur.'

His eyes navigated along my body, and a pleasurable shiver caught me. 'Are you disappointed we didn't reach Haworth?'

'No, you tried to change our reservations. Another time.'

His willingness to go with me was what mattered. Anyway, there was no need. Haworth lived alongside us in Hill House.

Hope Porter knocked on the bedroom door. She was already capable of running the household, and did the chief part of Mrs Foley's work.

'I have a wedding present for you, Miss Mary.'

'Why, Hope, you shouldn't be spending your money on us. But it's very kind of you. Shall I fetch Master Arthur to open it with me?'

'It's just for you, Miss.'

She gave me a substantial cream envelope sealed with dark blue wax. I took in the rightwards slant of the handwriting, the uncharacteristically extravagant Cs for Cuba Court, and my heartbeat speeded up. The letter was addressed to me at our previous home. 'I don't understand.'

'I found it inside an old umbrella. It was with some walking sticks from the parsonage, in a box in the attic. I was tidying the place while you and Master Arthur were away. Took the umbrella outside to give it a shake, see if it was watertight. And out falls the letter.'

I stared at the envelope. 'It's like a message from Charlotte. It *is* from her, isn't it?'

'I think it might be. I looked at some books she signed, in the glass case in the drawing room. No stamp on it. Maybe she meant to send the letter, but mislaid it. Aren't you going to open it, Miss?'

A sprig of dried white heather tumbled out when I slit the wax seal. I was conscious of Hope watching me while I read the letter, but didn't send her away – she'd earned a share in its news.

Haworth Parsonage,
Bradford,
Yorkshire
Monday 1st October 1854

Dearest of Marys,

To write and receive letters from friends is my chief entertainment, and so it was with great joy that I read yours, my lass. It was an elfin gift, all the more welcome because I ought to have written first to you, as promised. You must forgive me. Life is busy here in Haworth – a curate's wife has a great deal to occupy her, and time has to be stolen for my own pursuits. I keep telling myself I must not allow my literary faculties to rust from want of exercise. Yet I do not wish myself single again – even though, for now, all I can manage are letters. Arthur says I must do as I please. Either write or stop writing – it is all one to him so long as I am happy. ~~I wonder if I need to be unhappy to write?~~ I must turn my mind to another book soon.

My lass, when we were in Banagher I bid you come and visit us, and repeat that invitation

157

here. I can't promise dramatic scenery or glittering society, but the moors I place at your disposal. Like a person, they have moods. They can be light-hearted, meditative or gay. Sullen, mostly, when the mists are down! As for our wild little hill village of Haworth, despite its soot-dark houses and smoking mills, it has its charms.

Either come at once, before the winter sets in, or leave it until Easter when the moors deck themselves in their finery and the sun can be counted on (occasionally) to burst through our low, troubled, yet fascinating skies. I am happy, Mary, among the Haworthites, but I would be happier yet to see the sweet face of my cousin from Banagher, and cosy by the fire with her. There is no better place to be when a cruel east wind blows, as it does today. There is no better place to sit and gossip, although I haven't forgotten how you teased me about converting every story I heard to fiction if I was let – and even if I was not. We novelists are shameless!

Haworth is twenty miles from Leeds, which is easily reached from any point by railway. From there, you take a train to Keighley and either walk for four miles to our village, or hire a conveyance at the Devonshire Arms. Naturally, we would meet you in Keighley.

As regards my vanity set left behind by mistake, please don't trouble yourself to post it. It gives me pleasure to picture it sitting on the Blue Room dressing table, awaiting my return. As well, I should be loath to think of it getting lost or dented on the road. Emily and Anne pooled their resources to buy it for me at a time of trouble and unhappiness. I felt a failure because I came home early from Brussels, where I was a pupil-teacher — you may recall my mentioning it. How long ago and unimportant those times seem now! I know you will keep the set safe for me, dearest Mary. I have the utmost faith in you.

I close now by inserting a spray from the heather nosegay you presented me with in Dublin three months ago — sharing the luck your gift has brought me. I know how fortunate I am to have your cousin as my husband. Arthur and Papa join with me in sending our compliments to you and your worthy family, especially your mother. Arthur says to tell Hope she must work hard at her lessons so that she can read my books!

I am, cousin Mary, yours truly,
C.B. Nicholls

P.S. I add another page because I cannot seal up this letter without sharing some intelligence which Arthur told me in confidence after our return to Haworth. He does not suspect I am breaking it. I struggle with the idea of keeping this secret because I feel you should know. Hope Porter is your brother Richard's child — Mary, she is your niece and your mama's granddaughter. Richard wanted nothing to do with her, but Arthur forced him to see that he must take some responsibility for the girl. It was Arthur who concocted the fiction about a foundling left on the steps of the porter's lodge at Trinity College, after hearing of infants abandoned in similar fashion elsewhere. Hope's mother was a flower girl who agreed — with what reluctance, we can only imagine — to surrender her baby in the child's best interests. A sum of money was paid and she renounced all claims. It preyed on Arthur's conscience, and the following year he made inquiries about the mother, thinking she might welcome a report on Hope's progress. Unfortunately, he discovered news of her death. As to whether Aunt Harriette should be told, I leave that to your discretion. In years to come, Hope may wish to know something of her mother. All I can

glean is that her name was Nora, she had red hair
and sang like a thrush.

I looked from the letter to Hope. Her eyes crinkled. 'What does she say, Miss? If it's not wrong of me to ask.'

'That, that all's well in, ah, Haworth. Master Arthur inquired after you. The letter is full of ... plans and, and promises ... for all of us to meet again. But no real news.'

'Oh, Miss Mary! Promises to meet. Promises the poor lady couldn't keep. How sad!'

I found myself staring at Hope. She had inherited her father's pink and white complexion. The dimple on her chin was his, too. Was that his way of standing, weight balanced on one foot?

'You look pale. I'll skip down to the kitchen and brew you up a nice strong cup of tea.'

She had the door open before I found my voice. 'Are you ...' I cleared my throat, coughed and tried again. 'Are you contented here with us, Hope?'

'Such a queer question. To be sure I am, Miss Mary. You and Mrs Bell and Master Arthur, you've given me a home. It's an honour to serve you.'

The words felt like an explosion. I must have made a sound, because she hurried to my side. Before I knew it, she had sat me on the bed, unbuttoned my dress and loosened my corsets. My head buzzed. Why tell me, why not Mama? But no sooner did the question form than the answer came to me.

Mama knew already.

It explained why I had seen her sometimes, gazing at Hope with an odd expression on her face. As if simultaneously horrified by the girl and drawn to her. It explained her lenience with Hope, compared to the other staff, allowing me to educate her and Arthur to spoil her. Why she took pains to correct her speech, and insisted she pronounce her words properly. Why she advanced no argument when Richard left our household to take up a living in another parish, after incompetence and disorganization lost him the headmastership. It meant Mama was relieved of the necessity of seeing her son and his love child in a master–servant relationship.

'Hope, would you do me a favour?'

'You've only to ask, Miss Mary.'

'Don't tell Arthur or Mama, or anybody, about finding the letter.'

'Why not, Miss? Wouldn't it be a kindness to let them read it?'

'I'm afraid not. It would only make them miserable.' She looked perplexed. 'You see, it's as if Charlotte Brontë is still alive in the letter, full of chat about Yorkshire and her moors. But the tragedy of it is – she's gone. Arthur, in particular, would be terribly unhappy. Remember that time after he left Haworth? How he stopped eating, hardly slept? That's how he'd be again.'

'That would be dreadful!'

'I knew you'd understand.' I laid a finger against my lips. 'Let's just keep the letter between us.'

1861–2

CHAPTER 14

Arthur's letter coincided with the chimney sweep's annual visit, which meant the house was all at sixes and sevens because of his kit and caboodle, and Mama was busy checking the servants had covered everything against soot.

'Read it for me, Mary. I'm too busy to stop.'

It was dated Wednesday, 18 September 1861. My eyes fled along its lines, reading the news he shared without frills: following Mr Brontë's death, the trustees of Haworth Church had rejected Arthur as a replacement, and he must vacate the parsonage immediately to make way for the preferred candidate. Could Aunt Harriette take him in until he formulated a plan? Perhaps the missions. But he was in too much mental distress to decide on his future at present.

'He says he's lost his position at Haworth, Mama.'

'What's that, Mary? Those curtains really need to be taken down.'

'Arthur's coming home. Yorkshire's turned him out.'

Now I had her attention. 'After all his drudgery? The boorish! The odious!'

'He's been doing the job since the old minister died. Every day for the past three months.'

'And the lion's share of the work for the sixteen years before that. Show me the letter.' Mama's colour mounted as she read. 'He built them a school. Christened their babies. Married and buried them. Ungrateful wretches!'

'He was convinced the job was his.'

'Never mind. He's coming home to us now.'

'I never thought he'd leave. England held him tight.'

'We'll hold him tighter, Mary.' I felt the weight of her gaze. 'And you can play your part.'

*

Arthur's arrival to live with us sent a tidal wave through our becalmed lives, now that Richard and his dramas were no longer our concern. My brother had discovered a previously unsuspected inclination towards the Church, studied divinity, and been taken on as curate to a vicar friend of Papa's. As far as I was concerned, the less said about that the better.

Hill House was no Cuba Court, but it was a substantial property, and there was plenty of space for Arthur to join Mama and me, along with our household staff. Mama designated a large bedroom and dressing room (on another floor to ours) for Arthur's use, along with a study at the side of the house, thinking they would be ample. But she winced at the quantity of boxes and trunks stacked on a cart when he arrived. 'He must have emptied out the parsonage!' she said to me in an undertone. One box made a bonging sound as two men carried it into the house.

'Watch out! That's valuable!' The voice was Arthur's, but the ashen crumple of a human being barely resembled him. He looked baffled by the trick life had played. Worry lines netted his eyes, his shirt collar flopped in exhaustion, mud clung to his boots and coat skirts. Haworth had sucked the vitality out of him.

'Never you worry, your honour. It's safe with us,' said the man in charge.

A lean woman a few years my senior, with robin-bright eyes and hair looped over her ears, climbed down from the plank placed as a crossways seat on the cart. She batted away the driver's attempt to help: 'You keep yus hands to yuself!' She turned out to be Martha Brown, the parsonage servant. Arthur had forgotten to tell us she was accompanying him. Also in his entourage was the parsonage dog, Plato. He'd neglected to mention him, too. A series of woofs reminded Arthur to give Plato the command to jump down. 'Stay,' said Arthur, and the enormous black hound sat back on his haunches in our stable yard, sniffing the air. Hope Porter glowered at Martha Brown, who folded her arms and paid no heed to her.

'Arthur's a scarecrow. We must make it our mission to fatten him up,' murmured Mama. 'Widowers never look after themselves.'

'Beggin tha pardon, Ma'am, but I always fed Mr Nicholls proper.' Martha turned out to have sharp ears. 'Mutton and beef and what not. But e went down'ill after old parson wur taken. Then when e wur done out o chapel, tossed aside by them as should a thanked their lucky stars to ave im, you could get im to eat nowt. Wunt lift a spoon.'

'No one doubts you did everything in your power for him,' said Mama. 'Go into the kitchen and have Mrs Foley give you a cup of tea and something to eat. Travel's exhausting.'

Martha squinted at the way the cart was being unloaded. 'Nay, I'll eat after I've watched them gobs o men do job proper, Ma'am. Dog'll want feeding, though. Girt beast eats better nar minister. Dunt tha, Plato?'

He pricked his ears at his name, but kept his eyes on his master.

'Aye, ignores me now, but I wur one saw to im on ship when minister wur poorly. E wunt fit for owt once we left port. Dog yowled for im, down wi cargo.'

'Take him around the back. Mrs Foley will find him a mutton bone or something,' said Mama.

'Soon as e's fed I'll mek a start on unpacking.' Martha snapped her fingers at Plato, who lumbered to his feet and followed her.

'Will that one who talks funny be staying long?' asked Hope.

'A very good question, Hope,' said Mama. 'We haven't been told.'

'She'll need a bed for a few nights, at least, Mama.'

'Mary, perhaps you might help Hope and that person – what was her name?'

'Martha.'

'Martha unpack. I'll see what can be done with Arthur.'

I was curious about the boxes' contents, and pleased to lend a hand. I thought I'd be supervising Martha, but the reverse was true. Still, she was a storehouse of information about the Brontës. In one chest, I found a medallion silhouette – all chin, collar and fluffed-up hair. 'Who's this fine gentleman?'

'Branwell,' said Martha. 'Ee, lad wur a peacock. They wur a clever ouse. But Branwell wunt ardworkin like girls. Could apply imself to nowt. He wur like me da, not a man to shirk is liquor. Ad winnin ways, I grant you. But too much wur expected of im and it made im wretched.'

'What's that you have?' Arthur loomed over us.

'Master Branwell,' said Martha.

'It's not worth tuppence – leave it in the trunk.'

'I've taken a fancy to it,' I said. 'I know the perfect spot for it, on the landing wall.'

He wrinkled his mouth. 'Where's Plato, Martha?'

'Stable block. E's to sleep there, mistress says.'

'I'd like a bed made up for him in my room, please.'

'Arthur, you know Mama doesn't allow dogs upstairs.'

'If he sleeps in the stables, so do I.'

Arthur had his way, and space in his bedroom was made for the parsonage animal. Making space for Martha was trickier – Hope's attic room went to her, which meant Hope had to share with Delia, the parlour maid who replaced Lizzie. 'It's only temporary,' I told Hope, although none of us knew for sure. It seemed Martha would stay as long as Martha chose.

We could hardly understand her Yorkshire speech, but she expressed herself with such determination we acquiesced to almost everything. However, I put my foot down when Martha said Hope needed her ears boxed, after Hope inquired if she was still waiting for her missing front teeth to grow in.

'Hope's like one of the family,' I told her.

''Lass sits i kitchen not parlour, dunt she?' countered Martha, and I had no answer to that.

*

And so Arthur, Martha and Plato joined our lives, along with the contents of Haworth Parsonage. Some of the furniture was useful, but we expected Arthur to make a bonfire of the papers. Instead, he left them in the box room and attic to moulder, and descended into a slump, the weight of the world crushing his shoulders. That huddle of belongings was all he cared about, and he handled them like a miser counting his gold. Any art of conversation he once possessed had evaporated. Arthur wallowed in his sorrow, which had become his pleasure.

He particularly liked to sag before Charlotte's portrait – the first item unpacked. Mama agreed to it being hung in the drawing room, and consequently we spent our evenings with Charlotte Brontë. Richard visited for a few days, and sat with us there, fidgeting at his pipe. He'd taken up smoking because someone told him he looked magisterial, pipe in hand. I thought he should have taken it out to the garden, but Mama was inclined to humour his fads.

Richard jabbed his pipe stem towards the picture. 'A winsome sketch. Maybe not an exact likeness. But he captured her expression.'

'It's Charlotte to the life,' rumbled Arthur.

'If you say so. How long has it been since …?'

'Six-and-a-half years.'

'Quite some time, old fellow.'

Arthur fired a look of unadulterated dislike at Richard, who missed it because he was tamping tobacco into his pipe bowl.

But Mama noticed, and patted Arthur's arm. 'Her loss was sudden. Just like my dear Alan's.'

Arthur heaved a sigh. 'She was gone without warning. A flame snuffed out.'

Richard tested out some recently discovered man-of-God waffle: 'The Bible tells us we die at the appointed hour.'

Arthur left the room.

'Go after him, Mary,' urged Mama.

I found him in the conservatory, pulling dead leaves off plants. 'You should know better than to let Richard provoke you, Arthur.' He nodded, and continued stripping foliage. 'Had you no notion of how frayed Charlotte's health was becoming?'

'None. One day, I was the happiest man in the kingdom. The next, a wi …' He couldn't bring himself to say the word. 'And then to lose the parish, too. I never dreamed I'd have to leave Haworth.'

'At least you don't have to dance to old Mr Brontë's tune anymore.'

'Ah no, Mary, we only had one serious difference in our lives.'

'Arthur, it's me you're talking to. I saw how his long arm stretched across the Irish Sea during your wedding tour. I remember your panic when her uncle –'

'Enough! We were the best of friends, Mr Brontë and me.'

Out of sorts, I returned to Mama and Richard.

'He needs to find another parish,' said Richard. 'I'll speak to him tomorrow, before I go back to Kilkenny.'

*

I happened to be there when Richard raised the question of Arthur's plans for the future.

'I'm through with parsoning,' said Arthur. 'I can't speak to people about God when He's robbed me of everything I love.'

'I thought you wanted to be a labourer in God's fields?'

'God's fields will have to flourish or go to seed without me. Is that Plato I hear barking?' He lifted his farming manual and went to investigate.

'No harm,' said Richard, when we were alone. 'The deadening tramp of Arthur's sermons are duller than November. He'd empty the church.'

I giggled so immoderately, I almost forgot my hostility towards my brother. 'All the same, he has to do something.'

'He could take up teaching again. Mama says he was a natural, that time Papa had to keep him home from Trinity to help with the school. Had the boys reciting Latin verbs for hours. Every time she opened a window, *amo, amos, amat* came sailing in. Mama almost became a Latin scholar herself, simply from exposure.' I laughed again, and he draped an arm around me. 'Perhaps I should go into the schoolmaster business with Arthur.'

Alarmed, I shook him off. 'Don't, Richard. It wouldn't be fair.'

'Oh wouldn't it, Miss Prim. But him floundering about here doing nothing is fair.' He sat down, long legs stretched out. 'He seems uncommonly attached to that opinionated little servant he brought with him from Yorkshire. Fine eyes, but she's a shade long in the tooth for my taste. Proud as Lucifer, too. Still, pride comes before a fall.'

'I see putting "reverend" in front of your name hasn't changed you one iota, Richard.'

'Says Miss Prim.'

*

Richard left later that day, to pursue his hedonistic ways, and Mama and I settled into life with Arthur. October gave way to November, and still the sunshine dawdled as if it could not bear to make way for winter. Flowers bloomed even as leaves drifted to the ground. But Arthur was deaf to efforts to help him, and blind to the weather's unexpected bounty.

Mama took to cupping his cheek, as if he were a small boy. 'You'll have good times again, I promise, Arthur.'

'Good times, bad times, all times are soon spent,' he said.

Even she began to lose patience with him.

Only the need to exercise Plato persuaded him outdoors. Sometimes, Hope accompanied them on their walks, but Martha preferred to sit hatching in the kitchen with the other servants, who were spellbound by her.

'Has Master Arthur said anything about his plans, Hope?' I asked.

'He says maybe he'll go to Australia, Miss Mary. That's a shocking long way, isn't it?'

'A shocking long way. We must do everything we can to keep him in Banagher.'

'Yes, Miss.' She dipped a hand in her apron pocket and plucked out a little wooden swan. 'Look what he brung me from England.'

I recognized it instantly. 'He never forgets you. May I see?'

She surrendered it into my hands, and I traced my finger pads across the wood. It was a crudely carved item, yet had an undeniable grace. When I turned it over, I found its maker's initials carved on the base. The hardiness of man-made objects in comparison with God-made flesh never failed to surprise me. 'You must treasure this, Hope. It belonged to his wife. Her uncle made it as a wedding gift. See this HB? That's him.'

'What's HB mean?'

'His initials. Hugh Brunty was one of Patrick Brontë's younger brothers. It's quite the compliment Arthur gave it to you. His Charlotte held it dear.'

Hope's cheeks crinkled with pleasure. 'She sewed a cloak for Marigold. So she wouldn't get cold.'

'Who's Marigold?'

'My doll, Miss Mary.'

'Oh yes, I remember. Do you still have her?'

'Of course!'

'You must show me the cloak.'

'It has purple flowers and the collar stands up. Mrs Arthur had a dress the same. She said there were leftover bits for making patches. In case her dress got tore. She took one out of her sewing box to make Marigold a cloak.'

A guilty nip. It had never occurred to me to make doll's clothes for Hope.

'Arthur always brings me presents from England. A skipping rope, a box of marbles, now this.' She held out her hand to reclaim the swan. 'But Marigold's the best one he give me.'

'He gave you, Hope, not he give you.' Mama rustled into the room.

'Yes, Ma'am.' Hope slid off.

'We're due to call on the Neales, Mary.'

'Mama, Arthur is talking about going to Australia. To the missions.'

Mama's face stiffened. 'Where in the world did he come up with that notion? Wait, he has a sister who lives there. But he hasn't laid eyes on her in donkey's years. It's a ridiculous idea.'

'Perhaps he wants to gather souls to God, Mama. He's a clergyman, after all.'

'Mary, there's nothing I don't know about men of the cloth. I was married to one. A missionary must have unwavering faith, but it's clear as daylight Arthur doesn't.'

'Because of losing Haworth?'

'Because of losing his wife.'

She ruminated as we tied on our cloaks and bonnets. 'Our Arthur is becoming maudlin, Mary. But I'll keep coddling him, and you'll help me.'

'I see no reason why.'

'Well I do. Arthur must tuck Banagher around him like a quilt, and you'll be one of its patchwork squares. Comfort matters in a relationship.'

'Mama, stop matchmaking.'

'How else am I meant to pass my time?'

'Do good works. Embroider tray cloths. Fiddle about with your hives.'

'I prefer matchmaking.'

'Seriously, Mama, what's to become of Arthur?'

'I mean him to run the Hill House farm – he has a bent for it. When all's said and done, he's a farmer's son. I'll say our all-female household can't manage and needs his help. That'll buck him up. The fact is, Arthur lacks the requisites to succeed in the Church: charm and fluency. Yet we love him for his faithful heart. Don't we?' I pushed out my lower lip. Mama raised her voice. 'Yes we do!'

*

Despite our combined efforts, pockets of silence widened around Arthur.

'In Yorkshire, e were all bustle and business, but now is grief weighs im down,' Martha told me, checking a shelf of ornaments for specks of dust.

'All griefs are unwanted.'

'But some's eavier than others.'

Martha liked to have the last word. Heaven knows how that fared in the parsonage. She was always as direct as a hammer blow on a nail. Generally, she was on the verge of flitting from one spot to another, but late one afternoon, when she carried in the lamps, I saw her gaze drawn to Charlotte's portrait.

'Sit down for a minute, Martha. What was it like, packing up the parsonage? You must have felt a pang.'

She sat in a circle of lamplight, and rested her chin on the palm of her hand. 'Ee, I could a wept, Miss. But there wunt no time fo tears. We ad too much to do. Minister wur given four days to leave parsonage. E wurnt ardly able to decide what to tek and what to leave, so e took near enough all. Except Misss Charlotte. Ad to leave is wife behind, poor gentleman.' She dabbed her eyes with her apron hem.

'I'm sure you did your best for him, Martha.'

'Someone ad to sort im out. E wur sat there like a statue while we wrapped and boxed. Not fit to give us orders. And when e wunt sitting e were trampin moors wi blessed girt ound. Give me some odds and ends. Rest wur auctioned off. First two days in October. Kitchen stuff and furniture, mostly. Grieved minister to do it. Felt it let folk spy on is life.'

'Horrible for him.'

'Made im some brass, mind.' Martha rubbed forefinger against thumb. 'But e shrank from sellin bed she died in. Med ma uncle chop it up and bury it.'

It occurred to me that Charlotte's death bed was probably their marriage bed. What must it have been like for Arthur, continuing to sleep in the bed where his wife had died?

'Best thing could a happened im, bein thrown out. Least e's got company in I'land. In parsonage, when day's work wur done, e wur sat there on is own.'

'You're a good friend to him, Martha.'

'It's what Miss Charlotte would a wanted, Miss.' She stood up. 'I went to work for Brontës when I wur nobbut a bairn.

Some folk's born to dance through life like they're in a ballroom. And some's born to labour. But at least there's life's small pleasures. Treacle toffee, fo one.' She grinned, holding her work-chapped hand over her mouth to hide the lost teeth.

'Did you have a favourite Brontë?'

'I wur partial to all o them. Never no airs nor graces wi a Brontë. They mucked in. Anne wur gentle. Patient, like. A curate took a shine to er but e died young. Emily wur a law unto erself. Charlotte and Anne called er the Major. Charlotte, she wur headstrong, but learned to ide it. And Branwell.' She clicked her tongue. 'Wunt all is fault. Round peg in square ole.'

'What about the Reverend Brontë?'

'Parson wur strict but fair, remembered me in is will. E were sharp enough to ave Yorkshire folk's measure. Young minister stepped on folk's toes.'

'You must miss Haworth and your sisters.'

'Aye, Mother wants me to live with er. She's lonesome for Father – e died same year as Miss Charlotte. Dust on is lungs. I miss Brontë lasses a sight more, tell thee no lie. But naw use cryin over spilled milk.'

'Haworth was home to Mr Nicholls for sixteen years. It holds dear memories for him.'

'E's proper knocked back but e might recover. E wur good to parson. Miss Charlotte would a been reet pleased.'

'Mr Nicholls has told Mama he wants you to stay here in Banagher, Martha. Make a home with us.'

'So e says. I'll stay a bit longer. Not forever, mind. Not enough for me to do ere.' She re-tied her apron strings. 'They never would a turned im off if she wur alive. Must a spun in er tomb at what they done. Dumped like pigswill.'

'Maybe she was used to life's fluctuations, Martha. She'd more experience of setbacks than most.'

'Nay, Miss Charlotte never stopped oping fo sunshine. That's why she writ er books. So as to mek up er own appy endins.'

1854

CHAPTER 15

Sunlight through tall windows glossed the dining room as we waited for the guest of honour to join us. Alan Nicholls' house and its contents were evidence of his success in business. He operated his shipping office from the ground floor, but upstairs was a gentleman's residence. A Turkish rug in turquoise and crimson covered the floorboards, the furniture was polished cherrywood, and caged songbirds burbled in the background. Arthur threw a glance at their bars, and I knew what he was thinking because he said it often to me. *It's a sin.*

We had just arrived there from the railway station, after meeting the newlyweds, and Charlotte had gone to bathe her face and hands. Now she entered the dining room. With her bonnet off, I saw she wore her hair in a bun coiled like a seashell, a few curls positioned on her forehead.

'Come and sit beside me, Charlotte.' Arthur stood up from the table and pulled out a chair for her. She took her place, pink-cheeked because everybody was looking at her.

'Please help yourselves,' urged Julia, Alan's wife. 'Don't stand on ceremony. We're all family here.' Despite being close to her time, with the under-eye shadows of a sleep-deprived expectant mother, Julia had excelled herself. The best china, silver and linen were on display, and the table was weighed down by boiled ham, sliced chicken, black and white pudding and boxty. Charlotte's eyes skittered across the array.

'My wife doesn't have a big appetite,' said Arthur. 'She'd live on air if she could. But we won't permit that, will we dearest?'

Alan patted his wife's stomach. 'My Julia is eating for two, aren't you my love.'

'I'll say grace first, if I may.'

We bowed our head while Arthur asked for God's blessing.

'Try some chicken, Mrs Nicholls.' Julia spoke up as soon as everyone repeated 'amen'. 'It's light on the stomach.'

'I eat very little meat, Mrs, ah, Nicholls.' I could swear I saw a smile lurk – the replication of their names seemed to tickle her.

Julia's eyes rested on Charlotte's narrow waist. Women who laced tightly were unable to manage more than a mouthful or two at mealtimes. The same thought had occurred to me, but I discounted it. Her waistline must be due to nature, rather than corsetry, because the rest of her was diminutive. I was an elephant beside her.

'Charlotte, you might like to try one of our soda farls,' suggested Arthur.

Charlotte accepted a buttered triangle, and he passed her a bowl of strawberry jam to spread on top. She nibbled. 'It's soft!' She bit down on the slice with more enthusiasm.

Already, I'd noticed she was missing several teeth, and one or two others were loose.

At the head of the table, Alan announced a toast. 'It feels measly without a splash of something in the tea to mark this happy occasion.' He reached for a bottle of brandy on the sideboard, looked at me, and when I shook my head, passed the bottle to Arthur.

'Not for me.'

'Always abstemious,' chuckled Alan. 'Unlike our father, who enjoyed his whiskey punch. But you could make an exception for your wedding toast.'

'My marriage needs no strong spirits to turn it into a celebration.'

'How about Mrs Arthur?'

Charlotte looked bewildered. 'My brother is offering you a dash of brandy in your tea.' A shudder, quickly subdued. Arthur covered her hand with his own.

Alan splashed in a dollop. A cheerier version of Arthur, but with the same dark-haired, blue-eyed good looks, he rose to his feet and tapped his cup with a spoon. 'Here's to the bride. Welcome to the land of your forefathers.' Charlotte blinked. 'Also to the Nicholls clan. Which includes the Bells, our nearest and dearest.' A bow towards me. 'And good luck to Art, a prince among men and king among brothers.' Hear-hears were scattered, and we clinked teacups. Alan reached along the table corner to clap his brother on the shoulder. 'We'd have travelled to Yorkshire for the wedding, if you'd given us any warning.'

'Was your wedding day everything you hoped for, Mrs Nicholls?' asked Julia.

Faces turned to Charlotte, expectant.

'Yes.'

We waited. There was no elaboration.

'Did you carry flowers?' Julia persisted. 'I married in January and had to make do with some evergreen. Even so, there's nothing I'd change about that day. I'm sure it was the same for you, Mrs Nicholls.'

An emotion flicked across Charlotte's face. 'I carried a Bible. Friends stood in for my sisters.'

'And there were wedding bells, and kisses, and cheering well-wishers lining the churchyard. Followed by a wedding breakfast at the parsonage with cake and speeches. I was the proudest man in all Yorkshire,' cried Arthur. 'You see how I crow? Won't you tell them yourself, Charlotte, how perfect it was? They might think I'm putting words in your mouth!' Laughter rippled around the table.

'I'm fortunate in my choice of husband,' said Charlotte. 'Every day, I'm reminded of it.'

Alan banged his knuckles on the tabletop. 'Long may it last! Our newest family member is diplomatic. You took your time finding a wife, Art.'

'I took my time persuading the one I wanted to accept me. Not quite the same. But for years, I knew where my heart inclined.'

'You'll be next, Mary. Weddings lead to weddings,' said Julia.

Everybody was looking at me – colour crept upwards from my neck. 'Mama doesn't want to part with me yet.'

'Whoever wins Mary will be fortunate,' said Arthur. 'A man needs someone sensible to share his load with him.'

Alan guffawed. 'Sensible isn't the first quality a man looks for in a wife. Luckily, our Mary has beauty as well as prudence. More tea, Mary? Richard tells me you drink it at the drop of a stitch.'

Alan was a man of business, not just a shipping agent but manager of the Grand Canal from Dublin to Banagher. A good heart beat inside him – he'd give you the bread out of his mouth, as our servants say – but he was always teasing me. Just like my brother.

The door was nudged open, and a King Charles puppy raced in.

'Kildare! No! Bold dog!' Julia pulled a mock-severe face at the chestnut ball of fur with a white muzzle and forehead.

'Oh, let him stay!' Charlotte was suddenly animated.

'I warn you, he'll beg for scraps. Very well, Kildare, but if you don't behave out you go.' Pop-eyed at the smell of food, the spaniel positioned himself by Julia's chair leg.

Charlotte leaned down and tugged one of Kildare's ears. When he licked her hand, she begged to be allowed to hold him, giggled when his tongue lapped at her face, and fed him morsels from her plate.

'You've made a conquest. He'll want to go home with you,' said Julia.

'He might be too refined for the Yorkshire moors. Only the hardiest survive there. But I'd find room for him in my luggage if he'd come with me.' She dropped a kiss on the bridge of Kildare's nose.

'It would break my heart to part with Kildare. But he has littermates, if you'd like one? Consider it a wedding gift.'

'Please don't trouble yourself. We have tough Yorkshire hounds in the parsonage. They might not take kindly to an Irish newcomer. Especially such a fetching specimen.' Charlotte scratched the pup's neck, and he wriggled with pleasure. 'But I do thank you for the offer, Mrs Nicholls.'

'He has a fine pedigree, unlike the Nicholls family,' said Alan.

'You aren't descended from high kings and celebrated bards? I thought everyone in Ireland was.' Charlotte's eyes twinkled behind her spectacles.

'Madam, I confess it freely – Art and me, we're of mean extraction. We come from a long line of beggars, not to mention a forebear who died on the gallows.'

'I can't believe Arthur has disreputable ancestors.' She was shaking with laughter now. 'Surely he'd have confessed it before our marriage!'

Arthur joined in the joke: 'I couldn't risk it. You might have changed your mind. But it's true. Granda's brother was a highwayman, and hanged for it.'

'I can claim no relative who was hanged – to my knowledge – but some who deserved to be,' said Charlotte.

Alan stamped his feet in appreciation, Julia's stomach wobbled, and our lively chatter drowned out the chirping birds in their cages. But Arthur muttered something beneath his breath, which only Charlotte and I heard. A sentence I turned over in my mind later.

'If Mr Brontë had known, he'd have used it against me.'

*

That afternoon, Arthur set off on a walking tour of Dublin with Charlotte and me. Alan had explained his intentions before we left. 'Art wants his wife to see Ireland as civilized. He's afraid she may have picked up some unfortunate ideas. The English newspapers can be unkind about us.' We skirted the Liffey quays, where Arthur spoke about the Wide Streets Commission, and the vision for Dublin as a substantial city. But his words were drowned out by a fish woman pushing a barrow: 'Fresh herrings! Dublin Bay herrings!' He steered us away from the dingy grey river and into Great Brunswick Street, past stately, gable-fronted terraces.

Arthur stepped into a chemist's shop to collect a package ordered by Alan for Julia, and while he was inside, we were obliged to make way for a band of sailors with rolling gaits, their ship's name stitched onto their caps.

'Did you hear?' Hands clasped, Charlotte's block-shaped face was altered.

'Hear what?'

'They're speaking French! A glorious sound!'

Arthur reappeared and gave the sailors a disapproving look. I knew he spoke no French, and was inclined to be suspicious of that pleasure-seeking nation. 'What a din!'

'It's certainly noisy, dear. But London has ten times the hullaballoo.'

'You must be a seasoned traveller, Mrs Nicholls,' I said.

A conspiratorial flash of the eyes in my direction. 'Mrs Nicholls is a person I don't yet know. She's only lately come into existence.'

'Do you mean a woman becomes someone else when she marries?'

'It allows for the possibility. Sometimes, this life I have now as Arthur's wife feels unreal. Like a scene glimpsed from the window of a train.'

'Come along, we need to cross the road,' said Arthur. 'Careful there. Now, this is College Green. That's Trinity College behind the railings.'

We sidestepped a steaming mound of manure, and were marshalled through the university's imposing oak gates.

'Mary, that's the porter's lodge on the left.'

'Hope Porter's doorway?' I looked left, imagining the scene. Her mother, weakened by childbirth, dragging herself to a place where a solution might be possible. Did she kiss her infant daughter as she laid her down? Did she hide in the shadows to see who found her? Why choose Trinity? I glanced at Charlotte, wondering what a novelist might make of such a story. But Charlotte was listening to Arthur, marching us across cobblestones. 'Limestone,' he said, and 'quadrangle'. 'Chapel. Examination Hall. Granite and Portland stone.'

We stopped outside a building, where he gave a magician's flourish with his hand. 'Behold, the Long Room Library. Pride and joy of Trinity College.' We climbed to a room made splendid by wood panelling and a domed ceiling. Its tall walls were lined with ancient volumes, ladders propped against each alcove for access by the library servants. Dust and age thickened the air, and Charlotte and I sneezed in unison. 'The longest single-chamber library in the world,' whispered Arthur. Up and down the galleries we walked, trying to be inconspicuous because of the scholars copying passages from books.

'Can you smell almonds?' I murmured to Charlotte.

'Yes! And vanilla, too. It's something to do with old books.'

A clerk behind the desk laid a finger against his lips. I pointed to the rows of marble busts, and mimed a question to Arthur.

'Philosophers, writers, and the like. There's Socrates with his boxer's nose.'

'Shakespeare's rather dashing,' said Charlotte. 'A shame ruffs have gone out of fashion. You'd suit one, Arthur.'

'Did you expect to find such devotion to learning here in Ireland, my love?'

'There's something chilly about marble statues. Give me wood. It doesn't weather as well as marble, but it's friendlier.'

Arthur looked dissatisfied, as well he might. Charlotte was no easy woman to impress.

'It's agreeable to see the dean, all the same.' She nodded towards the bust of Dr Swift, with his complicated turban hat. 'I'd like to visit the cathedral where he preached.'

'Then we'll go to service in St Patrick's.'

'And I'll feel his presence there.'

'Be warned, St Patrick's is knee-deep in marble statues,' I whispered. She giggled, eliciting a chorus of shushes.

'Let's visit Trinity's new museum,' suggested Arthur.

Accompanied by the tumble of birdsong, we walked along paths laid out between lawns. 'There's a cricket pitch over that way. I played a little, as a student.'

'We could almost be in Kew Gardens,' said Charlotte.

'Miss Brontë! Miss Brontë, I say, wait!' A gentleman in a painter's smock, easel under his arm, was chasing us. 'Forgive the intrusion, Miss Brontë, I know it's presumptuous. I met you at the Pensionat Heger. Professor Heger introduced us.'

Charlotte quivered, but quickly controlled it.

'Arthur Nicholls. How do you do, Sir? The lady you're addressing as Miss Brontë is, in fact, my wife.'

The bearded Englishman bowed. 'Oliver Evershed. I'm afraid I didn't hear the news of your union – congratulations on such a distinguished wife. Madam, you've taken the literary world by storm. May I shake your hand? And yours, Sir?'

Gratified, Arthur accepted the outstretched hand, but Charlotte's was offered reluctantly. She behaved as if she wanted to blot herself out.

'I don't suppose you remember me. I gave art lessons to the mademoiselles for a month, and a few English lessons to the professor and his brother. But you took over the language lessons, and I was out of a job!'

'I remember.'

'You loved the French language. Do you keep it up?'

'Love given is never a guarantee of love received.' Her eyes blazed momentarily. Surprise at her vehemence travelled around the group. Mr Evershed took a step back, while Arthur placed a hand under her elbow, as though to steady her. As for me, I had to remind myself not to stare.

Mr Evershed moistened his lower lip. 'Madame Heger terrified me, always popping up where you least expected her. Of course, she was responsible for the young ladies – the school was her project, he married into it. I was sorry to leave Brussels. But I read *Villette*, and saw you made more profitable use of your time there than I did.' A nod acknowledged the compliment. 'Do you ever hear from Madame? Or any of your pupils?'

'Never. Nor would I expect to. The pupils were spoiled girls – I didn't care for them. And Madame Heger and I were not *sympathique.*'

'Monsieur Heger, then? Fascinating individual. I keep meaning to look him up.'

'The professor and I are not in touch.'

Charlotte's clipped tone was riddled with some subterranean emotion. Mr Evershed looked disconcerted, while even Arthur – not the most perceptive of men – shot her a puzzled glance. Pitying her acquaintance, I enquired whether he was sketching in the Trinity grounds, and he told us he was drawing the new Campanile. Charlotte began to tap her foot on the cobblestones, each rat-a-tat a protest.

Oliver Evershed took the hint. 'I've trespassed on enough of your time.'

'Not at all, but we must be getting along,' said Arthur. 'We're planning to inspect the museum collections.'

'Venetian in spirit. Quite the triumph.' A tip of the hat. 'Ladies, Mr Nicholls, enjoy your walk.'

Arthur swept us off to the museum, with its row of arched windows grouped into bays, and strips of intricate floral carvings. 'Now then, the highlight of the –'

'Dear, I don't feel able to do it justice today. A migraine is starting to slop through my head.'

'I'll whistle us up a hansom. There's a way out onto Nassau Street here.' Arm at her waist, he steered her towards the side gate, me lagging behind, which sometimes happened when other people moved too fast.

'I'm sure I could manage the walk to your brother's house.'

'I'm sure you couldn't. Come along, Charlotte. You, too, Mary.'

He shepherded us onto a busy street lined with buildings, a world apart from the serenity of Trinity. All was stimulus and commotion, and Charlotte rallied, more attentive to humanity than museum collections. Arthur signalled to a cab pulled by a roan horse, and dashed forward to ensure the driver's attention.

'I hope you're not disappointed at the premature end to our excursion, Miss Bell. But perhaps these sights are familiar to you. It may be tedious to see them again?'

'I live in the midlands. I'm not often in Dublin. But please don't worry. Enough is as good as a feast.'

'Thank you for understanding. Oh goodness me, Arthur's looking cross.'

He stamped back. 'Cabbie wouldn't stop. Let's walk in the direction of Westland Row.'

I put two fingers in my mouth and let rip with a piercing whistle. A cab pulled to a halt beside us.

'Hidden talents, Mary.' Arthur's surprise was visible as he handed us into the hansom. Inside, he canted forward and instructed the driver.

'When were you in Brussels?' I asked Charlotte.

'A long time ago. In another life.'

Arthur settled back in his seat opposite us. 'Did you remember that artist fellow?'

'A little.'

'I thought you didn't much care to talk to him, so I carried you off.'

'People were staring.'

'Were they?'

'Yes.'

'If you say so, dearest.'

She turned to me. 'I've always shrunk from the thought of being known publicly. I've an ostrich impulse towards concealment.'

'I suppose the gentleman simply wanted to express his admiration.'

'I can't abide being lionised because I'm sure to disappoint. Being unable to roar when bid. Also, I dislike being reminded of Brussels.'

Arthur turned to me. 'Where did you learn to whistle like that, Mary? You'll have to teach me.'

'The year I was laid up with my leg. Denis showed me how.'

'Denis Coughlan is the coachman at Cuba Court, Charlotte. You'll meet him when we go to Banagher.'

'Mama wasn't pleased when I went about the place doing it. She says it's not ladylike.'

'Aunt Harriette's always right. But that whistle's mighty impressive, Mary. Who knew my little cousin was so talented?'

'I'm nearly as tall as you.'

'And twice as accomplished.'

Charlotte blinked at us. 'What friends you are. It reminds me of my brother … before …'

'Don't think about Branwell. It makes you sad.'

'It would be sadder if I forgot him.'

'Sometimes forgetting's for the best, dearest. I have brothers I had to forget.'

'But yours are still alive, Arthur.' She touched a hair bracelet, the plaited strands held in place by a purple amethyst the size and shape of a raindrop. Backwards and forwards, she twisted it.

'I never saw them again after Alan and I moved to Banagher.' Arthur's mouth turned down.

I was sorry to see him reminded of the years before he joined our family, and cast around for oil to pour on troubled waters. 'What a pretty ornament on your wrist.'

'My sisters' hair. Two of my sisters: Emily and Anne. I scissored it from their heads, after they … after the worst.'

'Charlotte.' Arthur drew out the name, a warning note in his voice.

'I saved their hair as a memento. One day, I noticed Mrs Smith, my publisher's mother, wearing a plaited hair bracelet. She said it was a relic of her mother, and recommended a hair-worker in Regent Street. So I posted off Emily and Anne's hair, and this came back. It means I have my sisters with me always. I touch them when I touch it. This bracelet cheats the grave.'

Arthur cut in. 'It's morbid, this idea of cheating the grave. You have my permission, Charlotte, not to wear my hair in any kind of jewellery if I go to meet my Maker before you.'

'Don't be a crosspatch, Arthur. Emily and Anne deserve to be remembered. All of them do – Branwell, too.'

'How could anyone be cross with you? But there are other ways to keep loved ones in mind. Aren't there, Mary?'

'I'm named for Grandma Bell,' I offered.

His face cleared. 'Exactly! We'll call our first daughter Emily Anne.'

CHAPTER 16

The hansom clopped to a halt outside Alan Nicholls' house on Sir John Rogerson Quay, with its row of pert flowers in boxes on each of the front windowsills. While Arthur settled up with the driver, we climbed out and I rapped the knocker. The door opened, and their breathless maid Tilly bobbed a curtsey, still trying to jam her stormy frizz under a cap. We brushed past her into the red-tiled hall, and handed over our cloaks and bonnets.

Arthur stamped in a few moments later. 'Fellow has the cheek to tell me he has no change. I said he must give me something back – his promise to stop taking alcohol. Stank of strong drink. Didn't you notice? He said, "A shot of the cratur's needful for a man who earns his living outdoors. On account of the weather." Charlotte, you should lie down. The sights will still be there tomorrow.'

'Mrs Nicholls, there's a letter for you on the hall-stand,' said Tilly.

'From Papa!' Charlotte laid the envelope against her cheek. 'I wonder what he's written about our wedding day? His impressions are always noteworthy. Papa's speech at the wedding breakfast was so droll. My friend Ellen Nussey developed a stitch in her side at the way he kept pronouncing et cetera, et ceterorum in a comical voice.'

'Humour isn't my forte, I'm afraid,' said Arthur.

'But your speech was sincere, dear.'

'And best of all, brief. Now, upstairs, Charlotte. Lean on me.'

'Why not look after Miss Bell? She's a perfect angel and everyone's ignoring her.'

I was sitting in a chair, massaging my throbbing knee through the skirt. 'Really, you mustn't mind me.'

'Mary's fine. I want you to rest, Charlotte.'

She tugged at his elbow to make him lean down, and whispered something. His face darkened. 'As you prefer.' She slipped away.

'She wants some time alone. To read her letter in privacy.' A pause. 'She's devoted to her father.'

'I imagine, with only the two of them left, it must make people … I don't know, cling to one another.'

'There's me. I'm part of their family now. New blood.'

'I expect he's glad of you. I can see she is.'

'Mr Brontë, glad of me? As a curate, I suppose. Not as a son-in-law.'

'But you've been his right-hand man for years. He must value you.'

'Mr Brontë is ambitious for his daughter. He hoped a man of substance might make an offer. And who can blame him? I don't own a publishing house, I've no sway in literary circles, and church mice have more money than me.'

'Arthur, come to Ireland where you're appreciated. Find a parish near Banagher. Bring Charlotte to live here.'

'It's impossible while Mr Brontë is alive. His roots are wrapped around hers. She'd never let me transplant her. One of the reasons she married me was to keep me in Haworth.

Her father's too old and blind to run the parish – I do most of the work.'

'All the more reason for him to appreciate you.'

'Reason doesn't come into it. He didn't want me marrying his precious daughter.'

'He gave his permission, surely?'

'But not his blessing. He wouldn't give her away. Refused at the last minute. But she went ahead and married me. My Charlotte has pluck.'

Shock spidered through me. I'd never heard of such a thing, except with elopements. 'I – how – well, it's done now, and can't be undone.'

'No.' His smile set aside dark thoughts. 'I love her, Mary. I mean to do everything in my power to make her happy.'

'How could she not be happy, married to my favourite cousin?' I wasn't yet ready to surrender the idea of the two of them living in Ireland. 'Mr Brontë is elderly, I think?'

'Late seventies. Well past the biblical three score and ten.'

'He can't live forever. And then …?'

'I hope to replace him.'

'Or you could come home to us.'

'You know why I went to England in the first place, Mary. Ireland has fewer parishes for Anglican priests. And the grip of the Roman Church remains strong, despite our best efforts.'

'But you've experience now. Plus, a wife is an asset to a minister, I've heard you say so yourself. Couldn't you try again?'

'There's no one with influence to plead my case. Your father would have helped me, but …' He shrugged.

'Poor Papa. Mama's convinced he worked himself into an early grave.'

'Better than drinking himself into an early grave, like mine.'

'Charlotte's name is bound to assist you.'

'I'm not looking for reflected glory.'

'Forgive me. That was clumsy. I only meant –'

'No, I'm the one who should apologize for being a bear.'

'Perhaps your wife will fall in love with Ireland.'

'If not with Ireland, then hopefully with my family.' He patted my hand. 'I'm determined to show her the sights while I have the chance. Goodness knows what's in that letter. Mr Brontë's capable of telling her to turn right around and return to England.'

'Selfish old man.'

'Frightened old man. One by one, he's buried a wife, sister-in-law and five of his six children. If I take Charlotte from him, what's left?'

'Don't you resent him, Arthur? Even just this much?' I held my forefinger and thumb a smidgen apart.

'His reluctance to lose her is understandable.'

'She finds it so, at least.'

'She's all forbearance where he's concerned. I'll have to practise it when I move into the parsonage after our trip.'

'It's too bad you won't have your own establishment. Even a cottage would be preferable.'

'Charlotte can't leave her father. And I can't leave Charlotte.'

'And at least you have her to yourself on your honeymoon.'

'That's why I want it to last as long as we can stretch it. This month in Ireland will be summer on our tongues during winter, which outstays its welcome in Yorkshire.' He cleared his throat. 'By the by, don't tell Aunt Harriette about Mr Brontë's refusal to give Charlotte away. Your mama will be cross on my behalf.'

'I'm cross on your behalf.'

'No need, I captured the castle.'

'You two look very cosy here. What are you talking about?' It was Charlotte.

'Family gossip,' said Arthur. 'What news from Haworth?'

'Martha Brown's sister toppled out of a tree and broke her arm. The parsonage dogs miss their daily walks with you – substitutes are tolerated but not encouraged. Oh, and Papa asks for confirmation of our return date.'

*

That night, noises awakened me. They pushed through the adjoining wall from Arthur and Charlotte's bedroom, a metallic scraping which I identified as bedsprings. At first, I covered my head with a pillow to block out the sounds, but then I removed it and put my ear to the partition. The low rumble of a male voice. Disjointed words. Gasping sounds. I slid from my bed and edged open the door. I listened, drew back, but something drove me on. Barefoot, I tiptoed the corridor, taking care to distribute my weight evenly to avoid creaks.

Now I could hear a kind of whimpering, soft but insistent, brimming through the bedspring clatter. It came from Charlotte. I knew nothing of passion and its urgency astonished me. Yet it transfixed me, too, and my pulse accelerated, as hers must have done.

'Say it. Who do you love?'

'You.'

'Who?'

'You.'

'Say my name.'

'Arthur.'

The knocking sound speeded up.

'Who?'

'Arthur! You! Arthur!' Charlotte's moans emerged from deep inside her.

The rhythmic scraping stopped with a crash. A muffled groaning, a run of sighs, the smack of lips. A gush of laughter drove me away. I discovered toes really did curl with embarrassment, and knew I had no business eavesdropping. Back I glided to my room, but slept no more that night – guilty, yes, but also consumed by my stolen glimpse into the mysteries of married life. And by the way Charlotte had abandoned herself to pleasure.

*

Next morning, I studied her face covertly, to see if the previous night's events were stamped on it. She looked the same as ever. Later that day, I walked into a room where Arthur had her sitting on his knee. I backed away before they saw me, but stood outside and eavesdropped on their conversation.

'I'll share a secret with you, Sharlie. But promise never to tell your papa. I feel closer to God on the moors than in the pulpit.'

'Emily felt the same way.'

'But she wasn't a minister.'

'All of us learned to love the moors because of Papa.'

'They help me preach. To find the words I need in front of those expectant faces, I conjure up the walk to Lumbfoot or Skipton. When I see you looking up at me from the Brontë pew, you mustn't smile and give me away! A twitch of your lips will be enough. I'll know you're beside me on the heath, your hand in mine.'

'That deserves a kiss, Arthur.'

CHAPTER 17

'Would you be Miss Brunty?' An upright man, several years into his seventies, touched his hat brim to Charlotte. He was standing at the bottom of the steps to Alan's house, in hobnailed boots and the bawneen jacket farmers wore to market.

'Yes. No. I used to be.'

The slouchy hat was removed to reveal a head covered by springy white hair. 'I'm your Uncle Hugh. Your father's brother.'

She advanced a couple of paces. 'You're ...' A current ran through her and her voice choked.

He held out a hand that was arthritic from labour. 'Girl-dear, you're a credit to the Brunty name, so you are.' Her hand was encased in his, pale blue eyes creased into a smile, and she returned it. 'We've been reading your books. Our Pat sends them over. You're a born shanachie, lassie. Like all the Bruntys. Your granda Hugh – I'm named for him – was fit to hould folk in the palm of his hand when he'd spin a yarn.'

Charlotte and I had ambled back from a short excursion to St Michan's Church, famous for the centuries-old mummies in its crypt, preserved because of gases, or limestone, or the Lord's own mysterious reasons. Arthur escorted us there, but had an errand to attend to, and gave us into the care of a talkative guide. Charlotte was enthralled by the spectacle of coffins crumbled away to reveal their inhabitants. The attendant called one 'the crusader' – a giant of a knight with broken leg bones. Another was 'the nun', while he dubbed a third 'the thief' because he was missing a hand, and the guide suggested it might have been cut off as punishment. How Charlotte had stared at them! It wasn't hard to guess she must be thinking about her family, buried in a vault below Haworth Church. But the expedition invigorated rather than saddened her, and she wanted to converse about nothing but the mummies on our walk home. She was still speculating about them when her Uncle Hugh made himself known.

'It's such a coincidence to meet you here,' said Charlotte.

'No coincidence, lassie. Our Pat writ and give us your address.'

'Papa? He supplied my whereabouts?'

'In a manner of speaking, aye. Said he cudn have it on his conscience for you to be in Ireland and us not knowing.'

'And he told you where to find me?'

'Here's the how of it. Pat says in his letter you're staying in Dublin with a shipping agent be the name of Nicholls. So me and your cousin Welsh took a lift off a neighbour bringing cattle to market here.' He pointed to a thin, lanky man watching a ship on the Liffey have its rigging assembled by a squad of sailors. 'Thon's Welsh, my brother William's boy. He lives along wi me and James. At the docks, they were fit to tell us Alan Nicholls' place of business. I wasn't to know his house and office was one and the same. But handy for us when we went looking for you, oh aye, handy.'

She clapped her hands. 'You tracked me down! I'm gratified!'

'I don't mind telling you I'm stiff as a board from rattling over them roads. But here I be, still in one piece. We're waiting this past hour. The maid said you were out.'

'Didn't she ask you in?'

'Closed the door in our faces, truth be tould. I dare say she thought we intended for to make a nuisance of ourselves. Hugh Brunty of Ballynaskeagh, says I. Thinking me name would be enough. But divil the bit of it.'

'I'm extremely sorry. I'm sure you'd have been invited in if they'd known who you were.'

'But I give in me name, I could do no more.'

'I'm very glad you waited.'

'Aye, well, I wanted for to salute me own flesh and blood. It'd be a mortal shame to think of you here, and not a Brunty to welcome you. That's why Welsh and me, we said we'd endeavour to get the length of Dublin to make your acquaintance.'

'Thank you.' A catch in her voice. 'How like Papa you are! You have his eyes.'

'Folk allus say I'm the spit out of his mouth. Tarrible full o' cleverality, was our Pat. Still is, I dare say. All gab, like a young crow. The da used to tell him he was smart enough to meet hisself coming back.' Hugh beckoned to his nephew. 'Welsh, where's your manners? Come and say good day to your famous cousin Charlotte Brunty.' He pronounced her first name with a hard *ch* sound, to rhyme with bar.

Welsh Brunty shuffled over, removed his cap, and mumbled a greeting.

'You're the image of Branwell!' exclaimed Charlotte. 'But taller.'

'Welsh gets his red hair from your granny Alice McClory,' said Hugh. 'Pat, the same. You're a wee scrap of a thing, so you are. Like your granny. A breath of wind would a twirled her like a leaf. She was hardy, mind. Had to be, to rear ten of a family.' Light raindrops began splatter us, but he kept talking. 'Pat's first, I'm number three. But sure you know all that. Pat'll have tould you his seed and breed.'

'Charlotte! Mary!' Further up the street, Arthur called our names. He was out of breath when he reached us. 'It's starting to rain! Why are you standing outside? You'll get wet.'

197

'Arthur, this is Papa's brother, Uncle Hugh, and my cousin Welsh. Uncle, Cousin, this is my husband, the Reverend Arthur Nicholls.'

Arthur leaned the oblong package he was carrying against the steps, and pumped their hands. 'How do you do, Mr Brontë, and you too, Mr Brontë. What a – an agreeable surprise.'

Welsh Brunty hung his head and kicked his boots against the ground, but Hugh spoke up. 'I have your name in me head as our Pat's curate. But I believe you're a sight more, forbye, if the news is true. Oh ho, you knowed a good thing when you see'd it. Not a body could blame you. Am I right, Welsh, or am I right?'

His nephew eked out a self-conscious smile. 'Aye, Hugh. Right you be.'

Arthur's tone warmed. 'It's like hearing my father speak when I listen to the two of you.'

'A County Down man, is he?'

'Antrim. But you bring him back to me.'

Hugh turned back to Charlotte. 'And how's our Pat? He fairly made his way in the world. But he's had a sore time of it, burying wife and childer.'

'Papa is stoical. But he feels it, of course. Uncle Hugh, what was he like as a boy?'

'Full of stories, lassie. Once he'd start to tell one, you wudn hear a mouse squeak. And the memory he had! He oney had to hear a thing the onest and he'd be fit to repeat it back.'

The rain became more insistent, causing Arthur to cast an anxious look at Charlotte. Rivulets were beginning to stream from her bonnet and darken her cloak. It occurred to me to whisk into the house for an umbrella, but I was loath to miss this scene. Besides, I thought we were all on the brink of going inside.

'I must apologize, Mr Brontë, but I need to get my wife indoors. The rain will bring on her cough.'

'Sure you'd harly call thon skiff rain. Tisn't but a wee taste of spit.'

'The only creatures immune to this kind of rain have webbed feet,' snapped Arthur.

'Arthur!' protested Charlotte.

'Forgive me, Sir, I spoke sharply. But my wife's health is delicate. Charlotte, you need to say goodbye to your uncle and cousin. Mr Brontë, I'm sincerely sorry but we can't dally. We're on the brink of leaving Dublin.'

'Surely we can spare a little –' began Charlotte.

'There's packing to finish, and the quays are busy.'

Hugh Brunty gave Arthur a direct look. 'I'm not a young man. I've hauled a right step to meet me own flesh and blood.'

'Believe me, I wish it could be different. But it can't be helped.'

'Couldn't we invite them in for some tea?' said Charlotte. 'My relatives are getting soaked.'

'We simply don't have time, my dear. Our schedule is fixed.'

'But –' said Charlotte.

'Time, tide and trains wait for no man. I'm truly sorry, gentlemen. Unfortunately, we're under pressure to make our travel connections. It's an honour to meet my wife's people. Charlotte, we need to go.'

'Well then, Charlotte, I'll bid you goodbye. But first I have a wee wedding present for you. Welsh, give it here.'

A tin box was produced, the sort used for storing a pipe and tobacco. Hugh put it in Charlotte's hand and closed her fingers over it. 'I made it meself, lassie, from a piece of bog oak Welsh here found on our land. Might-maybe be hunnerds of years old.'

'You're a woodcarver?'

'Now and again, when the humour takes me.'

She lifted the lid. A carved wooden swan nestled in sawdust. Its neck made the bird's signature arc, its body glided on the rough outline of water. Although no more than six inches square, it was a vivid representation. 'It's beautiful. Isn't it, Arthur?'

'Magnificent. You're a talented artist, Sir.'

'I just fell to whittling, so I did, and this here's what showed itself.'

'Really, Uncle Hugh, I can't believe how lifelike it is. If I set it on water, I wouldn't be surprised to see it shake out its feathers and glide away.'

'Aye, I heated the point of a knitting needle to blacken its pupils. You'll make sure our Pat sees it?'

'Of course. I wish my sisters could, too.'

'Poor lassies. They'd a hard fate.'

I spoke up. 'Why a swan, Mr Brunty?'

'We see them round our way a right bit, young lady.' He returned his attention to Charlotte. 'And there's swans in a legend I dare say Pat tould you about. *The Children of Lir*. About four childer turned into swans. A big sister the eldest. Like you four wee wans beyond in Haworth.'

'It represents all of us? Me, Branwell, Emily and Anne?'

'Aye, that was in me mind. Thon's a piece of the Brunty homeplace for you to keep. So's you know you're part and parcel of us.'

'Goodbye, Mr Brontë,' said Arthur. 'We'll give your best regards to your brother.' He edged Charlotte away. 'Mary, would you knock on the door for us?'

'God bless you, Uncle Hugh. You too, Welsh.' Charlotte was hustled up the steps. 'I'm glad to have met you.'

'Tell our Pat there's a place be the fire for him any time he wants to come home to Ballynaskeagh,' called Hugh.

Tilly answered the door with a curtsey, and stood aside to let us enter.

'Was that really necessary, Arthur? We were horribly discourteous.'

Arthur made vigorous use of his black eyebrows to suggest Charlotte wait until they were alone. 'Thank you, Tilly. If you'd just take our coats and put them somewhere to dry.'

'Very good, Sir. The mistress is resting. Will I call her?'

'No, leave her in peace.'

Conscious of being superfluous, I tucked myself in by the window. The two men remained outside, impervious to the rain. Welsh had his eyes on his uncle, shoulders hunched, while Hugh stood beside a gaslight pole and stared up at the house, the picture of bafflement. Raindrops weighed down his hat brim and he shook his head to dislodge them. Something Mama always said struck me: in Ireland, we like to chart the social and geographic map of the people we meet. The Bruntys were a fit for Ballynasomewhere, but not for the Nicholls of Dublin or the Bells of Banagher.

Behind me, Charlotte and Arthur were bickering. I didn't often see how Arthur behaved when he wore his ministerial authority – with us, he was always on holiday.

'You told an untruth. You said we're about to leave Dublin.'

'I gave Mr Brontë my solemn promise not to let you visit your family.'

'You'd no right!'

'He said they'd try and dun money out of you.'

'They asked for nothing except to shake my hand. In fact, they gave us something.' She held up the tobacco box. 'Made with wood from Papa's homeplace. I wish …' Arthur began to speak but she held up her hand. 'Don't even think about stopping me! I never should've left them standing there.' She whirled around and darted outside, the front door banging behind her. 'Uncle Hugh! Welsh!'

Arthur slouched over and gloomed beside me, hands jammed in his pockets. The muffled sound of a ship's horn carried through the window. 'I bought a doll for Hope Porter while you were at St Michan's.' He indicated the package he'd been carrying. 'A proper doll, with a china head. She shouldn't have to make do with a stuffed sock and a face embroidered on it.'

I nodded to show I'd heard, my attention fixed on Charlotte and her relations, engrossed in conversation. How demonstrative she and her uncle were – each of them almost acting out what they were saying.

'I know how this must look, Mary. But I'm honouring Mr Brontë's wishes. He's violently opposed to his relatives making any claims on Charlotte's goodwill.'

'Why tell his brother Charlotte was in Ireland if he didn't want them to meet?'

'To save face.'

'I don't understand.'

'I warned him the newspapers might write about her visit. He said even if they did, she'd be home again by the time his brothers knew about it. Do you want your family hearing it like that? I asked. Second-hand from an old report in the papers? I suppose he picked at it in his mind after we left, and decided to send a letter to Ireland. To cover himself.'

'Poor old gentleman. His nephew, too. The trouble they took to come and see her.'

'I know. But I promised Mr Brontë we wouldn't go to the north of the country. Who'd have thought his brother would up and come to Dublin?'

'It's a crying shame you gave that promise.'

'He worked himself into a state. His veins were popping, and I thought he'd have a seizure if I didn't agree. He didn't even want us visiting Ireland – kept saying France or Italy would be more suitable. I explained my new wife had to be introduced to my family. But it was a sore business.'

In another room, a clock chimed a musical tune and Julia's caged birds sang back, as if determined the timepiece shouldn't rival them.

'He sounds a right tyrant!'

'Don't say that, Mary. He has some peculiarities, but Mr Brontë's a decent man. The parishioners like him – better than they like me. It was foolish of him to say Alan has a shipping business. He couldn't help boasting, but that's how they found her. Otherwise she'd be a needle in a haystack.'

'Promise or not, we should've invited Charlotte's relatives into the house. They're your family now, too. It was badly done, Arthur. Badly done.'

'I'm not proud of it. Mr Brontë's ashamed of his origins, that's why he harassed me into giving my word. Not because he's an Irish peasant. He can live with that, although he doesn't relish it – changed his name from Brunty to Brontë fifty odd years ago, when he wasn't a wet week in England. But it's his Catholic mother – Alice McClory – that really vexes him. Even the Brunty side are only Protestants for a generation or two. His people are Catholics under the skin. Not ideal for an Anglican minister.' A rattle of loose coins in his pocket, a toe kicked against a skirting board. 'But not enough to explain his attitude. Who knows what else is there to be dug up? Irish rebels, I shouldn't wonder.'

Outside, a team of drays pulling a cart lumbered past, blocking the view. 'She'll blame you for this insult to her family.'

'Better me than her father.'

'Why do you indulge him, Arthur?'

'Self-preservation. Mr Brontë and I are going to be living under the same roof. He already thinks I'm an appalling sneak for stealing away his daughter. I need to regain some ground.' Reluctantly, I nodded. 'For her sake, too,' he added. 'She doesn't always agree with him, but in her heart she hero worships her father. Charlotte needs someone to look up to – it's her nature.'

Footsteps clicked along the tiled hallway. Charlotte stood in the doorway, dress muddy at the hem. 'I'm going to lie down.'

*

That night, their argument penetrated the bedroom wall.

'You dislike them because you think they're peasants.'

'Not true.'

'Farmers with black under their fingernails.'

'My father was a farmer.'

'Why did you stop me getting to know them?'

'There wasn't time.'

'We could have made time.'

Back and forth, they quarrelled. I waited for Arthur to exonerate himself by revealing the promise extracted by Mr Brontë, but he never mentioned it. Then I heard a soft thudding, as if fists were pounding against someone.

'Shush, my heart's darling. Shush, my Sharlie.'

The pop-pop of lips. The squeak of bed springs.

CHAPTER 18

Arthur's yelling woke the household. I tumbled out of bed and opened the door. He was barefoot on the landing in his nightshirt.

'She's gone! Stolen away in the dark!'

'Where?' cried his brother Alan, also in nightwear, Julia peeping around his back.

'Gone to Yorkshire?' I asked.

Arthur crushed a note in his hand. 'No! To the north, with her father's people. She says she'll be away a day or two. It's something she has to do.' His voice sharpened. 'I can't allow it – I'll have to fetch her back.'

The men threw on their clothes and clomped downstairs. Julia and I dressed and followed. The brothers sat at the dining table, waiting for Tilly, who was rubbing sleep from her eyes, to carry in an early breakfast. Arthur was in such a rush to retrieve his wife, he even mentioned borrowing a horse and riding after her, but Alan reminded him he was no horseman. 'How can you effect a rescue if you break your neck?' He scratched his stubble. 'Have something to eat, Art, and we'll draw up a plan.'

'I'll help Tilly.' Julia Nicholls disappeared, but I stayed put.

'She didn't even consult me!' growled Arthur.

'Aye, but she's not your common-or-garden wife, is she? You need to tread carefully here.'

'What I need is to bring my wife to her senses. When Mr Brontë hears about this …'

'Maybe he won't.'

'If Charlotte doesn't tell him, one of those Ballynaskeagh Brontës will. He and the brothers appear to write to each other.'

'Cross that bridge when you come to it. Now, here's Julia with bread and cold meat. Let's eat.'

The brothers consulted a map, and considered hiring a driver and gig. 'You'll be fleeced,' said Alan. 'Why not use the stagecoach? The Dublin to Belfast route's a reliable service, and the coach bowls along at a fair lick. Look here.' His finger traced a route. 'Travel as far as Banbridge, it's a decent road, then hire a gig or a man with a horse and cart to cut across country to Ballynaskeagh.'

'Won't the coachmen have to make stops to water and rest the horses?'

'They do, but they have it down to a fine art. In and out in jig-time. The stage does a good ten miles an hour, at least. You'll be there in, say, seven hours, eight at a push allowing for a break.'

I made a polite hawing noise. 'I have a suggestion.' Alan's hand stalled in the middle of buttering a slice of bread, and Arthur lowered his cup. 'Charlotte's departure was so sudden, it indicates a disordered state of mind. She might need a woman. I should accompany you, Arthur.'

'I'm afraid you'd hold me up, Mary. Speed is of the essence.'

'She went willingly, Arthur. She wasn't kidnapped. Both of us, travelling together, could be presented as a spontaneous desire to join the Brunty party. You alone makes it look like a rescue mission. Imagine if there was any suggestion of a forcible abduction – the newspapers would make hay: "Jane Eyre Seized by Irish Brigands".'

'Mary's right. Discretion gains the day,' said Alan. 'It's less dramatic if you arrive with Mary – travellers taking in the sights. Your wife just went ahead, for a little extra time with her people.'

*

Shortly after breakfast, Arthur and I were waiting near Carlisle Bridge for the stagecoach. It clattered up, a coachman with a cocked hat and face ruddy from weather at the reins. The guard clambered onto the roof and began tossing down the baggage of exiting passengers, while a team of horses snorted behind their blinkers, flanks heaving and sweat steaming off them.

'Excuse me!' Arthur called to the guard in his braided jacket.

''Tis a madhouse today, so it is. I'll be down to you directly, Sir.'

Arthur turned his attention to the coachman, who nodded in a stately way but declined to climb down to discuss tickets. 'I darsent leave the horses. The ones in front are mannerly beasts, but the brown one has the divil in him this day.' He wagged a finger at the near-hand horse. 'I'm watching you, me boyo.'

As the Belfast coach filled up, the guard leapt down, agile as a squirrel, and agreed to sell us two seats rather than send us to the ticket office, a delay which meant we'd miss the coach. Other passengers' bags were heaved up and strapped on the roof, but we were travelling light and had none. Two bench-style seats inside could accommodate six passengers, more at a pinch, and there was straw on the floor to soften the jolting and soak up mud from boots. Arthur put me at one end, and suffered being jostled in the middle.

'First stop Drogheda,' intoned the guard. A click of the coachman's tongue, and the carriage pitched forward. It was tolerably comfortable, except for the joggling on downhill stretches, and when wind stole through gaps in the window frames to pinch our ears. The coach drove close to the coast – winking glimpses of the sea separating Ireland from England on our right. Some of the towns we passed though had graceful, bow-windowed houses and shops, people wheeling in and out of them like a school of fish. But whether a place was elegant or down-at-heel, it had a regiment of raggle-taggle stick figures – as in Dublin. The country still hadn't recovered from the Famine.

'Would Charlotte have taken this route?' I asked Arthur.

'Presumably. It's the main road north from Dublin.'

'The shoreline is worth seeing. But I suppose she can't have seen much, travelling by dark.'

'Like a thief in the night.'

His snappishness prevented further conversation.

It was late afternoon when we saw Carlingford Lough, where a vapour was suspended above the water. Window catches rattled as passengers lowered them to marvel at the landscape. A dour-faced Arthur cracked his knuckles, refusing to be impressed, his silence a wall.

'Keep an eye out for the horse eel beyond on the lough, young miss.' A passenger with white hair and pink-rimmed eyes, like a sugar mouse, unclamped his pipe from the side of his mouth – he'd kept it unlit, to my relief.

'What's that?'

'A sea serpent with a horse's head and neck, and the long, slippery body of an eel. Nails like iron that dig into a body and never let them go.'

Like Arthur's hold on Charlotte, was my disloyal thought. If he'd played fair by old Hugh Brunty and his nephew, she wouldn't have gone tearing off.

In Banbridge, the coach jangled up to the Downshire Arms, a long white coaching inn on the main road. Arthur spoke to a stable man, and established it was only four miles or so from there to Ballynaskeagh, where the Bruntys lived. He toyed with walking, but decided against it when he learned it was along country lanes, and wrong turns were likely.

'It'd be different if it were daylight, Mary. Best if I hire a cart and driver. This fellow says he can take us.'

'Arthur, we don't exactly know where Mr Brunty lives, or even if Charlotte's staying with him. Why not spend the night here and present ourselves in the morning? Dashing up by moonlight makes us look like a rescue party.'

Arthur saw the wisdom of this proposal. We had supper in the inn, where a fellow diner regaled us with stories about fairy hurling matches and strong men who died mysteriously after dallying to watch them – no sight for mortal eyes. Before retiring, I said something that had preoccupied me during the journey.

'I know you want to protect her, Arthur. But you can't wrap her in tissue paper. She won't take it from you.'

'No. She's an odd mingling of needy and independent. I understand my wife better than some give me credit for. Herself included. Charlotte wants love. That's what I give her.'

I reflected on it in the bedroom, where I removed my cloak, bonnet and shoes to rest on top of the bed, without undressing further – wary of bedbugs. His love wasn't in doubt, but was it love that had sent him in pursuit of her? I was unconvinced.

*

Next day, without delaying for breakfast, we set off walking. The County Down landscape was a place of moss green fields and rolling, misty mountains, slipping burns and couches of blazing gorse. The odd whitewashed cottage or one-and-half-storey farmhouse poked its thatch through the bushes. Overall, there was a sense of space and order. 'Good, fertile farmland and healthy livestock,' said Arthur. From behind a hedge, we heard the lowing of cows overdue their milking, a mournful sound. He tutted, always a farmer's son despite his minister's collar.

On the track, we encountered a fisherman swinging his catch, and Arthur inquired after Hugh Brunty's residence.

'Thonder it is. Not the cottage hard by the side of the road, thon's a McClory house. The two-storey place fornenst it.' He indicated a substantial property in the style of a manse rather than a farmhouse.

'Did you catch those perch just now?' Arthur nodded at the striped fish.

'Aye, the burn here does be hopping wi them.'

The Bruntys' house was masculine-looking, with two chimneys either side of the roof and a plume of smoke from one indicating its occupants were awake. In front, fields sloped down to a stream where rushes kissed the bank, and behind that was a glen. The Bruntys might be as wild as hares, but they lived in an idyll.

In the yard, an insolent rooster flapped up to block our approach.

'Ignore him, Mary. He's just attempting to convey his dominance. If we keep walking forward he'll know we're not afraid of him.'

The black-and-white rooster lowered his head and made a mock charge at me, but stopped several yards away, clawing the ground, neck feathers fluffed up. My stomach lurched. 'But I *am* frightened of him, Arthur.'

'Stand your ground, Mary. If you back away he'll chase you.'

'Help!' I shrieked.

Welsh Brunty emerged, fiery red hair standing on end, picking at his teeth with a twig. He reached the rooster in a couple of strides, pounced, and secured the bird's wings with one hand. With the other, he pinned down his legs, and held the bird at arm's length to keep the beak at a safe distance. 'Henry Joy McCracken here's fair scundered wi visitors. We'd a party last night. McCracken's a crabbit boy, but better nar any guard dog.'

'I've come for my wife,' said Arthur.

'Who's outside, Welsh?' A voice from the house.

'Themmuns from Dublin. Charlotte's folk.'

Hugh Brunty was outdoors almost before Welsh had finished speaking. An effusion of welcomes poured forth, which Arthur interrupted.

'Is my wife inside?'

'She's out for a dander wi her Aunt Alice.'

Colour mounted Arthur's neck and face. 'Your sister?'

'The very same.'

'But Mr Brontë told me. I mean. His sister. She's unstable!'

'Not at all, man. It's fair to say Charlotte's Aunt Alice is essentric, but she's not mad. Or to put it another way, if she's mad, then so be the rest of the family.'

'I understood she was in an asylum.'

'Naw, naw. We wudn lock away wan of our own. Our Pat's lost the head if he thinks we'd do the like of that. She lives here wi Welsh and me, and my brother James. He's away into Rathfriland – faith, he'll be sorry to miss you. All of us, we keep an eye on Alice.'

'And my wife is with your sister now?'

'Never you fret, man-dear, she'll come to no harm. There isn't an ounce of harm in Alice.' He produced a handkerchief and blew his nose into it. 'We're all a wee bit the worse for wear. On account of last night. I'd say there's many's the head birling in this townland the-day.'

'I don't understand why Mr Brontë would lead me to believe his own sister's insane, when you tell me she's not.'

'She's disordered – thon's the best way to put it. Her thoughts tumble this way and that. Sometimes the world's sadness is too much for her to bear. But today's wan of her good days. She took a shine to her niece the minute they met.'

'Where are they?'

'They went for a ramble up towards Drumballyroney churchyard.'

'Which direction?'

'Ach, it's oney a stretch of the legs up beyond. You might-maybes meet them coming back.'

Without another word, Arthur set off.

'Now, Miss, I don't believe I caught your name, but I mind you well from Dublin. Could you fancy a wee taste of milk fresh from our cow? Welsh, don't stand there like a turnip, put thon bad-tempered bird in the outhouse and fetch a stool for our guest. It's a sin to sit indoors this gift of a morning.'

'The house hasn't been redd up since last night, e'ther,' said Welsh.

While I was given a three-legged stool, followed by a beaker of milk, Hugh propped himself against the wall of the house and gazed into the horizon, pale eyes reflective. 'You know, Miss Bell, our Pat only come home the onest, after he went to England.'

'Do you mean Mr Brontë? Charlotte's father?'

'Aye, when he finished in Cambridge, he trotted back for us to admire him. Preached for the first time above in St John's, where thon ticklish boyo you come wi is headed now. Powerful it was, Pat's sermon – you darsent stop listening for fear o what you'd miss. I mind well it was a windy day – strong enough to blow the horns off a goat. And then away the wind blowed our Pat to England and never blowed him back.'

'How so?'

'Ach, he was headstrong, and wanted more nar we could offer. But never content, was Pat. The sort of man, if you give him Ireland, England, Scotland and Wales for a garden, he'd hand them back and ask for the Isle of Man. It's just how he is.' He withdrew into his thoughts.

'Looks like he's met them on the road.' Welsh pointed with his thumb.

I shaded my eyes with a hand, and three approaching figures became visible.

'Is Alice wi them, Welsh?'

'Aye.'

'A good sign. I was afeared she might-maybes a gone off on her lonesome, to brood and whatnot. Fetch out some more seats. Our house was as busy as market day last night, Miss Bell. We put on a right céilí for Charlotte.'

'Mary! You're here too?' Charlotte's face was rosy, her hair tousled by the air. I'd never seen her look so vibrant. 'What do you make of my father's glen?'

'Picturesque.'

'This is Aunt Alice. Aunt, meet my husband's cousin, Miss Bell of Banagher.'

She was as tall as me, with iron-grey hair and a waist-length veil pinned at the back of her head, its net moving in the breeze. Her black dress was heavy for July, fashioned from bombazine, and unrelieved by ribbons or lace. An odour I recognized drifted from the material – it was caused by the chemicals used to remove the sheen from cloth intended for mourning clothes, so it was absolutely without lustre.

'Miss Brunty. How do you do?'

'Mrs Lambert,' she corrected me, and lowered herself onto a stool with the equilibrium of a duchess. But such a face! The eyes were sunken, smouldering like coals.

I recoiled – other people's sorrows are hard to take – but managed to gather myself. 'Forgive me, Mrs Lambert. You were showing Mrs Nicholls some of the local attractions, I believe?'

'Graves,' she said. 'No shortage of them in these parts. Themmuns asleep in the earth depend on me to visit.'

Arthur had been standing with his arms folded, more or less patiently, but now a tic started up on his jaw. 'High time we were off, Charlotte. Tell me where your bag is and I'll collect it.'

'So soon?' she protested.

'We need to leave.'

'Sure we haven't got acquainted yet,' said Hugh. 'I ax you, man, aren't we all family now? We need to have a bit of an aul blether. Tell them, Alice.'

'Thon man knows his own mind, Hugh. Her bag's upstairs, first door on the right. Mind you don't wake my husband. Mr Lambert needs his sleep.'

Arthur was gone before she'd finished speaking.

'Uncle Hugh, I never asked which bedroom was Papa's.'

'Pat never lived here in the better house. He growed up in the lower house, over Lisnacroppin way. Near-hand where he taught school. But he knowed the glen.' He nodded towards the trees beyond the field. 'Did Alice not show you our old cottage when you were out tramping the roads?'

'No, may I go back and see it now? I'd love to picture him in it. Is it far?'

'Sure it's no distance at all. Welsh, take you your cousin to the lower house.'

Arthur emerged with her bag. 'We haven't time, Charlotte,' he cried.

'What did I warn you about not making a clatter!' protested Alice.

Hugh scratched his chin and studied Arthur's face. 'You've a long road ahead of you, lassie. You can look at it another time. There's McClorys living in it now. They'd be connections of ours on your granny's side.'

'Say goodbye now, Charlotte,' said Arthur.

She turned to Alice Brunty. 'I won't forget the phantom house story you told me, Aunt Alice.'

'Tell it to our Pat, forbye, girl-dear. He'll know the bones of it.' A feather-ball of a bird shrilled from a branch overhead and Alice arched her neck to find it. 'You've picked yourself a shady perch, young fellow-me-lad. Strange, to think how these trees will still be reaching for the sun when every wan of us here is meat for the worms.'

I must have gasped at the image, because she fastened those lambent eyes on me. ''Tis nature's way.' She shifted her attention back to Charlotte. 'Show me your hand, Charlotte.'

'Alice has a gift,' said Hugh.

Alice peered at the lines on Charlotte's palm. 'I see a great love. But it's dead to you. Far away over the sea, where it needs to stay.' A shadow crossed her face.

'What else, Aunt Alice?'

'Your name's going to pass down the generations. Far into the future, folk'll be reading your books. But if it's childer you want …' She was on the verge of adding something, but shook her head. 'No more. Let's take a look at yours, Miss.'

'We'll never make the next Dublin coach at this rate,' complained Arthur.

I held out my hand to Alice.

'A long lifeline. Good enough health. Nothing you cud rightly call heartbreak.'

'What else?'

'I see a marriage for you, lassie, but not soon.' Her eyes flickered from me to Charlotte, and back to me. 'You know your husband already.' She dropped my hand. 'That's enough.'

'Your turn for a reading, Arthur,' I said, a shade impishly.

His heavy eyebrows met in the middle. 'Even if we had the time – which we don't – I've no inclination for it.'

Alice barked a laugh and stood up. 'Please yourself. Hey-ho, if Charlotte's being carried off by thon impatient man of hers, I might as well go on about my business.' She placed her hands on her niece's shoulders and bent towards her. 'Misfortune's a relentless hunter, daughter-dear. But maybes you can give him the slip.' Alice Brunty pulled her veil over her face and walked away.

Everybody watched her leave. Hugh cleared his throat. 'Grief clogs our Alice's insides like undigested meat. But she is as the Good Lord made her.'

Amid the lull, a commotion erupted. The black-and-white rooster escaped from the shed where Welsh had him penned up, and raged his way into the yard. Charlotte was nearest, and he flew at her. She screamed, and covered her face with her hands, thinking he meant to peck at her eyes. Arthur made a run at the bird, which bolted onto the roof of the house. Thwarted, Arthur shook his fist at him, while Hugh and Welsh added their voices to the racket. 'Ye hallion, Henry Joy McCracken!' was flung at the rooster.

Loose feathers were still swirling in the air when I reached Charlotte's side. 'Are you hurt?' She held out her hands. Beads of blood welled up. 'We need bandages,' I shouted at the men.

'We wudn have the like of that,' said Hugh. 'An eel skin would do her scratches a power of good, but I doubt we have wan. A big dock leaf or two will have to serve. Welsh, fetch a lock o them.'

'No!' My tone was sharp. 'I can cobble together an alternative. I'd like some clean water, though.'

'There's a pump behind the house,' said Welsh.

For privacy, I stepped into the hallway. The interior was dim, but I detected a rush-bottomed chair with a long back, and rested one leg on a rung. I lifted my skirts, ripped away a long strip of petticoat, and divided the cloth into three pieces.

Back outside, Charlotte's face was blanched. Someone had helped her to a stool, and Welsh waited there with an enamel basin of water. I crouched beside her and used one length of cotton to wash the blood from her hands. She winced at each dab, but once they were clean, it became apparent the injuries were superficial. Around each hand I bound the remaining strips, and knotted them at the thumb. 'There now, good as new.' She managed a wan smile, and I put my arms around her – she was as delicate as foam on warmed-up milk.

'You're for the pot the-night, McCracken,' scowled Hugh Brunty.

'Promise you won't harm the creature,' said Charlotte. 'He was maddened by something. Who hasn't acted hastily in pain?'

'Aye, maybes. But Henry Joy McCracken has a right temper on him. You boyo, you! Aye, let you shrink from me voice. You shud be shrinking from a damn sight more!'

'Charlotte needs to lie down, Mr Brunty,' I intervened. 'Bed rest is the best cure-all. May I help her inside?' He gave his permission, and I led her indoors. At the end of the hall was a kitchen with a banked-down fire and wooden settle bed, not yet tidied away. The room smelled of turf, livestock and milk that had gone off. But the bed looked comfortable, and Charlotte stretched out on it. When I returned, Arthur was holding forth.

'My wife is easily fatigued. This trip north was too much for her.'

'She was grand till McCracken took a run at her.'

'She was exhausted even before that.'

'Not at all, man. She was the life and soul of last night's revelries.'

'You had a celebration for her?'

Hugh squinted at him. 'Aye, to introduce her to the neighbourhood. There was singing, and fiddle-playing – folk's kind enough to say they likes my playing – and Welsh here partnered your wife in a fairy reel.'

'Charlotte danced?'

'She did, aye.'

'Charlotte told me she never dances.'

'Sure all the Bruntys is dancers. We're famous for it.'

'I've never danced with her.' Arthur lashed a furious look at Welsh Brunty, who was stroking a smear of beard.

'Not even on your wedding day?' Arthur shook his head. 'Then it's high time you did. As the Bible says, and you should know, *A time to weep and a time to laugh, a time to mourn and a time to dance.* Some of the party danced their way right across the road and into the field thonder.'

'No wonder her strength is taxed.'

'We give oursels a rest wi some storytelling when the night wore on.'

I spoke up. 'What kind?'

'Ghost stories, young miss. Best kind, if you ask me. Headless horsemen, skeleton bridegrooms, and the like. Charlotte tould us a couple herself. She has the Brunty knack for it. Thon lass is an attic room crammed wi stories.'

Mama's voice tumbled into my head. *Only servants tell ghost stories.* But I wished I'd been there last night to hear them.

Arthur changed the subject abruptly. 'I suppose, Sir, you'll be writing to Mr Brontë about Charlotte's visit?'

'I cannot think of a single reason why I wudn tell our Pat.'

'No.' A sigh.

'It's a mortal pity he wudn come hisself, and pray at his parents' graveside.'

There was silence, which sharpened as it lengthened. I slipped into the house to check on Charlotte, expecting a forlorn figure after the ruckus, but she had rallied.

'What did you make of my Aunt Alice, Mary? She has Emily in her. They have the same walk, flinging out their arms and legs. And that knack of pinning you to the spot with their gaze!'

'Your aunt scares me, Charlotte.'

'Why?'

I shivered, and rubbed my arms to warm myself. 'Just … I don't know.'

'Don't be silly. She's my father's sister.'

'Is she disturbed in her mind?'

'She's been unfortunate.'

'How?'

'Aunt Alice is in pain. It sets people apart. I know the locals avoid her, in case whatever's unhinged her mind rubs off on them. But I understand grief, so I understand her. Dear Mary, don't look so worried. I'm among my family. People I hardly knew I had – but you've no idea how glad I am to discover them. Some are a little awry, in their way, but when I look at them I see Emily, Anne and Branwell. I don't feel like the last Brontë after all. It lifts a weight from my mind.'

*

While Charlotte rested, Hugh Brunty organized a lift for us back to Banbridge with a neighbour – a man with a beard like a stork's nest. He hupped to his horse, and Charlotte waved at the Bruntys, full of smiles and promises to write, but noticeably cool towards Arthur, whose face was carved from flint. An argument was brewing about her flight to Ballynaskeagh, that much was apparent.

En route, the wagoner had to stop off at a church with an arch above the door, indeterminate creatures rearing from it, as though bursting through the stone – gargoyles and what not. Beyond it, a green slope with buttercups like buttons, spindle-stemmed poppies, and fat blobs of purple clover.

'Let's take a stroll, Mary,' said Charlotte.

'We don't want to delay the driver,' warned Arthur.

She refused to acknowledge him. Bending her will to his would have as much success as tying up the wind, I thought. 'I think we should walk, Mary. Just for a few minutes. We'll be a long time in the coach.'

It was a strangely mute setting, the hush caused by tall grass. We wandered under lichen-furred branches towards a shade-dappled graveyard, pausing to read dissolving inscriptions on humped slabs, traces of a date here, a name there. Most of the stones were upright, although listing to one side, but there were a few flat markers, which reminded me of beached sea creatures tossed out by tidal forces. It was a world like no other, secrets buried in those graves, but a world, too, where pain had evaporated. Life had lost its power to cause unease.

All of a sudden, sobbing could be heard. We rounded a corner and discovered Aunt Alice lying full length on a large grave, convulsed by grief. She had pushed back her weeping veil – I suppose she couldn't easily breathe inside its weight – and her cheek was pressed against the earth, fingers clawing at the clay. For a few moments, I imagined she was trying to dig up whoever was buried there.

I made a movement towards her, but Charlotte placed her hand on my shoulder. 'Leave her be.'

'Who does she mourn?'

'Nobody. Everybody.'

Our voices must have penetrated Alice's fog of misery, although we took care to whisper, because she pulled herself upright, and turned her head in our direction. We helped her to her feet and she gestured towards the headstone.

1847

Here be many
Safe in the arms of Jesus

There had been a line of writing along the bottom, but it was chiselled off.

'Not safe,' she said. 'Stolen.'

'Charlotte, Mary! Time to go.'

Charlotte hugged her aunt. 'Mr Lambert needs his bread baked, Aunt Alice.'

'Yes, I'd best go home and see about Mr Lambert.' She picked off some plant stalks caught in the folds of her dress, and strode off, purposeful as a cat.

By unspoken consent, neither of us mentioned the incident to Arthur. But while he was in the stagecoach office in Banbridge, arranging our return journey, Charlotte spoke to me about Alice.

'Her weeping began in the third year of the Famine, the worst one.'

'Did she lose family members?'

'No, but what she saw unbalanced her, according to Uncle Hugh. He says that was the year evictions mounted, because the people had no money for rent. They died on the road, grass stains around their mouths. Some made it to the workhouse. But Famine fever swept it empty. Bodies began to pile up, too numerous to bury.'

'Your Aunt Alice isn't responsible for what happened. How can she be?'

'She's not. But they started putting the bodies into communal graves. No coffins. A tangle of human flesh. That's a mass grave where she does her weeping. No one knows why, but Aunt Alice has appointed herself chief mourner for those deaths.'

I noticed the wagoner watering his horse, and approached him, Charlotte following. 'Excuse me. That place where we stopped. There was a large grave with a missing line on the headstone. Do you know what it said? It seemed to be scratched out deliberately.'

The man transferred a wedge of tobacco from one cheek to the other, a wary look on his face. I held out a shilling and he pocketed the silver. 'Ireland thanks England for her help in our hour of need.' He touched the broken brim of his hat to us, and led away the horse.

'We prayed for Ireland,' said Charlotte. 'Every day, in the parsonage.'

I nodded. 'Charlotte, do you think grief can make people mad?'

'It's possible.'

'Your Mrs Rochester was mad.'

'Bertha Rochester was a sinner before her marriage. And sin's a form of madness. Temptation catches people and tosses them about. It makes them contemplate doing things they'd never ...' Charlotte began to pant. 'Things I know are wrong. But somehow I wanted to ... I mean ... people ...' A series of tremors shook her. When they passed, she rested one bandaged hand across her eyes. 'I don't know what came over me, Mary. What were we talking about?'

'Your Aunt Alice, I think. Or maybe not.'

'You know there's no Mr Lambert? She imagines herself a wife. But it's all in her head – Papa says she has a spectral bridegroom.'

'Your father knows about her imaginary Mr Lambert?'

'He sends money to help with her upkeep. Papa calls Aunt Alice the madwoman in the glen.'

CHAPTER 19

Back in Dublin, Charlotte's injury meant she had to rest her hands, so I volunteered to write any letters she wished to send.

'There *is* one piece of writing I'd be grateful for you to do on my behalf.'

'Of course. Any small service I can carry out for you gives me pleasure.'

'The phantom house tale my aunt told me – I've been turning it over in my head, embroidering it here and there. I believe I have a story suitable for Mr Dickens' *Household Words* or some such publication. May I dictate it to you, Mary?'

Excited at any role, however insignificant in Charlotte Brontë creativity, I fetched paper, pen and ink, and prepared to transcribe.

'Now, here's my Irish ghost story. Are you ready, Mary?'

Arthur squeaked into the room, trying out a pair of boots which Alan had offered him. 'Where's Julia?'

'Resting.'

'Quite right, in her condition. What are you two doing?'

'Telling ghost stories,' I said.

'Ghost stories are irrational. Impossible to give credence to,' he said.

Charlotte's eyes bounced off his. 'For my part, I make it a rule to believe impossible tales. Remember your *Hamlet*, "There are more things on heaven and earth, Horatio."'

At least they were speaking again.

'I just think it's nonsense, Charlotte. There are better ways to spend time.'

'There's no possibility of a walk today.'

The three of us listened to wind snuffle down the chimney breast, and rain drum against the window.

'Well, I'll leave you to it.' Arthur squeaked out.

'Now then, my lass. You're the first to hear this tale, or my version of it, at least. My storyteller is a housekeeper living alone in an ancient, empty property she's paid to maintain. Let's call it Cuba Court. A memorable name. And my housekeeper can be a Mrs Bell. Mary Bell.'

'Should I be writing this down?'

'In a minute. Give it a title – "The Phantom House" – and don't worry if I go along too fast for you. Think of this as a rough draft to get my ideas on paper. Just write down everything I say, even if it doesn't always make sense, and I'll polish it up later. Start now. Mary Bell, a young widow without family and forced to rely on her own resources, had filled the role of housekeeper at Cuba Court for six months without ever meeting her employer. She understood from the agent that he was overseas, and that he rarely visited Cuba Court, his ancestral seat in the northern part of Ireland. One day, she received a letter from her master with instructions to make a visitor welcome – a cartographer charged by government interests with mapping that section of the countryside. She should also arrange a local man to act as his guide. Mrs Bell carried out his orders, and everything was made ready for the visitor. The gentleman arrived as night drew in, and she answered the door to him holding an oil lamp.'

On went Charlotte, conjuring up pictures in my mind as she told of this fictional Mary Bell out walking and getting lost when a mist descended, forced to take refuge in an isolated farmhouse with an uncanny brother and sister. There, she encountered a chilling story about unbaptized babies, an inflexible minister, and a mother who defied his hellfire-breathing rules.

When Charlotte stopped speaking, I laid down the pen, blotting the paper by accident, and clapped my hands together. 'Oh Charlotte, I didn't want it to end!'

'Truly?'

'I expect it to give me nightmares!'

A faint smile pointed to the author's gratification. 'Emily would have loved to get her hands on that source material. *Wuthering Heights* came from an old story in Papa's family, you know. Of course, she worked it up into something her own.'

'I'm flattered you put me into it, as your housekeeper.'

'All of us liked ghost stories. Papa's would make the hairs stand on your head.' A sudden slump came over her, as the energy required for storytelling winnowed away. 'A writer can mimic God. But it's only play-acting, Mary. Our powers have limits.'

'This story's different to your books.'

'I suppose so. "The Phantom House" needs more work. But there's something in it – my sixth sense tells me so.'

On an impulse, I held out my pen. 'Why not sign your name at the end of the pages, Charlotte? If it won't cause your hand too much pain?'

She managed a lumpy version of her signature, and blew on the ink to dry it.

'You found your Ballynaskeagh relatives inspiring. I believe you mean to use some of them as characters in a book. Aunt Alice, perhaps?'

Charlotte gave me back the pen, but kept the pages. 'I had an already-seen when I met my aunt. As soon as those eyes of hers fixed on me, I knew!'

'Knew what?'

'That we'd met in my dreams. That I was meant to hear her story.'

'I don't know what an already-seen is.'

'Mr Dickens writes about it in *David Copperfield*. He tells of a feeling that ambushes us occasionally – we know what's coming next, as if we suddenly remember it. But something's off-kilter. Emily had them, too, but not Anne.'

'I don't think I'd like them.'

'It's not something you can choose to have or not. It just happens.'

'And then?'

'Your heart twists inside your chest, and your stomach swoops. An eerie feeling overtakes you. It's as if one of your dreams has been sucked out and set to play in front of you.'

'Do you get them often?'

'The last already-seen was the morning of my wedding. My friend Ellen was hooking me into my wedding dress while I watched her in the mirror. She stood behind me, getting everything just so. When she pinned the veil to my bonnet, she asked, "Will I leave it off your face until you leave the house?" I said, "Do, Ellen." Something tickled my left wrist, and I saw the bottom button on that sleeve was hanging by a thread. "I'll sew it on for you, Sharlie," said a voice. It was Anne's. At that exact moment, my heart skipped its rhythm. And I knew I'd dreamed this scene where I dressed for my wedding, but with Emily and Anne's help. Except my sisters were gone. I'd seen every detail before, including the loose button. My mind recognized it. But it wasn't quite right, because Anne and Emily had died and Ellen was attending me. I grew light-headed, swayed and lost my footing.'

'Did you faint?' That would be bad luck, but I didn't say so.

'Thankfully not. Ellen caught me, forcing me to sit. Our friend Miss Wooler heard us and hurried in with some smelling salts. She had Martha produce a cup of sweet tea, and became very motherly about how I'd eaten no breakfast, and shouldn't go to the altar with nothing inside me. Imagine if you get woozy and frighten your poor bridegroom half to death, she said.' Charlotte closed her eyes. 'Often, my already-seens happen when I'm fasting. Have you really never experienced them?'

'Never. I'm too solidly of this world.'

'This wasn't a starry-eyed moment because my truelove waited for me in the church. It happened because it was foreordained I'd marry Arthur. We think we can control our fate, but some things are predestined.'

'You believe Arthur was intended for you as you were intended for him?'

'Nothing so romantic. Life is about choices, after all. But certain choices lead to outcomes. You'll discover that in time, Mary.' She widened her eyes and gave me a significant look, as though passing on knowledge.

'I have no truelove,' I admitted.

'But you're so pretty.'

I squirmed. 'I'm lame.'

'What difference does that make with your bonny face and golden hair? Besides, it's barely noticeable. But perhaps you don't want to wed? You have your mama, and a home with her.'

'I suppose I'd like to run my own household one day. I've had offers. But none I cared about.' I tried to sound modest rather than boastful.

'Were you born this way?'

'A riding accident when I was sixteen. My mare stumbled and threw me. She rolled on my legs, and when I tried to stand, I couldn't move. The doctors ordered bed rest for a year, and I regained some movement, but the left knee won't bend. I'll always be lame. She was a beautiful, dappled grey mare with a white flash on her forehead. Starlight. I loved that horse. I never saw her again. Mama couldn't bear to look at her, and sold her to a bishop for his twin daughters to ride.'

'Was anyone with you when the injury happened?'

'No, but Arthur found me lying on the ground. He picked me up and carried me home. Five miles, and not a word of complaint.' *His blurred face bends over me. I feel his thumb press my inner wrist. When he lifts me, a rushing sound fills my ears, then darkness. I come to with my cheek nestled in the hollow of his shoulder, breathing his heathery smell. Nearly home, Mary, he says. And I know I'm safe.*

'Arthur's a man you can rely on,' said Charlotte.

'He's always been the same.' A gusty sigh escaped from me. 'I don't ride any more. Do you?'

'We never had the money to keep a horse. We trudged everywhere, my sisters and me.'

'You must have missed them dreadfully on your wedding day.'

'I miss them dreadfully every day. Perhaps I'd never have married if they were still here. I was happy among the Womenites. But they're all gone now. Once I had four, then two, and now none.'

'Who was your favourite?'

'I couldn't choose. Emily, Anne and me, we grew together in the parsonage like your shamrock – three leaves on one stem. Emily was striking-looking, courageous. Byron might have said of her, *She walks in beauty, like the night*. Anne was goodness made flesh. She endured.'

'You've endured, too.'

'There were times I felt deserted. But now I know our Irish Brontës ...' She bowed her head. 'And perhaps I won't be the last, for another reason.'

'You'd like to give your father a grandchild,' I guessed.

'It's hard on Papa to have buried a brood of children. But he's stoical. Still, a grandson or daughter ...'

'I thought he opposed your marriage.'

'Has Arthur been complaining?'

'He speaks nothing but praise of Mr Brontë.'

'Then how do you know?'

'I put two and two together. I've known Arthur all my life.'

'Papa thought nobody was good enough for me. But I'm no prize. Papa's reconciled to our marriage now. They've a great deal in common, Papa and Arthur. They'll rub along well enough. Even better with a child to share.'

'Childbirth can be dangerous.'

'Yes.'

'Although Arthur's always been fond of little ones.'

'Yes.'

'And children are God's blessing on a marriage.'

'Yes.' Her gloom intensified with each response.

'What's wrong? Perhaps the risk troubles you?'

'Other women manage so I dare say I could. Aunt Alice doesn't seem to think it's a good idea. I'd chance it, though. Except …'

'What?'

'It's a lot of expectation to dump on one small set of shoulders. To seal the friendship between its grandpa and papa. And the parsonage is a peculiar place for children to grow up. My friend Mrs Gaskell insists it's a supernatural setting. A house of blackened stone hemmed in by moors on one side and gravestones on the other.'

'A child might send the ghosts packing. Especially if it had playmates.'

'One child, perhaps. It seems excessive to hope for more. I'm old for motherhood. But not too far gone, I trust.'

'As our housemaid Lizzie Nolan likes to say, you're the youngest you'll ever be.' Charlotte reached out and squeezed my arm. Having pleased her, I displeased her: 'Is it like *Wuthering Heights*, your parsonage?'

She made an impatient movement. 'Why must people always think we write from life? It's nothing like Emily's novel. We four were happy there. But it's no place for a child alone. And yet I must have one.'

Conversation petered out. While I cleaned my inky fingers with a pen wipe, I heard her begin humming. 'That sounds familiar.'

'It's an Irish lullaby. A speck of a fellow sang it for me in my uncles' house. He was carried in to a party they had for me. I don't know the words, but the tune is haunting – it keeps running through my head.'

'I had a nurse who used to sing it. There's one line which goes, "My jewel, my joy, my pulse, my boy."'

Charlotte's voice was a whisper. '"My jewel, my joy, my pulse, my boy."' A smile transformed her face. 'I'd like to sing that to my baby one day.'

CHAPTER 20

'Are you sure you don't mind me going back with you?' I asked.

'Don't be silly, Mary,' said Charlotte.

'I've never travelled alone – I don't know if I could. Typical Richard, leaving me behind when we were meant to do the journey together.'

'It's a nuisance being fetched and carried, isn't it? Like a parcel. But we can surprise ourselves with what we're able to manage. I went overseas on my own.'

'I'm not like you.'

'Necessity taught me. But it's a relief to have Arthur in charge of our arrangements. He's so …'

I waited.

'… efficient.'

'You make him sound like a train!'

'But I like trains. They're a convenient way to get about.'

We were at Kingsbridge station, black with the grime of decades. Clanging doors and clanking railway carriages, coupled and uncoupled, were noisy competitors with steam jets. Arthur had found our seats, and disappeared to check the bags were stowed safely in the luggage car. He returned as whistles blew.

The engine wormed through the city, but picked up speed outside Dublin, when our carriage shook disagreeably at times and bucked us about on bends. I inhaled the worn leather smell of the seats, and settled to watching Charlotte watching Ireland over the course of our four-hour journey westward. The haunting melancholy of the landscape gave her particular pleasure – greens, browns and purples flowing into one another, especially when we rode through heather-rich fields into the Great Bog of Allen. There, the train slowed to a halt, and two guards leapt out to remove a blockage on the track. She drew our attention to several pairs of curlews poking around in rushes with their long curved beaks. One gave their distinctive piping echo, flapped its wings and took flight.

At Athlone, the train huffed carefully into the station over an iron bridge. We had to disembark there, to transfer to a paddle steamer – a more leisurely form of transport. Carriages and carts jostled in the station yard, and we sidestepped children playing leapfrog. As in Dublin, a clamorous shoal of beggars descended on us, and we had coins ready to distribute. A porter with a barrow wheeled our luggage to a conveyance laid on to bring train passengers to the quayside, where our steamer idled. We waited to board, smells of river bilge, black earth and burning turf assaulting us. Arthur looked glumly at the broad Shannon bisecting the town.

'What's wrong, dear?'

'I wish we were in Banagher already.'

Charlotte patted his sleeve. 'A river voyage is different to travelling by sea. There's no tidal pull and consequently no sea-sickness.'

'Tell that to my stomach. Even on a good day, the Shannon's a surly stretch of water.'

She caught my eye. 'Arthur was horribly nauseous on the voyage over from Wales, although it was quite a calm crossing.

I'm mesmerized by the sea – it must be my Cornish roots. On my mother's side.'

'Charlotte insisted on standing on deck holding the rail for almost the entire voyage from Wales,' said Arthur.

'It was exhilarating! The briny smell. The sea's hollow boom. Its camp followers.' She pointed to some gulls floating on the Shannon's surface.

We embarked and settled ourselves on the quarterdeck, where Charlotte kept a close eye on the crew's preparations for casting off. Men unpacked creels of turf from donkey panniers, and passed them to sailors who loaded them on to power the steamer, a modest vessel with a wheel under the stern. A brace of languid lieutenants in scarlet and white boarded, all frogging and brass buttons. One produced a spyglass to inspect the far riverbank.

'What a pair of dandies!' whispered Charlotte. 'Jackets cut to perfection and not a wrinkle on their trousers. There's no vanity to match a young officer's.'

Arthur frowned. 'If those bucks went next or near a battlefield they'd drop down dead in a faint. You're not looking at them, Mary?'

'As Mrs Foley in the kitchen says, sure looking is free,' I teased. Arthur harumphed.

'Is it far from here to your home, Mary?' asked Charlotte.

'Two hours down-current. Mama's already watching the clock and making sure everything's ready to receive you.'

'I hope she approves of me.'

'Aunt Harriette has a heart as big as all outdoors,' said Arthur. 'Of course she'll approve.' He cupped a palm under her chin. 'Look at those roses in your cheeks, dearest. Ireland agrees with you.'

I was uncertain what Mama would make of her. Charlotte was refined, which would please Mama, but sometimes outspoken, which wouldn't.

At the landing stage in Banagher, the carriage and pair sent from Cuba Court was easy to spy. Denis Coughlan lurched into a bow to Charlotte, a courtesy he'd never extended to me. 'Welcome, Ma'am. May every hair on your head be a candle to light you to glory, and let you be as happy as the month of May. You're in the middle of Ireland now so you are.'

'The middle? How interesting.'

'The very middle.' Our coachman made even the most humdrum remarks appear portentous.

'How's your son, Denis?' asked Arthur.

'Thriving, praise God, Master Art'ur. Ben's a grand help to me in the stable yard.'

The countryside around Banagher put on its Sunday finest for our visitor. Our landscape was unassertive, and most landscape painters pronounced us bland and pushed westwards to Galway. But King's County had meandering rivers, rolling hills and ancient ruins. Charlotte took in our lush fields with daisies, harebells and clover, each patch of land separated from its neighbour by low drystone walls. 'Not a factory chimney stack in sight!' she marvelled. 'Does Ireland have no industry, dear?'

'You have to go north for that. As you must have noticed on your own odyssey.' He wagged a playful finger, and her lips twitched in a demure half-smile. The pair had patched up their differences. 'Linen and shipbuilding, mainly. It's all distilleries and tanners down here.'

'We have bogland instead,' I said. 'Animals stray onto it and don't come home. Swallowed whole.'

The carriage jolted to a halt, and Arthur climbed down to open a pair of iron gates. Charlotte couldn't hide her surprise when the horses trotted along a wide avenue of lime trees. 'Extensive grounds.'

'Over there's a walled fruit garden, and Cuba Court has a vinery, too. You'll see the lawns in a moment. Look, the house!'

First impressions were of grey stone and an abundance of chimneys, bays and windows with triangular pediments above them.

'Arthur grew up here?' Charlotte's eyes were saucers. 'Such classical proportions!'

I knew she'd be impressed because visitors always were. Cuba Court was more than a hundred and twenty years old, symmetrical and formal. Even we – who took it for granted – knew the house was constructed on a majestic scale.

'I never imagined a gentleman's country seat,' she added.

'Not exactly. It's a school as well as a house. The school buildings are behind the house, beside the stables.'

'I'd no idea it was so magnificent. He's always so modest.'

'This was Arthur's home from boyhood. He loves it, Charlotte.' I couldn't resist adding, 'Love runs in deep channels with him.'

'I learned that during our courtship. Cuba Court's a strange name for an Irish house.'

'A former governor of Cuba built it in the 1700s.'

'Aunt Harriette!' cried Arthur.

Mama had heard the carriage and was standing on the front steps like a tranquil abbess. Beside her was my smiling brother, sunlight gilding Richard's hair.

The carriage hadn't halted before Arthur sprang off to be hugged by Mama. He was always her favourite. 'Where's your bride, Arthur?' He raced back, boots crunching on gravel, and handed her down, while Denis helped me to alight, to the scolding of corncrakes and drone of bees. A flicker of surprise crossed Mama's face when she saw Charlotte, but vanished as quickly as it had appeared. She clinked forward, household keys dangling from their chain at her waist, to catch Charlotte's hands between her own. 'You're most welcome to Cuba Court and the Bell family.'

'Thank you, Mrs Bell.'

An auburn-haired wisp of a child in a pinafore apron darted around the side of the house from the servants' quarters. She had a nosegay in one hand which she dropped, retrieved, and shoved at Charlotte.

'That's Hope Porter,' said Arthur.

'Yellow rosebuds. How perfect. Thank you, Hope,' said Charlotte. 'Did you pick them yourself?' Transfixed, Hope stared at her.

'How's my favourite bundle of Hope?' Arthur knelt in the dust beside her. 'What's that?' He pretended to see something scamper up her arm and hide under her rope of hair. 'Shoo! Shoo!' His hand flicked across her neck and produced a pink sugar mouse. 'Is this yours?' She shook her head. 'I think it must be.' He presented it to her, prompting giggles.

'T'ank oo, Art'ur.'

'Master Arthur,' Mama corrected her.

'Master Art'ur.'

'Good girl. Hope and I are both from Dublin, aren't we, Hope? Not like these others,' said Mama.

Arthur winked at Hope. 'I've something in my luggage for you. Come and find me, by and by.'

She scampered after Denis Coughlan, who was leading away the horses. Arthur stood up, dusting his knees. 'Still only knee-high to a tadpole. She doesn't grow.'

'Give her time.' Mama directed her attention to Charlotte. 'Arthur needs a wife. Someone to mind him. That boy pays no heed to creature comforts, but the body has requirements as well as the spirit. Am I right, Arthur?'

'Always, Aunt Harriette.'

Richard cuffed me lightly on the shoulder. 'You haven't said hello, Mary.'

'Hello.'

'Mama missed you.'

'I'm back now.'

'Do much socializing in Dublin?'

'Just sightseeing. I thought I'd be coming home with you.'

'I fixed it up with Arthur for you to travel with him. I needed a day or two in Athlone. Thought I might be able to drum up new business for the school. And I had to see about a teacher who can take arithmetic and history classes.'

'Any luck?'

He pulled a face. 'How about you? Don't suppose you found a brilliant young professor in Dublin, and used your wiles to lure him into living in Banagher?'

'Marriage doesn't interest me.'

Mock-indignant, he cried, 'How can you be so heartless when the school needs another teacher!'

'More pupils, too, from the sound of it.'

'Always so abrasive around me, Mary.'

'I wonder why, Richard.'

He turned away and began to quiz Arthur on the news from England.

Arthur broke off to tell Mama, 'Alan sent down a crate of Dublin Bay oysters. He says eat them while they're fresh.'

'We'll have them for supper tonight. But what are we all doing, standing outside? Come in, come in, you must be tired and hungry. The tea things are set out in the parlour. Arthur, Mrs Foley baked barmbrack for you.'

Charlotte was still absorbing Cuba Court's grandeur. She seemed to believe we were in possession of the property. But the Bells were tenants, not owners – it was only ours while my brother had the mastership. I waited for Richard to correct her, but he allowed the misunderstanding to take hold.

'It's a barracks of a place,' he said. 'Cuba Court was full of rats and ghosts when we moved in. We keep the rats down with cats but can't do much about the ghosts.'

'You have ghosts?'

'Don't all old houses? Just the usual skeletons clashing their chains. We hardly notice them.'

'Don't,' groaned Arthur. 'My wife will spend our week here ghost-hunting.'

'Take no notice of this blackguard son of mine, Mrs Nicholls. Ghosts, indeed. As if I'd tolerate them. Inside, everybody.' Mama made a sweeping motion, and in we trooped. Our parlourmaid, Lizzie Nolan, a sturdy girl of nineteen with a flyaway dark mop, stood waiting to take everyone's dusty coats. She was warm-hearted and willing, well-liked in the household.

'By the way, there are two letters for you, Mrs Nicholls,' said Mama.

'From Haworth?' Her head, too large for the slight body, bobbed eagerly.

'I only know they're from England.'

'Our honeymoon is quite crowded out by the march of letters,' said Arthur.

'Don't exaggerate, Arthur.'

'You wrote to Miss Nussey on our wedding night!'

'You must be longing for some refreshments,' said Mama.

'Could I rinse my hands please? They're sticky from the journey.'

'Mary, show our guest where she can wash.'

Charlotte gave her posy to Arthur, and we walked the length of the wood-panelled main hall, with its collection of hunting horns suspended from hooks. I led her into a small room off it. A table with soaps, jug and ewer of water stood under a stained-glass window. She removed her bonnet. 'There's a mirror here.' I knew she'd want to pat down her hair. Already, I realized she liked to be neat – not just in appearance, but with possessions arranged in perfect order. She told me the habit was formed early by her papa.

Charlotte bathed her face and hands, and I gave her a linen towel to dry off.

'You're waiting on me like a lady's maid,' she protested.

'Like a sister.'

She stilled for a moment. Light from the window striped her face yellow, and I wished the words unsaid. But she stroked her plaited bracelet, gave herself a shake, and smiled. 'Mustn't keep everyone waiting. I'm ready now for Cuba Court and all its Bells.'

Mama's parlour smelled of freshly washed curtains and furniture polish. Immediately, she began playing hostess to Charlotte. 'Sit down, Mrs Nicholls. Over there, it's more comfortable. Will you have tea or barley water? Made to my grandmother's recipe. Mary, pass around those curd-cheese tartlets.'

Arthur was still holding Charlotte's roses, and he carried them over and rested them on her lap. Always looking for ways to please her. She touched the polished wooden arm of her chair. 'Beeswax. I love the smell.'

'I keep beehives,' said Mama. 'Wouldn't be without them. What's a sting or two compared to the bee's gifts?'

'I've heard it can keep wrinkles away. My friend Miss Nussey – she was my bridesmaid – smooths it onto her hands and throat every night.'

'Wrinkles are part of life.'

'Aunt Harriette's the wisest woman I know.' Arthur was always convinced those he loved were paragons. He was grinning now to see his two favourite people in the same room.

'I almost called Richard Ambrose, after the patron saint of beekeepers, whose words are sweeter than honey.'

'Ouch!' cried Richard. 'A narrow escape!'

'Even so, soft words flow readily from you, Richard,' I said. 'Miss Prim.'

'Don't squabble, children,' said Mama. 'By and by, I'll send for Hope Porter, to give her the honour of showing you to your room.'

'Am I not in my usual berth?' asked Arthur.

'Certainly not, you're in the Blue Room.'

'We've been upgraded, Charlotte. That's the best in the house. Marriage has its perks.'

'Summer or not, I had one of the maids set a fire in it, to drive out any chill. This house is a magnet for draughts, and our flagstone corridors are cold underfoot. It won't bother Arthur, but might not agree with you, Mrs Nicholls.'

Ahead of their visit, Mama and I had hurried to finish off a cobalt-bright counterpane we were quilting, a series of interlocking diamonds with flowers stitched at each northern and southern point. 'Is it too blue?' I had wondered. 'Blue is never too blue,' Mama had said in her decisive way. 'Light or dark, it's the colour of innocence.' I thought of the coverlet now, lying on their bed – and an image flashed into my mind of the two naked beneath it, making the bed creak as they had in Dublin. Our quilt would witness their lovemaking.

'Is Hope a family member?' asked Charlotte.

'A foundling. But we do our best by her,' said Mama.

'She does little jobs about the house to earn her keep,' I said.

'Nothing strenuous,' Mama put in. 'We make a pet of her, really.'

'I'm teaching her to count and recite her A, B, Cs, Arthur.'

'Good for you, Mary. Education will stand to her.'

'But she can't be educated above her station in life,' cautioned Mama. 'It will make her discontented.'

'She looks like a child of four. Not – did you say six or seven, dear?' asked Charlotte.

'She'll be seven on the last day of August. Hope was born in one of the worst of the Famine years. Black Forty-Seven. I suspect her mother's body couldn't give her the nourishment she needed.'

'She's never wanted for food or a roof over her head since the day you handed her to me, Arthur. If you're ready to go to your room, Mrs Nicholls, I'll ring for the child now.' Mama stood up and pulled the bell cord by the window, half-hidden by curtains.

'Your Hope Porter is lucky. In Haworth, the week before Arthur and I were married, a newborn boy was found in a shallow grave. A dog dug him up. The mother was a mill worker who said she gave birth on her own on the moor. No one seemed to know she was with child. Had the baby, went straight back to the mill, lost only half a day's pay.'

'Gracious me,' said Mama.

'Was a charge of infanticide pressed?' asked Richard.

'No. The girl said the baby never drew breath. There was no proof she killed him, so the inquest recorded "found dead in a field". The moor accepts all. Even tiny corpses.'

Mama, who never fidgeted, began knocking her fingers together. Her eyes alighted on Charlotte's cut hands. She had left off her bandages, saying the air would help them to heal. 'Did you have an accident, Mrs Nicholls?'

'It was no accident. At least not on the part of the rooster who was attacked me.'

'Evil creatures.'

A smile. 'He was defending his territory.'

'Where did it happen?'

'Never mind,' said Arthur quickly. 'They're just scratches. Look, here's Hope now.'

She tripped into view, cupping one ear with a hand.

'Hope, are you forgetting something?' asked Mama, but gently. The child bobbed a curtsey. 'Very good, pet. Now, show Master Arthur and Mrs Nicholls to their room. Mrs Nicholls, you must want for nothing. Our ways are rough and ready compared to what you're used to, I suppose. But if any comfort is missing, please let me know.'

'I'm used to no great comfort, Mrs Bell.'

'Is your ear hurting?' Arthur hunkered down, took hold of Hope's lobe, and looked into it. 'It's red-looking, Aunt Harriette. Can't we do something for her?'

'Spooning warmed olive oil into a sore ear works wonders,' Charlotte volunteered. 'Papa swears by it.'

'Will you ask Mrs Foley to look out some for her, Aunt Harriette?'

'Hope, you have a persistent champion in Master Arthur,' said Mama. The little girl twiddled the corners of her apron. 'After you show them to the Blue Room, go back to the kitchen. I'll attend to you there myself.'

'Best of aunts,' said Arthur.

As soon as they left, Mama said, 'Arthur's wife's as skinny as a hairpin. And I don't like the look of those wounds on her hands. After I sort out Hope, I'll mix her up one of my honey salves. They'll stop scarring.'

'Should I go after our guests, Mama? In case they need anything?'

'All they need is each other, Mary. My old nurse used to say, Love and a cough are two things you can never hide. Leave these lovebirds to their own devices, my pet. Now, I must find that olive oil.'

With Mama off on household business, I decided to unpack. My bedroom window overlooked the front lawns, and before long Arthur passed along the path holding Hope's hand. She had a strip of material tied over her ear, and her face was trustful as it never was with anybody else. When he was home on holidays, the two of them paraded up and down Banagher's lanes together, Hope often on his shoulders clinging to his black hair. No empress could have been more contented with her transport.

Now the two of them were on the grass. Arthur removed his jacket and waistcoat and began flapping his arms like a bird and running on the spot. Hope hopped about, copying him.

'What are you looking at, Mary?' Mama materialized in the doorway.

'Arthur doing his exercises.'

'Your papa was a great believer in them. I'm pleased Arthur keeps them up. Richard should take a leaf out of his book. You still do yours every day, don't you?'

'Most days.' Routines were adrift because of Charlotte's visit, but I promised myself I'd go back to them.

'We don't want your leg getting rigid.'

'No, Mama.' She joined me at the window, and automatically my hand crept through the crook of her elbow. Sometimes, she irked me, but I admired her, too. She could have gone to pieces when we lost Papa, but had stayed strong for us.

'Richard needs to find a suitable wife soon,' said Mama. I gave a noisy intake of breath. 'Your turn will come, Mary.'

'That's not what I –'

'Richard's problem is he can't settle on just one woman, when every girl with a pretty face catches his eye. I wish your papa were alive to have a stern talk with him.'

'I don't see why everyone has to be matched off.'

'Not everyone. But a woman, in particular, doesn't have much choice. What will you do if you don't marry, you goose? Go out governessing like Arthur's wife before she hit on writing novels? Your brother would never permit it.'

'Which would he forbid? Governessing or novels?'

'Both.'

'I'm not fit for much but marriage. I wasn't trained for work.' I numbered my talents on one hand. 'Embroidery, flower-arranging, instructing servants, presiding at table, making agreeable conversation – that's how you coached me.'

'The last of those accomplishments leaves much to be desired.'

'There are no gentlemen in the room. My pleasant chit-chat is meant to be directed at them, to ease their precious leisure time.'

'I can see I've spoiled you.' She adjusted my collar, stroking it smooth. 'I know Banagher is dull at your age, and you want to spread your wings. Of course you do. Perhaps we could manage a London season. But you need to remember you're one of the Bells of Banagher, and it's your duty to wed someone suitable. Even Jane Eyre chose marriage.'

'Don't you mean Charlotte Brontë?'

'I wish you'd stop fighting me, Mary.'

CHAPTER 21

'Will you take a turn in the grounds with me?' said Charlotte. 'The twilight hour shouldn't be spent indoors.'

'Where's Arthur?'

'Inspecting the schoolroom with your brother, who wants his advice. Come on, my lass. Will you? That's how friends address one another in Yorkshire.'

Arm in arm, we matched our steps, and I felt accepted by her.

'My lass. It sounds cosy.'

'We work hard at cosiness where I'm from. It's defence against the landscape. The elements. The King Learness of it all.'

I threw back my head and laughed.

'You remind me of Arthur – you thrum with life. I admire that,' she said.

'It feels as if my life's suspended. As if I'm stuck under a bell jar, waiting for it to get started.'

'Youth's an impatient age, Mary. As I remember.'

'You willed things to happen. All I do is observe them.'

She touched my cheek, halfway between a tap and a caress. 'The watcher has their role to play, too.'

'What do you make of Ireland, Charlotte?'

'It's a place where unexpected things seem likely to happen.'

'Is that good or bad?'

'Perhaps good *and* bad. Growing from the one tree.'

We walked further, breathing the scents from Mama's flowerbeds, following a scarlet butterfly which danced onto a stone, where it spread its wings to soak in the last of the day's warmth.

'The evening air has magic woven through it. My brother Branwell used to say the gods come out at dusk.' A sigh. 'He'd talent to burn. And that's what he did – set it on fire and reduced it to ash.'

'Were you near in age?'

'A year to the difference. We were like stepping stones, all of us, and good friends as children. After Branwell grew up, it was less –' She wrinkled her nose in search of the word '– congenial. At least in his final years.'

'Look.' I turned her around, and pointed to the outline of the house glowing rose-pink against the setting sun. 'Like the roses on your shawl.'

The sight cheered her, as I hoped. 'This was part of my going-away outfit. Chosen to match my bonnet. I trimmed it with pink roses, you see, on Papa's advice. He said they were bridal.'

'Your papa has knowledge of haberdashery?'

'There's nothing he doesn't know. He's the smartest man in all England.' A tiny frown. 'And now I've seen Ballynaskeagh, I respect him even more. Such determination to better himself! Not that the place he comes from isn't ... I mean ... well, you saw it, too.'

'Yes. Though I wonder if he ever regrets what he left behind? To achieve his position in life, I mean.'

'He gained more than he lost.'

'What will you tell him about Ballynaskeagh?'

'That the glen is a place of beauty, and the people are full of stories. Nothing he doesn't know already. But I won't write to him about it – best if I wait till we're back in Haworth.'

'Do you wish you'd visited his homeplace with your papa?'

'Not Papa. Emily. I think she'd have been moved by it.' Her brow knitted, and she bent over a rose, taking a moment to collect herself. When she straightened, I went to snap it off for her, but she held up a hand. 'Let it flower on its stem.'

'There's a whole garden of them.'

'But they begin to die once they're picked. Let it live, Mary. There's too much death in the world.'

'Mama loves her roses. They appeal to her extravagant side. Because they're utterly shameless in their opulence.'

'Rightly so. Every house should have a rose garden. I believe yours is my favourite corner of Ireland so far.'

'Do you have a big garden in Haworth?'

'My goodness, no, there's nothing you could safely call a garden in our parsonage. A few scraggy shrubs and currant bushes are the best we can rise to. Haworth is on the edge of the moors, and winds whip off it to scourge our gardens. But when Arthur and I returned from the church, at the head of our little bridal procession, roses peeped up from all over the house. And not just roses but sweet pea, scented stock and cornflowers. Martha, our maid, begged flowers from every garden in Haworth. I came back to a bower. It was her wedding gift to me.'

'She must be fond of you.'

'She's lived with us since the age of twelve. When our old servant Tabby needed help.'

'Everyone's pet lamb, then, like Hope Porter.'

'Martha's no one's pet! She's a straight-talking Yorkshire girl. A rough diamond. Muscles like cords on her arms. We rely on her.' She fingered her hair bracelet. 'When Arthur and I were leaving after the wedding breakfast, my friend Ellen snatched up armfuls of roses, and tore off their petals to scatter underfoot.

Poor Martha's face was like thunder. She disapproves of waste. But it's traditional for a bride to walk on rose petals.'

'For luck?'

'I suppose. Luck needs to be courted.'

'When you talk about your wedding, you make me feel as if I was there.'

'It was the quietest possible day. The quietest possible wedding. We posted no banns to make sure of it. But in spite of everything, word spread. Outside the church, the whole of Haworth, near enough, was standing there whooping. Women waving. Men throwing their hats in the air. If I hadn't held tight to Arthur's arm, I believe my legs would have gone from under me. So much goodwill was heartening.'

'Arthur says hardly anything about the wedding, apart from how wonderful it was of providence to arrange it for him. Won't you tell me about it all?'

Her face brightened, and she recounted the specifics as though laying out a plot in a novel: a cloudy summer's morning; the bridegroom and his best man in dark, clerical clothes walking across the moors; a small boy watching for their arrival to alert the bellringer; a bride and two loyal friends slipping out of the parsonage side gate to the church beyond the garden; a wedding breakfast for eight guests, in the same room where Arthur first proposed to her; the bride's papa the life and soul of the party.

'People love weddings – Mama especially. It makes them hopeful.'

'Or sentimental.'

'And your gown?'

'Organized in record time, like the wedding. My friends helped me choose the cloth. There was a silk tulle they tried to coax me into buying, but I couldn't justify the expense. Muslin was good enough for me. And I absolutely, positively wasn't wearing white. Except I did! Such frivolity!'

'A wedding without fripperies is a sad affair.'

Charlotte tilted her head, allowing the point. 'And before I knew it, I was in a carriage and pair, crossing the moors to Keighley station to start our honeymoon. Which has brought me' – she extended her arms – 'to Ireland.'

'So everything was perfect.'

She didn't answer at once. Instead, she felt the crown of her head, checking the parting. 'I'd have liked a keepsake of my mother's to wear. A necklace or piece of lace. Even a handkerchief. But there was nothing. I carried Aunt Branwell's Bible. They were sisters – it was a link.'

'Arthur says your aunt raised you.'

'Mama was from Penzance, but staying in Yorkshire when she met Papa. After they set the date, she wrote home for a wedding veil of French lace she intended to wear. Her sister sent a box by sea, but a storm blew up and the ship sank. Mama had to borrow a veil. Papa insisted she didn't mind the loss of her things – Christian fortitude, et cetera, et cetera. But Aunt Branwell said she was bitterly disappointed.'

'Your poor mama.'

'I suppose things get lost in life. We shouldn't attach too much significance to possessions.'

'You treasure your souvenirs of your sisters.' I let my eyes rest on the bracelet at her wrist.

'Not as much as I treasure my memories of them.' She touched the twist of jewellery. 'One day, this will be a leftover. Someone will look at it and see a tattered old piece of junk. And they'll throw it away. They won't understand its emotional weight.'

'I'm sorry you'd nothing of your mama's for your wedding day.'

'Don't feel sorry for me, Mary. I had my mother with me.'

'She looked down from heaven and saw you make your vows?'

'No, I felt her presence – and my sisters'. In the church, when I walked across the flagstones, I passed over the vault where they lie buried.'

I shuddered, and tried to mask it with a cough. She caught the shawl slipping from her shoulders, and linked me again, the bones of her forearm as hollow as a bird's.

'Love is meant to fill an emptiness inside,' she said. 'We have such high expectations of it.'

'Does it fill you, Charlotte?'

'Happiness didn't just arrive for me. I willed it, waited for it, recognized it when it came. I made it happen. Not with foolish fancies. But determined to seize what was offered. You must grab what joy you can, Mary. Store it up against the winter.'

'I'm not unhappy.'

'Aren't you?'

'Restless, maybe. I feel as if there has to be more to life than sitting in Banagher being Mama's daughter and Richard's sister.'

'Your brother protects you. Poor Brannie couldn't take care of himself, never mind anybody else. Circumstances forced me to be self-sufficient, and on the whole I don't regret it. But there's a price to pay for experience.' Her voice dropped. 'When I went out into the world, it scorched me.' She blinked hard.

'Being Arthur's wife will keep you busy now. Although a successful authoress must have plenty to occupy her, too.'

'My books weren't enough for me. Arthur won me with his constancy. He fills a void within me.'

'Is that why you love him?'

'His certainty in wanting me – I found it compelling.'

'He's handsome, too.'

'You think so?'

'Of course. Don't you?'

'Appearances are irrelevant to me. I look for character.'

'Arthur has that in spades.'

'But no inner life.'

I gave her a sidelong glance. 'Isn't that good? What you see is what you get. No nasty surprises.'

'Whereas I'm full of them.' She laughed. 'Just teasing. My life is dull, it's why I turn to fiction. Arthur's worth twenty intellectuals or literary types tied in a bunch.' Shadows were beginning to thicken, but we meandered on. 'Has your heart ever been broken, Mary?'

'Only by the loss of Starlight.'

'Heartbreak is productive if you learn from it – it pruned my expectations. I was lonely before Arthur. The parsonage reeked of absence. Empty chairs and closed writing desks. Oh, there were trips. To the Smiths in London. Mrs Gaskell – my kind Elizabeth – in Manchester. But the Haworth evenings were dismal. Papa in bed, the wind muttering against the windowpanes. And me, alone with my thoughts. It became a house of silence and shadow.'

The swerve of Charlotte's mind fascinated me. I imagined a Dutch interior in an oil painting, introverted people lost in thought.

She went on, 'I felt as if my skin had been peeled off like orange skin, Mary. The air itself stung me. We weren't just sisters, you see, but fellow writers. They understood me. No one will ever fathom me like them.' A click of her tongue. 'But I have a husband now. A companion. A foothold on the world. We're poles apart in some ways. But with Arthur, I'm no longer solitary.'

'He's convinced the sun rises and sets with you.'

'I won't forget what I owe him. Despair was unravelling within me. Arthur put out his hand and stopped it.'

Stillness settled between us, so absolute I was convinced I could hear the beating of her heart. We turned back for the house.

'Sometimes, my lass, it's as necessary to hear something as to share it. You've listened. You've a gift for it.'

*

Over lunch the following day, Mama set about charming Charlotte, seating our guest at her right hand, serving Apple

Charlotte in her honour. When Charlotte thanked 'Mrs Bell' she was corrected. 'Mrs Bell, indeed! Call me Aunt, like Arthur.'

'I'd be honoured. And you must call me Charlotte. There aren't many people left who can Charlotte me. I've lost so many members of my family.'

'But gained a new family through marriage,' I said. Her eyes were lustrous, like phosphorescence, reaching across the table to me.

Arthur was deep in conversation about fishing with Richard. My brother wasn't yet thirty, and young to run a school – Mama always said he should have been a botanist, more interested in the small treasures of nature, from snowflakes to insects, than educating boys. He was given a magnifying glass for his twelfth birthday and loved nothing better than to pore over some found object.

'What did you do this morning, Charlotte?' asked Mama.

'Arthur showed me his boyhood spoils. An old sledge seems to be his pride and joy – apparently, not a winter went by but he'd play truant, and race Alan down hills. I'm learning new things about my husband every day.'

'He was the kindest brother to a small girl. More patient than my own,' I said. 'When he left Banagher for the university, I was grief-stricken. But a man must make his way in the world.'

'He was never one for mitching from school,' said Mama. 'It was Alan put them up to mischief. He's two years older. If ever Arthur went astray, we always knew where to look for the source. But Arthur got up to very little badness, in truth. Dr Bell and I never had much worry with him.'

'You make a Goody Two-Shoes of me!' Arthur protested, catching the tail end of our conversation.

'What else did he show you?' I asked.

'Baubles of local colour,' said Arthur. 'You wouldn't be interested.'

'I want to hear it from Charlotte.'

'He took me out promenading. We saw a holy well, with scraps of coloured cloth tied to the thorn bush beside it. Sewn together, they'd have made a coat to match Joseph's in the Bible.'

'They'll stay on that thorn bush till they fall apart. No one would dream of touching them. It would bring bad luck,' said Arthur.

'We live cheek by jowl with the good folk here,' said Mama. 'It doesn't do to get on their wrong side.'

'I thought Ireland was in Rome's grip.'

'Arthur told you that?'

'Papa. He says the people are under the control of their bishops.'

'There's a pagan strain in the people no religion can shift. They mixum-gatherum to suit themselves.'

'It's not how my imagination sketched it beforehand. Yet I feel at ease here. Not a belonging exactly – but a connection. As if I've breathed this air before.'

'I'm glad you feel a link, pet. We'd be delighted if you took root here. Transplanting can happen, as any gardener knows.'

'I could never leave my moor. It's meat and drink to me.'

'It's not our old homes we miss when we move on. It's our childhood.'

A shake of the head. 'I'm addicted to my moor. To its silences and rages. In winter it has a stark beauty, and in spring it pulses with life. You should hear the song of the skylarks there!'

'Ireland has skylarks,' Richard put in.

'The West Riding spoils you for anywhere else. Anyway, my family are there. The dead may be invisible, but they aren't absent. The shades of me, my sisters and brother will haunt the moors for all eternity – our talk hanging in the snap of the air.'

Mama rounded her eyes, while Richard pretended to drop something and hid his face beneath the table.

Arthur cleared his throat and changed the subject. 'We didn't make much progress on our walk. Everybody wanted to be introduced to my wife.'

'Notable visitors are rare here,' said Mama. 'And brides always cause interest. We've a tendency to marry cousins in this family. First cousins for preference, second cousins at a push.'

'Then I've thwarted a match by making off with Arthur.'

'Plenty more cousins in the sea. Aren't there, Mary?'

'I'm content as I am.'

'Don't let your cousin Joseph Adamson hear you say that. You'll break his heart.'

'He has a head shaped like a boiled egg!'

'Marriage isn't the Promised Land for a woman,' said Charlotte.

'What is?' asked Richard.

'The knowledge she can make her own way in the world. On an equal footing to any man.'

Mama's eyebrows vanished into her hairline. 'To be queen of her household is enough for any woman.'

Charlotte murmured in Arthur's ear, before addressing Mama. 'Would you excuse me if the meal is finished? I need to fetch something from our room.'

'Certainly.'

'I'll go with you,' said Arthur.

After the door shut, Mama said, 'What a pair of turtle doves.'

'Not her, she's as self-contained as a seagull,' Richard contradicted Mama. 'Ungainly as one, too.'

'Odd, for such an elfin creature. A lady should always glide along. It's a pity Charlotte lost her mother so young, or she'd have taken her walking in hand. You know, if I say so myself, your limp is hardly noticeable, Mary. I'm pleased I made you do those exercises. You did say you're keeping them up, didn't you?'

'Yes, Mama.'

She steamed on, pinned to the chug of her thoughts. 'High time we found Arthur a landing place in Ireland. The Rosses might help him to a living.'

'You heard how she talked up the moors,' I pointed out.

'We women go where our men place us.'

'What about Arthur's career? He can't be a holy orders underling all his life. How will he provide for a family?' asked Richard.

'It's a pity she's not scientific. The Rosses prefer science to literature,' said Mama.

'Astronomy mad, the lot of them,' said Richard.

'Still, a literary lady in their midst would please the countess. Especially when their London cousins visit. I wonder if we might be invited to one of their dinners. Imagine who you might meet there, Mary!'

'Shush, Mama, I hear footsteps.'

Charlotte and Arthur returned with something wrapped in muslin, and presented it to Mama. It was a hunk of their wedding cake. 'I'm sorry there's not more of it, Aunt Harriette. I didn't realize how many it would need to share around. Arthur says the servants will expect some, because of knowing him from boyhood.'

'They'd be hurt we left them out,' said Mama. 'But I can make it stretch.'

She tugged the bell rope for Hope Porter, used as a messenger between the household and its staff. Hope was to tell the servants, indoor and outdoor, to assemble in the drawing room in fifteen minutes.

We left the table to join them there. 'Who's that with Denis?' Charlotte whispered to me. A man and a boy stood just inside the door, caps in their hands.

'His son, Ben, the stableboy.'

'A playmate for Hope.'

'Ben doesn't play. He's ten years old. He works. He and his father have a cottage on the grounds.'

'Just the two of them?'

'Denis is a widower. Counts himself lucky to have one child left. He had five.'

'The Fa –?' Charlotte stopped her mouth with her knuckles, and went over to shake their hands.

Mama made a ceremony of those morsels of fruitcake. She sliced up parings, and had Richard pour everyone sherry or whiskey to toast the bride and bridegroom. Arthur refused a glass, abstinent even on such an occasion. The servants oohed and aahed over Master Arthur and his bride, whose crimped forehead suggested a struggle to follow the local dialect. Charlotte curled like a comma towards him, reliant on his presence among such a fleet of strangers.

Hope Porter was cradling a doll in a red woollen dress and black boots with side-buttons. 'Where did you get that, Hope?' I asked.

'Art'ur give me her.'

'May I hold her?'

'Don't break her.' Hope handed over her doll, and watched me narrowly. She had a white glazed porcelain head with painted-on hair and puckered pink lips, and a body made of cloth.

'Have you named her?'

'Art'ur showed me her name on the box. Marigold. That's a flower.'

'What a pretty name. I wish I was called Marigold. Did he bring her all the way from England?'

'Dublin.' She held out her arms for the doll, and I had no choice but to return it.

'Hope, don't be making a nuisance of yourself with Miss Mary, now.' Our cook wheezed over to us, her cracked voice belonging to someone twice her age. 'When I was your age, if I annoyed the grown-ups I'd be beaten with nettles.'

'She never annoys me, Mrs Foley. Do you Hope? We're the best of friends.'

The little girl hugged her doll close.

'Ah, but Master Art'ur's her favourite.'

'That's as it should be.'

Mama appeared. 'Mrs Foley, let Lizzie come up now for a piece of wedding cake like the others,.'

Mrs Foley creaked off, scolding under her breath about the dangers of spoiling young servants. 'Worthless as tatie peelings, some of them.'

Hope Porter tugged my sleeve. 'What is it, Hope?'

'Lizzie says tatie peelings would a kep' her family alive.'

'Now, now, Hope,' said Mama. 'No harm will come to anybody in Cuba Court while I have the running of it.'

Charlotte and Arthur approached us. 'Do you like the cake?' Charlotte asked. 'Martha Brown made it. Her mother is Arthur's landlady.'

'Former landlady. I have a new berth now.' His hand pressed Charlotte's waist.

'Delicious,' said Mama. 'Most considerate of you to bring us some. It's the next best thing to being at the wedding. Look how happy it's made the servants.'

Personally, I thought the sherry and whiskey were contributing to their gaiety because Richard had poured everyone second glasses. There he was, teasing two of the maids. When Mama spotted it, she flew over to intervene.

Lizzie Nolan arrived, face starry with freckles under the frill of her cap. I went to speak to her, and noticed how her eyes took in every detail of my gown and the arrangement of my hair.

'What's the news from Banagher since I've been away, Lizzie?'

She filled me in on a new baby son for the Earl and Countess of Rosse at Birr Castle. A travelling preacher who'd drawn huge crowds after people said his prayers could nearly turn hell into heaven. And her best friend, Mona Scully, was emigrating to Boston.

'You'll miss her. But you'll make another.'

'Real friends don't grow on trees. Mona and me, we come through sad times together. I'll be nothing to nobody once she's gone.'

'You're not nothing to us, Lizzie,' I protested.

'I haven't the money for the fare or I'd away to Boston with her. I've a chance of bettering meself there. Sure there's nothing for me here.'

I tried again. 'There's a home for you.'

Her expression turned blank. 'Yes, Miss.'

'It's not the same as home, though.' Charlotte joined our conversation.

'We try to be good to the servants, here at Cuba Court.'

'Earning your bread among strangers is sore work,' said Charlotte.

'You were never a servant, Mrs Nicholls?' said Lizzie.

'A governess. I know how it is, guarding your tongue with your employers. Bridling your very thoughts. It wears you out.'

'Lizzie, come and have some sherry,' called Richard.

Lizzie's nut brown eyes shone. 'Your brother has a smile that would tame a bull, Miss Mary.'

She went towards him, and something in the way their gazes connected made me uneasy.

'You can tell a lot by a person's shadow,' said Charlotte.

A clock chimed in another room. 'I beg your pardon?'

'I've noticed your brother, Mr Bell's. His ... well ... it spreads itself.'

CHAPTER 22

Charlotte, Mama and I were sewing together in the library to keep Arthur company while he gave Hope a geography lesson. Mama admired Charlotte's pocket-sized stitches.

'Thanks to Aunt Branwell. Stitches that were too big were called cat's teeth, and had to be unpicked.'

'Look at these, Hope. You could learn to sew like that. Much more useful to you than geography,' said Mama.

'The needle does be hurting me fingers,' cheeped Hope.

'The needle hurts my fingers. You mustn't talk like the servants.'

Perplexed, Hope looked up at Arthur, who patted her head.

'I ought to have been stricter with your stitches, Mary,' Mama went on. 'Or told your governess to be.'

'You had a governess?' Charlotte's eyes fastened on me.

'Two.' A snowstorm of qualms closed in on me. I'd hidden when they called me. Mocked their clothes and manners. Daydreamed during lessons. I looked over at Hope and Arthur, who was turning a globe borrowed from the Cuba Court school.

'Show me on the map where Haworth is, Art'ur. Can I go and live with you there?'

'And leave Banagher? You'd be homesick.' She pouted. 'But if you apply yourself to learning your letters from Miss Mary, you can write to me.'

'And you'll write back?'

'Every day and twice on Mondays. Now, let's look at the countries in Europe. Can you show me Greece?'

Charlotte took off her spectacles and rubbed twin pinch marks at the bridge of her nose. 'Don't have Hope memorizing countries, Arthur.'

'I won't, dearest. We're going to make a rhyme out of it like you suggested, aren't we Hope?'

'What's wrong with memorizing?' I asked Charlotte.

'Memory's best developed by association of ideas. Cramming children with facts is no use. They need to learn to reason, not parrot.'

'Have you seen much of the world, Charlotte?'

'I've been to Scotland, Wales and Belgium. And now Ireland.'

'What's Belgium like?' I asked.

'A land of churches, convents and confessionals.'

'Same as Ireland, then,' said Arthur.

'I'd love to go to Paris. Or Venice. Or anywhere!' I burst out.

'Your cousin Joseph Adamson would bring you there on a wedding trip, if you'd accept him.'

'Mama, you know perfectly well I don't care for him in that way.'

'Life isn't a romantic novel, my pet. Is it, Charlotte?'

'No.'

Arthur opened his mouth, and closed it without speaking.

'Your Mr Rochester bears a resemblance to our Arthur. All of us thought so. Didn't we, Mary?'

'We did.'

Charlotte's forehead pleated. 'How so?'

'Middle height with a broad chest. Strong features. Firm mouth – all energy and decision. It's Arthur on the button.'

'Without the country estate. Or the wealth. Or another wife in the attic,' protested Arthur.

'Cuba Court has attics,' said Mama.

Charlotte clapped her hands. 'Then I must inspect them for my own peace of mind.'

A knock on the door was followed by Lizzie Nolan, waving a letter. 'A footman from Birr Castle's just landed in, Ma'am. With a message for you from Lady Rosse.' She produced the name as though it was a pocketful of gold sovereigns.

Mama examined the envelope with the Rosse family crest, two leopards rearing up on either side of a shield.

'Don't keep us in suspense, Mama,' I said.

Everyone watched as she broke the sealing wax and shared the contents.

My dear Mrs Bell,

May I invite myself for tea the day after tomorrow at three pm. to meet your guests? I do hope this proves convenient. Perhaps you'd kindly send back word with my footman.

Sincere regards,

Mary, Countess of Rosse

'What an honour! Lizzie, make sure the castle footman is offered refreshments, and ask him to wait while I compose a reply. I dare say she wants to throw her eye over your bride, Arthur.'

Charlotte coloured and turned to Arthur, who said, 'People mean it as a compliment when they visit a bride, dearest.'

'Arthur, tell Charlotte about the Rosses,' said Mama.

He described the family. Scientists and astronomers … the earl's giant telescope at Birr Castle … known as the Leviathan …

curiosity of science … so large a man can stand upright inside its mouth.

'I'd like to see that,' she admitted.

'I expect Lady Rosse will invite you to pay a return call,' I said. 'The visit shows she means to take you up.'

'Another conquest for the authoress,' said Arthur. 'But it might also be a courtesy from one Yorkshire woman to another. Lady Rosse was formerly Mary Field of Heaton Hall.'

'Near Haworth?' I asked.

'Bradford direction. But she wouldn't know us,' said Charlotte. 'We move in different circles.'

'Yorkshire isn't high and mighty,' said Arthur. 'People there are thrifty whatever their means. Even the millowners.'

'I must write to Lady Rosse,' said Mama. 'Come along, Hope. I need your help.'

*

That night, preparing for bed, I remembered I hadn't done my leg stretches, and decided to make up for it before going to sleep. I opened my bedroom window for some fresh air, and settled to the tedium of flex-hold-release. Halfway through, voices floated up from the garden.

'I'd move to London tomorrow if I wasn't stuck with this school!' cried Richard. 'I'm only doing it for Mama and Mary.'

I abandoned my exercises and listened.

'You don't mean that,' said Arthur.

'Don't I? What would you know about it?'

'I know Banagher's a decent town.'

'It's a living death! There's nothing to do here! It's all work and tedium!'

'London's overrated, Richard.'

'It has theatres. Clubs. Card games. Prize fights.'

'It's like all cities. Full of careless, gay people living cheek by jowl with desperate souls.'

'You can't put me off. I'm withering here!'

'You're feeling restless. Give it time. It'll pass.'

'Cuba Court's an albatross around my neck! To hell with the house, the school and everyone in them!'

They moved on, and I heard no more, but their conversation niggled at me. I shut the window and went to bed, where Richard's bitter words ricocheted and prevented sleep. Finally, I touched a match to an oil lamp's wick and went downstairs to the library to find a book. A fire was still smouldering there, extending an invitation, with another oil lamp's yellow flare on the mantelpiece. The maids must have forgotten to extinguish it, I thought.

A movement at the window seat caught my attention, its curtains opened and Charlotte emerged from inside them. 'You're up late, Mary.'

'So are you. Can't you sleep?'

She pointed to a table by the fireside, where a writing case sat. 'I thought I'd catch up on my correspondence. Except the moon distracted me.'

I glanced at the wooden box with a star pattern inlaid in brass on the lid. 'That looks well-travelled.'

'Wherever I go, it goes with me. It gives me solace to know I have paper and ink to hand. The tools of a writer's trade.'

'It must be hard to invent people.'

'I invent people, of course, but I'm always myself when I do it. The myself of me is always present in a novel.'

'May I?' I opened the lid, which revealed a brown velvet writing slope. In perfect order inside various nooks in the case, a cornucopia was arranged: metal nibs, pots of ink, beaded pen wipes, India rubber, sealing wax, blotting sheets and notepaper.

I threw some logs on the fire, and used a bellows to encourage the flames. Firelight and shadows turned the room into a cave. I plumped down on the leather fender seat. 'Come and join me by the fire.'

Charlotte sat on the rug, legs hugged against her chest, four curl papers hanging on her forehead where she was training her fringe. She looked about nine years of age. The creator of *Jane Eyre* was someone I longed to know. She must be a Sphinx – secrets locked away. I found her almost mythic: the incarnation of that fictional governess who had her happily ever after.

'Will I go to the kitchen and forage for a midnight feast?' I offered.

'I'm not hungry.'

'Wait, I know where Richard keeps his secret store.'

I liberated a bag of nuts from a drawer, and we sat splitting them with his nutcracker, watching orange and yellow flames undulate in the grate.

'What will you do when you go back to Haworth?'

'Become a Mrs Parson, I suppose. Although the Mrs Parsons I meet bore me.'

'I don't believe you! You'll write an Irish novel.'

'Maybe. But I write slowly. I'll need time to mull over what I've seen.'

The clock struck one. 'Arthur will think you've run off to Ballynaskeagh again if he wakes up and finds you missing.'

She giggled. 'The entire house will be roused. He'll call in the militia.'

'That's love.'

She peeked sideways at me, fidgeting with the woollen shawl around her shoulders. Beneath it, twin rows of lily-of-the-valley were filigreed on her nightdress yoke. 'He's livelier here than in Haworth. The village thinks him a silent man. When he called to the parsonage, he'd say good day and go straight in to Papa about parish business. The first time he proposed, it was the longest speech he'd ever made me.'

'He had to propose more than once?' She nodded. 'How many times?'

'I lost count.'

'Double figures?'

'Depends on what you consider a proposal. Some were along the lines of, May I at least hope, Miss Brontë? That kind of thing.'

'Was he a friend of your brother's?'

'Heavens, no. Brannie called him Mr Flat-Earth because he's such a traditionalist. And Arthur thought Brannie a rake. Anne and Arthur were civil to one another. But out of all of us, Emily had most in common with him.'

'He never mentions her.'

'He didn't know what to make of her. Emily was a true original, and established her own boundaries. She was more suited to poetry than novelizing. Her verses were a string of gemstones, they emerged strand by jewelled strand.'

'She and Arthur don't sound at all similar. He's no patience with poetry.'

'No. When we were courting, he tried to recite a piece of doggerel to me. I had to forbid him from continuing!' Her smile flickered, like a candle guttering.

'Arthur and Emily?' I prompted.

'Both loved the outdoors, and had an affinity with animals. Emily used to come back from her walks carrying some injured creature or other, determined to nurse it to health. She had an inflexible will, and Arthur's is like iron, too, when he's convinced he's in the right. Yes, they were alike in various ways.'

'But you're the sister he loved.'

'The heart is a mysterious organ.' Tawny eyes latched on to mine. 'We can choose to love, of course. But choosing not to love is impossible – the heart won't be overruled by good sense.'

A log shifted and collapsed in the fireplace, and she gave herself a shake. 'Look at your hair – it's honey-thick. My sisters and I used to trade gossip about the day's events while we plaited our hair at bedtime.'

I fingered my blonde braid. 'You must miss them.'

'They're gone like dreams.' Her voice was freighted with a harsh note. 'Winnowed away, one by one.'

'Mama says we'll be reunited with lost loved ones in heaven.'

'I must believe in heaven, for how else are we to meet again?'

'But you have your sisters' work. You can hear them speak through their novels.'

'Their work is misunderstood. Critics call Anne's immoral. Crude and coarse-minded. And Emily's is barbaric, they say. They're blind to the honesty and power of *Wuthering Heights*. Its vibrant storytelling. They accuse both my sisters of salting their books with savagery, but they didn't exaggerate. They portrayed life faithfully.'

'*Wuthering Heights* puzzled me the first time I read it. But the novel improves on closer acquaintance. Even so, I found it shocking, at times. Singular and vigorous, undeniably.'

'There are no wrong books – only wrong interpretations. Those noodles think *Wuthering Heights* is about unfulfilled love. It's not!'

'What then?'

'Good and evil. The primal theme.'

'Richard told me *Jane Eyre* was attacked. But that the critics' arguments were sham.'

A snort. 'They said a woman couldn't possibly have written it.' She toyed with her sisters' bracelet of plaited hair. 'There was another novel by Emily. Her second. All but complete.'

'I'm afraid I haven't read it.'

'It hasn't been published. I can't allow it.'

'Why not?'

'We always discussed our work in progress, and read passages aloud to one another. But Emily refused to do it with this book. From the start, she was secretive about it – wouldn't even reveal its title. After her death, I searched her papers, and found a complete draft of *Though Earth and Moon Were Gone*. Naturally I read it, and gave it to Anne to read – then I burnt it.'

'No!'

'Yes, I burnt it – and I'd do it again. I knew people would judge my sister.'

'And Anne agreed?'

Charlotte's breathing grew laboured, and she shifted in her seat. When she spoke, there as a catch in her voice. 'Anne wept. She said it was wicked of me, and begged me not to do it. But I reduced it to ashes in her presence. I did it for Emily – an act of love. For Branwell, too, despite the misery he rained down on us.'

'Branwell – why?'

'He was one of the subjects. She called him Maxwell, but there was no mistaking our brother. Boastful, excitable, easily led, too fond of spirits. A sour-breathed fantasist who believed his own lies.'

'But surely –'

'I tried to re-work the novel. I altered his red hair, his name, his nature – but his behaviour drove the plot. It was impossible to change him. Maxwell had no capacity for self-restraint, and no concern for those he hurt. A firecracker. Anyone who knew us would recognize him. The only thing Emily changed was his deathbed conversion. Papa pleaded with Brannie, until he submitted and prayed at the end. But Maxwell refused – he died unrepentant.'

'But why would Emily expose your brother like that in a novel?'

'Her mind was burdened writing the book. Emily took on most of Branwell's care during his final months. He soiled his sheets and she cleaned him. He had hallucinations and she held him down.'

'It's painful watching those we love suffer.'

'It wasn't sad, it was brutal. He was out of control. Lied, begged, tricked and stole to feed himself with gin and opium. To drown his distress of mind. It was a slow death by his own hand.' Her face sagged, the weight of her past visible on it. She jerked to her feet. 'We should go to bed, Mary.'

I stood, too, and she trailed alongside me on her little felt slippers, head bobbing at my earlobe. On the staircase, she touched my arm. 'When Brannie told stories, his eyes danced and his charm was irresistible.'

'I know you loved him, Charlotte.'

'I've grown scar tissue over the Branwell place in my heart. But sometimes it tears.

*

'Lizzie's sad,' said Hope, when I found her playing with her doll in the summerhouse. Eyes without guile met mine. 'She put her apron over her face and cried.'

'Why?

'Mrs Foley told her off.'

'Poor Lizzie. Did she smash something?'

'Mrs Foley says she's to stay away from Master Richard.'

I seized Hope by the arm. 'What else did she say?'

She screwed up her face. 'Ouch! You're hurting me!' I relaxed my grip. 'Mrs Foley says you can't trust him.'

'Then what happened?'

'Lizzie says, But he won't give me no peace and Mrs Foley says, Tell the mistress. And Lizzie says, She'll blame me. I'll be sent away without a ... a word I don't know.'

'Reference?' A nod. 'Is that all?'

'Mrs Foley said, So you won't be told. You foolish, foolish child. You'll come to a bad end. And Lizzie, she run away and I see'd her crying.'

Hope wriggled free and darted off.

*

'I hear you're bothering the servants, Richard.'

'Your information is incorrect, Miss Prim.'

'Leave Lizzie Nolan alone. I'll tell Mama if you don't.'

'And what will Mama do? Send me to bed without supper? The only reason you and Mama are still living in Cuba Court is because of me. I keep this roof over your head.'

'You'll ruin Lizzie. And then what will you do? Find another girl to destroy?'

'Nobody's forcing Lizzie. If she spends time with me, it's her own choice.'

'Don't you understand what she's suffered? It's a wonder Lizzie can put one foot in front of the other after everything she's been through. She was twelve years old, Richard. In the space of a month, every last member of her family died. You're preying on her – on her need for some light in her life. What's going to happen when you tire of her?'

He shrugged. 'Haven't the foggiest. We amuse one another. That's enough for now.'

I searched his lean face, skin without a blemish, trying to recognize my brother in this indifferent stranger. 'That's not right!'

'Amusing one another isn't right? Mary, you've grown up to be a moralizer and killjoy. You don't know a finger's snap about worry, and drudgery, and putting your shoulder to the wheel of life. Your wants have always been supplied from our father's purse.'

'Don't make excuses, Richard. And don't mention Papa because you aren't fit to clean his boots.'

'Stamp your feet all you like, Mary, Mary Quite Contrary. But I hold the purse strings. I might accidentally forget to pay your allowance this quarter. I might tell Mama the estate hasn't the money, and we'll have to carry it over to the next quarter. Or even the one after that.'

'I'm ashamed of you, Richard!'

His blue eyes flattened, and I shrank from their contempt. 'And I'm bored of you, Mary. I'm bored of the school and its grubby little pupils. I'm bored of Banagher and this blasted provincial life. So save your lectures, concentrate on dress trimmings and flower-arranging. And don't meddle where it's none of your business.'

*

I watched for a quiet moment with Lizzie Nolan. On the morning of the Countess of Rosse's visit, she passed Mama and me in the hall, Mama's prized triple-branch candelabra between her muscular arms.

'Mind that silverware, Lizzie,' said Mama. 'It was a wedding present.'

'Yes, Ma'am. I'm taking it to the pantry for cleaning.'

I followed her. 'Lizzie, I can let you have the money to go to Boston with your friend. Not right away. But when I get my allowance.'

Lizzie's eyes were like lamps. 'Oh Miss Mary! You're an angel straight from heaven! I'll pay you back. No matter how long it takes, you'll get every penny back.'

'Can your friend wait for you?'

'No, Miss, her passage is booked.'

'You can follow after.'

'I'll have to give notice to the mistress. She won't let me have a reference if I just disappear.'

'I'll write you a reference. Disappearing is exactly what you have to do, Lizzie. But until I raise the cash, you must promise to stay away from my brother.' Troubled, she folded her arms around her body. 'I know how buttery he can be, but you're not to listen to him. Are you still, I mean – he hasn't touched you, has he?'

She lowered her eyes. 'He helps me forget the sad years, Miss. When I lost everybody belonging to me. He makes me laugh.'

'You'll lose your position because of him, Lizzie. He'll do nothing to help you if ...'

'He's promised to stand by me, Miss Mary.'

'He's lying.' She shook her head, and I clutched her by the shoulders and made her look at me. 'Richard can't be trusted. He'll let you down. He lets everyone down.'

Her speckled skin flushed. 'Tell me what to do!'

'Keep Hope with you as much as possible, Lizzie. She'll be your shield.'

'She's only a child, Miss.'

'Do as I say. Don't get separated from Hope. Share your bed with her.'

'She sleeps in Mrs Foley's room.'

'Say you're having trouble sleeping. Say you need company. Say you're troubled by visions of your dead family.'

'Ah no, Miss. They're at peace now. Death was a release for them. From the hunger pains 'ating them alive.'

'Lizzie, you can't be too particular about this. You have to use any weapon you can. Say whatever comes into your head. But reach for Hope Porter and keep her close by. The sight of her will push Richard away.'

'Why, Miss? Doesn't he like the child? I don't understand.'

Some peculiar fold of loyalty to Richard, despite everything, prevented me from sharing my brother's secret. 'Her innocence will shame him.'

CHAPTER 23

The entire household collected on the steps to meet the Countess of Rosse. A carriage and four pulled up at the front door, that distinctive leopard crest on its sides picked out in paint. A liveried coachman and footman sat above the matched black horses. The footman handed out the countess, triggering a wave of curtsies and bows. In her slipstream came two self-possessed boys. Lady Rosse seemed planted there on the gravel, her gaze traversing Cuba Court. A nod suggested it passed muster. Mama and Richard hurried forward to greet her, she offered her hand as though it was a precious possession, and was led indoors.

Lady Rosse should have governed a colony, or commanded armies to advance, or made speeches in Parliament. Instead, she said, 'I've come to meet the newlyweds.' This was the cue for Arthur and Charlotte to be presented. He merited no more than a brisk handshake, but Charlotte was thoroughly inspected. 'The authoress,' she said. 'We have your novels in the Birr Castle library. They do you ...' A temporary halt. 'Credit.' A communal sigh of relief. There was no knowing what Her Ladyship might have said, and no one would have been able to dissent.

My turn came next, and I dropped another curtsey. 'Charming,' she pronounced, a waterfall of lace at her throat. 'Just so, Miss Bell. A young woman should always look ever so slightly overwhelmed. You'll make a suitable match. But perhaps your mama isn't ready yet to part with you.'

'How could any mother stand in her daughter's way?' parried Mama. I knew the cogs in her brain must be clacking through possibilities in the Rosse circle.

Introductions were made to her two elder sons, Lord Oxmantown, the heir, and the Honourable William Parsons – boys of about thirteen and ten respectively, after which, with casual efficiency, Lady Rosse press-ganged Richard and Arthur into bringing them outside for a tour of the grounds. 'If these scallywags misbehave, take them to the schoolroom and set them to copying out a passage from *The Aeneid*,' she instructed. Everyone chased off like lambs.

Charlotte sat on a dark grey horsehair sofa, the lowest piece of furniture in the drawing room. It meant her feet could reach the ground. She flashed me a knowing glance before dropping her eyelids. She was the exhibit. I imagined this was how she'd taken instructions from her mistress as a governess. All compliance on the outside and unruliness on the inside.

'I don't normally read novels, Mrs Nicholls, because I regard them as a waste of time. But I made an exception for yours,' said Lady Rosse.

'I'm honoured, Your Ladyship.'

'Yes, and profited by them.' Lady Rosse eyed the company, daring anybody to question it. 'They're not milk-and-water stories – yours have meat on their bones. I believe you were a governess before your marriage?'

'For a time, yes. Also a schoolmistress.'

'I have fond memories of my governess, Miss Curran. We treated her like one of the family. She impressed upon me the importance of the work ethic, and encouraged my interest in science.'

'Your Miss Curran is fortunate to be remembered with affection. Is she still with your household, Your Ladyship?'

'Sadly, no. Upon my marriage to His Lordship, she took employment with another family. If I could, I'd have packed her in my luggage and taken her with us. Like these.'

She bent to a basket at her feet, and one after another, like a conjuring trick, produced *Jane Eyre*, *Shirley* and *Villette*. Charlotte was commanded rather than requested to sign them, and obliged with good grace. It was, after all, a compliment, and Her Ladyship wasn't the type to scatter them willy-nilly. Charlotte Brontë Nicholls was reproduced on each fly leaf, and Charlotte blew on her signatures to dry the ink. Just as well. Her Ladyship wouldn't have tolerated a smear, just as she wouldn't have stood for C.B. Nicholls, or Charlotte Nicholls, or any such glossing I'd seen her do with other visitors.

'Do you have a favourite, Lady Rosse?'

'Among your fictional novels?'

'All my novels are fictional.'

Lady Rosse blinked, but let it pass. 'None in particular.' She consented to drink tea, and finger by finger her gloves were removed. A porcelain cup and saucer from Mama's prized ivy-leaf service was accepted, one sip taken, and the tea discarded. Mrs Foley's plum cake met a similar fate.

Obligations fulfilled, Her Ladyship settled to business. 'Mrs Nicholls, I've recently developed a passion for that pioneering artform known as photography, and those who understand this subject better than me are kind enough to say I show a flair for it. I've made some studies of my children. I'm immodestly proud of them, I confess.'

'The studies? Or the children?' inquired Charlotte.

'The studies. There's one in particular of the dear boys with Spot, their pet rabbit. Although the silly creature dropped down dead last month when one of His Lordship's hounds took it into his head to tease it. Such a nuisance, the younger boys were fearfully upset. The dog was only playing.'

'I suppose the rabbit didn't know it was a game,' said Charlotte.

'Quite.'

On high alert, Mama's glance fluttered between the two.

'Do you spend much time in London, Mrs Nicholls?' asked Lady Rosse.

'Once, I went fairly regularly. But I'll have too much to do now as a parson's wife.'

'My husband and I have a house there. Feel free to call on us when you're back.'

'How kind. I really can't say when that will be.'

'You must be careful not to go to ground in Yorkshire – and I speak as a Yorkshire woman. The intellect needs feeding, and the great cities do that in ways the countryside can't manage.'

'In the city, you can profit by meeting like-minded people.'

'Just so.'

'But London is a belching Babylon. Enthralling, granted. But it gobbles up its inhabitants.'

'There's plenty of belching, as you put it, Mrs Nicholls, in the manufactories and mills of our native county.'

'When I was a schoolgirl in London, I watched the illuminations to celebrate the Battle of Waterloo,' Mama put in.

'You were educated in London, Mrs Bell?' said Her Ladyship.

'Briefly. I was homesick, and my father fetched me back to Dublin after a few weeks.'

'Indulgent.' Lady Rosse's lips almost disappeared.

'I did benefit from a visit to the Great Exhibition in the Crystal Palace,' said Charlotte. Perhaps Your Ladyship was there?'

'Numerous times – His Lordship was enamoured of it. A splendid world's fair. On one occasion, we encountered Mr Charles Darwin. Perhaps you know him, Mrs Nicholls?'

'Not personally. Naturally I'm familiar with his work.'

'And what did you make of the exhibition?'

'I stood in line to see the Koh-I-Noor diamond from India.'

'Who wouldn't!' said Mama.

'It was a shop window for works of industry,' said Lady Rosse. 'Everything from medical instruments to musical instruments. Diamonds were beside the point.'

'There were so many *things*,' said Charlotte. 'It felt excessive.'

'They had a purpose. To show off Britain's place in the international pecking order, Mrs Nicholls.'

'We read about it in the newspapers.' Mama wasn't going to be trounced by Her Ladyship's lack of interest in her. I felt a spark of pride.

'It was strange to see so many objects piled high. And their inventors or manufacturers beside them, as gratified as though they'd designed Adam and Eve. Naturally, I understood their pride. But it made me wonder …' Charlotte paused.

'Yes?' prompted Lady Rosse.

'If creations may not just outlive, but outshine, their originators. Become something the creator never intended.'

I gathered together my courage and spoke up. 'To be outlived by your books is a form of immortality. I mean … I suppose … some would think being outshone by them is a price worth paying.' Conscious of the room's gaze, I wriggled and sat on my hands. Mama's frown made me shift again and fold them on my lap.

Charlotte tilted her head, spectacles catching the light. 'I'm not interested in immortality. I write because this is my one mortal life and I want it to mean something. My sisters felt the same.'

Lady Rosse squared her shoulders. 'May I ask, Mrs Nicholls, have you ever been photographed?'

'Never, Your Ladyship. I dislike seeing my image, no matter the artform.'

'Even so, I have a great favour to ask. I have a studio in the castle, where I develop my photographs using the waxed paper method. Your face has character – it intrigues me. Mrs Nicholls, may I take your photograph?'

'I regret to disappoint Your Ladyship. But no.'

'Oh, but Charlotte,' protested Mama.

'Your modesty becomes you, Mrs Nicholls. But I know you've posed for a society portraitist because I've seen the result reproduced in one of your novels.' She snatched up *Villette* and flourished it.

'I was persuaded to sit for Mr Richmond against my better judgment. The result is the artistic form of blarney.'

'That's where a photograph's honesty leads the field. Wouldn't you prefer people to know your true face rather than an artist's interpretation? Especially if he means to flatter?'

'I cannot control how an artist depicts me. I can only sit, and allow them to do their job.'

'Naturally. Even so, Mrs Nicholls, won't you reconsider? Photography is a noble invention. It replicates rather than embellishes. It allows a person's likeness to lie fixed forever on paper.' Charlotte shivered, but the countess pressed on. 'Posing would inconvenience you very little. I'd place you in the castle grounds – outdoor photographs have a freshness lacked by indoor ones.'

'Indoors or outdoors, it makes no difference. I can't agree.'

'I'd be pleased to give you some copies as a gift. You could use my photographic portrait for your books, if you chose. I understand Mr Dickens has posed for a daguerreotype, which seems to be greatly admired.'

'Mr Dickens may do as Mr Dickens sees fit.'

'Charlotte will think it over, won't you Charlotte?' appealed Mama.

'I do have one idea Your Ladyship might like to take up.'

'Yes?'

'Miss Bell would make an excellent study. She has the face of a Botticelli angel.'

Lady Rosse narrowed her eyes, and allowed that I might be worth photographing. Flattered, I longed for her to make the arrangements. But Her Ladyship turned brisk again. She thanked Mama for the tea, pulled on her gloves and departed amid a flurry of activity.

'Does she never smile?' Charlotte hissed, standing on the steps to see off the Rosse carriage.

'I don't believe she ever formed the habit.'

We stifled our giggles, and Mama reprimanded us for setting a bad example in front of the servants. The following day, a whole salmon and brace of wild duck arrived with the compliments of the castle, along with an invitation to call three days later.

'You see,' said Mama. 'We made an impression.'

*

Next morning I entered the breakfast room to find Charlotte immersed in a newspaper, a glass of milk in front of her.

'All alone!' I protested.

'But it's so lovely to sit here catching up on the news, with the flowers nodding in at me through the window.'

'You're reading the foreign intelligence section?'

'The Crimean War. Now that Britain and France have entered it, Imperial Russia won't have everything her own way. One of our soldiers has been awarded the Victoria Cross for bravery at a battle on the Black Sea coast.'

'If I were to read that, my head would explode.'

'I like to know what's happening in the world. From our nursery years, Papa discussed things with us, and encouraged us to have opinions.' She busied herself folding the news-sheets.

'Where's Arthur?'

'Supervising some ditch-building on the estate. Hope's out with him. Your brother was meant to go, but cried off.'

A knock on the door preceded Lizzie Nolan with the hot breakfast dishes. She walked without haste in a wavering, sideways motion – the way a snowflake descends. Mama often said it would be delightful in a lady, but in a servant it was a nuisance. 'The mistress says to go ahead without her, Miss Mary. She's moving her hives and it's taking longer than she thought.'

'Thank you, Lizzie.' I passed the bread and butter to Charlotte.

'Is it true you write books, Mrs Nicholls?'

'Yes. Do you like books, Lizzie?'

'I don't read so well, Mrs Nicholls. I never had much schooling. Mrs Foley says there's enough sorrow in the world without looking in books for more.'

'Sometimes there's happiness in books.'

'If you deserve it?'

'Happiness isn't deserved, Lizzie,' I intervened. 'It's either given. Or not.'

'But you can be receptive when it's offered,' suggested Charlotte.

Lizzie raised her shoulders and dropped them. Not so much a shrug as an admission of powerlessness.

'If Mama finds you standing about, she'll give you a piece of her mind,' I warned.

Lizzie flitted away.

'She talks as much as our Martha Brown,' said Charlotte.

'We'd be lost without Lizzie.'

'And we'd be lost without Martha. I don't suppose either would be lost without us, though.'

'Lizzie's the only one of seven to survive the Famine. The labouring classes had a hard time of it when the potatoes rotted in their drills. Black as pitch, and a smell off them to turn your stomach! Some people thought the blight was a punishment from God.'

'How did Lizzie make it through?'

'Mrs Foley knew her people, and asked Mama to find a place for her here. She'd have starved otherwise. There were two sisters old enough to work, but Mama only had space for one. She told Mrs Foley to choose. And so Lizzie came to us. The rest of her family died of hunger or Famine fever.'

'I suppose Lizzie lives for all her family now.'

I lifted the woollen cover to study a nest of speckled eggs. My appetite had deserted me. I looked at Charlotte, who shook her head.

Lizzie coasted back with a pot of tea and another of hot water. Charlotte stirred sugar into her cup, and gave Lizzie a sympathetic look. 'How old were you when you were orphaned?'

'Eleven, Ma'am. Mam was first. Her and Breda, the baba she was nursing. Then Kathleen, the two boys next, and Dada was last. All gone now.'

'Like me. Except for Papa,' said Charlotte.

'Was there the hunger beyond in England?'

'No, it was something else. They fell ill. But death is death.'

'Ah no, Ma'am, there's hard ways to die and 'asy ways to die. The hunger's not … it's …'

'Lizzie,' I said. 'You'll never go hungry with us.'

'You've a heart of corn, Miss Mary.'

'I was five when my mama was taken,' said Charlotte.

'You'd remember her, so. You've that at least, Ma'am.'

'It's a shadow image. Like a figure standing behind a blind.'

'I gets sad about my family. I do be thinking about them. Wondering why they were taken and me left.'

'You'd to grow up fast, Lizzie.'

'You grow up fast when you lose everyone belonging to you, Miss.'

'They're at peace now,' I said. 'And haven't you a good place here.'

'I have, Miss Mary. Mrs Foley is training me up to be a cook. But she does be suffering with her teeth and it makes her cross.'

'I loathe cooking but I'd make a good parlour maid: I can iron, sweep floors, make beds, black-lead stoves and clean out grates,' said Charlotte. 'I've done it all at the parsonage.'

'Try doing it all day every day, Mrs Nicholls. Then you'd see how well you like it.'

'Lizzie! What's got into you!'

'Sorry, Miss Mary. Sorry, Mrs Nicholls. I spoke out of turn.' She faded from the room.

'She reeks of melancholy, poor girl. All that misfortune in her family. I don't know how she puts one foot in front of the other.'

'Mama says some families are born under an unlucky star.'

Charlotte tensed, and I realized what my words must suggest. But it was too late to take them back. 'At least she doesn't suggest misfortune is a punishment for sin,' she said. 'Some people think so. I've wondered it myself.'

'Don't say that,' I blurted out.

She lowered her eyelids and I saw a pulse beat against the tracery of veins. 'Once, I thought I'd die for love. But I came closer to dying for lack of it.'

'After you lost your sisters and brother?'

'Long before. There was a time in my life where I might have sinned with a man who wasn't my husband. But I was spared that fate.' Her eyelids sprang open, her gaze drilled into me. 'I've scandalized you, Mary.'

'No.' My voice was tight, I could barely force it out through my throat.

'I can see it in you. Once, I might have been shocked, too. But life has taught me not to judge.'

I swallowed. 'You – didn't – ?'

'No. Only because he refused me.' She monitored my face. I tried to make a mask of my features, recognizing I was being tested.

'I'm a daughter of the parsonage, Mary. My life hasn't been' – a twist of her mouth – 'Byronic. But I *have* known the scorch of passion. It's a fever. I'm relieved those days are past. That my emotions no longer tumble about like unchecked weeds.'

'Does Arthur know?'

'Not unless you choose to let him know.'

'Why are you telling me this?'

'Oh Mary, if I don't tell someone, I'll be obliged to do like King Midas's barber and whisper it into a hole in the ground. But even holes don't hold secrets forever.' She caught my wrist and pulled me close to her. Her eyes hooked mine, exacting an unspoken promise. 'I trust you, Mary. I'll take my chances with you.'

In the distance, I heard my name called. For a few moments, it didn't register. It sounded again. 'Mary!' It was Mama, her voice shrill with pain. Charlotte and I ran outside, and found her with neck and face covered in bee stings. Hope was dawdling about, and I called to her to bring ointment to the parlour. By the time we'd pulled off the net Mama wore looped around her head, Hope was back.

I rubbed the salve on the swellings. 'You need to take care with bees, Mama.'

She held her breath as I tended to her, but didn't moan or gasp. 'It's my own fault I was stung. I should know better than to open the hive when it's damp out.' She addressed Charlotte. 'Bees are like people – they prefer a clear day.'

'I hope you're not in too much pain, Aunt Harriette.'

'Pleasures must be paid for. I think I'm going to need a helper. How would you like to learn about looking after bees, Hope?'

The small face registered alarm. 'No, Ma'am. I'm afeared of them.'

'Afraid of them, Hope. Not afeared.'

'Yes, Ma'am. I don't like them, Ma'am.'

'But they're such diligent insects. Think what you could learn from them, Hope.'

Her lower lip wobbled, and I intervened. 'Ben Coughlan could help you, Mama.'

'I suppose so. Very well.'

'We should order you some sweet tea for the shock,' said Charlotte. 'Would you like me to read to you while you rest?'

'That would be lovely, pet.'

'Come along, Hope,' I said. 'Time to get your slate and practise your letters.'

She slipped her hand into mine. 'I's sleeping in Lizzie's bed,' she whispered.

'Good girl.'

'Master Richard got mixed up and come into our room last night. Lizzie and him was standing in the dark whispering. They woke me up. When he see'd my eyes open, he said a bad word and went away. Lizzie got back into bed and she was crying. I asked, What's wrong, Lizzie? But she wouldn't tell me.'

CHAPTER 24

It was a sultry afternoon when Denis Coughlan was instructed to bring the carriage around to the front of Cuba Court for our jaunt to Birr Castle. 'Them horses is like slugs in the heat,' said Denis. 'Lizzie Nolan's been looking for you, Miss Mary.'

'Will it wait?'

'It's something for the Rosses. She's in the back kitchen.'

'Don't be long, Mary. We mustn't be late.' Mama tweaked my straw bonnet with pink ribbons tied in a bow at my chin. It matched my pink-and-white striped summer dress. Charlotte's had tiny purple flowers, and her hat was in the latest fashion, shaped like the bowl of a spoon. It had felt pansies pinned on the crown, jewelled centres sparkled in the sunshine, and the hat sat back on her head, revealing some of her pretty hair.

I found Lizzie in the pantry wrapping a honeycomb in greaseproof paper. 'For Lady Rosse, Miss.'

'Well remembered. Why Lizzie, what's the matter? You're not crying, are you?'

She palmed her eyes. 'I'm being silly, so I am.'

I went closer, smelling the sweat from her armpits, and put my hand on her shoulder. 'Tell me, Lizzie.'

'Did you manage to get the money you said you'd lend me, Miss Mary?'

'I tried for an advance on my allowance, but Richard is being difficult. Soon, hopefully. I know your friend's American wake is tonight. But remember what we talked about? You can follow her over, if you still want to go.'

'It's not for a fare on a sailing ship I need the money now. Something else.' She pushed out her lower lip. 'I'm going to have a child.'

I let my arm fall away. 'Have you told Richard?' I managed to gasp out.

Her eyes took on a faraway glaze. 'He made my hopes rise like a loaf in a hot oven them times I lay down with him.'

Alarm spiked my voice. 'Have you told him, Lizzie?'

She turned her head and looked directly at me. 'He says it's best I don't have it.'

'I don't understand.'

'That's what he says.'

'But if you … you can't … how do you stop it coming?'

She lowered her eyes, her voice a wisp. 'There's ways to lose a baby if you're not far along.'

'Surely that's a sin, Lizzie!'

She flinched. 'I've sinned already. I'll lose my position once I start to show. Then how will I feed myself? Or the child?' A solitary tear trickled down her face. 'I'm desperate, Miss. I need money for what has to be done.'

'Could you ask Richard?'

'I did. He says the school's up to its ears in debt. He can't help me.'

Typical of my brother, I thought. Convinced the problem will disappear if he ignores it. 'Do you want to keep it, Lizzie? Maybe we could find a way.'

'No, Miss. Master Richard's right. Best if I lose the baby.'

'My mammy lost me when I was a baby.' It was Hope Porter, eyes like cartwheels.

Lizzie's honest, freckled face coloured. 'It's only a game, Hope.'

'I was lost. But Art'ur found me.' A wobble. 'Did my … did my mammy want to lost me?'

'Your mammy loved you, Hope,' I said. 'But she wasn't able to keep you. So she left you where Arthur was sure to find you. And here you are, snug as can be, and a big help to us. We wouldn't be without you.'

Denis Coughlan appeared. 'So this is where you're all colloguing. Hope, you were sent to fetch Miss Mary.' He nodded at me. 'The mistress is mad keen to get going.'

'I'll be right out, Denis. Would you bring Hope outside, please? Hope, you're a great girl.' I watched him tramp away with her, and turned back to Lizzie. 'I have to go now, Lizzie. But we'll speak again when I come back – together we'll find a solution.'

'If you say so, Miss.'

'I'll help you. I promise.'

'Yes, Miss.'

A resigned note in her voice made me look hard at her. Lizzie's hands were knitted together, bone showing through the knuckles. I set my hand on top of them. 'You need to sit down with a nice cup of tea. Things won't seem so dark by and by.'

'Mrs Foley'll have something to say about me drinking tea and the work half done.'

'I'll smooth her over on my way out.' I wished I didn't have to leave, but Birr Castle was waiting. 'Lizzie, I give you my word. You're not alone.'

'Should I maybe have another word with your brother, Miss Mary? He might have had second thoughts. Could be, it was just the shock made him …'

'You could try. Today's a good day to speak to him. The house will be quiet. Have your tea, then go and find him. He's in his study upstairs.'

'I'll do it at once, Miss. He's not heartless, is he?' Darkened with emotion, her eyes met mine, the skin around them pinched.

'Oh, Lizzie. No, he's not heartless. But don't pin your hopes on him.'

I left her there and hurried to Cuba Court's main kitchen, where Mrs Foley was basting a meat joint. I told her Lizzie had an upset stomach and was having a rest. When she reappeared, she should be given tea with plenty of sugar in it. The cook heard me without protest, an unusual state of affairs, but the wary look on her face suggested she'd guessed Lizzie's condition. 'Go easy on her today, Mrs Foley. Please,' I added. A nod.

Now I went quickly outside to Mama and Charlotte, who were sitting in the carriage with doors and windows open, fanning themselves.

'About time,' said Mama.

I held up the package. 'The honeycomb. You promised Lady Rosse.'

'Shut the carriage doors. We'll be late if we don't leave this instant.' No sooner was I in than she tapped the roof. 'Move on, Denis.'

We clip-clopped down the avenue, and I closed my eyes and tilted my face into a ruffle of air which stole past our bonnets to stroke against skin. Money would have to be found for Lizzie, with or without Richard's help, but I'd think about it later.

We swayed past sights which were normal to Mama and me, but I saw how Charlotte noticed them. Uninhabited cabins, roofs like birds' nests, their former occupants dead or emigrated. Others which looked derelict but smoke showed them to have squatters. A number of the houses still had horseshoes nailed on their doors for luck – which had passed them by.

At the approach to Parsonstown, some freckled, barefoot children playing in the dust of the road scattered before our wheels, but when we waved at them they waved back. On, we trotted, through the town's wide streets lined by tall buildings with fanlights above the doors. Harness creaking, the horses skirted the square. A litter of sunken-faced men gathered, as usual, near Dooly's Hotel, sharing around a clay pipe. '*Dia duibh*,' Denis Coughlan greeted them, and they called out replies, hands raised.

Beyond the town, at the approach to the castle, we passed a long, whitewashed building, two storeys high. An overhanging thatch covered the main house, with an extension tacked on at the end under a slanting slate roof. The yard was swept, and flowers made a bright show in wooden barrels either side of the door. It was well-maintained, unlike the cabins we'd passed.

'That's how Arthur describes the house where he grew up in Antrim,' said Charlotte.

'Memory can play you false,' said Mama. 'It was never as prosperous – that's why we took in Arthur and Alan.'

'Two of their brothers run the farm now,' I said. 'Arthur's never been back.'

'Why would he?' said Mama. 'His parents are long gone. Arthur belongs here.'

'Arthur's made his home in Haworth.' Charlotte radiated certainty.

The carriage lurched and clattered into an avenue. 'Here we are!' carolled Mama, transparent in her triumph at being invited to Birr Castle.

It was a mock-medieval vision, swarming with turrets, battlements and multipaned windows, its outer walls ivy-covered. A footman opened the monumental curved door to us, and a woman in a black dress, trim as a candle, appeared almost at once.

'Welcome to Birr Castle. I'm Mrs McAndrews, the housekeeper. Her ladyship will be with you directly.' We followed her into a cathedral of a reception room, gloomy despite a profusion of gilt – the arched windows were almost floor to ceiling, yet light barely penetrated its thick walls. A crystal chandelier with trembling pendant points was suspended from the vaulted ceiling.

Charlotte examined some portraits hanging from a picture rail. 'Ancestors?'

'Naturally. The Parsons have lived here since 1620. His lordship is the third earl. May I offer you refreshments? Tea, sherry, elderflower cordial?'

'Cordial, please,' said Mama.

'It revives after a journey, Ma'am.'

'It's a thousand pities my husband is in London, and cannot be here to greet you.' The Countess sailed in, and her housekeeper slipped away.

Her Ladyship chatted graciously about the grounds, which she told us were filled with rare specimens of plants and trees, while a maid served cordial, bowls of cherries and star-shaped almond biscuits.

'Don't you love Ireland, Mrs Nicholls?' said Lady Rosse. 'The tumble and gallop of the wind. The crumbling towers. The wildness, the shapes, the colours. The legends attached to every patch of woods and valley. The outlandish superstitions.'

Charlotte gave a non-committal answer, which Lady Rosse took for agreement, and Her Ladyship led Mama to the far wall to view a portrait of a lady at her spinet.

'*Do* you love Ireland?' I asked quietly, while they were occupied.

'I'm still deciding,' she whispered back.

It pulled me up short. I thought we'd found favour with her.

'This is the earl's grandmother.' Lady Rosse pointed to a lady in a wig, wearing an old-fashioned gown with square-cut neckline. 'She was musical. I've heard you're fond of music, too, Mrs Bell. We have her spinet, said to be a fine example of its type. Unfortunately, I don't play. I'm at a loss what to do with it. I'd welcome your advice.'

Mama, who liked nothing better than dispensing advice, expressed a willingness. The bell was rung for Mrs McAndrews to return, and Mama was spirited away.

'Come and see my darkroom.' Lady Rosse hustled us along corridors and into a tower room full of camera paraphernalia, including glass plate and waxed paper negatives. 'May I show you some of my photographs?' She produced a study of two young boys sitting on a donkey, with a nursemaid holding onto the younger one who looked in danger of toppling off. It was followed by a photograph of Lord Oxmantown playing chess with a lady, shadows thrown up in dramatic fashion. The Great Rosse Telescope was next, against a backdrop of the castle walls.

'Your castle looks exactly as a castle ought,' said Charlotte.

'I should hope so. This one' – a leafy oak filled the photograph – 'was taken by Lord Oxmantown. He's following in my footsteps.' We made appropriate noises. 'Once, I'd have scrambled up that tree. When I said as much to my sons, they chortled. Positively chortled. Girls don't climb trees, they said. Don't they, though, I replied. But when my interest in science took over, I stopped climbing them.' She puffed out her cheeks. 'I should have kept it up. What do you think, Mrs Nicholls?'

'I was never any good. My sister Emily was the climber. But the odd time I made it up a tree, I liked where I was. The world looked different. A useful corrective.'

'Quite so. Mrs Nicholls, I won't beat around the bush. Let me ask you again. May I take your photograph? There are far too many studies of pompous gentlemen and cherubic infants. Where are all the ladies, that's what I want to know?' Charlotte's silence was a wall, but Her Ladyship pressed on. 'Miss Bell, can't you persuade your friend?'

My cheeks rouged with embarrassment. 'If she doesn't – I mean …'

Lady Rosse took pity on me. 'Her will is forged from metal. Very well, I'll take your photograph, Miss Bell, and Mrs Nicholls shall be my assistant. Perhaps she'll change her mind when she observes the process.' If a countess can be said to wink, she did.

Three footmen were summoned: one scooped up a box of props, another lifted a three-legged stand, while a third took possession of the camera in a wooden box with leather strap and brass attachments. We trooped outdoors to a lawn. I was posed holding a fan. 'Too predictable,' said Her Ladyship. Reading a book. 'Too sedentary,' said Her Ladyship. Stooping to scissor some sweet pea. 'Too delightful!' said Her Ladyship, who approved of the pose because it implied activity. She frowned at us from behind the tripod. Beside her, a footman stood to attention holding equipment whose function I couldn't begin to fathom. 'In a moment, I'll tell you when to start counting out loud, Mrs Nicholls. That's for the exposure.'

'How high do I count? To twenty? Thirty?'

'The light is favourable today so I think a count to ten will be sufficient. Keep absolutely still, Miss Bell. No blinking or fidgeting.' Lady Rosse ducked under the camera cloth. 'Ready, Mrs Nicholls.'

'One, two, three, four, five …'

The requirement to hold my position proved too much for my stiff leg. I swayed. We tried again. I kept wobbling. Impatient sounds floated from under the camera cloth.

'May I make a suggestion?' said Charlotte.

An overheated Lady Rosse ducked out from beneath the heavy cloth, and huffed some air up her face. 'Well?'

'You could have Miss Bell lean on the trunk looking up into the tree, as though she spies something.'

'Such as?'

'A bird's nest? A little girl balanced on one of the branches? It doesn't really matter. What's important is the idea of something just out of sight, catching your subject's interest. That way, your photograph tells a story. But people are free to imagine its shape.'

Her ladyship let fly a whoop of laughter. 'Let's move you over there, Miss Bell. By the oak. Now, can you pretend to be watching an intrepid little minx shimmying up like a monkey? Unless you'd like me to give you a leg up, Mrs Nicholls? And you could act it out for Miss Bell?'

'I believe Miss Bell can manage without me going to those lengths.' Glee lurked in Charlotte's voice.

I shaded my eyes and gazed upwards. 'There's a magpie on one of the branches. Look! There really is. You conjured him up, Charlotte.'

'Assume the position, Miss Bell. And do try to hold this one. I mean my image to convey curiosity, an adventurous spirit, and a sense of happiness.'

'The secret to happiness is to be happy already,' said Charlotte.

*

We met Arthur on the avenue at Cuba Court, jacket off and shirtsleeves rolled above the elbow. He leaned in at the carriage window. 'Come down to the riverbank. It's too hot for indoors.'

'Is there time before supper?' Charlotte asked Mama.

'Certainly, pet.'

Arthur lifted her out of the carriage and spun her about in his arms, his grip sure. 'All dressed up for the Countess of Rosse.'

Hands on her bonnet, she protested, 'Silly boy! Put me down! This hat's already been raided. I don't want it dented, too.'

'Charlotte's hat was attacked at Birr Castle,' I said. 'By a magpie.'

'No one told me,' said Mama.

'It was sitting on the tree where Lady Rosse was taking my photograph. Spotted something shiny on Charlotte's hat, swooped down and helped itself.'

'How vexing,' said Mama.

'Lady Rosse told her footman to fetch a groundsman and shoot the thief. But Charlotte prevented it.'

'Why shouldn't the magpie have my bauble if it fancied it? Besides, it was funny.'

Mama tapped the carriage roof. 'I'd have shot it. Move on, Denis.'

The idling carriage began to roll forward, and I pulled shut the door Arthur had left lying open.

'Aren't you coming Mary?' he cried.

I looked at Mama.

'Take my parasol, dear, you don't want to freckle.'

Arthur gave me his hand to step out, and the three of us ambled towards the river, past fields where puffball sheep munched. At our approach, a scattering of swallows emptied out from a tree and took to the air. Yards of talk spilled from Arthur about a black-legged vixen he'd seen with her cubs. 'They were like human children, the way they wrestled each another.' The riverbank was a counterpane of cowslips, buttercups and dandelions. Charlotte and I sat on a slope, hands clasped around our knees, and Arthur pulled off his tattered sunhat to fan us.

'I've never seen you in a straw hat, dearest.'

'Not mine. Borrowed from the hatstand at Cuba Court.'

'They let you do as you like there.'

'They always have.' He jammed it back on his head. 'I'm off to catch a trout.'

'Without a rod?' asked Charlotte.

'If you're patient, you can do it by hand. And I'm a patient man, Charlotte. It's how I won you.'

'I hope I was worth the wait.'

He lay full length on the riverbank, hands in the water. 'Fishing for a compliment, Mrs Nicholls?'

Not a single daub of cloud smudged the sky. Herons wheeled overhead, and a flash of bright blue and orange streaked past. 'Look! A kingfisher!' cried Charlotte.

It should have been idyllic. But a complaint was wrung from me. 'You're leaving soon and I'll never see you again.'

'Don't fret, my lass, I'm certain we'll meet again. It has to be. You must come to Haworth on a visit. And we'll write to each other – I'll be relying on you for all the Banagher news.'

'There's never any news in Banagher. Nothing to interest you.'

'Everything about Arthur's home interests me. We'll come back to see you all, by and by. You'll be married, with a home of your own.'

'I don't think so.'

'You will.'

A trout landed inches from us, gills flapping.

'Ireland, land of flying fish!' cried Charlotte.

'Sorry!' Arthur scrambled to his feet. 'I threw him farther than I meant.'

'Throw him back, dearest. Today's a day where nothing bad can happen – not even to a fat fish.'

'I promised Aunt Harriette some trout for tea.'

She stood on tiptoe and rested her hands on his shoulders. 'Tell her you humoured your soft-hearted wife.'

While they kissed, I grabbed the quivering fish between both hands and heaved it back into the Shannon.

Charlotte broke away. 'Arthur! You're soaking my dress with your wet hands!'

'I can do better than that.' Arthur jogged to the water, made a container of his hands, scooped, and tossed the contents at Charlotte. A shout of laughter, and she grabbed Mama's parasol and pretended to beat him with it. He picked her up and dangled her at the river's edge.

She kicked her legs, squealing with laughter, and dropped the sunshade. 'Put me down, Arthur. Now! This instant!' As she wriggled, her sun bonnet slipped off and rolled on the ground.

'One, two, three!' He swung, as though preparing to toss her in, and she shrieked and clung to his neck. They collapsed on the bank, where he began tickling her.

'Stop! Stop that! Mercy!' Charlotte was breathless with merriment. 'I'm not one of your fish.'

'You're as slippery as one. I can hardly get a grip on you.'

'Mind my bonnet! You'll flatten it!'

'I like you better without.'

Her face was radiant with love. While they were absorbed in one another, I sat back on the rug and occupied myself with daisy chains, taking pleasure in Charlotte and Arthur's joy-swirl – it was enough for me to be here with both of them. A fish somersaulted in the river and Arthur raised his head at its splash. He noticed me, and pulled me down onto the grass with them. Lulled by river sounds and warmed by sunshine, the three of us mingled together in a tangle of limbs and laughter.

CHAPTER 25

Lizzie Nolan went missing that night. By the time we returned from our river walk, she'd left for her friend's American wake. To our surprise, she wasn't home by breakfast. One of the other maids had to serve us, and Mama's face wore a sour-apple look over Lizzie's absence. She sent Denis Coughlan to make inquiries of Mona Scully, who said she'd left the party shortly after midnight to walk home along the riverbank. Refused all offers of company. Said her head was fizzing, and the night air would cool it.

Mention of the riverbank sent up a distress signal.

'We need to organize a search party,' said Arthur. Richard's face crumpled and he chewed on the ball of his thumb. Arthur threw an arm around his shoulders and squeezed. 'I know you feel responsible, as head of the house. Don't worry, we'll find her. I'll ask Denis to round up some of the locals.'

'We should ask for help from the military at the Bridge Barracks, too.'

'Good idea. Will you ride over?'

Volunteers were soon assembled and a hunt began, while Mama, Charlotte and I waited at home. I imagined the men beating the riverbank, splashing through the shallows and calling Lizzie's name. Perhaps she'd fallen and hurt herself. With each hour that passed, we feared the worst, but no one wanted to name what we dreaded.

A knock on the parlour door revealed Mrs Foley. 'Ma'am, there's a trick I've heard tell of, to turn up a body from the river.' She blessed herself. 'You lights a candle. Places it on a good, strong leaf. That's our boat. Then you floats it down the river. The candle's caught by whatever twist in the current has the body trapped. If it's a body we're looking for, God help us all.'

'Mary, fetch a candle,' said Mama. 'A half-burnt one from a candlestick, nothing too tall. It's less likely to topple over. Make it two, just in case.'

Returning from my errand, I encountered Hope Porter, hair snarled and eyes swollen. 'We'll find Lizzie. I promise, Hope.' I stooped down, wiped her face with my handkerchief and held it to her nose. 'Blow. Good girl.'

'I wanted to help. But Art'ur said go home,' she sniffled.

'He knew we needed you here.' I took her hand and led her to sit with us.

'Send Ben Coughlan down to the men with those candles, Mary,' said Mama.

'He's out looking for Lizzie. Everyone's helping. Why don't I carry them down?'

'I'll go with you,' offered Charlotte.

'Very well,' said Mama. 'I'll stay here in case Lizzie turns up.'

'Lizzie's been ate up be the river,' whimpered Hope.

'Nonsense,' said Mama. 'Now, Hope, I want you to keep me company. So I'm not left alone. Wouldn't that be a good idea?' A half-nod. 'That's my girl. I'll show you how to do embroidery. Would you like to learn? But first, we have to do something about those knots in your hair. Mary, fetch me a brush before you go.'

'I'll get one. My room's closer.' Charlotte sped out and returned with a case lined in pink silk, containing a matching mirror, brush and comb made of bone. She saw me notice some of the comb's teeth had snapped off. 'Emily threw it at Branwell when he wasn't himself,' she whispered. 'She'd a bit of a temper.'

*

Charlotte and I made all speed towards the searchers, and I was glad of her company because the suck of water caused me to shiver. We followed the sound of Lizzie's name tossed through the air – the men, who were working in pairs strung out at intervals, called it aloud. Some waded through the shallows, swiping at rushes with sticks. The soldiers were methodical, but the locals who knew Lizzie looked dispirited, and communicated a sense of misgiving. A huddle of women bunched nearby, several with shawls over their heads as though already in mourning. I regretted not bringing food as well as candles. Arthur saw us first and stamped over in rubber boots.

'Any news?' I asked.

He shook his head, tension crowding his face. 'Is Hope above in the house?'

'Aunt Harriette's looking after her,' said Charlotte.

'Don't worry, she won't let her come down here again,' I reassured him.

'It's no place for her,' said Arthur.

Richard heard our voices and joined us. I gave him one of Mama's candles, repeating what Mrs Foley had said. He took it without a word – and without being able to look me in the eye.

Charlotte produced a sturdy oval leaf. 'I found this on our way down, I think it should hold the candle's weight.'

Arthur went to speak to the army sergeant further up the riverbank. The searchers fell silent, watching while Richard lit the candle, placed it on the leaf, and set it afloat. It bobbed about, disturbing some wading birds. Arthur returned to gather Charlotte towards him, but when Richard put out a hand to console me, I warded him off with my eyes.

A sudden movement, and the candle was pulled forward by the current. All of us, searchers and local women included, followed after. Its light was extinguished by a splash of water, but on it sailed, and led us to poor, drowned Lizzie Nolan wedged in and hidden by a clump of reeds. A hush that was almost solid matter fell as Arthur and Richard, along with two soldiers, lifted her out and laid her on her back on the riverbank. It was a sight that clenched my insides. Our Lizzie was a flesh-and-blood creature turned to alabaster. Her hair stuck to her face in clumps, her mouth drooped open, her eyes stared at nothingness. A stripe of weed was folded around her neck like a scarf. Lizzie's sodden gown was muddy, and one shoe had gone missing – her big toe stuck out through a hole in the stocking.

Arthur bent and brushed shut Lizzie's eyes, smoothed the lank hair off her face and unhooked the weed. Then he knelt and began praying aloud over her body, and Richard went on his knees beside him. Other voices joined in the prayers, ours included. Throughout, I kept my gaze fixed on Lizzie's wet face. Thank God the fish hadn't nibbled her flesh. All at once, the prayers were interrupted by a sound, once heard, you'd never forget. It was an opera of shrieks, and came from the women.

'What's that?' Charlotte's voice in my ear.

'The *caoine*.'

Arthur and Richard knew better than to continue prayers while the people's lament was ululating. Arthur straightened Lizzie's limbs, folded her arms in front of her, and tugged down her dress where it had ridden up. A bulge below her hips became apparent. He put his hand into a side pocket of her skirt, and out came a fistful of rocks. The other hand probed the opposite pocket – more rocks.

'Suicide.' The word flew from mouth to mouth. The *caoine* faltered, a shudder passed through the throng.

*

'What did you say to Lizzie?' I hissed at Richard.

His face was blotchy, as if he'd been crying, but now his eyes were flat – he seemed determined to brazen it out. 'I don't know what you mean.'

'She went to see you yesterday.'

'Don't try blaming this on me.'

'Of course you're to blame.'

'Nobody asked her to throw herself in the river. She'd a melancholic streak, everyone knew she did. I suppose she was depressed because her friend was emigrating.'

'Don't take me for an idiot. She was at her wits' end because of the baby.'

Tight-mouthed, he seized my arms, fingers pressing in. I tried shaking him off but his grip was inexorable. 'What did she tell you?'

'Enough.'

He shook me. 'Answer me!'

'You did it again, didn't you, Richard?'

'I don't know what you're talking about.'

'Yes, you do! You can't leave them alone, can you!'

'Watch what you're saying, Mary.'

'I know about Hope Porter. Hope Bell, she is really.'

'Keep your voice down!' In his agitation, his fingers bit deep, and I winced. 'Hope living here was Arthur's idea. Not mine.'

'It was a good-hearted act from a good-hearted man. But yours is black, Richard Bell. Rotten to the core.'

'If this gets out, I'll lose the headmastership. And you and Mama will lose your home.'

It gave me pause. I didn't care for myself, but our mother loved Cuba Court – who was I to turn her out of the house?

298

Deprive her of its conservatory and rose garden? Dispossess her of the parkland and wooded walkways? I stared at my pleasure-seeking brother, fearful only about his loss of status. Not a word of contrition over Lizzie Nolan. But what would happen to Mama and me if Richard's reputation and livelihood crumbled? Where would we go? Lizzie's drowned face, eyes dulled by hopelessness, came to mind and I pushed away my selfish thoughts. 'You took your pleasure, then washed your hands of Lizzie. And she'd nowhere to turn. No family, no money.'

'I never pretended ...'

'You did! You let her believe something that wasn't true! And when it was over, you didn't lift a finger to help her!'

'I couldn't.'

'You turned your back on Lizzie. She trusted you and look where she ended up.'

'It wasn't my fault!'

'Then whose, if not yours?'

He released me, and I rubbed my bruised arms. More to myself, than Richard, I said, 'There must have been a way for poor Lizzie to keep her baby.'

His mouth thinned, and maybe some self-loathing was clotted through the self-pity. 'Fill Cuba Court with my bastards? Now there's a solution to the servant shortage.'

*

Lizzie's body rested on a table in a room off the hall in Cuba Court, dressed in my best nightgown, her hair combed and plaited. Mama and Mrs Foley had laid her out. Mama's tallest beeswax candles were at her head and feet, and Mrs Foley had worked a set of rosary beads through the stiff fingers.

The house was at sixes and sevens. The coroner had ridden over with a surgeon, both men examined the body, and the coroner said it was an unnatural death, which required an inquest. He insisted one should be convened in our house for convenience, and sent out a summons for a dozen 'good and honest' men from Banagher and neighbouring parishes, who were now kicking their heels in our library. They had already been taken to see the spot where Lizzie was found. Proceedings were due to start as soon as the coroner, deep in private discussion with Richard, was ready.

Mrs Foley was agitated at the idea of having to give evidence, but Arthur reassured her it wouldn't be necessary.

'Apart from anything else, you can't rely on the people's word in any kind of legal proceedings,' I heard him tell Charlotte. 'They don't regard those oaths as binding. Family promises are more sacred to them.'

'Emily used to say God's law takes precedence over man's,' said Charlotte.

'Hmm. In principle, yes but, it's not particularly helpful in court.'

Mama rustled over to join them. 'Poor Lizzie. I wish I'd known she had troubles. Self-murder!' Mama winced.

'At least her family are all gone – there's no one left to feel the shame,' said Arthur.

'Maybe it's the loss of her family that drove her to it,' said Mama.

My eyes drilled into Richard, a ball of anger expanding inside my chest. He must have felt me stare at him because he glanced up, and an imploring expression took hold of his face.

'Quiet, please, let's make a start,' said the coroner.

The surgeon gave evidence of death by drowning. Richard stuttered through an account of the search for Lizzie, while the sergeant from Banagher barracks described her retrieval from the river, and mentioned the stones found in her pockets. Members of the jury exchanged looks. The coroner uttered the word 'suicide' and the verdict appeared to be inevitable.

Charlotte stood up. 'It wasn't suicide.'

'You are?' asked the coroner.

'Mrs Arthur Nicholls. A guest in this house, and family member by marriage.'

One hand kneaded the material of her dress. I edged closer and squeezed the free hand.

'And do you have evidence you wish to lay before the court?'

'I do, Sir. Miss Nolan was gathering the stones on my behalf. I told her I wanted them for a rockery in Haworth. As a souvenir of Banagher. She promised to find me some specimens.' The coroner looked sceptical. 'Miss Nolan said riverbank stones were the fittest for purpose.'

'Can anyone corroborate this conversation?' asked the coroner.

I stood up. 'I can. I heard it. Mary Anna Bell, daughter of the house.'

'Very well. I direct the jury to take account of this evidence entered into the court.'

The verdict was death by misadventure.

*

It meant Lizzie was allowed to have a Christian burial. The priest would come from Birr to say the Romanist prayers, and attend to the various trappings that matter to those of Lizzie's persuasion. We kept her in Cuba Court until she went into the ground. Charlotte wanted to delay their departure to attend. Everybody told her it was quite a sight to witness an Irish wake and funeral – the people were rowdy in their display. But Arthur and Charlotte left before it. Arthur had steamer tickets to take them on the Shannon to Limerick, and onwards by rail to Kilkee.

The household gathered on the steps for their leave-taking. Hope stood holding Mrs Foley's hand, watching Denis and Ben load luggage into the carriage. Mama was giving instructions about regular letter-writing to Arthur and Charlotte, but he extracted himself and came over to me.

'Charlotte's attended too many funerals. She doesn't need to see another young woman shouldered by neighbours to her grave.' I nodded. 'Keep an eye on Hope for me, Mary. She'll take Lizzie's death hard.'

'Arthur!' called Richard, and he excused himself.

I beckoned to Hope. 'After they leave, let's you and me pick some flowers for Lizzie.'

'Should I give her Marigold? So she's not alone.'

I crouched down to bring my face level with hers, noticing shadows under her eyes. 'No, Hope, Marigold's yours. Lizzie wouldn't want you to lose her.'

Charlotte finished her farewells and came last to Hope and me. Speechless, Charlotte and I hugged, bone against bone. When we separated, she bent down to Hope, hooked a forefinger under her chin, and tilted her face. 'Keep practising your reading, Hope. To read is to fly!'

*

From Haworth, Mama had regular letters from Arthur, and a thank-you note from Charlotte, but I looked in vain for a letter to me. The disappointment made me wonder if I'd imagined our friendship. Then a letter with the Birr Castle insignia was delivered to Mama, which triggered the usual excitement caused by any interaction with the Rosses. It contained two photographs from our visit there.

Mama studied the shiny black-and-white images. 'It's too bad we can't see your face properly, Mary. Why are you leaning on that tree? What are you looking at?'

'A bird. It's called a pose, Mama.'

She clicked her tongue. 'And the other one is fuzzy. I thought Lady Rosse was meant to be good at this.' She set them aside to parse Her Ladyship's note again.

I picked up the discarded photographs. They were as small as art miniatures, two inches wide by an inch-and-a-half long.

One showed the rear view of a girl in a summer dress, bonnet dangling by its ribbons between her shoulder blades. Her gloved palms rested on a tree trunk, and she was gazing into the branches. The other photograph had the same girl in profile, facing a woman in spectacles standing over to the side. These figures were out of focus.

'Lady Rosse says one of the photographs is ruined because you're both moving and it's blurred,' Mama read aloud. 'But she thought you might like it anyway.'

My eyes rested on the image. The smaller figure was pointing at something in the tree, and holding her hat with the other hand. The taller person was reaching out with an arm towards the other – so close they were almost touching.

Both women were laughing.

Epilogue

1928

HAWORTH, YORKSHIRE

The elderly woman didn't stand out among the throng of sight-seers, and initially the guide was too busy fielding questions to pay attention to her.

Was she Jane Eyre?

Which sister was the best writer?

Was there a real-life Mr Rochester?

Out of the corner of his eye, he noticed her response to a solemn-faced engraving of Charlotte Brontë near the front door. It seemed to bedazzle her. She reached out a gloved hand as if to touch it, before pulling back. Such behaviour wasn't unusual at Haworth Parsonage, however, where emotion brimmed up. Brontë disciples flocked there to breathe the air inhaled by the doomed sisters, as he liked to characterize them, and trail their fingers along walls which had sheltered literary genius. Brontë-ites tended to be demonstrative. Even borderline hysterical. He'd been offered bribes for anything belonging to the family: a snippet of their handwriting, a ribbon, a scrap of sewing. An unscrupulous person could take advantage of the Brontë fetish.

As he finished fielding questions, the woman caught his eye again. Not because of her appearance – slightly stooped, hair like tarnished silver under a grey felt hat, bright eyes in a creased face – but because of the way she cradled her elbows in her hands, making it seem as if she were hugging a secret.

'Thank you, ladies and gentlemen. We have a gift shop with Brontë souvenirs, including handsome editions of their novels. Anything you purchase here will be used to keep the parsonage running. It may be one of the smallest museums in England, but I'm sure you'll agree its charms are on a considerable scale. Any final questions before we part company?'

'Who did you say Charlotte was married to?' asked one of the party.

'The Reverend Arthur Bell Nicholls, her father's curate.' He reeled off facts. *Brief but happy marriage … died upstairs in this very house … whom the gods love die young … widower remained devoted to his bride's memory ... stayed in Haworth to care for his elderly father-in-law.*

The woman in the grey hat had a gaze that was crowding him. With an effort, he collected his train of thought. 'After the death of Patrick Brontë, coincidentally both the first and last of the Brontës, the Reverend Nicholls returned to his native Ireland.'

'You mean Haworth turned him out,' said the woman. A factual tone of voice. An Irish accent.

'Most regrettable. As you say, he must have had expectations. But he wasn't appointed to the living after the Reverend Brontë's passing.'

'It's like a time capsule in here,' said another visitor. 'Did the family leave everything to the nation?'

'Unfortunately not. The parsonage was Church property, and after Patrick Brontë's death it went to the next incumbent. When Arthur Nicholls left, he emptied it out.'

'He took what belonged to him,' said the Irishwoman, conversational rather than confrontational.

The guide, who was also the museum's deputy director, fingered uneasily under his collar. 'Many of the exhibits you see here were transported to Ireland by him. As Patrick Brontë's heir, he inherited more or less everything. But towards the end of his life, he sold some items. His widow sold more. There have been auctions. We buy what we can. We've also acquired relics from the family of Martha Brown, the parsonage servant. But as you can imagine, competition in the salerooms is stiff.'

'Money talks,' said another voice.

'We compete with private collectors and their deep pockets.' The deputy director looked rueful. 'The museum is a work in progress. But we're proud to have the world's largest collection of Brontëana. And now, ladies and gentlemen, your tour is at an end. Feel free to visit the shop before you leave.'

He had to pass the Irishwoman.

'I can't help wondering,' she said.

'Yes, Madam?'

'Can a museum ever own too much?'

'I suppose it can house surplus objects in its storerooms.'

'That's not what I mean.'

'Everything can't go on show.'

Her forehead furrowed. 'How is it something is treasure one day and storage the next?'

'Better examples come along. Good day.' He continued on his way.

Ten minutes later, a volunteer knocked on the office door. 'Sorry to disturb you, Mr Warburton, but there's a lady here I think you should meet. She's something to Charlotte Brontë's husband.'

He turned hot, then cold. 'Elderly? Irish? In a dark green coat?'

'That's her. We fell to chatting. Turns out she knew Arthur Nicholls ever so well.'

'Would you be good enough to show her in, Miss Skelly?'

'Might be better if you invite her yourself, Mr Warburton. She's in the gift shop.'

He straightened his tie and went in search of her, past window seats and walls heavy with wainscoting. She was queuing to buy postcards.

'My dear lady, no need to wait in line, allow me to present them to you on behalf of Brontë Parsonage Museum. Won't you share a pot of tea in my office? You'll find it less packed than the village establishments.'

He ushered her into a cluttered room, calling over his shoulder to Miss Skelly to organize a tray.

'I regret, Madam, that the director is not with us today. He'd be honoured to welcome you personally. Allow me to give you my card. May I inquire your name?'

'Miss Hope Porter.' She took a seat, her eyes roaming the room.

'And what do you make of our little shrine to the Brontës, Miss Porter?'

'I've often walked these rooms in my imagination. It's strange, finally, to set foot in the place. Master Arthur wasn't a talkative man, but he spoke about the parsonage. Always fondly. And about the people from around here, too. Less fondly.'

Ah, a servant, he thought. From the way she spoke, he'd taken her for a lady. 'Was your master Arthur Bell Nicholls?'

'He was.'

'Most unfortunate about the living. He was the Reverend Brontë's right-hand man.'

'All water under the bridge now. Maybe he was better off in Banagher. Where he was appreciated.'

'I trust you've enjoyed your visit, Miss Porter?'

'I see familiar friends at every turn. None of them were museum pieces to us. They were just Charlotte Brontë's things. I know that portrait like my own face. And the grandfather clock you showed us – that stood on the landing in the house where I worked. Clanging away the hours for half a century. Master Arthur was particular about it. Wound it at nine o'clock every evening.'

'As Patrick Brontë did before him. We're delighted it made its way back to its original home. The portrait's only a copy, sadly.'

'I dare say there's sense to the clock being here. But it's a crying shame to see the way people snoop about, poring over her belongings. I don't mind her sketches and books. But her dresses, her shoes, her sewing box, her jewellery. It's indecent!'

'That's a harsh assessment, Miss Porter.'

'There's people here never read one of her books, and never will. But they pay their money and that gives them the right to stare at what she wore, used, mended, valued. Things that were part of her life.'

'They come to worship at a site of literary genius.'

'They come for a right good nosey.'

'Oh surely –'

'Making an exhibition of her bits and pieces is just plain wrong.'

Warburton blushed. 'We give the public what it wants. Just so I'm clear in my mind, Miss Porter, how long did you work for Arthur Nicholls? This was in Ireland, I presume?'

'I worked for the Bells. All my life, from when I was old enough to shell a basin of peas or polish a stair rod. Master Arthur, he always did right by me. I helped to nurse him in his final illness, Laid out his wife, Miss Mary, and followed her coffin to the graveyard. She was the second Mrs Arthur Nicholls. After Charlotte Brontë.'

'Ah, Mary Anna Bell, I was forgetting her.'

'People do.' A sharp inhalation. 'Both of them dead and gone now. I know time stands still in this parsonage, but it trots along in the outside world.'

'It was before my time here, but I understand the lady in question was good enough to give us first refusal on various items of memorabilia in her possession. She said her husband would have wished it.'

'Miss Mary had a sense of delicacy. She valued Charlotte Brontë's things because Master Arthur did, and took care of them. But circumstances forced her hand.'

'Is it long since …?'

'Nineteen-fifteen.' A beat. 'She was kind to me in her will.'

Instantly, Warburton fathomed the significance. 'Is it possible you have some Brontë artefacts?'

'A few things.'

'The museum would be most interested in acquiring anything belonging to Charlotte and the other Brontës – anything at all.' A pause, while he waited for a response. None came. 'We maintain our exhibits in perfect conditions. We'll hand them over, intact, to future generations.'

'I don't have anything against this museum, as such – it's nicely done.'

A knock rat-a-tatted. 'Enter.' Miss Skelly carried in a tray with a pot of tea and a plate of gingerbread. Warburton's leg jiggled while she served it. Hope Porter unpeeled her gloves and set them on her lap, accepted a cup and saucer but refused food. Miss Skelly was disposed to dally, but Warburton sent her on his way.

'We know he took her wedding dress to Ireland.'

Hope swallowed a mouthful of tea. 'I used to look after it. Made sure the moths didn't get to it.'

'Oh, Miss Porter! You know it?' A nod. 'It's an item our lady visitors never fail to inquire after. A cultural artefact of great significance. Charlotte Brontë set out from this very house wearing those bridal garments. Think how fitting it would be to bring them home again!'

'To let the world and his wife look them over? Feeding their fancies? Brontëmania, Miss Mary called it. A cult. Unhealthy.'

'Don't rush to judgment. Consider, Miss Porter. She slipped out of the parsonage one summer's morning, two dear friends by her side. When she returned for the wedding breakfast, she entered on the arm of her husband, her name changed to Mrs Arthur Nicholls. The dress would be the centrepiece of a breathtaking display – we'd recreate the bridal party. People could marvel at how so much greatness came from such a tiny frame.'

'You'd make a peep show of something sacred.'

'Don't think that, I beg you! We'd honour the bridal clothes. As we honour her. That family of prodigies lived and laboured together inside these four walls. And the moors from which Charlotte drew her inspiration lie just beyond them. Her essence is here.'

'That's as may be. But ask yourself this. What would Charlotte Brontë make of her belongings going on display?'

'Why, I imagine she'd be flattered. She's revered in Haworth.'

'Then you imagine wrongly. She was a private person who shrank from attention. I may not know much, but I know that.'

'How do you know?'

'I met her in Banagher. I was only a small-little girl but I've never forgotten her.'

He stared. 'You talked to her?'

'A few times.'

'About what?'

'Nothing important. I was barely seven years of age.'

'Even so, Miss Porter! You're a bridge to her!'

Hope made an impatient gesture with her hand. 'I'm telling you, she'd be aghast at strangers trooping through her home. Everything laid out for people to goggle at.'

'Objects have always fascinated humankind. The Greeks had a name for it. *Charis.*'

'You're using her to put Haworth on the map. She's the jewel in your tourism industry. The reason your streets are full of visitors. Meals ordered, rooms rented, souvenirs sold, all because of Charlotte Brontë. Is it only about respect? I wonder.'

Warburton stiffened. 'We celebrate her life and work. We pay her the attention she deserves. Why are you here, Miss Porter, if you feel so strongly about it?'

'Yes, you may say I'm as bad as the rest. But I didn't come from idle curiosity, although I inspected everything in your display cases. Haworth was a place I grew up hearing about. It was always in my head to take a look at it. To see if the stories measured up to the reality. And I have another reason.' She drummed her fingers on her lap. 'To make up my mind. I'm not getting any younger. I'd like it settled before I pass on.'

'The Brontë memorabilia you inherited?'

'If you want to call it that. It's something Miss Mary gave me a year or so before she passed away. Small, but important.'

'Which Brontë is it connected with?'

'Charlotte. But I don't know that I want to say any more about it just now. I'm still turning it over in my mind. Maybe that portrait on your wall is enough.'

Excited, he exclaimed, 'You have another portrait?'

'No. It's just something Lady Rosse of Birr Castle had a hand in. But I've said too much.'

'Your hesitation is understandable. May I arrange for you to meet our board and one or two of our principal donors? Sir

James Roberts in particular? He bought the parsonage from the Ecclesiastical Commission several years ago, and handed the deeds to us. It would be a privilege to demonstrate how seriously we take this duty – this privilege – of preserving Charlotte Brontë's legacy.'

'I'm only in the area for another day.'

'It would be our honour to host a dinner for you. There are people who'd consider it an honour to hear your memories of her.'

'They'd be sorely disappointed, Mr Warburton. I've nothing worth telling.'

He bit his lip and regrouped. 'About the relics you mentioned. At least tell me you won't let some other institution have them.'

'I can't make any promises.'

'Irreplaceable artefacts have been scattered abroad. To private collectors who make miser's gold of what they buy. Ours is a democratic treasure house – we share what we have. Dare I hope … is the wedding dress in your possession?'

'No, that's gone.'

'To America?'

'To ashes.'

'Burnt!'

'I'm afraid so.'

'That's a sin!'

'Sin or not, it's gone.' She began putting her gloves back on. 'My friends are expecting me. I must say goodbye. Thank you for the tea.'

Warburton accompanied her to the front door of the parsonage, and down three steps to the path. Ahead sat a square-towered church. 'You must be careful on the hill, Miss Porter. It's easy to slip. But perhaps you're planning to walk on the moor? Visitors often do.'

She glanced skywards, then down at her umbrella. 'Looks like rain. I think I'll go by Sexton House, to see where Master Arthur lodged before his marriage.'

'Allow me to arrange a personal visit. It's just up there on Parsonage Lane.'

'I'm happy enough to stand outside and look.'

'Why don't I step over with you? It's beside the National School where Arthur Nicholls taught the children scripture. He kept treats in his pocket for them, so the villagers say.'

'I'm not one bit surprised. He did the same for me, back in the day. Master Arthur had a great fondness for children, and a sweet tooth himself. I remember him crunching sugar lumps.'

Warburton kept pace with Hope Porter through the modest front garden of the parsonage. Its perimeter wall separated it from the churchyard, where mossy gravestones jostled one another. 'They might as well have lived slap bang in the middle of the graveyard,' said Warburton. 'But at least the moor was at their back.' He stood aside at the garden gate, allowing her to precede him, then guided her along a passageway. They arrived at a cottage a few doors from the church, and he indicated an upstairs window.

'Arthur Nicholls rented that room from John Brown, the sexton. Who was also the gravedigger. And drinking companion to Branwell Brontë. Martha Brown was his daughter.'

'Funny to think of Master Arthur up there, pining for Charlotte Brontë.'

He pointed back at the parsonage. 'He could see the light in her bedroom window from his room. Would you like me to bring you into the church, Miss Porter? St Michael and All Angels. It's where Charlotte and her family are buried. They're in a vault below the floor. I can show you the spot.'

'I stopped off there first. Saw the plaque.'

'She'd have worshipped there every Sunday. Listened to her father preaching, and later her husband.'

'The master had a lovely voice. A touch of melancholy in it. I must be going now, Mr Warburton.'

'Do you know your way? You mentioned friends.'

'We're lunching in that public house.' She stabbed her umbrella towards the Black Bull.

'It's been a privilege, Miss Porter. I hope we meet again. Won't you let me have your address?' He scribbled down what Hope dictated, and floated the idea of visiting her in Banagher, a proposal to which she neither agreed nor disagreed. 'Miss Porter, may I shake your hand in parting? After all, it's the hand of someone who met the great Charlotte. Can you recall anything she said to you?'

'I remember she was kind to me.'

'In what way?'

'In ways that belong to me, Mr Warburton. Nobody else. Miss Mary told me that. Ever such a long way ago.' She wrinkled her nose, struck by a thought. 'Yet it feels like yesterday.'

Gripping her umbrella's carved ivory handle, Hope tapped across the uneven cobblestones. At the pub door, she turned back to see if Warburton was still visible. He understood she had something further to add and hurried to close the gap. 'I do have something else you might be interested in. A story Charlotte Brontë wrote in Ireland. I don't think it was ever published.'

'An unpublished story?' The palms of Warburton's hands felt suddenly moist. 'Are you quite certain?'

'Miss Mary told me. She found it in her papers and recognized it. I've been thinking maybe other people have a right to read it. Makes more sense than prying into her things.'

He had a handkerchief out, mopping at the back of his neck. 'Can you tell me anything about the story?'

'It's called "The Phantom House". I've read it many's the time. A ghost story she heard from an aunt of hers.

'You must mean Aunt Branwell.'

'Not her. An Irish aunt.'

'I wasn't aware she had contact with any Irish aunt.' Warburton felt his legs begin to shake, and realized he needed to sit down. 'Miss Porter, this is tremendously exciting. May I make arrangements to view the manuscript?'

'As a matter of fact, I have it with me. My friends are minding my bag. Come inside with me now, and I'll let you take a look at it.'

1932

BLANCHARD'S AUCTION HOUSE, THE STRAND, LONDON WC1

Note made by proprietor Thomas Blanchard, 7th July 1932

THE PHANTOM HOUSE is an unpublished story found among Charlotte Brontë's papers following the death in 1930 of Hope Porter, a household servant to the Bells of Banagher. It was put up for auction but failed to make its reserve. Subsequently, it was offered for private sale and bought by an anonymous collector using an intermediary. Thereafter its whereabouts are unknown.

Scholars are unconvinced of the authorship for four reasons. First, the hand-writing has been identified as that of Mary Anna Nicholls, second wife to Charlotte Brontë's husband Arthur Bell Nicholls. Second, the signature at the end, although in a different hand, is a clumsy rendition of Charlotte Brontë's. Third, the story is located in Ireland, and apart from a piece of juvenilia as a child, the authoress used no Irish settings. Fourth, the tone is somewhat different to her known work.

The general consensus is that Mary Nicholls rather than Charlotte Brontë is the author, and the work is an act of homage, or possibly wish fulfilment, rather than a genuine example of Brontë literature. This copy of the tale was made before its sale and has been kept as a curiosity.

*

THE PHANTOM HOUSE

by Charlotte Brontë

Mary Bell, a young widow without family and forced to rely on her own resources, had filled the role of housekeeper at Cuba Court for six months without ever meeting her employer. She understood from the agent that he was overseas and rarely visited his ancestral seat in the northern part of Ireland. One day, she received a letter from her master with instructions to make a visitor welcome – a cartographer charged by government interests with mapping that section of the countryside. She should also arrange a local man to act as his guide. Mrs Bell carried out his orders and everything was made ready for the visitor.

The gentleman arrives as night draws in. She answers the door to him holding an oil lamp. At his request, she shows Mr Logan some of the ground-floor rooms – the drawing room, dining room, and so on. They are high-ceilinged and spacious, with handsome furnishings, but the passages have a despondent air. He settles into the library, where a turf fire burns, its earthy

perfume conjuring up ancient oaks and mossy glens, and asks
for his supper to be served there on a card table. When Mrs Bell
returns to collect his empty tray, he detains her with questions
about the area. She does her best, but tells him a farmer's son has
been hired as his guide, and can give fuller answers.

'Does your master visit often?'

'We never see hide nor hair of him, Sir. He's as rare as a white
blackbird. If that's all, Sir, I'll be on my way. John Eccles will be
here for you bright and early in the morning.'

As she prepares to leave, a gust of wind sends a shower of
soot tumbling down the chimney, causing the fire to crackle.

'If any house has a ghost, it must surely be this one,' says
Logan.

'I've heard nothing in that line, Sir.'

'Of course not, I was joking.'

'Though there's a phantom house a half dozen miles from
here. I've seen it with my own eyes. Well, good night to you, Sir.'

'Mrs Bell! You can't leave a statement like that dangling in
the air! Sit down, I implore you, and tell me the story.'

Logan pulls up a chair to the fire for the housekeeper, and
returns to his seat. 'Wait, now, till I light my pipe.' Soon, he is
puffing out tobacco fumes, boots on the fender.

Mrs Bell stares into the flames.

'I was only in my present position a matter of weeks, Sir.
One afternoon, I was tramping the bogland – truth be told, I'm
never happier than when out and about. I love to see the maid-
enhair, with those starry flowers, and maybe catch a glimpse of
a hare. But that day a mist blew up, and I went astray. I knew to
take cover, and looked for an animal byre, but there was none to
be seen. Then I spied a faint glow and made my way towards it.
It was a lantern, hung beside a gate post. Stone acorns the size of
kitchen stools were set on top of the posts.

I peered past them and made out the shadowy outline of a
yard. All was quiet, not even a dog's bark, which I took to be
on account of the mist. The animals must be indoors, I said to

myself. Even so, there was an odd stillness about the place – as though even the air was holding its breath. I hesitated, but urged myself onwards. Maybe there was a house at the end of the path, or some kind of shelter. After all, somebody left out that lantern. I lifted it down, and used it to pick my way through the swirls of mist. My hand touched a wall, then a door.

I knocked, and was relieved to hear footsteps. The bolt was shot back, and as the door groaned open, a thought caused me a flash of unease. Not all houses welcome strangers. But what choice did I have? A respectable-looking woman stood there, aged seventy or thereabouts. I introduced myself, apologized for taking the lantern off the gatepost, and threw myself on the stranger's mercy.

–The lantern was left for you. To help you find us. You'd best come in. My brother's in the kitchen.

The room was shadowy with candlelight. Her brother was the mirror image of the woman who'd admitted me. Grave, handsome, resilient. The Good Book was held between his hands.

–She's here now, Enoch.

–We've been expecting you, he said.

Three chairs were arranged in a semi-circle. Enoch indicated one to me, she took another, and he sat upright in the middle seat. At once, he was all business. On went a pair of spectacles, and he read aloud from the Book of Kings.

–*And the word of the Lord came unto him saying, "Get thee hence, and turn thee eastward, and hide thyself by the brook Cherith that is before Jordan. And it shall be that thou shalt drink of the brook. And I have commanded the ravens to feed thee there." So he went and did according unto the word of the Lord. And the ravens brought him bread and flesh in the morning, and bread and flesh in the evening; and he drank of the brook.*

Enoch Alcorn closed the book.

–We must learn to await the Lord God's designs. Just as He appointed the ravens to feed Elijah, we must trust to His care.

The Lord God never disappoints. But he expects His people to have faith amidst tribulation.

–The Lord God could have sent His angels with food for Elijah, but chose to use ravens, said Enoch's sister. It was His way of showing He can serve His own purposes by the meanest creatures as easily as the mightiest.

–And now, let us reflect on the Lord God's ways in private prayer.

They bowed their heads and closed their eyes, hands clasped. I couldn't resist a peep around the room, and spotted that each chair-back had an acorn design carved into it. The man's eyes fastened on me, catching my inattention.

–Supper time, sister, he said.

They returned the chairs to the table, after which hot milk, bread and cheese were produced. Despite the peculiarity of my situation, I was starving and made a hearty meal.

–What name do you go by, Sir? I asked.

–I'm Enoch Alcorn. This is my sister Leah.

–And your house? Has it a name? I haven't noticed it before on my rambles, but perhaps I strayed further than I realized.

–Alcorn Farm. He drained his mug and said he had to tend to the livestock.

–Won't you lose your way in the fog?

–None is lost who trusts in God's mercy.

Alone in the kitchen with his sister, I tried some further questions.

–Miss Alcorn, would you mind –

–I'm no Miss Alcorn. I was wed. Mrs McDowell is my name.

–And Mr McDowell?

–Gone to meet his Maker this many's a long year. His death was a release.

–Was he in a great deal of pain?

–A release for me, young lady. He wanted a son to carry on the family name, and I was able to give birth to none but dead childer. Year after year, I carried them, growed them and delivered them. But never a one saw a full day of life. Some drew breath on their own for a matter of hours, mewling their thin cries. But they took fits, nobody knowed why. And some couldn't utter even a single cry. It was fit to kill me, this endless birthing of babes. I couldn't thole it for the grief it laid on me, never mind being dangersome. But Mr McDowell, he give me no respite. On and on I must go.

–That must have been …

–Aye, it was.

She carried the crockery and cutlery to the sink, added hot water from the kettle suspended on a crane above the fire, and began to wash the dishes. I wiped them and put them away, seeing by the gaps on the dresser where cups and plates belonged. We worked in silence. But when we were finished, Leah McDowell took up the threads of her tale again.

–All my childer was perfect. Not misshapen in any way. Years went by. I grew weaker. It breaks a body's spirit, a hard fate like that.

–*God in your mercy set aside a hard fate*, I said, a quote I heard often in the house where I was reared.

–There were no mercy for me. On and on, nine little markers over thirteen years. Till I cried, "Enough! I'll have no more!" Watch my babes turn blue in my arms? Choke and struggle for breath, and lose the fight? I'm done wi childbirth! And I locked my bedroom door agin him. So he got the parson in to me. Mr Spottiswood. I couldn't refuse my husband, says he, casting up my marriage vows. It was God's will our infants died.

–Maybe it was God's way of saying stop trying for a child.

–Aye, you have the right of it. The childer are buried side by side in a plot of land at the back of the house. Facing a stretch of water we call the Cat's Cradle. Nine wee markers planted there, nine wee souls beneath. I wasn't let bury them in the churchyard.

–I'm sure where you chose is as good as any churchyard. God cares nothing for such niceties.

–We must hope so.

–I'm convinced of it, Mrs McDowell.

–Bless you, lass. I begged Mr Spottiswood to tell me we'd all meet in Paradise – that the Good Lord so willed it. Pleaded with him to show me that mercy. But it were beyond his power, he said, because my babes were born with original sin on their souls. They needed baptism for to remove the stain. I told him I'd shifted for myself as best I could be the time the fourth child was born. When the birth pangs was splitting me asunder, I asked the woman tending to me for a beaker of water. I poured it between my legs, wetting the top of the head, and cried, "I baptise thee in the name of the Lord our God." Not knowing was I baptising a boy or a child, but in hopes it would do the job. I did it for all the babies after that. "The Good Lord will take it into account," I said. "The child was innocent inside me." Mr Spottiswood said it counted for nothing. I was in error – it wasn't done proper. I turned wayward, then. Put my two hands flat on his chest and give him a push. And I screamed at him. "I spit on you and your cruel God!" Mr McDowell, he put me in a madhouse. But he died two year on, and my brother come and fetched me out. We don't go to chapel any more, we says our prayers here.

She pressed her hands together, as though praying, but her eyes were stormy. I searched for words to comfort that fierce creature, and found none.

–I didn't do what I were meant to. I can pray till I'm blue in the face. But I failed.

–Failed at what, Mrs McDowell?

–To keep them safe from harm.

–You aren't answerable for what happened.

–If a mother isn't meant to keep her babies safe, who is?

–A mother isn't God. Only God is God.

–And He's cursed me.

–God doesn't curse people. That's not His way. He's merciful.

−If He was merciful, He'd a left me one of my wee mites. Just one. That's not too much to ask. But He took every last bairn. Blown out like candles. As surely as if they never existed.

−You'll be reunited with your children one day.

−Maybes. I can but hope. Would you like to see their graves tomorrow?

−Yes. We could say a prayer there. You could remember them.

−Not a day goes by but I remember them. I can still see every one of their wee faces. I'll make you up a bed now, lass.

I'd prefer to doze in the seat here by the fire, if it's no trouble.

−No trouble to me. I dare say you'll rest sounder in the kitchen where it's warmer.

Enoch Alcorn came back in, bid me good night and disappeared. His sister delayed a little longer.

−There's light from the fire, but I'll leave a candle burning on the dresser. In case you'd be nervous in a strange place.

−Thank you, Mrs McDowell. You've shown great kindness, feeding and sheltering a stranger.

−Naw, naw, you're the one should be thanked. You've given me comfort, lass. I had it in me head God withheld His grace. But He give me some mercy − He never took my babies' faces from me.

I was convinced I wouldn't manage a wink of sleep, but it was daylight when I woke up. Picture my astonishment when I found myself in an empty byre. Outside, I saw a tumbledown farmhouse, its roof caved in. When I walked around the back of the house, I saw the stretch of water Leah McDowell called the Cat's Cradle.

Nine small crosses with chiselled-on names faced it. Where once there must have been mounds, now the ground was flat − the earth had reclaimed them, heathers and clovers roaming freely over the graves. I passed from one roughly-made wooden marker to the other.

Lord in your mercy look kindly on Jeremiah Alcorn McDowell
Born 7 January 1737 died 7 January 1737

Lord shed your grace on Robert Alcorn McDowell
Born 15 November 1737 died 15 November 1737

Lord take Enoch Alcorn McDowell home to Thee
Born 30 December 1738 died 30 December 1738

Lord into your hands we commend Ruth Leah McDowell
Born 22 February 1740 died 22 February 1740

And so on. I gathered some nodding bluebells and scattered then across the row of graves, speaking the babies' names aloud to recognize their existence. Finally, I looked for headstones for Noah Alcorn and Leah McDowell, but found none.

Back across the cobblestoned yard, to the gateposts with an acorn on top of each. John Eccles and his brother Peter met me on the path home – they set out at daybreak looking for me. I told them the story as we made our way back to Cuba Court. A look passed between them.

–You've seen the phantom house, said John Eccles. It appears maybes the once in a year.

–Them that sees it, never forgets it, said Peter Eccles.

–What does it mean?

They shrugged, unable to answer.

Later, I went back looking for those wee graves but could never find them, search though I might. They were lost in the mist. But I had a thought about what the phantom house might mean – it could be a sign that people linger on in some shape or form. Death is never final.'

Charlotte Brontë, July 1854, Ireland

Author's note

I have taken a novelist's licence with some facts and characters.

Mary Anna Bell Nicholls was from a large family and had a number of brothers but none called Richard – the master of the Royal Free School at Banagher was James, who bears no resemblance to Richard.

Patrick Brontë was one of ten children, and had a brother called Hugh and sister named Alice, but she was not mentally disturbed.

There is no evidence Charlotte Brontë ever visited County Down or that the Bruntys travelled south to meet her during her honeymoon in Ireland in 1854.

Charlotte and Mary did spend time together in Dublin and Banagher, and Charlotte mentioned her favourably in a letter, as well as the other Bells she encountered – especially Aunt Harriette.

After being widowed, Arthur returned to Ireland, married Mary, and for decades they shared their home – Hill House, Banagher, Co. Offaly – with many of Charlotte's possessions.

Over time, these objects, ranging from clothing to manuscripts to artwork, were sold or given away. Arthur asked for Charlotte's wedding dress to be destroyed after his death and this wish was carried out. However, both Arthur and Mary helped to preserve much of what might have been lost.

Acknowledgments

Sincere thanks are due to:

Seán Farrell for insightful editing

The Lilliput Press team for unflagging support

Professor Jarlath Killeen of Trinity College Dublin

Dr Robert Logan of Brontë Ireland

James Scully of Banagher Brontë Group

Nicola Daly, owner of Charlotte's Way guesthouse, formerly Hill House in Banagher

Gráinne Shannon of Birr Castle for Rosse family fact-checking

Jon Smith of the *Irish Independent* for guidance on Yorkshire dialect

Cathal Póirtéir for Irish language advice

Carlo Gébler and Justin Blanchard who read early sections

All my valued writer friends with whom I spoke about *Charlotte* on walks or over coffee.